For my father

KRISTALLNACHT

"Leave it Benjamin. We'll clear it up later. I fear there's more to come. Take cover under the table with Saul and your mother," whispered Jakob Lindenheim, as loudly as he dared.

Outside, they could hear the jackboots on the cobbled street, the counterpoint to a cacophony of barked orders and shattering glass.

"There's no point in hiding. All we can do is hope that they don't come looking," continued Jakob, sitting down on the floor, in the corner of the room, with a dining chair tilted against the wall to afford him some protection from flying glass.

The brick which had just broken the kitchen window lay in front of the cooker. Ben had started to pick up the shards when his father stopped him. Only now, as they sought refuge under the furniture, anticipating the sitting room window succumbing to a similar fate, did he realise he was bleeding.

As he tried to remove the handkerchief from his trouser pocket he leaned backwards into his brother.

"Keep to your own side!" muttered Saul, who was already feeling squashed against one of the table legs.

"Stop it, boys," came the exasperated reprimand from Miriam Lindenheim.

She noticed the blood on Ben's hand.

"My poor boy," she mothered him, her frustration changing to concern.

Miriam took the handkerchief from Ben and bound his hand, which was helpful, as he was left-handed, and the cut was to his left hand.

"I don't think there's any glass stuck in there," she reassured him.

Ben was sixteen and trying to be brave, but the truth was, he was terrified. Both the shouting and the sound of breaking glass were getting louder, until it was obvious, the Lindenheims' block was next. The soldiers were right outside. Thankfully, the flat was on the first floor, so at least the soldiers couldn't peer in through the window. A short burst of submachine gun fire and the windows in the flat below disintegrated. Bracing themselves, the Lindenheims waited fearfully for their sitting room window to shatter. Nothing. Another barked order, and the soldiers moved on, accompanied by more gunfire and breaking glass in the block next-door.

"We have to get the boys away from here," declared Jakob in a low voice, as soon as it felt safe enough to talk.

"Where?" responded Miriam, mournfully.

"Anywhere," replied Jakob.

"What about the cousins in Wiengarten?" suggested Miriam.

"I'm not sure the towns will be any safer than the cities. The Nazis will hunt down all of us."

"But it's got to be safer than here in the city. Surely? Even for a few weeks or months."

Miriam would never have dreamed of arguing with Jakob, but she was desperate.

Miriam and the boys wriggled out from under the table and Jakob replaced his chair in the space they had vacated.

"Shall I get some newspaper and glue?" offered Saul, "To fix the window."

"Thank you," replied Jakob, unsure whether it would be wiser to leave things as they were, to give the impression no one lived there, but he knew he was just kidding himself. Either way, the soldiers would be back soon enough, this week, next week, searching the blocks from top to bottom.

Miriam started to gather up the larger pieces of glass from the kitchen floor, placing them on the table on several layers of newspaper. Once the big shards had been retrieved, she set about sweeping the rest of the glass up.

"Just don't walk around in bare feet," she reminded the boys.

"No mother," responded Saul.

"Do we really have to move away?" asked Ben.

"Your father and I think it's for the best. Until this all blows over. God knows when or if it will ever be over. You and Saul are the future of the Lindenheim family. We have to keep you safe. One day, you'll understand."

"I'll never understand why people hate us so much," retorted Saul.

Four weeks later, just before the start of Hanukkah, when Jakob returned from a brief but perilous excursion to buy whatever basic food items were available, he had a resolute look in his eye.

"Miriam, Saul, Benjamin, come and sit down. I have some news."

The family each took their place around the dining table.

"I've heard they are organising transport out of Germany for minors. Trains. And boats to England. We need to get Saul and Benjamin on one of those boats. There's a train leaving for Rotterdam tomorrow."

Miriam stared back at him. Her mother's heart ached, even though she knew it was their only hope.

"The matter's settled then. Boys, you need to pack your small cases with a change of clothes and something to remember us by," instructed Jakob, adding, "Until we meet again. Tomorrow, we will take you to the train station and register you with the latest group of children."

Thankfully, in the eyes of the law, Saul was still a child, a few weeks shy of his eighteenth birthday, the older of the two brothers by twenty months. Jakob knew he and Miriam might never see their sons again, but he wasn't about to reveal his deepest fear.

The following day, after a breakfast of bread and slightly hardening cheese, Jakob and Saul left the flat. They set off through the back streets, on foot, heading for the central train station. Ten minutes later, Miriam and Ben carried their bicycles down the stairs. Ben ran back up to the flat, grabbed his suitcase, took a last look round, locked the door and ran back down to where his mother was holding the bicycles. He handed her the key and planted the suitcase, corner first, into the basket which was fixed to his handlebars.

"It's not very safe, is it?" he mused.

"Ride with care," responded Miriam.

The risk of being stopped and shot seemed far greater than the risk of the suitcase falling onto the wheel. Safety had become a relative term. They cycled off in the direction of the train station, with the intention of meeting Jakob and Saul there.

In spite of the melee of frantic parents and children jostling on the forecourt, Miriam and Ben found Jakob and Saul without any difficulty. No sooner were they together than Jakob strode off to talk to a woman with a clipboard, pressed by a group of adults waving papers in her face. Jakob joined the back of the group.

"Please try to wait your turn," pleaded the woman with the clipboard. "We will process all of you."

Eventually, Jakob found himself standing in front of her.

"Good morning. I have my sons over there," he stated, pointing vaguely over his shoulder. "Benjamin Lindenheim, sixteen years old and his brother Saul, seventeen years old."

The woman wrote down the boys' names and handed Jakob a pair of labels attached to long loops of string.

"I'm afraid you cannot join your children on the platform. Say your goodbyes out here. Write their names on the labels and send them through onto the westbound platform. Next!"

"Thank you," smiled Jakob, moving away to create space for the next parent.

Once back with his family he realised he didn't have a pen.

"I don't suppose either of you packed a pen?"

"I have a pencil in my pocket," replied Ben, taking it out.

"Write your name and date of birth on the label and put it round your neck. They won't allow us onto the platform. We'll have to say goodbye here."

Miriam was already fighting back her tears. Ben wrote Saul Lindenheim on one of the labels, with his brother's date of birth, and handed it to him.

"Thanks," grunted Saul, pulling it over his head.

Ben filled out his own label, returned the pencil to his pocket and put the label round his neck. The four of them stood looking blankly at each other.

"Send word, when you can," Jakob instructed them.

He held out his arms to hug Saul, a gesture reciprocated somewhat robotically by his son. Miriam hugged Ben and kissed him on both cheeks. They swapped, with Ben enthusiastically hugging his father.

"Look after your brother," Miriam spoke quietly into Saul's ear as she put her arms round him.

"I will," Saul mumbled into her shoulder.

The boys picked up their suitcases and walked into the station without looking back. Miriam and Jakob got on the bicycles and rode home, the tears flowing freely down Miriam's cheeks. Inside the concourse, a crowd of children, of all ages, were advancing like lava onto the westbound platform, to where a train was waiting.

"You OK?" asked Saul, as he and Ben were ushered into a carriage.

"Yes. You?"

Saul nodded and claimed the two seats either side of the window. He lifted his case onto the luggage rack and sat down. Ben did the same, although it was more of a struggle to reach high enough and he ended up half throwing his case up. Saul was staring out of the window, deep in thought and hadn't noticed his brother struggling.

Saul and Ben had a strained relationship. To be fair to Saul, Ben had a bit of a temper and was generally the first to fly off the handle when diplomacy failed. Up until his bar mitzvah, Ben had looked up to his older sibling. Once his status had changed, he began to think he knew as much, if not more than Saul, and resented any guidance or help from his brother, always wanting to work it out for himself. Saul was the more level-headed of the two. He had learnt, for the most part, to let Ben do his own thing and only offered advice or assistance when it became absolutely necessary. Ben was more practical and helped their father with maintenance jobs around the house. The family owned a small cabinet which Ben had crafted the previous summer, with mitred joints and bevelled edges, polished until you could see your reflection in the walnut veneer. Jakob was hugely proud of Ben's achievement, a cabinetmaker himself. Saul found himself wrestling with bouts of jealousy. His own career could have been a doctor or a lawyer, if they had stayed in Germany, although his studies were now unexpectedly interrupted. Three years in succession, Saul had won the school prize in humanities. Jakob's heart was bursting with pride when he watched his older son receive the certificate, and yet Saul had got it into his head that their father must love Ben more than him, because Ben was like their father. But family is everything, and Saul had promised their mother to look after Ben on this adventure into the unknown.

Outside, a guard blew his whistle, and the train pulled out of the station, sluggishly at first, gathering speed as the sulphur infused air wafted in through the open window. Ben stood up to close it, looking at the other children as he did, but receiving no contrary responses, mostly because none of the other children in his immediate vicinity appeared to be old enough for their bar mitzvah. He couldn't work out if it was fearful denial or resilient defiance in their empty gazes.

The journey would be longer than six hours, and he felt he should do something, at least say something.

"Hello. My name is Ben, and this is my brother Saul," he introduced them, smiling.

Silence.

"What are your names?"

"Aaron. This is my sister Freida."

"Samuel."

"David. He's Levi."

"Are you brothers?"

Levi nodded.

The little girl in the corner opposite didn't answer and pulled a handkerchief from her coat pocket.

"Don't cry. We'll get through this," Ben consoled her.

"I forgot Moshe. I want my teddy," she blurted out, her tears flowing down her cheeks.

"You can write to him and tell him about all the fun you're having. I'm sure he'll be waiting for you."

Ben was far less convinced by his supposition than the girl, who nodded and blew her nose.

"Let's play a game," proposed Ben. "Can you all count?"

All the children nodded.

"What about your five times table?"

They nodded again.

"And your seven times table?"

Ben was relieved to discover that the other children also knew their seven times table.

"Let's play Fizz-Buzz, then. Do you know how to play Fizz-Buzz?"

"One, two, three, four, fizz, six, buzz, eight, nine, fizz," replied Samuel, proudly.

"That's right," Ben affirmed him. "Fizz if it's a multiple of five, buzz if it's a multiple of seven, and fizz-buzz if it's a multiple of both. If you make a mistake, you drop out."

To Ben's amazement, the game lasted almost an hour, with different winners each time. Once or twice, it was obvious to Ben that Saul deliberately made a mistake, because he didn't want to win. Ben picked up on the tactic and also let the others win several times, most importantly, when he found himself head-to-head with the little girl, whose name they still didn't know. Winning a game of Fizz-Buzz seemed finally to break down the walls.

"I'm Ruth," she giggled.

"Well Ruth, I'm going to keep an eye out for you, and make sure you get on the boat to England. It'll be Hanukkah soon. Has anyone brought their dreidel with them? inquired Ben. "I'm pretty sure it would be alright to play the game early. Given the circumstances and all that."

"I've got mine," responded Levi.

"Me too," added Freida.

"Then, let's have a game. We can spin them on the floor, here," suggested Ben.

"I think I'll sit this one out," announced Saul, unsure that they should be playing with the dreidels yet.

In the end, it proved to be a great idea, because the children were kept entertained for another hour.

"I'm hungry," complained Ruth.

"Did your mother pack you something to eat?" responded Ben.

"I don't know."

"Let's have a look in your case," Ben encouraged her.

She opened the case, but there wasn't anything to eat in there.

"What about the rest of you?" asked Ben, looking around at the other children.

"We have some bread and jam," offered Aaron.

"We don't have anything," admitted David, a little embarrassed.

"Biscuits," came Samuel's response, "Dried ones."

"We have some bread and jam as well," confirmed Saul. "Don't we Benjamin?"

Benjamin nodded. Saul reached up for his suitcase, opened it and took out a paper packet.

"Shall I pass you your case?" he asked his brother.

"Yes. Thank you," replied Ben.

Saul reached down the case, without having to stretch, and handed it to Ben, who took out a similar packet to Saul's, except that the jam had leaked out onto his clean shirt.

"It'll wash," he declared nonchalantly, picking up the shirt and sucking out the jam.

Saul stood watching, shaking his head with an ironic smile on his face. Ben replaced the shirt, closed the case again and passed it back to Saul.

"There's eight of us and five of us have something to eat. I say we share it all out evenly and have a picnic," insisted Ben.

Samuel relinquished his biscuits and Aaron handed over the tin in which his and Freida's lunch was packed. Ben got out his pocket-knife and started to cut the bread whilst Saul broke the biscuits in half. They piled all the jam onto one piece of paper and sat it on the floor.

"Help yourselves," Ben invited the others.

Everyone hesitated, trying to let the others go first. Considering all the Jewish families in the Lindenheim's immediate circle had been struggling for several months, this was an amazing demonstration of community.

"Try to chew each mouthful slowly and for a long time," suggested Ben, sounding a little like his mother.

The children fell silent as they ate. Unfortunately, there was nothing to wash down the bread and jam and dried biscuits.

"I'll go for a walk along the train and see if I can find us something to drink," suggested Ben, getting up from his seat.

He staggered slowly along the aisle, passing some children who were sleeping, some who were reading books, and others who were staring out of the window. There was an absence of grown-ups. Opening the carriage door he stepped between the carriages, an involuntary sense of vertigo clouding his mind as he imagined the sleepers rushed past beneath him. In the next carriage he found a middle-aged couple.

"I don't suppose you know where I could get hold of some water. The children I'm seated with are thirsty."

"I'm afraid I don't," replied the woman, kindly.

Ben wondered if they might be able to find some at the next station, but he couldn't see any containers. In any case, an awful lot of water would be needed if all the children were to be satisfied. Frustrated, he gave up on the idea and returned to his seat. Surely, there would be something to drink once they got on the boat, even though that was still several hours away.

Samuel, Freida, David and Ruth we all asleep when he returned. Saul looked up at him. Ben shook his head.

"Perhaps we should all try and sleep for a while," proposed Saul, leaning back and closing his eyes. Ben continued to peer through the window at the landscape rushing past. When would they cross the border into Holland? As Ben was pondering their current location, houses started to flash past. Very soon the train decelerated into Cologne station. Ben's window came to a stop opposite a standpipe and fire bucket. Without weighing up the pros and cons, he jumped up, rushed to the door, ran across to the standpipe, filled the bucket and ran back over to the train.

"What do you think you're doing?" came a shout from somewhere along the platform. He ignored it and climbed back on board.

"Wake up," he whispered loudly, shaking Aaron's shoulder, followed by Freida's. "Here, drink some water. Quickly."

He woke Samuel, David and Levi, whilst Aaron and Freida were drinking.

"Quick. Drink from the bucket, before the train leaves the station again."

Saul had woken, disturbed by the movements around him.

"Drink some water, quickly," Ben instructed him as he tried to wake Ruth up by squeezing her arm.

She jumped, was disorientated and let out a gasp.

"It's OK, Ruth. I've got us some water, but you need to drink it quickly."

The guard's whistle blew just as everyone's thirst was quenched, apart from Ben's. The train started to move. He took a swig of water, pulled down the window and dropped the bucket out onto the platform. There was a loud clang, the bucket bounced twice and rolled to a stop in front of the guard.

"Thank you!" Ben shouted, pushing up the window again and flopped back into his seat.

"You're completely nuts," laughed Saul. "But thank you."

The children were all wide awake again, now.

"Who knows the story behind why we celebrate Hanukkah?" asked Saul.

"I do," responded Levi.

"Me too," added David.

"I think I do," added Aaron.

"Shall I tell you the story of the Macabees?"

There was a general chorus of 'Yes' and 'Please' with Ruth the loudest.

"Once upon a time in the city of Jerusalem there was a temple belonging to God, where our ancestors went to worship. There was a beautiful seven-branched menorah in the temple and every evening the cups were filled with oil so the menorah could be lit. The Jewish people loved it, but the king was very unhappy about it. His name was Antiochus, and he was a very mean king. He didn't like the Jews, so he made laws to stop them going to the temple or reading from the Torah. Worse still, Antiochus told his soldiers to go into the temple, fill it with rubbish, smash everything up and take away the menorah. The soldiers got rid of all the oil as well. There was a man call Judah Maccabee who said to the other Jews, 'This has to stop! We have to fight back.' 'But we have no weapons,' someone said. 'Then we will have to be very brave and very clever,' replied Judah Maccabee. Amazingly, the Macabees managed to chase the soldiers away. Judah Macabee and the others went into the temple and cleaned up the rubbish and fixed the broken things. They made a new menorah but there was no oil because the jars had all been smashed. All except one. After looking high and low in a temple, they found a tiny little jar of oil. 'That's not going to last very long,' someone said, 'And we need the menorah to stay lit for eight days.' That was when the miracle happened. The oil didn't run out for eight days. And that's why every year we light our menorahs for eight days and celebrate the miracles God did for Judah Macabee and the Jews."

Freida, Samuel and Levi had all fallen back to sleep, by the time Saul finished the Hanukkah story.

"Please, tell us another story," pleaded Ruth.

"Your turn'" laughed Saul, looking in Ben's direction.

Ben thought for a moment and began, "There was once a prophet called Elijah."

"What's a prophet?" asked Ruth.

"Good question, Ruth," responded Ben. "A prophet is a man called by God to tell other people messages from God."

"What sort of messages?" Ruth pressed him.

"That's another excellent question. If our ancestors were doing things that made God angry, he would send messages to tell them to stop. Sometimes he gave the prophets messages about what he was going to do in the future."

Ruth didn't have a third question, so he carried on with the story.

"One day, there was a contest between the prophets of Baal and Elijah. Elijah built an altar, and the prophets of Baal built an altar. They both soaked their altars in water.

The prophets of Baal couldn't get their sacrifice to burn, but God let Elijah's sacrifice burn. The king and queen and all the people could see that Elijah's God was the true God of our people, and this made the king and queen mad. Elijah ran for his life, and he ended up a long way from home. He was scared and tired and hungry and confused. An angel gave him food and he went to the mountain of God. He went into a cave and that was where God spoke to him. 'What are you doing here, Elijah?' Elijah was feeling sorry for himself. 'I've done what you asked me to do, they got mad, I'm all on my own, and now they're trying to kill me.' 'Go outside,' responded God. 'I will pass by.' So, Elijah went outside and waited for God. First there was a very strong wind, but God was not in the wind. Then, there was an earthquake, but God was not in the earthquake. After the earthquake came fire, but God was not in the fire either. Finally, there came a very quiet whisper. 'What are you doing here, Elijah?' Elijah was still feeling sorry for himself. 'I've done what you asked me to do, they got mad, I'm all on my own and now they're trying to kill me.' 'Go back again. Go to the desert of Damascus. Make Hazael king of Aram, make Jehu king of Israel and make Elisha a prophet to take your place. They will kill my enemies. And Elijah, you're not alone. There are seven thousand who still worship me.' So, Elijah stopped feeling sorry for himself and went and did what God had told him to do."

"I really like that story," enthused Ruth, "Pleeeeeeeeease, tell us another one."

"I have a better idea," responded Ben, pulling out a magazine which had been stuffed down the side of his seat. As he unfolded it, the glamorous, lipstick-bedecked face of a woman was revealed, propaganda for Hitler's 'Children, Kitchen, Church' policy.

"I think the best thing we can do with this is turn it into paper darts or boats," remarked Ben.

"How do we do that?" asked Aaron.

"I'll show you," answered Ben, smiling. "Watch."

He tore out a page, and folding over a thin border, he ran his nails along it to create a nice sharp crease, which he was then able to tear along to give a straight edge. After a few folds, he launched a colourful dart across the carriage at David, who caught it and threw it back, his face beaming. Ben tore out three more pages and handed them to David, Aaron and Ruth.

"Will you help me, please?" requested Ruth.

Ben spent the next ten minutes helping Ruth make her paper dart.

"Now, I'll show you all how to make a boat," remarked Ben.

Initiating the process in a similar way to the darts, Ben turned his paper rectangle into a single-sailed boat.

"It will float quite happily in a basin, until the paper soaks up too much water," he explained.

"Will you help me again, please?" whispered Ruth.

"Yes, but you can do the first part by yourself now, can't you," Ben encouraged her.

He watched as she neatened off her page.

"What do I do now?"

"Fold that edge to there and that edge to there."

Ruth folded.

"Now, fold that edge to here and the same the other side."

Ruth folded some more.

"The next bit's a little tricky because you need to get this part to stick up."

Ruth tried but her hands were too small.

"You do that bit, please."

Ben made the sail appear in the boat.

"Now, just fold down the edges around the sides of the boat. It'll make it stronger. See?" he added, folding the first one over.

Ruth finished it off.

"Thank you."

"You're welcome. Now I'm going to try and get some sleep," insisted Ben, leaning back into the corner between seat and window and closing his eyes.

The rhythmic rattle of the bogies and the gentle swaying of the carriage soon lulled Ben to sleep. At some point in his sleep, he drifted into a dream. His parents were present, but they weren't in their home in Karlsruhe. Their home in his dream lay in ruins, the morning after a bombing raid. Ben was searching for something in a pile of rubble. None of it made any sense to him. He woke suddenly to the sound of breaking glass. Disorientated for a few seconds, he surveyed the carriage and realised the glass was in his dreams. A quick glance at Saul's upside-down watch suggested the train was only about an hour from Rotterdam.

Outside, the style of roof on the buildings which flashed past was unfamiliar. Not far from the train track, a child was chasing a dog in a grassy field. He looked up at the train and waved. Instinctively, Ben waved back. He started to wonder where he and Saul might end up living. Would it be in a city, like Karlsruhe, or out in the country? The idea of living on a farm appealed to him, a bit like an extended holiday. Ben was trying to think himself into taking a positive stance to this entire painful experience. The great thing about a holiday was that you went home afterwards.

The woman Ben had asked earlier about something to drink was walking along the aisle carrying a clipboard and counting heads. Ben smiled at her, his cheeks warming to the guilty realisation that what he had done with the fire bucket was probably illegal. Did she know it was him? She smiled back and continued along the carriage. Ben turned back to the window, where the number of buildings was starting to increase, until the fields were swallowed up by cityscape. By now, the train had slowed, the rhythm of the bogies against the tracks decreasing from quaver to crotchet to minim. Their journey continued at this slower pace for another ten minutes, until the terminus platform slid silently alongside them. A few nerve-shredding squeaks later, and the train came to a standstill.

"We've arrived," confirmed Saul, somewhat stating the obvious. "We'd better get off the train and join the exodus."

Saul took down Ben's suitcase and his own, setting them on the seat. Ben was helping Ruth gather her things together.

"Are you going to be warm enough? Shall we get a cardigan from your suitcase?"

Ruth nodded. Ben opened the case and pulled out a cardigan. There was Moshe, hiding underneath.

"Moshe! Moshe!"

Ruth grabbed her teddy bear and hugged him tightly.

"Looks like you didn't forget him after all," reflected Ben. "May I hold him while you put your cardigan on."

The other children were making their way to the door. Saul was starting to get a trifle impatient.

"We need to get moving," said Saul.

"I know, I know. But I promised Ruth I'd look after her. We're almost ready."

Ruth fastened the bottom button and held out her hand, expectantly. Ben returned Moshe to her. She walked alongside Ben and Saul, her case in her left hand, her teddy bear in her right. Unfortunately, by the time the three of them alighted, they had missed the instructions. Swallowed up in the river of passengers, they were propelled along the platform in the direction of the dock, where two ships were moored. There were adults and children climbing the gangplank onto both ships. Saul was propelled in front of Ben and Ruth. Just as they were passing the stern of the first ship, Ruth dropped Moshe.

"Moshe! Moshe! I've dropped Moshe," announced Ruth, tugging at Ben's sleeve. Saul was in a world of his own and didn't hear so carried on walking, but Ben stopped alongside Ruth. Poor Moshe was in grave peril from the tramping feet. Going against the tide of people, even for just a few paces, was a struggle, but Ben was determined to rescue the teddy bear. Grabbing Ruth's hand, he dragged her with him, navigating their way back through the crowd.

"Sorry."

"Watch out!"

"Sorry. Lost teddy bear."

By the time Moshe was safely back in Ruth's relieved grasp, Saul was out of sight. Ben wasn't too concerned, though. He knew they would be able to reconnect on board the ship, whose gangplank he was now traversing. Meanwhile Saul, hemmed in by the crowd, was heading towards the second of the two ships and only realised Ben and Ruth were no longer behind him when he reached the gangplank. An official-looking man stood welcoming the passengers on board.

"Excuse me," asked Saul, politely. "Have you seen a boy about my height, sixteen, and a small girl?"

"Sorry. As you can see, there's rather a lot of people embarking. I can't remember them all."

"Oh. Alright."

Saul made his way up onto the main deck and started searching for Ben and Ruth, trying to imagine where Ben would take her to wait for him. Five minutes later, the gangplank was raised, and the ship moved slowly away from the quay. He worked his way down the ship, without success, convincing himself that Ben was also searching the ship and they kept missing each other. Meanwhile, Ben and Ruth were carrying out their own search, but on board the first ship which left port for Harwich, ten minutes later.

About thirty minutes into his New York bound voyage, Saul went to the first-class lounge to see if Ben and Ruth were there by mistake. That was when he overheard two middle-aged women talking about the Empire State Building.

"Excuse me," Saul interrupted them hesitantly. "I couldn't help overhear you mention you wanted to visit the Empire State Building. This ship is heading for England, isn't it?"

"No, my dear. New York."

Saul felt like he had been hit in the stomach with a flail.

"Is everything OK?" asked the other woman.

"Not really," responded Saul, his voice cracking. "I'm meant to be on the ship to England, with my brother. Somehow we got separated in the crowd."

"Let's get you a cup of tea, and think about what you can do about it," suggested the first woman, kindly.

"Thank you. This is nothing short of a disaster. I promised our mother I would take care of him."

The second woman disappeared for a few minutes, seeking out a cup of tea for the three of them.

"Is there any chance he made the same mistake and he's somewhere on this ship?" inquired the first woman, grasping at straws.

"I've been searching everywhere since I came on board. That's why I came here, to first-class. It was the last place I thought he might be, and that only by accident."

"Oh dear. Was no one taking a register? I mean, is there someone you can ask. Sorry. You probably already tried that."

"There wasn't anyone when I came on board. I should have realised then that something might be wrong. I'm so stupid."

"Don't be too hard on yourself. How old are you?"

"Seventeen. Saul Lindenheim, by the way. My brother's called Benjamin."

"Well, I'm Stacey Grainger and my friend is Renata Fischer."

"Are you American? You speak very good German. Sorry, that was impertinent of me."

"Not at all. It was very kind of you. I have been visiting Renata for years. Now it's time to take her to New York."

A brief pause as she glanced around to see how close the nearest passenger was.

"I don't like what is happening in Germany one bit," she continued, lowering her voice.

Just then, Renata reappeared, followed by a waiter carrying a tray with a pot of tea, three cups and saucers and three side plates bearing small cakes.

"Please join us. There's nothing like a bit of sugar to steady the nerves," she declared.

The waiter placed the tray on the low table they were seated at and walked off. Renata poured the tea.

"This is Saul, Renata. It appears he somehow managed to board the wrong ship. He thinks his brother Benjamin is on the other ship that was going to England."

"Oh dear. I'm guessing this means you don't have a cabin. We'll be on this ship for ten days."

"I don't have a cabin. To be honest, I have neither ticket nor money. I must be a stowaway."

"How exciting!" responded Stacey, lightening the mood. "You absolutely must stay with us, until we reach port.

There's not a lot we can do then, because you will have to pass through immigration. Right now, it would be our pleasure…"

"And an adventure," interjected Renata, giggling.

"Really Renata. This is a serious situation," continued Stacey, winking at Saul. "It would be our absolute pleasure if you would be our guest for this crossing."

"Won't that get you into trouble?" replied Saul, starting to become self-conscious about his status.

"Who's going to know, apart from us?" laughed Renata.

"Well, if you're quite sure, how can I refuse such kindness?"

"That's settled then. Let's get you to the cabin so you can freshen up before we have our evening meal."

Once their ship had left port for England, Ben had positioned himself with Ruth adjacent to the doorway through which they had entered the ship. After half an hour watching and waiting, hoping that Saul would wander across the deck in search of them, Ben's instincts were telling him something was wrong.

"Let's go and look for Saul, instead of standing here," he suggested to Ruth.

Ruth looked at her teddy bear and back up at Ben.

"Moshe thinks we should look for Saul, too."

"Good. I'm glad we're all in agreement. Let's go."

Halfway round the ship, they happened upon the woman with the clipboard.

"Excuse me. Somehow, I seem to have become separated from my brother. I don't suppose you have seen him. He's seventeen and looks quite similar to me.

I know there are lots of children on board, but maybe you noticed him because he was looking for someone also."

"I'm afraid I haven't. Let's go and find someone who can put out a call," responded the woman, helpfully. "What is your brother's name?"

"Saul. Saul Lindenheim."

"Come with me."

She led them to the other end of the ship and found a man wearing a uniform.

"Would you do us the kindness of putting out a call for Saul Lindenheim, please?"

"Certainly, Madam."

He walked off and a few minutes later, a distorted voice cut through the air.

"Is there a Saul Lindenheim on board? Please come to the bridge."

"I suppose we should just wait here," reflected the woman with the clipboard, and looking into Ben's eyes, added, "Was that you with the water bucket, by the way?"

"I'm afraid so. The children were thirsty. I didn't know what else to do."

"This is Ben. He is very kind. And he's clever," commented Ruth.

"Is Ben your big brother?"

"Yes," blurted out Ruth, before Ben could respond.

He didn't know what to say at this point. He was concerned for Ruth, but she wasn't his sister. Right now, his priority was finding Saul. Did it really matter if Ruth wasn't his sister? After all, when they reached England, none of the children knew where and with whom they'd be staying. What was wrong with spending a few months in the same house as this frightened little girl and her teddy bear, Moshe?

Ten minutes after the first announcement, the crackly voice repeated the call for Saul.

"Surely, he must have heard it," observed Ben, his stomach tightening, as he contemplated the improbable, that Saul had embarked on the other ship.

"You would imagine so. Is there any possibility that your brother might have got on the wrong ship?"

"I'm beginning to fear as much. Do you know where it was going?"

"America. New York. Did you not hear the instructions?"

"No. We were delayed by this little one. Case of the missing teddy bear. By the time we made it onto the platform, all we could do was join the flow of passengers. At one point, Ruth here dropped Moshe, and we had to turn and retreat several paces, against the flow, to rescue him. That was when we became separated from Saul. That still doesn't explain how he may have ended up on the other ship though."

The man in uniform returned to where they were waiting.

"I'm afraid no one has come to the bridge. I will put out another call just before we dock. I'm sorry."

"Thank you," responded Ben, choking back the panic.

It was in that moment that he decided to adopt Ruth as his sister.

"When the call goes out again, I will meet you back here," proposed the woman with the clipboard. "Probably best if we hang back and watch all the passengers disembarking. For now, try and find somewhere to settle down for the night. I'll come and bring you a blanket."

Ben nodded. Ruth tugged at his sleeve. How much of the gravity of their situation she grasped, Ben knew not, but she appeared to sense something was wrong. The tug was not demanding but consoling.

"Please, tell me another story."

Ben was glad of the distraction.

"Alright. But let's find somewhere to sit down."

He took hold of her hand and led them to a small space against the side of some stairs.

"Here. Put your suitcase against the wall and use it as a seat. Like this."

He set his own case down and sat on it.

"I want to lie down. I'm tired."

"I'm sure you are. Let me hold onto your case. You lie down here."

Ben used Ruth's case to form the back of a chair, resting on top of his own case, which was pushed lengthways back against the wall. Hardly had she laid down, Ruth was fast asleep, her face pressed against Moshe. The woman with the clipboard found them, about ten minutes later, with an army blanket.

"I'm afraid I could only find the one. It's probably large enough to cover both of you though."

"Thank you," replied Ben, taking the blanket, unfolding it, and placing one half gently over Ruth.

Settling back into his suitcase armchair, he drew the other half over his legs and closed his eyes. In silent murmurings to a God he no longer trusted, Ben articulated a cry for help.

"Why? Is it not enough that we have to be separated from our parents? Watch over Saul. Watch over our parents.

If you're there at all. And watch over this little one and her bear."

Ben fell into an uneasy sleep. His dreams were filled with a river of passengers, similar to the exodus from train to ship in Rotterdam, but Ben's subconscious was unable to place the unfamiliar station, and there were soldiers. 'Jews. Jews, Jews,' echoed around Ben's auditory system, loud and menacing, but from somewhere inside his mind. He woke, sweating. In the half-light, Ruth appeared as a picture of serenity, her innocent dreams undisturbed by prophetic imagination of the horrors to come. Across the floor, Ben could barely make out the grey, blanket-covered swell of sleeping children, breathing in, breathing out, rising and falling, the calm before the impending storm of war.

Ben had no idea what time it was, but from deep within the vessel he could hear metallic creaks and bangs. Someone turned on the lights.

"Wakey, wakey. Time to get up!" came the distorted voice.

The lady with the clipboard appeared in the doorway with a large sack, accompanied by the man in uniform who had helped put out the word for Saul. Spying Ben by the stairs he walked across the now choppy sea, as yawns and stretches and groans heralded bleary-eyed children sitting or standing and folding their blankets.

"Good morning. I take it your brother has still not appeared?"

"Good morning. No, he hasn't."

"I'll put out another call," responded the ship's officer, turning and walking away.

"Our very kind hosts have given you some biscuits," announced the woman.

A cheer went up and she started handing out the treats.

"Hopefully, these will tide you over until we dock."

She was interrupted by the tannoy, "If there is a Saul Lindenheim on the ship do not disembark. I repeat, do not disembark. Your brother is waiting for you."

Ben felt instantly sick and put his biscuits into his pocket. Ruth was slow to stir but became more enthusiastic when Ben handed her two biscuits.

"Good morning, sleepy."

Ruth giggled as she crunched on her first biscuit. The woman with the clip board had noted that the announcement did not mention Saul having a sister waiting. She came over to Ben.

"Do you really have a sister?"

Ruth looked up, her mouth full of biscuit, her eyes pleading.

"I do now," replied Ben.

The woman with the clipboard appeared to grasp what Ben was saying.

The ship seemed to take an eternity to dock. Ben and Ruth hang back, but Saul did not appear. The deck emptied slowly, until only Ben, Ruth and the woman with the clipboard remained.

"I'm sorry. You'd better make your way off the ship, before you miss any further instructions."

"Thank you for all your help," responded Ben, appreciatively, putting on a brave face and taking Ruth's hand. "Come on you. Have you got Moshe?"

Ruth held up her teddy bear.

"Will you carry my case?"

"Hmm. I think we're going to have to put Moshe in your suitcase. I only have two hands, as do you. We each have a case and I want to hold your other hand."

Without protest, Ruth handed Moshe to Ben, who opened her case and placed him under the edge of a woollen cardigan, tucking him in. Taking Ruth by the hand, they disembarked and joined the back of the crowd which was advancing towards the train for London. By the time Ben and Ruth got on, all the compartments were full, and they couldn't find two spaces to sit together. In the end, Ben sat Ruth in a compartment and stationed himself in the corridor, just outside the door. By now he had reluctantly and painfully accepted that Saul was on his way to America, and spent the entire journey standing, with both their suitcases at his feet, staring out of the window into the darkness. It was still dark as the train entered the London suburbs.

In the concourse at Liverpool Street Station, around fifty adults, some in couples, some alone, were waiting expectantly for the new additions to their families. Most had come forward from amongst the Jewish community in the East End, others were sympathetic to the plight of the Jews on mainland Europe. When news of the Night of Broken Glass had reached the British press, it had been a wake-up call for many, in the face of Hitler's increasingly dangerous and widespread discrimination against the Jews. The approaching train carried the hopes and fears of the next generation, transported to an indeterminate period of respite. No one quite knew when, or if, these children would be able to return home.

As the train crawled towards the buffer, Ben opened the compartment door and beckoned Ruth to step outside before the rush.

"Take your case. As soon as we get onto the platform, I want you to take hold of my hand, again."

Ruth nodded.

Other children were starting to spill out into the corridor, which was soon full. They shuffled along until they reached the door and descended onto the platform where Ruth immediately grabbed Ben's hand. The woman with the clipboard was waving everyone towards the concourse where a rambling queue was beginning to form.

"What's going on?" asked Ruth.

"I think we are being introduced to the families where we'll be staying," replied Ben.

"Can I stay with you?"

"I honestly don't know what's going to happen. It isn't really up to me."

Ruth's bottom lip trembled as she looked up at Ben.

"I'll do my best."

"Promise?"

"Promise."

Ruth smiled.

They arrived at the head of the queue.

"Hello. What's your name?" asked the kindly looking man sitting at a small table.

"Ben Lindenheim."

"I'm Ruth," chipped in Ruth, without waiting to be asked.

The man looked down his list.

"It says Ben Lindenheim and Saul Lindenheim here."

"It appears my brother got on the wrong ship. We think he's travelling to New York."

"That is most unfortunate. So, who's this?"

"This is Ruth. Saul and I were looking after her on the journey. I don't suppose we can stay together since my brother isn't here?"

"That would be most irregular, with you not being from the same family."

Ruth started to cry and grip Ben's hand even more tightly. The man looked back at his list.

"What is your family name, Ruth?'

Ruth gulped.

"I don't know."

"Do you have a label?" suggested Ben, trying to be helpful.

Ruth nodded and pulled the string and cardboard necklace from under her blouse and held it out for the man to read.

"Ruth Rosenkranz. I very much like that name, Ruth," responded the man.

Ruth giggled.

"That's more like it. According to my list, you and Ben, here, will be living on the next street from each other. You'll be able to visit each other, I'm sure. Now let's introduce you to your hosts."

Ben crouched down next to Ruth, so he was almost face to face with her.

"I promise I will visit you and Moshe often. You will soon make some new friends of your own age."

"You will make friends too," replied Ruth, with an empathy that was beyond her years.

"Mr Joe Draper and Mrs Dorothy Field!" called out the man.

A smartly dressed couple stepped forward from the waiting crowd.

"Hello. Mr and Mrs Joe Draper," the husband introduced them both, in German.

"Mrs Dorothy Field!" repeated the man at the table, his voice louder and more urgent.

A woman in her forties ran over to them puffing.

"I'm so sorry. The car broke down."

"Not to worry. You're here now. We have an unexpected situation. Ben here was meant to be travelling with his brother, Saul, but it seems there was a mix-up, and Saul got on the wrong ship. Perhaps he will be able to join you in the weeks to come. Benjamin, here, has been looking after Ruth and they would like to stay in contact. Benjamin is going to stay with you Mrs Field, and Ruth will be on the next street with Mr and Mrs Draper."

Ben hardly understood any of what they were saying. Up to now, the grown-ups had spoken with him in German, even if it was a little fractured.

"Please can Ben visit?" pleaded Ruth, tugging at Anna Draper's sleeve.

"I think that is a possibility," she replied, adding, "We'll try," in German.

"Shall we swap addresses?" suggested Joe.

The kind man at the table started to copy both addresses, using the bottom of the last page of his list, which he then tore off, and handed one to Joe Draper and one to Dorothy Field. Dorothy looked at the piece of paper and laughed.

"I think we've each got our own addresses!"

"So, we have," laughed Joe, holding out his slip of paper to swap.

"Why don't you come for tea, tomorrow. Four o'clock?" Anna suggested, and repeating the invitation in German, "Come and eat, tomorrow."

"Thank you, thank you, thank you," repeated Ruth, jumping up and down.

"That would be just perfect," replied Ben, looking across at Dorothy for approval.

"Of course."

"Good luck," the kind man encouraged them all.

Joe and Anna Draper, along with Ruth, turned and walked towards one exit, whilst Dorothy Field led Ben through a different exit to where her car was parked.

"I don't speak German. I expect you're tired and hungry?"

"I understand and speak a little English. Yes, I am tired. I sleep not much. I am not hungry, since my brother leaves."

"That is awful. When we get home, we must write two letters. One to tell your parents you have arrived in England and one to the immigration office in New York. It might take several weeks to reach your brother, but at least he'll know where you are."

"I'm sorry. I only understand 'two letters'."

"Sorry. You write one letter to your parents. You write one letter to America," explained Dorothy, making a writing movement with her hand.

"I understand. This is good idea."

"What do you like to eat, when you are hungry?"

"Cake," laughed Ben, "We cannot eat cake in the last weeks."

"Is it true what's happening to the Jewish people in Germany? I read about the Night of Broken Glass."

"It gets bad."

Nothing more was said, for the short journey to Ben's new home. In fact, he almost dropped off, his lack of sleep and food starting to overtake him.

"Do you like cats?" asked Dorothy, as they pulled up in front of a terraced house.

"Cats. I don't know. My family has no cat."

A man in overalls appeared at the door.

"That'll be Mr Field. He works nights at the local factory. Makes tractors."

Ben got out of the car and took his suitcase from the back seat.

"Bill, this is Benjamin."

"Hello, Mr Field," said Ben, extending his hand. "I am Ben. I am pleased to meet you."

Bill grabbed his hand and shook it firmly.

"I thought there were two of you. We were expecting two of you."

"Ben's brother managed to get on the wrong boat. We'll write a letter and perhaps he'll make his way here in a few weeks."

"I wouldn't put money on it," replied Bill. "I don't mean to sound unkind, but it's a bit of a long-shot."

Dorothy made a frown with her eyebrows.

"I don't understand," answered Ben.

"Come on in. Dot will make us some breakfast. Then, I have to sleep, I'm afraid. This week I'm on nights."

"Nights?"

"I work sometimes in the daytime and sometimes at night."

"I understand. Thank you that you wait to meet me."

"Do you like porridge? There's no porridge quite like Dot's porridge."

"You're embarrassing me, Bill. Ben says he likes cake, so I'm certain he will enjoy porridge."

"Porridge. It sounds good. Thank you."

Ben felt welcome, even if the language difference was a bit of a barrier. He was relieved to have arrived at the end of a long and traumatic journey.

"I'll show you to your room, whilst Dot sorts out breakfast. Come."

Ben followed Bill up the stairs. When they reached the landing, they continued up another flight.

"You'll be getting fit, here," laughed Bill. "Do you play sport?"

"Sport? I play boxing."

"There's a local club. I'll introduce you at the weekend, if you like?"

"A club? Thank you. I don't pack my shorts or my gloves."

"No matter. Dot and I have two sons and a daughter. They've all gone off to school. Simon is about your age. You can borrow some of his shorts."

They stopped in front of the doors to two attic bedrooms.

"That's Jessica's room. That's yours. Matty and Simon share a room down below, next to Dot's and mine."

Bill opened the door and ushered Ben in.

"There's a water jug and basin there. The toilet's outside. I'll leave you to sort your things out. Shout if you need anything else. The porridge will be ready in about ten minutes."

"Thank you."

Ben couldn't help noticing there were twin beds. Bill went back down to the kitchen and Ben sat on one of the beds. It wasn't too firm. Noticing the skylight, he stood up again and peered out of the window over a sea of rooftops and chimneys. Most were smoking. Ben started to wonder whether Bill had meant the toilet was really outside, as in out in the back yard. He had only grasped a little of Bill's last sentence. There was a polished wooden chest of drawers with two drawers, so he opened his suitcase and taking his clothes, arranged them in one of the drawers, holding onto the glimmer of hope that Saul might be able to join him, in a few weeks' time and fill the second. He had also packed a book of adventure stories and his textbook of furniture-making, both of which he placed on the bedside table. Dorothy had hung a towel on the end of each of the metal bedsteads. Ben poured some water into the bowl. There was a half-used bar of soap on a small porcelain plate, so he washed his hands and face, dried himself off and went downstairs.

"All sorted? All good?" inquired Dorothy.

"Yes. May I use the bathroom?"

"The toilet is outside in the shed. When it comes to baths, you can use the tin bathtub."

"Thank you," replied Ben, a little uncertain of what he would find in the shed. As he sat using the facilities, it occurred to Ben that the Field family were not well off. The Lindenheims had never been poor, up until now, and inhabited a comfortable flat. With the political upheaval in Germany, that had all changed and they had begun to experience scarcity. The Fields, on the other hand, seemed to be poor in possessions but rich in hospitality.

"Will I go to the school?" he asked on re-entering the kitchen.

"I sincerely hope so," laughed Dorothy, placing a bowl of porridge on the table at the vacant seat. "You can wash your hands in the sink."

Ben obliged and sat down, leaning forwards to smell the steam rising from the porridge.

"Mmmmm," he expressed his appreciation, taking the spoon and removing a portion of the creamy breakfast from the edge of the bowl.

Moving the ball of porridge round his mouth, Ben savoured the weird culinary sensation. Covered in sugar, the taste was sweet, but the surface of this hot, oaty mixture, against the cold milk in which it sat, created an almost glutinous texture.

"What time comes home Matty, Simon and Jessica?"

"Sometime around three o'clock. They all do chores and homework, we eat tea and then we play games or they read or entertain themselves. In summer they play out. Oh, that reminds me, Bill. Ben has been invited for tea tomorrow. He was looking after a little girl coming over from Germany and she has been lodged on the next street. Isn't that right, Ben. Tomorrow you eat with Ruth and her new family?"

"Yes. I think that she wants me as brother. I think it is good I visit her. One day she meet some new friends."

"That's the spirit. Let's hope you make some new friends too, especially at the boxing club. Ben boxes, Dot. He'll need some of Simon's shorts. Right, I'm off to bed. Thanks Dot."

Bill placed a hand on Dorothy's shoulder and left the kitchen.

"I help clean?"

"Not today. You can write those letters. Write to your mother and father. When I finish, I will help you write to America in English."

Dorothy took a notepad, two envelopes and an ink-pen from the shelf.

"There you go."

"Thank you."

Ben began to write, "Dearest Mother and Father. It was a long journey but ...." He was just about to write 'I' and felt a sudden pique of responsibility for sparing his parents the anxiety, especially if Saul was to return to England in a few weeks. He continued, "Arrived safe in London. It is a lovely family, but they have even less than we do now. I can box at a local club. The bedroom is in an attic, and I can see the smoking chimneys. I love you and miss you. Keep safe. Your loving son, Ben." Surely, they would wonder why there was no letter from Saul, so he added, "Saul will write soon. He sends you his love. You know what he is like with letters." Folding the letter in half, he slipped it into one of the envelopes and wrote his address on the front. As he wrote 'Germany', he began to wonder if it would ever be delivered, and whether even sending it, placed his parents in danger. Why had they asked him to send news? Dorothy was drying off her hands.

"I cannot send this."

"It's alright. We will buy the stamps."

"No. The address, it tells the soldiers to find my parents."

"I see. Perhaps it is better not to send it. But it'll be fine writing to the immigration services?"

"Immigration services?" repeated Ben, questioningly.

"When you arrived in London, someone had a list with names and addresses. The immigration services are the people who check your name and papers when you arrive in America. Let me write the envelope. Then you will be able to copy it."

Dorothy took the pen and wrote, "Immigration Services, New York City, United States of America." She handed the pen back to Ben.

"I speak a little English. Write English is difficult. Please, you write?"

Dorothy nodded, took back the pen and started writing her home address in the top, right corner, followed by the date. As she wrote, she read slowly. "Dear Sirs. My name is Benjamin Lindenheim. I am seeking information about my brother Saul Lindenheim. He left from Rotterdam on a ship to New York on 8th December. If you know his address from your records, please pass this letter to him. I am staying at the address above with Mr and Mrs William Field. Yours faithfully…." She handed the pen back to Ben. "Sign here."

Ben scribbled his best signature. Dorothy didn't hold out much hope of the letter ever reaching Saul, but she wasn't about to snuff out Ben's tiny glimmer of hope. She folded the letter, placed it in the envelope and stuck down the flap.

"I will go to the post office, this afternoon. Will you come with me?"

"Thank you."

Their breakfast was so late, Dorothy decided to miss out on lunch, and at one o'clock, they left for the post office.

"I have an idea," announced Dorothy as they walked. 'When we get back, how about we make a sponge cake? Do you like to cook?"

4 5

"I like cake. I don't know to make cake."

"That's settled then. We will make a Victoria sponge."

"What is Victoria sponge?"

"You'll see. It's delicious. Cake with jam in the middle."

"I like jam and I like cake," laughed Ben.

"What is your favourite subject at school?"

"What I like in school?"

"Yes."

"I like mathematics. My father teaches me to cut wood and to make things. This I like favourite."

"Bill is a practical man, too. He likes to make things with his hands."

"I understand."

"Matty is like his father. Simon plays the piano, like me. You haven't seen our piano. It's in the front room. Jessica likes to dance. I don't think any of them is a star in school subjects, but they all try their best. I can't ask any more than that. Their school stops at age sixteen. I think you will have to go to the grammar school. It's a bit of a walk. Did you understand all that I said?"

"I think so. I am happy to meet your children."

They reached the post office. Ben followed Dorothy to the counter where she asked for a stamp for America. Realising the stamp was quite expensive, Ben felt guilty. His thought also triggered a concern as to how he might have any money in England. The transaction complete, Dorothy handed Ben the letter.

"You can put this in the post box."

"Yes. I put this letter."

"You say, 'I put the letter in the box' or 'I post the letter'," smiled Dorothy.

"Thank you. I want to learn."

On the way home, they called in at the local corner shop where Dorothy bought some butter.

"I have flour, sugar and eggs, and jam, but I need butter for the cake."

"Good morning, Mrs F," the shopkeeper greeted her. "Is that one of those Jewish kids?"

"This is Ben. He's staying with us for a while."

"I am happy to meet you," added Ben.

The shopkeeper nodded in Ben's direction.

"What would you like today?"

"Half a pound of butter, please."

The shopkeeper breezed through the beaded curtain in the doorway at the back if the shop and returned two minutes later with a paper parcel.

"Anything else?"

"Not today, thank you."

Dorothy handed over some coins, without even asking the price.

"See you next time, Mrs F."

"Goodbye."

"Bye," added Ben.

"If we're lucky, the cake might just be ready to eat when Matty, Simon and Jessica come home."

"We eat cake today with Matty, Simon and Jessica?"

"Very good. Yes," Dorothy encouraged Ben. "You will learn English quickly."

"I hope this also."

Back to the house, Dorothy washed her hands in the kitchen sink, and left Ben to take care of his whilst she got out the ingredients and the scales.

"How are your weights and measures?"

Ben picked up a brass weight.

"What is 'oz'?" he asked.

"Of course, you have different units. That's about twenty-five grams, I think. This is one pound. That's about five hundred grams. One egg is about two ounces, so fifty grams. For the cake we need eight ounces of flour, eight ounces of butter, eight of sugar and four eggs."

"I weigh the flour?"

"Start with the sugar. Thank you."

Ben placed the 8 oz weight on one side of the scales and poured sugar into the bowl. Dorothy unwrapped the newly purchased butter and placed it in the mixing bowl. Taking a wooden spoon, started to cream it.

"Put that in the mixing bowl, now, and weigh out the flour."

Dorothy continued to cream the butter and sugar.

"Here, you try," she encouraged Ben, handing him the spoon.

Ben put some elbow grease into fluffing up the butter and sugar.

"This is difficult. My arm is tired."

"It will help your boxing muscles."

Ben made a strong-man gesture with his free arm and smiled.

"Now break the eggs in one by one, mixing them in as you go. Add just a little flour to stop them curdling."

"Curdling?"

"Separating, like milk when you pour in lemon juice."

"I think I understand."

Ben cracked the eggs into the bowl and mixed them in with a spoonful of flour. Eventually, the mixture became light and fluffy. Dorothy handed him a sieve and added a teaspoon of baking powder to the flour.

"Pour in the flour, through the sieve, and fold it in," she instructed Ben, demonstrating a folding movement.

Whilst Ben folded in the flour, Dorothy took two sandwich tins from the cupboard and rubbed the inside with the empty butter wrapper. She went to check on the oven temperature. Sprinkling a small amount of flour over the sandwich tins, she worked it around the inside, patting the rim as she turned the tins.

"Now pour the mixture into these two tins."

Ben obliged and Dorothy placed the tins in the oven. Ben started running his finger round the inside of the mixing bowl.

"It tastes good," he remarked, licking his finger. "I wash it?"

"Thank you. Use the kettle. It's just boiled."

Ben set to work washing up with water from the kettle. Thirty minutes later, Dorothy took the two nicely golden halves of Victoria sandwich from the oven and turned them out on a wire rack.

"We'll leave them to cool and add the jam when the children come home."

"Thank you for show me to make cake."

"My pleasure."

"Now, I go to read."

Ben went up to his room, lay down on the bed, took his book of adventure stories, and was asleep before the end of his second page. He was woken by the bedroom door flying open and three excited children bursting into the room. Although startled, Ben was able to name each of them.

"Hello. Jessica. Simon. Matty."

"Come downstairs and eat cake."

Ben followed the others down to the kitchen, still feeling slightly drowsy. A beautifully sugared sponge cake was sitting on a cake-stand in the middle of the table.

"You can cut it, Ben," said Dorothy, handing him the knife. "Ben helped me make the cake this afternoon."

Ben cut the cake into eight and placed a piece on everyone's plate.

"That's gigantic!" exclaimed Jessica.

"I like cake," laughed Ben.

The cake tasted particularly good.

When their plates were empty, the three siblings went to their rooms to do their homework.

"We can play in half an hour," promised Matty.

Simon was fifteen, going on sixteen, Matty thirteen and Jessica was ten. Ben collected the plates and washed them up. A tabby cat wandered in through the door. He only had one eye.

"Nelson, have you been hiding in Jessica's room all day?" inquired Dorothy, opening the back door.

Nelson rushed out.

"Are you looking forward to Hanukkah?"

"You have Hanukkah?"

"Yes. Bill is English through and through, so we celebrate Christmas as well. I am Jewish, like you. The children understand both traditions."

"You are born here?"

"Yes. I grew up here."

"Where you meet Mr Field?"

"I was a secretary at the factory. We've been happily married for eighteen years."

"My parents also."

Jessica appeared at the door, curious to get to know Ben.

"That was quick. Have you done your homework and your chores?" asked Dorothy.

"Yes. I dusted my bedroom. Do you want to play Ludo, Ben?"

"What is Ludo?"

"I'll show you."

Jessica went to the cupboard and took out a box. She had just finished setting up when Matty and Simon came in.

"Just shake the dice and move. We can tell you what to do each time," proposed a slightly impatient Matty.

They played their first game which Ben won.

"You are so lucky," groaned Matty, the most competitive of the three siblings.

Bill appeared in the kitchen doorway, having slept since breakfast.

"Good afternoon."

Jessica ran to him and threw her arms round him.

"Daddy!"

Bill kissed the top of her head.

"How was school Matty? Simon?"

I got 'A' for my spelling test," responded Matty.

"Well done."

"I finished my metalwork project."

"Poker, wasn't it?"

"Yes."

"I look forward to seeing it, at the end of term. And what about you, Jessica?"

"I can say my name in French."

"I teach you German?" offered Ben.

"Maybe."

"What's for tea, Dot?"

"Cottage pie."

"What is cottage pie?" asked Ben.

"Minced beef with potato on top. I put it in the oven when I took the cake out. Bill, you can have cake for dessert. Ben made it with me. The rest of us have already had some."

"Good. I'm going to go and wash."

Bill left the room and Dorothy checked in the oven to see how the cottage pie was progressing. It was good for Bill to have a hearty meal, before working a night shift.

That evening, as they sat together, tucking into cottage pie, Ben felt welcome. He had no idea how long he would be their guest, but he felt comfortable enough to stay as long as he had to. Simon put his empty plate on the floor and Nelson came running.

"He likes cottage," commented Ben.

"Not cottage," laughed Jessica, "Cottage pie!"

Ben laughed too, and everyone joined in. Dorothy was laughing so much that the moulded jelly which she had just taken out of the fridge quivered uncontrollably.

"I hope you like strawberry jelly, Ben?" she inquired. "Matty, please get a tin of evaporated out of the pantry."

Bill took a piece of the Victoria sponge, which was sitting underneath a square, umbrella-like fly screen.

"This is great," he complimented Dorothy and Ben as he got up to leave for work, the half-eaten cake still in his hand.

It was Simon's turn to do the washing-up.

"I help?" offered Ben.

"Thanks mate."

Jessica took a piece of folded newspaper tied to a length of string down from the shelf and started to play with Nelson.

"He sleep in your room?" asked Ben.

"Sometimes. Today he got shut in. Do you want him to sleep in your room tonight?"

"Door open? He come," responded Ben.

As soon as the washing up was finished, the four children settled down to a game of Monopoly, which Simon won. Jessica went up to bed followed by Matty and Ben. Simon stayed behind to polish his football boots. Ben left the door to his room ajar. He slept soundly, and when he awoke at five o'clock in the morning, Nelson was curled up on the bed which would have been Saul's.

"Hello, friend," whispered Ben.

The following afternoon, when the others came home from school, Ben went for tea at the Drapers' home, to catch up with Ruth. Dorothy walked him round to the house.

"Do you know your way back?" she asked.

"Yes. I think."

"If you're not back by six, I'll send out a search party."

"I think I understand. Thank you."

Dorothy turned and walked away. Ben flattened his hair, cleared his throat and knocked on the door. A few seconds later, it opened and there was Ruth, standing expectantly with Moshe in her hand.

"Hello," she beamed.

"Hello," replied Ben, crouching down to her level and holding out his arms for a hug. "How has Moshe settled in?"

"He's happy."

"Are you happy?"

"Very happy. They are lovely and they speak German."

"That's very good."

As Ben stood up, his hormones ambushed him. There in the corridor, a few steps behind Ruth, stood Betty, Joe and Anna Draper's fifteen-year-old daughter.

"Hello. I'm Ben, from Karlsruhe."

"Hello, Ben from Karlsruhe. My name is Elizabeth, but everyone calls me Betty. Except my parents, who call me Elizabeth, when I do something naughty."

Ben realised she was speaking in German, so he replied in his own language.

"And does that happen often?"

"No."

Anna appeared in the corridor.

"Hello, Ben. Welcome to our home. Ruth has not stopped talking about you."

Ben couldn't stop thinking about Betty's curves.

"You speak German?" reflected Ben, speaking to Anna.

"Yes. My parents came here in 1890. We are originally from Dusseldorf. Joe's parents are from Stuttgart. They came here one year earlier. So, yes, we speak German, but now we also speak English. Joe and I retain very little of our accent when we speak English. Betty is bilingual, but we only ever spoke German to her at home. It was not a good idea with the Great War. Joe was in the medical corps for the final two years. Praise God he came home. We haven't spoken German outside the home since. It's been nice for Ruth, to help her settle in, but she will soon pick up English at school. So will you, I'm sure."

"Thank you."

The house was detached. It had a small front garden, with a very young Buddleia planted in the middle.

"They have a garden," Ruth informed Ben, excitedly.

"Would you like to see it?" offered Betty.

Ben would not have refused any offer from Betty.

"That would be lovely," he responded.

Betty led the three of them outside, with Ruth grabbing Ben's hand and pulling him along. The rear garden was laid to grass a with few shrubs planted around the edge, not a huge space, but large enough to sit in during warmer weather and play games in. Ben noticed some wooden skittles lying in the grass and a child's tricycle.

"Look, Ben!" exclaimed Ruth, jumping on the tricycle and riding it in a small circle round the skittles.

"Amazing!" Ben encouraged her.

"And there's a bird table too," pointed Ruth. "We made some balls with lard and grain."

"Unfortunately, there's a resident pigeon which seems to drive the smaller birds away, at present," added Betty.

"Teatime!" came Anna's call from the kitchen window.

The children went back into the house and went into the dining room. Whilst they were in the garden, Joe had arrived home from the surgery.

"Hello. I'm Ben, from Karlsruhe," Ben introduced himself, holding out his hand, and immediately going red in the face with embarrassment, "But you already know that."

The last thing Ben wanted to do was look stupid in front of Betty. Joe, sensing Ben's embarrassment, took his hand and shook it anyway.

"Have you settled in Ben?" he asked.

"Yes, thank you. The Fields are very nice, and they have three children. I have my own room at the top of the house.

Yesterday we ate cottage pie. It was very tasty. And I made a Victoria cake with Mrs Field."

"A Victoria Sandwich? You have been busy," replied Anna.

"When will you start at school?" asked Betty.

"After the Christmas holidays, I think. At the grammar."

"I start school on Monday," interjected Ruth. "Moshe has to stay at home."

"Where do you go to school, Betty?" inquired Ben.

"The girls' grammar."

"Would you like to drink tea, milk or water, Ben?" asked Anna.

"Tea is fine, thank you."

"Help yourself to sandwiches," continued Anna.

"Thank you."

Ruth was sitting in between Betty and Ben, with the five of them equally spaced round the circular table. This meant that Ben wasn't quite opposite Betty, but he could watch her, without it being obvious. Her long dark hair was falling over her right shoulder, but the other side was pushed back behind her left shoulder. She wore a bottle-green cardigan with a round neck, and Ben could see her collar bone. He tried not to stare and looked back down at his sandwich. It was pilchard, an unfamiliar flavour to Ben, but not an unpalatable one.

"Betty and I made some scones for after the sandwiches," Ruth informed him, feeling pleased with herself.

"I look forward to these scones," responded Ben, uncertain of what they were, but fairly certain they would be sweet.

Ben washed the pilchard sandwich down with some tea and took a beef paste one. He preferred the latter.

When everyone had eaten two sandwiches each, Betty went into the kitchen and returned carrying a plate of scones. Ben had been wondering why there was a butter dish and a jar of jam sitting on the table and a knife at the side of his plate, but he soon discovered the joys of strawberry jam on buttered scones.

"These are very good. Well done, Ruth," Ben complimented her, "and Betty, of course."

There was an unmistakable glow gathering in Betty's cheeks. Joe caught Anna's eye, with that tacit recognition of parents who remember the awkwardness of their first romantic spark.

"You must come and see us on a regular basis, Ben," suggested Joe.

"That would be great," came the hopeful reply.

"Ooooo, please!" exclaimed Ruth, unaware of the grown-up significance of the conversation.

"Yes," added Anna. "Come a week on Sunday. Same time."

"I'll ask Mr and Mrs Field, but I'm sure it will be absolutely fine. Thank you. May I help with the washing up, before I leave?"

"What a helpful boy, isn't he Joe?" responded Anna. "No, thank you. There's no need."

"Then, on that note, I shall bid you goodbye. And again, thank you for a lovely tea."

"I'll show you to the door," proposed Betty.

Ruth took hold of Ben's hand and pulled him along the hallway. Betty followed. Crouching down, Ben looked Ruth in the eyes and said, "You are a very lucky girl to have met your big sister."

It came out awkwardly. Ben was frustrated with himself but took encouragement from the colour rising to Betty's cheeks again.

"It sounds like you've been a wonderful big brother to Ruth. And I'm sorry about what happened with your brother."

"Thank you."

As he walked back to the Fields, Ben didn't know whether to laugh or cry. All he knew was the hormone fuelled emotions he was experiencing were uncharted territory. A week on Sunday couldn't come round fast enough.

MAZEL TOV

On Thursday 5th January 1939, Ben started at the local boys' grammar school. He wore a second-hand uniform, but one with trousers which, thankfully, reached beyond his ankles. More practical than academic, he was a little nervous about the prospect, but he was keen to discover what woodwork and metalwork facilities the school might have, if indeed it had any. Confident in maths, he felt certain of building a good reputation with at least one teacher. What Ben was less confident about was the reaction of the other pupils. Would he be welcomed? Surely, there were others who lived in the catchment area, in a similar situation to him. Ben was determined to master the English language and settle in as quickly as possible. If anyone bullied him, he knew he could rely on his boxing skills.

With an air of determination, Ben left the house, a scribbled map in his pocket, having agreed it was too embarrassing, at sixteen, to turn up for the first day at school with a parent in tow. His letter of introduction was folded away in the borrowed satchel he now sported. To his immense joy and extreme awkwardness, as he reached the end of the street where the Drapers lived, he ran into Betty. Their paths would diverge as each continued to the girls' and boys' sites, but those first few streets would enable them to begin a conversation which needed neither to be mindful of Joe and Anna Draper, nor pitched to include Ruth.

"Hello, Ben from Karlsruhe," Betty greeted him.

"Hello. I'm trying to lose the 'from Karlsruhe'. I mean, they'll probably find out eventually, but I'd like to try and impress a few people before they realise that I'm a German Jewish kid."

He immediately kicked himself for challenging her.

"That's an excellent idea. Maybe we should speak in English, too."

Relief for Ben.

"Is Ruth happy with her school?"

Again, Ben felt awkward. he could have asked any question about Betty, but he chose to ask about Ruth.

"She is. I think she's made some friends."

"Good."

"And what about you?"

"Nervous but looking forward to getting back to some sort of normal routine," replied Ben in German, in a low voice, adding, in English, "I hope the school has a place to make wood and metal things."

"Is that what you're good at?"

"I learn to make wood from my father. I like it a lot. What do you like to do?"

"I enjoy school. My father wants me to be a doctor, like him. I don't think I'm cut out for it. I think I could teach."

"What can you teach?

"Children the same age as Ruth. I really like that age. Which means teaching a little bit of everything."

"I'm sure you'd be very good at it," responded Ben, in German.

"I think this is where we take different streets," announced Betty.

"Tomorrow, I can walk with you?"

Ben immediately regretted the question.

"I'd like that very much," came the reply.

Ben looked at his watch, working out how long they had been walking together.

"Quarter past eight, tomorrow."

"Have a good first day, Ben."

"Thank you. You, also."

Ben immediately felt stupid because it wasn't Betty's first day at the school, although as the two went their separate ways, Ben had a spring in his step. As he turned into the street on which the grammar school stood, two boys of a similar age came alongside him.

"Not seen you before. Are you new?" inquired the taller of the two.

"Yes, I am. I move house," replied Ben, hoping neither his accent nor his lack of tenses would give him away.

"You one of those German Jewish kids?"

"Yes," responded Ben, disappointed that his provenance was so quickly recognised.

"We'll look out for you," offered the shorter one. "I'm Stan and he's Max."

"I'm Ben."

"Is it true, what's happening to our brothers and sisters in Germany?" asked Max.

"Yes. One moment. Are you Jewish?"

"Born and raised here. Like Betty, who we saw you talking to earlier. She's a showstopper that one. Been chasing her for months."

Ben went red, partly out of embarrassment, partly due to the unfamiliar feelings of jealousy he was experiencing.

"I'm not Jewish," added Stan.

"I am happy to meet both of you."

"And may the best man win," joked Stan, winking at Ben.

They entered the school reception area.

"I register, I think so."

"Catch up at break," promised Max.

Max and Stan disappeared up the stairs and Ben knocked on the office door.

"Come in," came the muffled voice.

Nervously, Ben opened the door.

"Good morning. You must be one of Benjamin, Isaac or Joshua," affirmed the receptionist, kindly.

"I'm Benjamin Lindenheim. I like Ben."

"How have you settled in, Ben?"

"Good, thank you."

"You're with the Fields?"

"Yes. I have letter," responded Ben, taking the letter of introduction from his satchel.

"You'll be in Class 6C. Up the stairs to the first floor," she directed Ben, pointing through the closed door, "along the corridor, third door on your right. Mr Pankhurst is waiting for you. Don't forget to call him 'Sir' and not Mr Pankhurst."

"Thank you," answered Ben, attempting to picture the directions in his head.

On reaching the classroom, to Ben's relief, Max and Stan were sitting at the back. He nodded in their direction as he approached the teacher's desk.

"Good morning, Sir. I am Ben Lindenheim."

"Good morning, Benjamin," came the slightly stern reply. "Sit yourself down."

Ben hardly dared repeat his preference for the contracted first name. The desks were in rows, about a foot apart, with three feet between the rows, just about enough room to walk along the row when pupils were seated at the desks. There was an empty desk, right in the middle of the classroom. Stan jumped up, grabbed his books and satchel and moved towards the middle desk, vacating the desk next to Max.

"Where do you think you're going, Drucker?"

"Max and I met Ben earlier, Sir. I thought I'd let him sit next to Max, as it's his first day."

"Very good, Drucker. Carry on. Be quick, the pair of you."

Ben took his cue and approached the desk next to Max, nodding at Stan in appreciation.

"As many of you already know, and Lindenheim here is proof, there are political problems in Germany. Several children from Germany will be joining us in our school and I want them to feel welcome. With this in mind, I thought we might begin the new term with a brief history lesson."

A gentle groan indicated the level of appreciation for history amongst the boys gathered there.

"Now, now. I did say 'a brief history lesson'."

The groans dissipated.

"Actually, Lindenheim, please tell us, first-hand, what your experience is."

"I try, Sir. My English is not so good," replied Ben, clearing his throat as he stood up. "My family, we lose our business. There are laws. They stop the Jews to do business. We cannot buy food. The police can take away the Jews. People burn houses. They break windows. My parents hear stories. Children can leave Germany. I come to England."

"Thank you Lindenheim. Please be seated."

What followed was Mr Pankhurst's explanation of how Hitler came to power. He named some of the laws which marked out not just Jews, but Gypsies and Communists as criminals. He spoke about the building of the first concentration camps. He mentioned the annexation of Austria and the rise of the SS. Ben understood most of what Mr Pankhurst said. A stunned silence descended on the classroom, and several boys turned to look at Ben.

"You'll be alright, here," Max reassured him, whispering.

"So, Class 6C, your task, for the next three quarters of an hour, is to write your suggestions as to how the rest of the world might respond. And Sparks, you may help Lindenheim with his writing. In fact, you can all work in pairs. Forty-five minutes."

Mr Pankhurst sat at his desk and began to mark the holiday projects, as the air filled with animated discussion.

The bell rang.

"Homework is to complete your arguments in the form of an editorial in *The Times*. Bring it to class on Thursday. Off you go to your next lesson."

The boys filed out of the classroom. Ben had no idea what an editorial was or what style *The Times* was in or even if the Fields would have a copy. His concerns were soon forgotten as the next lesson was woodwork. Perhaps he could shine here. Not only did it not involve writing in English, but he had acquired a few carpentry skills back home.

"Good morning boys," Mr Simmonds greeted them. "We have a stranger in our midst, I see. Identify yourself, Sir Knight."

Mr Simmonds was considered by many to be a little eccentric. He didn't see it quite that way. In a school where there was constant pressure to perform academically, he presented his workshop as a kingdom of the imagination, where the boys had freedom to express themselves.

"I'm Ben, from Karlsruhe, Sir," Ben identified himself.

There was no longer any need to conceal his home city since everyone now knew he was 'one of those Jewish children from Germany'.

"You are welcome among us Sir Benjamin of Karlsruhe."

Ben stopped short of correcting his nomenclature. Something inside was telling him to play along. The boys separated into groups of four, congregating around a series of workbenches.

"Are you familiar with the tools of our realm, Sir Benjamin?"

Ben understood 'tools' and 'familiar' but not realm.

"I enjoy to cut wood," he guessed at a response.

"Well let's see what you're made of, then."

Mr Simmonds rolled down the rotating blackboard to reveal some chalked diagrams.

"Today," he began, holding up a block of wood, "you are going to turn this into one of these.

There was a sketch of an antelope, at the end of a series of staged diagrams.

"Just carve away everything that doesn't look like an antelope, a little piece at a time. You do not need to finish your antelope today. It is the first of several quests we shall accomplish this term. Take a block each from my workbench, and before you start carving, take a pencil, write your name on the bottom, and then, draw the rough dimensions of your antelope. Try and leave two inches for the horns."

Ben felt reassured that the diagrams on the blackboard were sufficient to guide him. There was a vice attached to each corner of the bench, space enough for four boys to work safely. A pile of wooden blocks sat precariously balanced on Mr Simmonds' desk. It was more a workbench strewn with books and papers, and at one end, Mr Simmonds also had a vice and a set of carving tools. His block of wood, already gripped in the metallic jaws, resembled an almost complete antelope, with only the scut to shape. One by one, the boys removed their blocks of wood, and the workshop filled with the percussion of wooden mallets against wooden handles of chisels. Mr Simmonds took the register by sight, and slowly wandered around the room. He watched Ben from the opposite end of the workshop and felt the deep satisfaction of a craftsman in the presence of his talented apprentice. All too soon, the bell rang.

"I look forward to your return in a week's time. I bid you farewell and safe travels."

After the boys had left the workshop, and Mr Simmonds started to tidy away their work, he stood for several minutes admiring the flowing curve on the back of Ben's antelope.

Next on the timetable was Mathematics, another subject where Ben excelled. On entering the classroom, the boys were confronted with a complicated looking equation.

"I like maths," whispered Max, as he and Ben took their seats at adjacent desks.

"I think this also."

"Good morning, Class 6C."

"Good morning, Sir."

"Baker."

"Sir."

"Brady."

"Sir."

Mr Stubbs worked his way through the register.

".... And last, but by no means least, Lindenheim."

"Sir."

Mr Stubbs looked up to see where the last Sir came from.

"Well, Lindenheim. Come to the front," he barked, beckoning Ben forward. "What is the answer to this equation?"

Ben looked across the line of numbers and symbols and brackets.

"Come on. We haven't got all day," Mr Stubbs chivvied him.

"Forty-two, Sir."

"Thank you Lindenheim. I take it Mathematics is one of your strengths. Perhaps you might now explain to the class how you arrived at forty-two."

For Ben, the maths was simple, the language of maths not so straightforward. He was embarrassed, and couldn't work out if the teacher was being deliberately sarcastic, trying to make him look stupid in front of the class. Out of panic, he started to explain the problem in German.

"Are you trying to be clever with me, Lindenheim?" inquired Mr Stubbs.

Ben misunderstood, hearing 'clever', and responded, "Yes, Sir."

Max lowered his face into his hands, knowing what was coming next.

"Hold out your left hand, Lindenheim."

Ben tentatively stretched out his hand.

"Let this be a lesson to you," hissed Mr Stubbs, thwacking Ben's knuckles with the edge of a wooden ruler. "Now go and sit down, Lindenheim."

Ben returned to his seat, his hand throbbing with pain, wondering what he had done to deserve the punishment. Was this how intelligence was rewarded? How could Ben have known that, secretly, Mr Stubbs was more than impressed by Hitler's rise to power and singularly unimpressed by the arrival of hundreds of Jewish children in his small, green and pleasant island? Thankfully, Mr Stubbs turned out to be the only teacher in the grammar school with whom Ben came into contact who was unsympathetic.

By the end of the day, Ben's hand bore a purply-pink weal, but the remaining lessons had proved uneventful. Max had been a good friend, throughout. They had met up with Stan during the lunch break, and when Stan had inquired about the already pink and swollen mark on Ben's hand, all Max had responded was, 'That Nazi sympathiser, again'. The afternoon geography lesson was all about volcanoes and the last lesson of the day, biology, was all about Mendel and his peas.

"See you tomorrow," said Max, as they left the school gates.

"Yes. Thank you. See you tomorrow."

Ben went straight to his room and completed his homework, hampered by the bruising to his hand.

"Tea!" came the invitation, echoing up through the house.

He almost collided with Jessica as she shot out of her room and hurtled down the stairs.

"Hey, Ben!" she greeted him, already on the stairs.

"Hello, Jessica."

"What on earth happened to you?" remarked Dorothy, as he took his napkin from its tarnished silver ring.

"It is nothing."

"It doesn't look like nothing to me," she pressed him.

"I have a good day at school but not with one teacher. He is Nazi sympathiser. He hit my hand with ruler."

"What did you do? Anyway, how do you know he is a Nazi sympathiser?"

"I make new friend. Max. He tells me. I try to explain maths with German. Too difficult with English."

"Well, I'm going to go and talk to the headmaster, tomorrow."

"Please. No. It gets badder afterwards."

"Alright, but I want to know if this happens again. 'Worse' not 'badder'."

Ben nodded and took the plate of beef stew Dorothy was holding out to him.

"I clean these?" suggested Ben, at the end of the meal, holding up his napkin-ring. "I have no chores, you say?"

The silver napkin-rings had been inherited from an aunt and were the only items of silver in the house. Dorothy rummaged in the cupboard under the sink and handed Ben a cannister of Brasso and the torn-off sleeve from a flannel shirt. Ben noticed that one end was blackened and the other hardly dirty at all, so assumed the blackened end was used for putting on the polish and the cleaner end for buffing. He set to work on the six slightly concave napkin-rings, bringing up a shine, which reflected his upside-down face back at him.

"Lovely job," Dorothy encouraged him.

"Thank you."

"No, thank YOU," she re-emphasised her appreciation, returning the Brasso and cloth to the cupboard whilst Ben put the napkins back in the rings.

The children played Monopoly until bedtime. Just before he disappeared up the stairs, Dorothy called him back.

"Let me have another look at that hand," she insisted. "I think we should put some Germolene cream on it, tonight."

"What is Germolene? It comes from Germany, no?"

"I don't think so. Miracle cure. You'll see," smiled Dorothy. "Don't move."

She went to her bedroom and returned holding a small screw-top jar, which she unscrewed and offered to Ben.

"Take some on your finger and rub it in gently, all over your hand."

Ben did as he was instructed.

"Thank you. Good night."

"Sleep well."

Ben fell asleep contemplating what he might say to Betty, if he met her on his way to school in the morning.

He was woken in the small hours by Nelson licking the residue from the Germolene cream on his hand.

"Nelson. I didn't see you in here," remarked Ben, in German. "Where were you hiding?"

As Nelson appeared not to understand German, Ben tucked his left arm under the covers and drifted back to sleep, with the cat snuggled against his leg. Ben was already becoming a cat-person.

Shortly before his alarm clock went off, Ben descended into a chaotic nightmare in which gaunt looking people were walking across a barbed-wire-enclosed compound. When they reached desks, a little like the desk where he met Dorothy, at Liverpool Street station, they held out handfuls of peas to a man in uniform. Some were sent to the left, others to the right. Suddenly, the depths of his sleep were filled with the sound of breaking glass. He woke sweating and turned off his alarm. Jumping out of bed, he poured some water into the basin and sloshed it onto his face. That was when he noticed the weal on his hand had almost disappeared. He went downstairs and joined the queue for the toilet, after which it was the usual porridge for breakfast. Now accustomed to the weird texture, Ben looked forward to this morning delicacy. He wolfed it down.

"Someone's in a hurry!" exclaimed Dorothy.

"I meet my friend before school."

Ben didn't indicate which friend, but he wanted to make certain he was waiting at the end of Betty's street, before she arrived, and although he was truly grateful to have met Max, he hoped he didn't run into him, before having the chance to get to know Betty more, especially as Max fancied her.

As luck would have it, Betty appeared only a minute or so after Ben had positioned himself on the corner of the street, a few minutes early herself, anticipating a similar encounter.

"Good morning, Ben from Karlsruhe."

"Hello, Betty. How are you?" responded Ben, quite liking the way Betty called him 'Ben from Karlsruhe', when no one else was around.

"I'm good. How was school yesterday?"

"I enjoy. Not one of teachers. He hits with ruler."

"What did you do?"

"I think teacher, he is Nazi sympathiser."

"That's terrible."

"I make friend, Max."

"Max Sparks?"

"Yes. He see me with you yesterday. He says you and he, if possible, he hopes together."

Ben was kicking himself for opening the door to the competition. Betty blushed.

"But I'm not interested in Max."

There was a momentary opportunity to explore the pause which followed, but the moment passed, and Ben satisfied himself with the knowledge that he might have a chance. This really was the great unknown for Ben, unsure of the etiquette required, which possibly accounted for the bold naivety of his next statement.

"I hope you and me, we can be together."

"I think I would like that very much."

A joy which Ben had not experienced before, erupted inside him.

"Can we go this weekend to the park?"

"That would be lovely. Sunday. I will meet you at the gates at two o'clock. If you come to the house, Ruth will want to come to the park with us," suggested Betty, heading off down the street towards her school, leaving Ben to reflect on what would be his first ever date.

At the end of teatime on Friday, just before leaving for work, Bill dropped a spanner in the works.

"I'll introduce you to the boxing club, on Sunday afternoon, if you like Ben?"

"Aagh. I say to meet with my friend, in the park."

Ben didn't really want to reveal his plans but adding 'in the park' seemed to deflect questions as to who, what or where.

"No matter. Next week?"

"Thank you," answered Ben, relieved.

"It's really nice that you have made friends," commented Dorothy, as Ben was drying up the dishes for her.

"Yes, I think this, also," replied Ben, hoping Dorothy's curiosity wouldn't necessitate further enquiries.

He felt the heat in his cheeks.

"If I didn't know any better, I would say you were blushing."

Thankfully, the other children had gone to their rooms or were doing their chores somewhere other than in the kitchen.

"I make friend, Max, in school. I go to park with Betty Draper."

"Awww," responded Dorothy, giving Ben an affectionate tweak of the cheek. "Your secret is safe with me. Make sure you're a good boy, mind."

"Thank you. And yes. Good behaviour."

On the dot of two, on Sunday afternoon, Ben was leaning against one of the gateposts at the entrance to the park, watching along the street. Families passed through the open gates, some with prams, others with children in pushchairs, still others with older children carrying balls and hoops, running and jumping. Ben felt a nostalgia for the visits his family used to make to the park in Karlsruhe, followed by a twinge of sadness at the realisation that Saul had still not returned from New York. Ben's thoughts had been too filled with Betty, these last few days, to think much about his brother, and now he felt guilty.

Around the corner at the end of the street came Ruth, pedalling manically on her tricycle, with Betty, walking briskly, a few paces behind. Ben's heart sank.

"Hello Ben," shouted Ruth, as she sped past Ben into the park.

"I had no choice," explained Betty. "I'm sure she'll be happy whizzing up and down the paths on her tricycle whilst we walk and talk, or even sit on a bench."

"She is happy. I think so."

"She has settled in well. So have you. I cannot imagine how difficult it must be."

"I cannot choose my life. I can accept it. I meet nice family. I make friend. I meet you."

"And I meet you, too, Ben from Karlsruhe."

At that moment Ruth whizzed past, ringing the shiny new bell, attached to the handlebars, and the tentative declaration was lost. They continued walking and chatting, their conversation interrupted every few minutes by the ringing of the bell.

"It's not such a bad thing, having Ruth here with us. No one will ask questions."

"I think this also," responded Ben, wondering how and at what point, he might begin to hold Betty's hand.

Next time Ruth whizzed past them, her back towards them, Ben grabbed Betty's hand and squeezed it. She reciprocated the squeeze. Just as Ruth appeared to circle for her return lap, Betty released Ben's hand. As if to reassure him, no sooner had Ruth whizzed away from them again, a few moments later, Betty took Ben's hand again.

"Do your parents know?"

"Do my parents know what? That I come to the park or that I like you?"

"I think both."

"They know I come to the park to meet you. They haven't said anything else."

This time, as Ruth approached them, she freewheeled to a stop, almost running into them.

"I'm tired. Can we go home?"

Betty looked at Ben and smiled.

"Yes, Ruth. We can go home. Shall we come to the park next Sunday?"

"Please, please, please!"

"Mr Field takes me next Sunday to the boxing club. We walk on Saturday?"

"It is the Sabbath. Maybe my parents let me come. They are not strict, but they may have plans after the synagogue."

"I can come to the synagogue?"

"But I will be with my mother and Ruth and you would be on the side of my father," laughed Betty. "Come, anyway. I will ask my parents if you can come and eat with us afterwards."

"I like this, also."

They made their way to the gate, strolling, due to a tired child dawdling ahead of them on her tricycle.

"I see you at the synagogue. Bye Ruth, Be good. Bye, Betty."

"Goodbye, Ben," giggled Ruth.

"Bye, Ben. See you next week."

The following Saturday, Ben went to the synagogue. He hung around outside until the Drapers arrived, whereupon Ruth ran headlong towards him and almost knocked him off his feet in her attempt to hug him. She hadn't done this at the park, possibly because she was on her tricycle, but Ben was convinced her actions were intentional, to draw attention to him, with a view to convincing the Drapers that he should be included in their weekly Sabbath outing. Ruth grabbed Ben's hand and dragged him back over to where Joe, Anna and Betty were standing.

"Hello Ben," Joe welcomed him. "It's good to see you're keeping the faith."

Ben felt guilty, knowing that his only intention was to meet with Betty.

"You'd better come with me. We'll re-join our lovely ladies in a short while."

Ben didn't remember packing his kippah, but when he had unpacked at the Fields, he found it in the pouch inside the lid of his suitcase. No doubt his mother was hoping he would remain faithful. He placed it on his head and followed Joe to the men's side of the congregation, catching Betty's eye as he turned away. Betty, Ruth and Anna entered through the opposite door.

"I expect you'll understand some of the service. I'm assuming you studied for your bar mitzvah and the same Hebrew is read in the synagogue in Karlsruhe?"

"I think this, also," responded Ben.

Throughout the service, Ben took his cue from Joe, although he struggled to concentrate on anything, as he could just see the back of Betty's head, beyond the decorated wooden screen separating the genders. At one point Joe had to nudge him to turn the page. Ben's face flushed. At the end of the service, they exited the building and found Ruth, Betty and Anna chatting to another family. Ben recognised the boy from school and wondered whether he was Isaac or Joshua, one of the other transported German boys, or whether the family were members of the substantial Jewish community, established in the east end of London. Anna noticed Joe and Ben walking their way and touched the mother's elbow. Ben couldn't hear what was said, but Ruth, Betty and Anna all peeled off together and came to meet them.

"Betty has asked if you can come for a meal. You are most welcome to.

"Thank you. I like this very much."

The family walked the short distance to where the Drapers' car was parked. Ben found himself squeezed in the back. To his frustration, he was separated from Betty by Ruth, who wriggled the whole journey home. In the house, everything had already been prepared the evening before, and now lay neatly arranged on the dining table under a fresh tablecloth. The tablecloth was folded and put to one side, Joe gave a blessing, and the family ate. It was a while since Ben had eaten challah bread and as he chewed, a wave of nostalgia engulfed him, and his eyes welled up. Anna noticed.

"Betty and Ruth made the challah this week," she said, in German.

"It is very good," responded Ben, somehow managing to choke on a crumb which legitimised his watery eyes, not that the salty expression of homesickness was to be ashamed of.

"They're looking to sell the land on which our synagogue stands. No one is quite sure where we will be meeting or when we will have a replacement site."

"This is difficult," replied Ben. "When will this take place?"

"In the next few months."

"Do the Fields attend?" asked Anna.

"I don't think so. Mrs Field is Jewish. Mr Field is not. We celebrate both Hanukkah and Christmas."

"You are more than welcome to come with us."

"Thank you."

Ben couldn't believe his luck, although, if they were separated and he wasn't able to sit with Betty, it might prove difficult to then talk about meeting up outside of school or synagogue. For now, Ben would satisfy himself with basking in Betty's beauty at a distance each Saturday.

At the end of the meal, Ben felt he shouldn't outstay his welcome.

"This is delicious. Thank you. I should probably go home, now."

"I play the piano, Ben," announced Ruth. "Can I show you?"

This little angel had again sensed an opportunity to facilitate Ben's time in Betty's presence.

"Go on, then, Ruth," Anna encouraged her.

Ruth ran to the piano and climbed onto the stool. Her legs didn't quite reach the pedals, but she had been learning the fingering. Slowly, but surely, 'Twinkle, twinkle, little star' emanated from the chords.

Everyone applauded, when she finished.

"I'll come to the door with you," proposed Betty.

"Thank you, again," repeated Ben.

"Come here next week and you can have a lift in the car," suggested Joe.

"You are very kind."

Joe and Anna were both really kind towards Ben. They also both rather hoped something might come of the budding romantic connection between Ben and their daughter.

"I will see you on the way to school," whispered Betty, as she opened the door for Ben.

"Yes. I think this, also."

Ben ran all the way home.

"Someone's acting like they're the cat that got the cream," joked Dorothy, when Ben walked through the door.

"I do not understand," responded Ben.

"Cats are meant to like cream. If you got the little bit of cream at the top of the bottle, and you were a cat, you'd be as happy as you seem right now."

"I am happy. Yes. I go to synagogue each week."

"This wouldn't have something to do with a girl, would it?" Dorothy ribbed him.

Ben laughed and carried on up to his room, where Nelson was happy to see him, although he had no cream. Ben gave him lots of attention and kissed him on top of his head.

The following day, courtesy of some borrowed shorts from Simon, Bill took Ben to the local boxing club.

"Wait here a moment," Bill instructed him, as they entered the building.

Bill continued over to the ring and beckoned the trainer to the ropes.

"I've got a new lad, one of the German Jewish boys who's staying with us. Any chance you could give him a try-out."

The trainer was an old friend of Bill's and he understood that Bill was asking for a free pass for Ben. The family couldn't really afford the weekly subs.

"Of course. Tell him to get his shorts on, grab some of the gloves from the shelf and bring him to the ring."

"Cheers."

Bill returned to where Ben was hovering nervously.

"Go get your shorts on and meet me by the ring," said Bill, pointing towards the changing room and the ring.

Ben nodded and trotted over to the changing room door. He was changed and back out in under two minutes. He stood patiently whilst Bill tied on a pair of boxing gloves, at which point the trainer nodded at the lad he was sparring with, who jumped out of the ring to make way for Ben.

"What's your name?"

"Ben."

"Well, Ben. Let's see what you've got."

Ben took up his stance.

"Ah, southpaw," commented the trainer.

They sparred for a good ten minutes during which time Ben jabbed away, doggedly, let go several left hooks and dodged several attempts by the trainer to floor him.

"You've got some skills, there, Ben," the trainer affirmed him, as he held up both gloves to indicate the session was over.

"Thank you."

"Would you like to fight Pete, over there?" he proposed, pointing at a gangly lad, pounding the punch-bag.

"I fight this boy, also?"

"Yes. Are you up for it?"

Ben nodded, and the trainer whistled at Pete.

"Pete, come and fight."

Pete jogged over and climbed up into the ring.

"Keep it clean lads. Box."

Ben and Pete started to fight. Inside two minutes, Pete was reeling from a left hook. He stumbled against the ropes. The two boys came together again, Pete bleeding from the nose. Angry now, he fought harder, but Ben was an accomplished boxer and not long after the first effective hook, he landed another, and Pete fell to the ground.

Ben stood watching as the trainer checked Pete's condition, slapping his cheek a couple of times, and taking a small bottle of smelling salts from his pocket, waved it under Pete's nose until he came round.

"You box well," groaned Pete, graciously.

"Thank you. I am sorry."

"Don't apologise," laughed the trainer. 'It's a long time, since someone with your talent, at your age, has boxed in this club. There's a tournament in a few months. I want to get you in peak condition to fight. You stand a very good chance of winning it."

Ben wasn't sure he understood everything, but Bill was standing watching, and overheard the whole conversation. He ruffled Ben's hair as he jumped down from the ring.

"Is that a yes, then?" Bill called up to the trainer.

"I'd say that's a definite!"

"See you next week. Thanks."

"Thank you," added Ben, as Bill untied his gloves.

"Where did you learn to box?"

"In Karlsruhe."

Bill didn't pursue the conversation to identify where in Karlsruhe. He was excited to have such a prodigy under his roof and couldn't wait to tell Dorothy.

Ben was back at the club the following Sunday, training and sparring. In fact, his life was settling into the most unanticipated, pleasurable routine. Meeting Betty on the way to school, trips to the synagogue on Saturdays, often followed by lunch at the Drapers, although they also had other guests to entertain, sessions at the boxing club on Sundays. He was managing to avoid giving Mr Stubbs an excuse to apply corporal punishment, not that Mr Stubbs needed any excuse to wind Ben up. Ben's English was improving, and his wooden antelope was nearing completion. His plan was to give it to Betty for her birthday, in July.

By the time Ben's own birthday came round, in May, he realised Betty had not yet visited the Fields. He and Betty were clearly an item by now, and it wasn't as if Dorothy hadn't been in on the romantic secret from early on.

"What would you like to do to celebrate your birthday?" asked Dorothy one evening as they were doing the washing up.

"You know that I have gone to see Betty Draper, for some months now. We are committed to each other. I would like very much that we invite her for a celebration meal."

Dorothy tweaked Ben's cheek, just as she had done when he first told her about his girlfriend.

"Nothing would give me greater pleasure. Your birthday falls on a Friday. We'll have a nice meal with a cake, before Bill goes off to work. You can even help make the cake. Seventeen candles!"

"I will invite Betty at five o'clock?"

"You can, indeed."

Delighted with Dorothy's response, Ben was both happy and nervous. The siblings didn't know about Betty and Ben didn't want to be ribbed about having a girlfriend, but he wanted to stop making excuses and meeting 'a friend' all the time. He was also a little sad that he couldn't tell Saul or his parents. Saul had not yet made it to England and Ben wondered if he had even received the letter. Surely, he would have tried to return, wouldn't he? Perhaps he had found a job and was saving up for the passage across the Atlantic.

The next morning, as he walked to school with Betty he invited her.

"It is my birthday on Friday. I asked Mrs Field that I can invite you for tea at five o'clock. Will you come?"

"I would love to come. Do Mr and Mrs Field know we are together?"

"Mrs Field, she knows all the time about you. She is very happy."

"I'm pretty sure my parents will say I can come. I will tell you tomorrow."

They separated to take the roads leading to their respective schools.

Three days later, on the Friday morning, Betty had a handmade card for Ben.

"Happy Birthday," she greeted him at the corner of her street.

"Thank you."

Ben opened the envelope.

"Did you make this?"

"Yes."

"It is beautiful. Thank you."

Betty had signed her name and added three kisses, arranged in a triangle.

"I can give you a birthday kiss?" suggested Betty.

Ben leant towards her and received a small kiss on the lips. He longed for so much more, but not here, not now. He glanced around, just to make sure no one had seen them. The coast was clear.

"I'll see you later. Five o'clock," confirmed Betty. "Have a lovely day."

"It is now so lovely. Five o'clock. Bye."

"Bye."

Ben could hardly concentrate all day and kept playing the sensation of that briefest of kisses, over and over again, in his mind. Five o'clock couldn't come round quick enough. The birthday cake had been made the evening before, and Dorothy had promised to buy candles today. When Ben arrived home from school, there was a small parcel on his bed. He opened it to find a stainless-steel razor, with a little note attached, 'Happy 17th Birthday Ben. My father gave me my first razor on my seventeenth. See you later. Bill'. Tears welled up in Ben's eyes, a confused response to his own father being absent and Bill demonstrating such kindness towards him. He poured water in the basin, rubbed his face with soap and started to shave the gathering fluff around his chin. The inevitable happened. He nicked the skin and was now bleeding. The only thing to hand, other than his hand-towel, which he didn't want to stain, was a newspaper, so he tore off the corner and allowed the blood to stick it to his face. When he went downstairs, Jessica erupted with laughter.

"I take it you got Bill's special gift," smiled Dorothy. "We'd better get some Germolene cream on that. With a bit of luck, it won't be noticeable by five o'clock."

"I am very happy for this gift. Thank you. I will practise."

The table was laid, and a pile of envelopes was sitting on Ben's placemat, along with three parcels.

"Are these for me?" asked Ben.

"Yes, but you must wait for teatime to open them."

Ben felt so accepted by the Fields. He was becoming increasingly nervous, as five o'clock approached. The aroma of a mutton stew filled the house. Ben's birthday cake, another Victoria Sandwich, but this time, covered in butter-cream icing, bedecked with seventeen candles, sat proudly on the sideboard, mounted on the cake-stand. Bill appeared in the kitchen doorway.

"Happy birthday, Ben"

"Thank you. And thank you for the razor. I cut myself."

"So, I see," laughed Bill, with Ben, not at him. "Have I got time to go and get shaved, myself, Dot?"

"If you're quick."

"Better make an effort for your girl," Bill encouraged Ben, winking, as he turned and skuttled off to the bathroom.

Just thirty seconds after Bill reappeared in the kitchen, his face now clean-shaven, the doorbell rang. Jessica started out for the door.

"Jess, not this time. Let Ben get it," insisted Bill.

Jessica stopped in her tracks, shrugged and snorted.

"I hope you're not being cheeky, my girl."

Jessica looked at him with her little-girl-can-wind-daddy-round-her-finger eyes and shook her head. Ben overtook Jessica and went to open the door. Outside stood Betty, wearing the bottle-green cardigan she had on, the day Ben met her, and for the second time, Ben couldn't help noticing the line of her collar bone. He was captivated.

"Happy birthday, again."

"Thank you. Come in. May I present to you, Mr and Mrs Field, Simon, Matty and Jessica."

"Bill and Dorothy is fine," responded Bill, "Although I call her Dot."

"Pleased to meet you."

"You're very pretty," observed Jessica, with a forwardness that comes from naivety.

"Thank you, Jessica."

"Come and sit down," Dorothy invited Betty, adding, "Jessica is right! You are a pretty girl."

Ben held out his hands in a sense of helpless agreement, and everyone took their place at the table, laughing.

"You will have to open your presents, Ben, otherwise there's no room for the plates," suggested Dorothy.

Ben opened the first which was from Jessica. He untied the ribbon and unfolded the paper to find his very own silver napkin-ring.

"I found it at the market. As we all have our own, I thought you should have one too, now you're part of the family."

Ben's eyes teared up.

"Thank you. This is lovely."

The second present was a little larger, but flat. Ben removed the paper to find a pair of boxing shorts.

"I think a champion needs his own shorts, don't you?" observed Simon.

"We bought them together," chimed in Matty.

"Thank you. I love this, also."

The third present was the largest of the three. Ben unwrapped it to come face to face with a pair of boxing gloves.

"They're not knew, but I've waxed them up and replaced the laces, so they look like new," explained Dorothy. "They're from Bill and me. A champion needs his own gloves too."

"Thank you. I am so happy. I have no words. Thank you."

Bill stood up.

"Allow me to put them on the sideboard for you," he offered.

Ben handed over his birthday haul and Dorothy served the casserole, which had been cooking on a low heat for the entire afternoon. She had removed the bones, after the meat had fallen off them.

"I've taken out the bones, but just be careful you done find a fragment lurking somewhere."

There was a satisfied silence as the family and their guest ate their first mouthfuls.

"You've done us proud, as usual, Dot," Bill affirmed his wife.

"This is very good, indeed," added Betty.

Simon removed a tiny piece of bone from his mouth and placed it on the side of the plate.

"Even the bones are tasty," he laughed.

He couldn't help staring at Betty's collar bone, understandably, as he was of a similar age to Ben. He tried not to be jealous.

"When is your birthday, Betty?" asked Jessica.

"Not for a while," she replied.

"How old are you?" Jessica pressed her.

"I'm fifteen. How old are you, Jessica?"

"I'll be eleven next month."

"Will you be changing schools in September?"

"Yes."

Ben and Betty came to the simultaneous realisation that Jessica would be going to the same school as Betty, which would mean no more walking part of the way to school together. Their eyes met.

"Have you all finished your casserole?" asked Dorothy.

Heads nodded around the table.

"Thank you, Dorothy," responded Betty, placing her knife and fork on the plate together.

Simon piled everyone's plate on top of his, not something he usually did so readily. Why he was trying to impress a girl who was clearly besotted with Ben, was beyond reason, not that hormones and sibling rivalry are based on any sense of logic. Bill caught Simon's eye with the briefest of disapproving frowns. Realising he was rumbled, Simon tried to recover.

"Ben made the birthday cake with our mother, Betty."

The plates were carried to the sink by Matty. Dorothy took a box of safety matches from the shelf and lit the candles. The cake was placed in the middle of the table, and the family, including Betty, sang 'Happy Birthday' to Ben. Jessica led the applause at the end.

"You have to make a wish when you blow out the candles," insisted Jessica.

Ben took a deep breath and extinguished the flames with a long breath. His wish was to marry Betty. How old did he have to be in this country? Would she want to marry him? Did he need Joe Draper's permission? The cake was cut, and everyone dived into the creamy, jammy delight.

"I've got to love you and leave you," announced Bill, standing up with his half-eaten slice of cake in his left hand. "Thank you, Dot. Ben. Lovely meal. See you tomorrow. Nice to meet you, Betty. I work nights at the factory."

Betty rose from her chair out of courtesy.

"Don't stand on ceremony. You're family."

"Anyone like another slice?" asked Dorothy.

"Full to busting," responded Simon.

Matty shook his head.

"Can I show Betty my room?" asked Jessica.

"Does Betty want to see your room?" responded Dorothy.

"I'll see if Nelson is in my room at the same time," added Ben.

"Go on then," came Dorothy's approval. "Matty and Simon, please will you help me with the dishes tonight?"

Neither brother protested. Jessica led Betty out of the room with Ben bringing up the rear. Ben hadn't ever been invited into Jessica's room, but why would he be? This was some honour for Betty. They reached the door.

"Ben, you have to stand at the door. Only girls are allowed in here. I have a dolls house."

"Alright, then."

Jessica was excited to show Betty her dolls' house. Ben hadn't seen it before. In fact, he wasn't aware Jessica had a dolls' house. He decided to make her a piece of wooden furniture for her birthday the following month.

"That is a lovely dolls' house," observed Betty.

"Do you want to play?"

"I probably don't have time today. Maybe next time. Ben was going to show me Nelson and then I have to go home."

Jessica looked a little disappointed, but she didn't argue. Ben opened his bedroom door to see a sleepy Nelson curled up on the bed which would have been Saul's.

"I present to you, Nelson."

"I love cats," exclaimed Betty, stepping forward to stroke the cat.

Nelson rolled on his back, welcoming affection. Betty sat next to him and rubbed his tummy, as Ben stood watching. If Jessica hadn't been there too, he might have been tempted to sit next to Betty on the bed.

"He's rather gorgeous. How did he lose his eye?"

"Don't know," replied Jessica, shrugging her shoulders.

"He passes many hours in my room," explained Ben. "Even in the night, he sleeps here with me."

Betty stood up.

"I really should be getting back, now."

"Do you want that I walk with you?"

"That would be lovely. Thank you."

"Goodbye, Jessica. I have a tiny doll I don't play with anymore. Shall I bring her for your dolls' house, next time I'm invited?"

"Ooh, yes please."

Jessica stood watching as Ben and Betty went back downstairs, before going into her room to make a space in the dolls' house for a new doll, even though she didn't know how long she would have to wait for the new addition.

"Thank you for a lovely meal. It was good to meet Ben's family."

"I hope you'll come and eat with us again, in the not-too-distant future," replied Dorothy.

"I hope so too," added Simon as he dried the dishes, emboldened by the lack of his father's presence.

"I shall walk with Betty to her house. I shall return straight away."

"See you in a bit."

Ben grabbed his jacket from the hooks behind the door, and he and Betty set off to walk the short journey to the Drapers'. There was never any question of her safety. It was simply an excuse to steal a few moments alone with her. In the end, they walked past the end of the street where Betty lived and made a three-street detour.

"How old must a person be to get married?"

"I think it's sixteen."

"When you are sixteen, I ask that you will marry me. I must ask your father also, I think so?"

Betty blushed.

"He's likes you. As does my mother. We are still very young. I'm not saying 'no' though. Where would we live? We're both still at school."

"I am not so practical. I am in love with you, Betty."

She stopped and looked at Ben.

"I think I'm in love with you too, Ben."

"I shall ask your father. If he tells us wait, we wait, but I want to be married with you."

Ben leant forward to kiss Betty, and she moved to meet his lips with hers. They remained in a kiss for several seconds, until Ben pulled away, for the sake of modesty. Taking her hand, they continued their journey, repeating the kiss, outside the front door.

"See you tomorrow, at the synagogue."

"Goodnight, Ben."

"Goodnight, Betty."

The next few weeks were busy for Ben. He finished his antelope, ready for Betty's birthday, and made a tiny writing desk and chair for Jessica's dolls' house, all beautifully sanded and polished, from some offcuts in Mr Simmonds' workshop. The desk even had a drawer which opened. Mr Simmonds glowed with pride when he saw the miniature furniture. Betty was invited, at Jessica's request, to her birthday party.

The boxing tournament would be the day after Jessica's party, and Ben had been putting in an extra training session after school on Wednesdays. He was feeling confident. He had been invited for lunch, at the Drapers again, and fully intended to take time to ask Joe for Betty's hand in marriage. Unfortunately, he sustained a black eye, a few days prior to the meal, and when he joined the Draper family at the synagogue, in spite of his liberal applications of Germolene cream, it was still purple.

"My, oh my!" reacted Anna.

"I train for the boxing championships. It's not a fight in the street and I was not attacked."

"Well, that's a relief," she responded.

"You stink!" announced Ruth.

"Is that a new aftershave?" Joe ribbed him, as the fumes from the ointment reached him, several feet away.

"It is the Germolene cream," laughed Ben, growing in his understanding of the British sense of humour.

As usual, Joe and Ben entered the men's section and Ruth, Betty and Anna went in through the women's entrance. This gave Ben an opportunity to speak of his intentions towards Betty.

"Can I ask you something?" he inquired nervously.

"Anything."

"I know that we are still young. I want to ask if you permit me that I ask Betty to be married with me."

"You are still very young. Are you sure?"

"I am certain."

"And Betty?"

"We love each other."

"I will give you my blessing, for the engagement, but I think you should wait until next year, when she will be seventeen. Then the marriage. I was hoping she would train to be a doctor. And you want a traditional Jewish wedding, of course?"

Ben was not about to point out that Betty didn't want to follow in her father's footsteps as a doctor.

"Perhaps you should ask her," continued Joe, "Or at least you should discuss your future. I mean, we don't know how long you will be in England, and I certainly hope you won't take Betty off to Germany and away from her studies."

"I understand. I want to live here, now. I will find work."

"Are you sure about that?"

"Yes. I am certain."

Ben couldn't have been happier. Nothing more was said on the matter, until the end of the service.

"Let me know how it goes. When you ask Betty, I mean," said Joe, placing his hand on Ben's shoulder. "I really do hope she says 'yes', you know."

"Thank you. I really hope this, also."

The day of the boxing competition arrived. The whole of the Field family turned out to watch, but Betty couldn't make it due to a family commitment. Although disappointed, Ben came to the conclusion he would not have been able to concentrate if he knew she was watching. He was nervous but confident in his abilities. The trainer met the Fields at the venue, which they had had to drive to.

"You'll be fine. In fact, I'm certain you'll do us proud Ben," he declared.

"Thank you," replied Ben.

"The spectators are through that door," he indicated, "The changing rooms are this way."

"Thank you," responded Bill. "Thank you for giving Ben this chance."

"He deserves it. He's good. Come on, Ben. Let's get you ready."

The Fields went into the hall and the trainer led Ben into the changing room. Once Ben had his shorts on, he handed him what looked like a bathrobe, except it was red and shiny, like satin.

"Put that on, to keep warm. Now, I've got some grease for your eyebrows. We'll put the gloves on last. Do you need the toilet?"

Ben nodded.

"Go on then. Before we put the gloves on."

When Ben returned, the trainer tied his gloves on, the ones Ben had been given for his birthday.

"These gloves will be lucky. I know it," observed Ben.

"Luck and skill. You make your luck, Ben. You can do this. If you make it to the final, that'll be the fourth match. Each match is three rounds. Let's go and see the draw."

There were four rings, set up in the hall, surrounded by several rows of chairs. Ben had never experienced anything quite like it. The draw was on a piece of paper pinned to a makeshift board. His name was halfway down.

"Looks like you're in Ring 2 against a Brendan McNeilly. Those Irish boys know how to fight. Just keep your guard up and jab until you're sure of an opening. They score punches landed, so you don't need to go for the knockout. Get your vision and your length in."

A bell rang and competitors started climbing into the rings.

"Off you go, then. I'll be ringside. Give me your robe."

What Ben hadn't yet realised, was that this was the All-London Junior Championships. If he had, he might have lost his nerve. His opponent was jumping from one foot to the other, shadow boxing. Ben had no intention of showmanship, and simply stood to the right of the referee, facing the show-off.

"Keep it clean lads. If I say 'separate' you separate. No holding. Box."

As instructed, Ben jabbed and ducked, moved and jabbed. McNeilly was good, and Ben took several punches, but by his own calculations, he was landing just as many. The bell rang and the boxers returned to their corners.

"You did well. I make that about evens," the trainer encouraged Ben.

Having studied his opponent during the first round, Ben was able to anticipate his combinations, and avoided more punches in the second round. His own punches were still connecting well, and at the bell, McNeilly's nose was bleeding.

"That's your round," declared the trainer. "Be careful, in the next. He'll know he needs to come at you with everything."

"I think this, also."

An intelligent boxer, Ben had his own strategy, and as soon as the third round got underway, before McNeilly had gathered himself, he landed a strong uppercut. McNeilly reeled against the ropes, and as he rebounded, Ben let loose a left hook. The referee stepped in between them and stopped the fight. The spectators close to the ring applauded, as the referee held Ben's arm aloft.

"Great work, Ben," the trainer praised him, handing him the robe. "Next match in thirty minutes. Keep warm when the next lot are fighting. You don't appear to have any wounds. Have a small drink and some chocolate."

The bell rang, bringing the other fights to a conclusion. As soon as the victors were announced, another group of boxers climbed up into the rings.

"We'll soon know who you're facing in the quarters."

"I think this, also."

Not wanting to sit, Ben started to pace up and down slowly. Eventually, the fights finished, and the names were written on the draw. The trainer pushed his way through the crowd that had gathered in front of the noticeboard. Ben waited a few feet away.

"Stephen Jones, in Ring 4," announced the trainer having pushed his way back through the crowd.

Another bell rang and they made their way to Ring 4, where Ben removed his robe and climbed in. Jones looked nervous. He was skinnier and taller than McNeilly had been, which meant he had a longer reach. Ben eyed him up and felt he could pass under Jones' guard. Again, the referee explained the ground-rules.

"Now box."

Ben jabbed away and noticed that Jones' often lowered his guard after a combination. That would be Ben's moment. He put together five jabs and brought round his left glove, landing heavily on Jones' right cheek. Jones tried to pull Ben in and hold him, long enough to take a breather, but the referee separated them. Unaware that he was lowering his guard, Jones regrouped, but received exactly the same combination from Ben. He was hurt. Again, Ben jabbed and threw a left hook, and the referee stepped in to stop the fight. Jones tried to protest.

"I'm alright."

"No, you're taking a beating. I'm stopping the fight."

The two boxers stood either side of the referee, and Ben's hand was held high. More applause.

"That was impressive."

"Thank you. He dropped his arm after the jabs. I saw he was open."

"I love the way you fight with your gloves and your brain."

Ben put his robe on and sat down, spotting the Fields in the audience, but escaping eye contact. The wait for the next round was not as long, because all the fights took place in the four rings. For the semi-finals, they would use Ring 1 and Ring 3 which were diagonally opposite each other. Ben soon discovered he was in Ring 1 which was the furthest away from where the Fields were sitting.

In the semi-finals, he was up against another Irish boxer, Sam Mullins. Ben recognised him from school, although he didn't attend the same boxing club. Mullins already had the makings of a cut under his left eye. Removing his robe, Ben climbed up and stood facing Mullins in the ring. Mullins stared at him, looking deep into his eyes, his gaze menacing. Ben focused on the cut. As soon as round one started, Ben jabbed almost for the full three minutes, and just before the end of the round, he put together a combination that landed two punches on Mullins' cut, opening it up so it bled. He repeated the tactic in the second round, causing a second cut to the opposite cheek. Mullins' trainer threw in the towel, much to Mullins' annoyance.

"You're not going to win this, Sam," insisted his trainer. "He's two rounds up and I can't see you knocking him out. He's too good."

Ben was filled with confidence, on overhearing the conversation.

"I must use the toilet," he informed his own trainer.

"Better get those gloves off. Be quick, mind. Can't have you late for the final."

Ben trotted out of the hall, returning just in time to have his gloves re-tied.

The final was to be contested in the ring in front of the Fields. Matty and Jessica were going wild with excitement and started chanting, "Ben. Ben, Ben!"

"Your opponent in the final is a Walter Stubbs."

The name connected with Ben like a right-hook to his jaw. His teacher, Mr Stubbs, the Nazi sympathiser who never missed an opportunity of causing Ben hurt, either physically or mentally.

"Everything alright?" asked the trainer, noticing Ben's expression change.

"It is nothing. I have a teacher. His name is Stubbs. He hates me. He hits me."

"Use it, Ben. Use it all. Turn the negatives into energy."

That was helpful advice. As Ben climbed into the ring, he found himself face to face with a seventeen-year-old boy who was the spitting image of his father.

"Lindenheim, you stinking little Jew," he muttered under his breath. "You're about to get what's coming to you. And then you can go back home with your tail between your legs."

Like father like son, Walter Stubbs was already a Nazi sympathiser. Ben felt sick, but he stayed calm and gave nothing away. Stubbs was about the same height and build, so they were evenly matched. He was good with his words, but how good was he with his punches? Ben wasn't listening, as the referee repeated the ground-rules. This was going to be anything but a clean fight.

After the first few punches, Ben thought Stubbs had a weak guard. He continued to jab throughout the first round, staying even on points. His plan for the second round was to hurt Stubbs, and he alternated between stomach punches and punches to the eyes. It was obvious he was succeeding, because at every opportunity, Stubbs pulled him in and muttered an insult into his ear, without the referee noticing. Again, Ben remained calm, and didn't let his anger show. As soon as they came out for the third round, Ben started throwing hook after hook after hook, with a wildness he hadn't yet revealed in the boxing ring, combining left and right, pummelling the sides of Stubbs' head. The referee allowed the punishment to continue, perhaps longer than he should, but this was the final, and he wanted to let things take their course. When finally, Stubbs was cornered, and Ben was landing all his hooks, the referee stepped in. He gave a standing count before allowing the boys to resume boxing. Ben wasted no time in bringing the sweetest of uppercuts onto Stubbs' chin. He crumpled in a heap on the floor, where he remained until the referee counted to ten. Ben felt satisfaction more than victorious. Stubbs wobbled to his feet and stood alongside the referee. Seeing Ben's arm raised hurt Stubbs more than the punches, but he felt sure, once his father knew what had happened, Ben's punishments in school would increase.

The Fields were cheering ecstatically. The trainer gave Ben an enormous bear-hug.

"Where did that come from?"

"He is the son of my teacher. He insulted me many times. He called me a 'stinking Jew'. He is Nazi sympathiser like his father. I was angry."

"Well, if that was how you use the negatives, well done. Champ! You realise you go forward to the Nationals, now, don't you?"

"I did not know this."

"Come on. It's time to receive your trophy."

By now Bill had joined them. He hugged Ben and started to untie his gloves for him.

"So proud of you," he said, holding Ben's face in his hands and looking him in the eyes. "So proud of you."

"And there's hardly a mark on him," responded the trainer."

"Thank you," added Bill. "I told you he was good."

Two weeks after his victory in the boxing ring, Ben was invited for Betty's birthday meal. As she didn't feel it was appropriate to invite Jessica, she had asked Ben not to tell his family that their usual family meal was, in fact, a birthday celebration. Ben had retrieved, from the waste-paper basket, the wrapping paper used for his own birthday presents, keeping it folded in his drawer. After cutting a straight edge, he carefully wrapped the antelope, tying the parcel with a length of bright blue wool which he borrowed from Dorothy's latest knitting project. Using a sheet of plain writing paper, folded into four, he designed a homemade card, sketching antelopes on the African plains. Not owning any crayons, and not wanting to borrow Jessica's, it had to be black and white, but the effect was stunning. He signed it with five kisses and placed it in an envelope which he slipped under the wool holding the parcel together.

Today was the day he would ask Betty to marry him. Freshly shaved, without cutting himself, he walked round to the Drapers' house and rang the bell. As usual, Ruth came running to the door and threw her arms round Ben. Betty followed her along the corridor.

"Happy birthday!" Ben greeted her, handing over the parcel.

"Open it, open it. I want to see what it is," insisted Ruth, jumping up and down.

"All in good time," responded Betty.

The table was set, and three vegetable tureens were positioned strategically. The aroma of roast beef filled the air.

"Hello, Ben," Anna greeted him, as she carried a gravy-boat to the table. "Do sit down. Joe is just about to bring in the meat."

"Hello."

At that moment, Joe appeared in the doorway, carrying a large rectangular meat server, piled high with a joint of beef and roast vegetables.

"Hello, Ben."

"Hello. That looks good."

Joe placed the roast on the table and began to carve. He put two slices on Ben's plate and positioned a small Yorkshire pudding, two pieces of potato, and two slices of roast parsnip next to the meat to allow room for vegetables.

"Serve yourself vegetables," indicated Anna, removing the lids from the tureens.

"I think roast beef is my favourite meal," announced Ruth.

"I never ate these Yorkshire puddings before I come to England," replied Ben. "I like very much."

"Don't forget to leave room for birthday cake," laughed Anna.

When everyone was served, silence prevailed for the duration of several mouthfuls.

"I hear you won the boxing tournament, Ben?" inquired Joe.

Ben pointed at his mouth and accelerated his chewing, swallowing prematurely, so as to answer the question in a timely fashion. Some Yorkshire pudding went down the wrong way and he started to choke. Betty passed him his glass of water. Eventually, red in the face, the choking subsided, and he was able to answer.

"Yes. Now I can box at the national championships."

"Congratulations. When are the national championships?" replied Joe.

"November, I think that my trainer said."

"It's a long way off," commented Anna.

"I must train, in this time."

"Well, I hope you win," added Anna.

"Thank you."

When everyone had finished what was on their plate, Ben helped carry out the plates. Betty followed him into the kitchen, carrying the remains of the meat.

"Can we go for a walk after the meal?" asked Ben.

"I should think so," replied Betty, just before Anna joined them in the kitchen.

"It's alright if Ben and I go for a walk after I've opened my presents, isn't it?"

"Of course. How about you open your presents, then, go for your walk, and we'll have the cake when you return.

I don't know about you, but I always feel full after a roast dinner."

"Good idea," remarked Betty.

"Ben and Betty are going for a walk after she's opened her presents and we'll eat cake when they get back," explained Anna, as they finished clearing the table.

"Ooooohhhhh," whinged Ruth. "Can I come?"

"Not this time, Ruth," replied Betty, quietly but firmly.

"Hmmph," came Ruth's reply, accompanied by folding her arms and frowning.

"Don't be silly. It's my birthday," Betty attempted to appease her.

"Alright. I suppose so."

Betty placed her presents on the table. She decided to save Ben's until last. Ruth had been learning how to embroider, and she had attempted 'B-D' in the corner of a handkerchief for her. Betty didn't have the heart to explain that 'Betty' was short for 'Elizabeth', and that her initials were 'E-D'. The monogram was a little wonky, but it had been sewn with fondness.

"I love it. Thank you, Ruth."

Ruth's frustration melted into giggles.

One of the two other presents, apart from Ben's, was tiny, and one large and round.

"I wonder what this could be?" questioned Betty, as she unwrapped the larger one, thinking it might be the hat she had seen, a few weeks previously, on a trip to Oxford Street.

Lifting the lid, hopefully, her face started to beam as her suspicions were confirmed. Taking out the pill-box style hat, she placed it on her head.

"Thank you so much."

"Beautiful," Ben couldn't help himself from observing.

Betty blushed and leaving the hat on her head, started to unwrap the tiny box. Of course, a hat needs a hatpin, and the little box contains a rather exquisite silver one. Taking it, she fixed the hat in place.

"Thank you, thank you. thank you."

It was the turn of Ben's present.

"Be very careful," he suggested.

"Is it breakable?" Betty asked.

"It has delicate parts."

Betty slowed down her movements and gently unwrapped the caring.

"Oh, my goodness! Did you make this?"

Ben nodded.

"Ben, that's amazing," exclaimed Anna.

"You have some skills, there, Ben," Joe affirmed him.

"My father, he taught to me woodwork. My teacher at school, he encourages me."

"I see what you mean by 'delicate'. These horns are so thin. I will keep it on my dressing table. Thank you. It's gorgeous."

That was just the response Ben had been hoping for. It was a triumph.

"Shall we go for our walk, now?" he urged Betty.

"Yes, let's."

Grabbing her cardigan, Betty led Ben to the front door. He held it open while she wriggled into the garment. Ben half wished she wouldn't do that in front of him but enjoyed seeing the contours of her figure move. At the end of the street, he took her hand.

"I have spoken with your father. Betty, will you be married with me?"

"Of course, I will."

"Your father says I may ask you, but we must wait until you have seventeenth birthday to be engaged and eighteenth for the wedding. He wants that you study. I told him I will not go back to Germany. When I finish school, I will look for work here."

"That's a long time to wait, but he's right. We are still young. I am happy, all the same."

"I am happy, also."

The walk was only about a mile, just long enough to walk off the roast beef and Yorkshire puddings and to have the conversation Ben had been anticipating. No sooner had they arrived back at the house, than Betty went running to her mother.

"Mummy. Ben has asked me to marry him, and I have said 'yes'. Daddy says we must wait, though."

"I'm so happy for you. Your father is right though. He did mention something to me before. Engaged on your seventeenth, married on your eighteenth."

"Congratulations," said Joe, giving Ben a firm handshake, immediately followed by a fatherly hug.

Ruth looked at Betty and then at Ben and her lower lip started to tremble.

"You will go away from here and I will miss you," she whispered.

"Firstly, they won't be married for another two years," explained Anna. "Secondly, it's highly likely Ben and Betty will live here, until they can afford a place of their own."

Ruth responded silently, taking her handkerchief from the pocket of her pinafore and blowing her nose.

"Let's eat celebration cake," suggested Anna. "Do you want to help me with the plates, Ruth, please?"

They fetched the plates, forks and cake, whilst Joe went to his study for some matches. No sooner were the candles lit than 'Happy Birthday' singing filled the room. Ben now knew this traditional song well and could join in with gusto.

"Make a wish!" Ruth reminded Betty.

As Betty extinguished the candles, with a series of tiny breaths, she wished that her father would change his mind and let the wedding happen sooner.

In making her wish, Betty could never have realised the developments in continental Europe. Neither could Ben, for that matter, although he read the newspaper, regularly. At first, he had worried about his parents, just as he'd spent much emotional energy wondering if Saul was ever going to make it to London. After a few weeks, he had adopted a coping strategy of shutting out thoughts of home. He found it easier to enjoy the present that way, and if he was being honest, since he had fallen in love with Betty, he had no desire to return to Germany. It was perhaps a blessing that Ben was ignorant of the situation, for at the same time as he had been celebrating his own birthday, his parents had been taken off to a work camp, and their home torched. Worse was to come.

It was 3rd September 1939, and the Fields were listening to the radio, like countless other British families. Two days previously, Hitler had invaded Poland.

"What is happening?" asked Ben, struggling to hear through the crackling.

"Hush. I'll explain in a minute," answered Dorothy, kindly but firmly.

Ben realised he needed to be quiet so that the others could hear.

"Neville Chamberlain, the Prime Minister, is about to make an announcement," added Dorothy.

"This morning, the British ambassador in Berlin handed the German government a final note stating that unless we heard from them by eleven o'clock, that they were prepared, at once, to withdraw their troops from Poland, a state of war would exist between us. I have to tell you now, that no such undertaking has been received, and that consequently, this country is at war with Germany."

There was a stunned silence. Ben understood enough to know what had just happened.

"What happens to me now?" he asked.

"You will always be welcome here. This is your home," insisted Dorothy, tweaking Ben's cheek.

"Thank you. This is my home, now."

"I've got an idea Dot," Bill interjected. "A lot of Jewish people in this country changed their names. We could get Ben's name changed."

It was a simplistic solution to a complex problem, but it was appealing.

"That is a good idea. What does my name mean in English? 'Heim' is my house. What is 'Linden'?"

"It's a tree," contributed Simon.

"How do you know that?" asked a surprised Dorothy.

"I'm not daft! I am interested in gardening and trees and things. It's the lime tree."

"Hmm. 'Limehouse' doesn't sound quite right," responded Bill. "We need to find out about names. Why don't you take yourself down to the library tomorrow and look it up in a proper dictionary? Ours is too small for that kind of thing."

"I will do this. Thank you."

"Right, I think this calls for tea and cake," suggested Dorothy, whose solution to most troubles was either cake or Germolene cream, and this was not a wound that antiseptic ointment could easily fix.

Ben wasn't hungry but he loved cake. He had also developed a taste for English tea, as long as it has lots of milk added. Most Sundays, there was cake or scones or shortbread, all of which Ben now knew how to make, although today's cake was made by Jessica and had dried fruit in it.

"This is very good, Jessica," Ben encouraged her, swallowing his first mouthful.

"Will we have to become soldiers?" asked Matty.

"I think you're far too young. Both you and Simon," replied Dorothy.

"Yes, but what if the war carries on? The last war lasted several years," persisted Matty.

The colour drained from Dorothy's cheeks at the thought of losing her boys, as had happened to a generation of young men in the Great War.

"Let's not think about that, now. We'll wait and see what happens. Maybe Hitler will change his mind," suggested Dorothy, naively trying to convince herself, more than anyone else.

"I want to fight," announced Ben, defiantly.

"Oh, Ben. I understand how this must feel, but I don't want to lose you either."

It was true, Dorothy was Jewish, but she hadn't experienced the first-hand persecution meted out under Hitler's rise to power, that Ben had begun to experience during the pogroms.

"Someone needs to stop him. This is not right, what Hitler does."

"Well, if you must go and fight, they won't let you join the army until you turn eighteen."

At this point, Ben suddenly remembered he was supposed to be getting married when Betty turned eighteen, by which

122

time he would be nineteen. He didn't know what to do. That night he slept little. Nelson snuggled alongside him, sensing he was troubled.

In the morning, after breakfast, he took himself off to the library, to look up names. He discovered that 'Linton' was the name of any settlement where flax was made, but also where there were linden trees. 'Linton' could be a place name, a family name, of those who heralded from a place called 'Linton', and in some cases, a first name. Through his research, Ben also began to realise that a doubled-barrelled surname carried a certain gravitas, a particular social standing. That was when he settled on his new identity. Benjamin Linton-House. What he didn't know was how to make it legal.

At lunchtime, he announced his decision.

"I read all about names, at the library. I wish that my name is Benjamin Linton-House."

"Very posh," laughed Dorothy.

"It will make a good reputation. I think this, also. But I don't know how the law does this."

"As far as I'm aware, we need to go to the registry office. I've also heard somewhere you have to put it in the newspaper, if you change your name. I think you are classed as an alien, though, so perhaps the only records of your being here are on the list when you arrived. We'll find out."

It felt like a very long time until Saturday and his regular trip to the synagogue with the Drapers. He didn't say a lot, all service, and Joe could sense something was wrong.

"You seem out of sorts. Is something the matter?"

"Yes. I must fight with Hitler. When I am eighteen. I will change my name to Linton-House. Most of all, I wish to be married with Betty, before I go to fight."

Joe frowned pensively, for a moment.

"I see. That is troubling. I have a very good friend who is in a similar position. His son is engaged and was going to wait until next year to get married. He is already eighteen, but his fiancée is sixteen. I believe they are going to get married next month, before the son goes off to the army. Why do you want to fight? Silly question. I suppose you will be called up anyway, the way things are going. I like the name, by the way. Let me talk to Anna."

"Thank you."

After lunch, Betty and Ben went for their customary constitutional.

"Betty. You know that I love you? I have asked to your father to be married with you during the next months, because when I am eighteen, I must go to fight with Hitler."

Betty was stunned.

"I do love you and I know you love me. It's true that I wished for us to get married sooner, but not under these circumstances."

"It is possible that I do not choose to be in the army when I am eighteen."

"I know. What did my father say?"

"He said he talks with your mother."

They held hands and finished their walk, in silence.

Back at the house, the table was set with cake. There were only four plates as Ruth had been invited to her best friend's house. After everyone had been cut a slice, Joe spoke.

"While you were out walking, Anna and I have been talking about the unfortunate situation that Hitler has brought us to. We have decided that you can get married as soon as possible. We are sad and proud of you and excited and a little afraid, but we think it is the right decision.

"Thank you," responded Ben.

"I love you Mummy and Daddy," answered Betty, getting up from her seat and hugging each of them.

"That's settled then. I'll talk to the rabbi."

The wedding was set for 12th November, the day after
the national boxing championships should have taken
place but which had now been cancelled, much to Ben's
relief. When asked what name should go into the marriage
contract, Ben announced himself as Benjamin Linton-
House. No one argued, not that he had any identity
papers. The Fields were there in their Sunday-best and
even Bill put on a kippah for the ceremony. Dorothy cried,
partly through nostalgia, partly through losing her 'son'. It
had been decided that Ben and Betty would live with
the Drapers until they could afford a place of their own, as
there was considerably more room than at the Fields'
house. In any case, Betty would need support, whilst Ben
was away fighting, especially if they were blessed with
children. It had also been agreed that, once married, Ben
would not continue with his studies, but try to find work,
until he went off to the army. Betty, on the other hand,

would continue until she matriculated, unless a baby came along.

Most of the day was a blur to Ben. He hardly heard the rabbi's words. He was intoxicated by the radiant sixteen-year-old standing before him, under the marriage canopy. She wore a bright blue floral summer dress, made by Anna, covered by a pale blue cardigan, which just like her bottle-green one, revealed the edges of her collar bones. Ben knew that tonight, he would be able to kiss the contours of her frame, and feast on the delights of their union, just as the Song of Solomon described. The ceremony ended with the traditional breaking of glass, as the couple trampled on it. A symbol of both joy and frailty, celebration and trembling, neither could have anticipated the ecstasy of their union or the way Ben's life would be shattered in the next two years. Shouts of 'Mazel tov!' echoed round the room, the musicians started to play, and the dancing began.

SHARDS

Over the next few months, as Ben and Betty settled into their new life together, it became increasingly obvious that Hitler had no intention of backing down. In fact, the violence towards the Jews only got worse, his plans to systematically cleanse society being worked out through ghettoization and transportation to concentration camps. And it wasn't just the Jews who were being persecuted. Hitler wanted rid of Gypsies and Communists and misfits, not to mention any political opponents or dissident voices. A British expeditionary force had been sent across the Channel, pretty much as soon as Neville Chamberlain had made his speech, but despite the declaration of war, echoed swiftly by France and countries throughout the British Empire, very little practical response was made. Poland was a lost cause. Hitler took the inactivity as a green light to invade Denmark and Norway. Ben followed the reports in the newspaper.

He had also started working at the factory where Bill worked, although they hardly saw each other, with Bill on nights and Ben working the daytime shift. Betty had avoided falling pregnant on their wedding night, more by luck than judgement. Although ignorant of his daughter and son-in-law's conjugal activities, out of concern that she continued her studies, Joe had broached with Ben, somewhat belatedly, the embarrassing, fatherly conversation about how to avoid making a baby. Ben and Betty agreed this was wise, and continued to enjoy each other passionately, whilst avoiding pregnancy. Betty always made sure she washed their bedsheets, to conceal their behaviour from her mother.

After three months of wedded bliss, quite unexpectedly, Ben ran into Stan Drucker in the canteen.

"I didn't know you worked here," observed Stan.

"Only for six weeks. I am married."

"You got married?"

"Yes. It should be two years later, but my father-in-law agreed, when war was declared with Germany."

"This weekend, I'm going to enlist with the Royal Norfolks."

"I want to fight, but my eighteenth birthday is in May."

"Why don't you come with me? Just tell them you're eighteen."

"I tell lies?"

"I don't think they're going to ask for proof. They'll just be grateful that you volunteered. Meet me here Saturday lunchtime. There's a recruitment event. I'll take you. Think about it for a few days."

Ben thought about it a lot in the ensuing four days. What troubled him most was whether to discuss it with Betty or just announce it. She had married him, knowing that he fully intended to go and fight. This would just make the inevitable come a few weeks earlier. He resolved to tell her after he had enlisted.

Saturday lunchtime found Ben in the canteen, waiting, if not a little nervously, for Stan to finish his shift. As Stan walked through the door a beaming smile came over his face, assuming that Ben was not there to tell him he had decided against enlisting.

"You've made up your mind, then?"

"I think this, also."

"Have you told Mrs Lindenheim?"

"Not yet. And I changed my name. Now, I am Linton-House."

"With a name like that you'll be up the ranks in no time?"

"I have promotion because of my name?"

"History of the British at war. Toffs are the officers. My sort make sergeant if we're lucky."

"What is 'toff'?"

"Posh people. People with double-barrelled surnames. People with titles. Upper classes."

"I just translate my name."

"Never mind. Come on."

They walked the short distance off the premises to where a makeshift army-tent, recruitment office had been set up in front of the factory.

"Good morning, gentlemen," an officer greeted them. "Are you willing to support the war effort by signing up for King and country?"

"Of course," replied Stan.

"When do we go to fight?" asked Ben.

"Your accent? Are you German?"

"I am Jewish. I came to England in December 1938. I escaped on a train with many children."

"So, you want to kill some Nazis, then?"

"Yes."

"Fill in these forms, gentlemen. There'll be a week of training, starting a week on Monday and then you'll be shipped across the channel to join the 2nd Battalion."

"Where is this training?" asked Ben.

"Norwich. Here's your train pass. Arrive by 10 am. You'll be picked up at the station. Any further questions?"

"Not from me," answered Stan.

Ben shook his head.

"Gentlemen, your King and country thank you, as do I. Good day."

Stan and Ben left the tent. Ben had to return to the factory, but Stan was off home to sleep.

"Meet me at the station at six o'clock, Monday week. We can travel together. Hopefully, we'll be in the same unit."

"Yes. Six o'clock."

Ben went back to work, wondering if he had done the right thing. Somehow, he was going to have to break the news to Betty, and he knew she would be upset.

Later, at the evening meal, Ben was quieter than usual.

"Everything alright?" asked Joe.

Although Ben and Betty had their own room, living with the Drapers meant little or no space for private conversations, as mealtimes were shared.

"I'm worried about this war," answered Ben, offering a half truth.

"Let him be, Daddy, please," insisted Betty, not normally accustomed to challenging her father.

Joe raised an eyebrow at his daughter but didn't seek further clarification from Ben.

No sooner was the washing-up completed, than Ben and Betty escaped to the privacy of their room.

"Would you like to tell me what's wrong, now?"

"I have joined the Royal Norfolk regiment, today. I'm sorry, but this means that I go to fight very quickly. First a week of training. Then across the sea to France. I know this is three months before my birthday."

Betty looked at him with a combination of annoyance, fear, pride and affection.

"You didn't think to discuss this first?"

"There is nothing to discuss. It happened. We both knew I will go in May. Now I go in one week."

"I'm scared of losing you, Ben. I know you have to fight. That's all."

Ben held out his hands to Betty, who took both of them in hers. He pulled her towards him and wrapped his arms round her, holding her tightly and kissing the top of her head.

"Can we try for a baby tonight?" asked Betty, into his shoulder.

"A baby?"

"If anything should happen to you, I want a part of you to go on loving."

"Are you certain about this?"

"Can anyone be certain of anything in these days?"

"And your studies?"

"Some things are more important."

That night they made love without Ben withdrawing prematurely. It was not the most passionate of encounters, on Betty's part, because she was far too emotional and distracted.

"We will do this every day until I leave," promised Ben.

"Tomorrow, we must tell my parents that you have enlisted earlier than planned. I'm sure they will understand."

Ben said nothing. He enfolded Betty in his arms and fell asleep within minutes.

At breakfast, as predicted, Joe and Anna did their best to offer understanding, when Ben explained what he had done.

"All we really want is for you to come home safe," responded Anna.

"Let it be known that I am both annoyed with you and extremely proud of you," added Joe. "You are both a son-in-law and a son to me."

"Thank you," answered Ben.

"We will pray for you every day," promised Anna.

"Thank you," replied Ben, still uncertain, these days, where his faith had gone.

Once his shifts at the factory started, Ben had stopped attending the synagogue regularly. He didn't work on Sundays, which was unfortunate for the Drapers, as they were practising Jews, who attended on Saturdays. If he were being honest, Ben had only started going to the synagogue to be able to spend time with Betty. He still had more questions than answers about where God was. Looking at Betty prompted him to believe. Remembering what had happened, what was still happening, to the Jews in Germany, evoked a lack of trust. Why was God allowing these things to happen to his people? Neither did Ben box at the club on Sundays anymore, as it was the only family time he had, not that boxing mattered much, since he had started contemplating going off to war. The young couple were also invited for a monthly tea at the Fields on a Sunday.

Going off to war was harder than leaving Germany, the farewell more heart-breaking. Betty and Ben had made love every night of their final week together, with the intention of making a baby, and the thought of not being there for her, was tearing him apart. There was to be no railway station embrace. Joe had insisted on giving Ben a lift, his offer only being accepted on the terms that goodbyes were said at the house. Apart from anything else, his rendez-vous with Stan was set for six o'clock in the morning, too early to be dragging everyone to the station.

Having spent lunch breaks over the last few days hastily carving and sanding a little wooden heart, engraved with the words 'I love you', which he placed on the dressing table, Ben had torn himself away from Betty, who was still fast asleep. He wanted to wake her and smother her in kisses, but it seemed kinder to let her sleep, so he slid out of the bed and got dressed in the bathroom. Anna stood in the hallway, her eyes welling up. Ruth, too, was still asleep.

"Thank you for everything," mouthed Ben to Anna, silently.

He slipped out of the door and joined Joe in the car. Nothing was said on the journey and halfway to the station, Ben realised he hadn't said anything to the Fields about going off to war. He resolved to write them a letter.

"I'll not get out," announced Joe, as he pulled up in front of the station, adding, "Write when you can."

"I will. Thank you."

Stan was waiting by the entrance and saw the car pulling up, Ben getting out, and the car driving off.

"You're a lucky bloke. I had to catch the bus."

They made their way to the platform, showed the rail passes and climbed on board the train bound for Norwich, which stopped at every station along the way. Ben had been watching out of the window and wondered how many of the young men getting on the train were heading for the Royal Norfolks' training camp. When eventually, the train stopped in Norwich, a group of around thirty men gathered by the entrance, waiting to be ferried to the barracks. Unfortunately, one of them was Walter Stubbs, and they had both spotted each other. Why was a Nazi sympathiser going to fight against Hitler? Was he going to swap sides?

No sooner had they arrived at the training camp, than Ben watched Stubbs sidling up to an officer and pointing in Ben's direction. The captain walked towards Ben.

"I'm afraid you'll have to come with me. Mr Lindenheim."

Ben followed the captain into an office.

"Have a seat. The man out there informs me that you are German. I'm surprised you were able to enlist."

"I was Lindenheim. Now, my name is Linton-House. Yes, I am German. But I am Jewish. I came here in 1938 after the Night of Broken Glass. My people are persecuted. I want to fight the Nazis. England is my home. I have a wife and a job here."

"I see."

"But I must explain. The man who came to you. He is called Walter Stubbs. His father is a teacher in the school I attended. The father hit me and insulted me because I am a Jew. The son insulted me also. We fought in the boxing championships. The father and the son are both Nazi sympathisers."

"Now, that is interesting. I should send you both home," asserted the captain, looking Ben in the eye. "Are you any good at boxing?"

"I won the championships. I had to go to the national championships in November. They were cancelled."

"The regiment could use a boxing champion. We have championships in the army, too, you know. You can go and re-join the men."

"Thank you."

"It's 'Thank you, Sir', from here onwards."

"Thank you, Sir."

Outside, the new recruits were standing in two lines, being shouted at by a sergeant. Ben joined the line but, because he was focusing on the sergeant, couldn't see the shock and annoyance on Stubbs' face.

"Nice of you to join us. What's your name?"

"Linton-House, Sir. Ben Linton-House."

"It's 'Serge'. 'Sir' is for officers. Which, come to mention it, how come you're not an officer, with a name like that?"

"Perhaps they will promote me, one day," replied Ben, not really knowing how to answer.

"And don't answer back, Linton-House."

Thankfully, their exchange was interrupted by a private marching over to the sergeant and saying something inaudible to the recruits.

"Stubbs. The captain wishes to speak with you. Go with Private Cleverley. At the double."

Stubbs left the group. He didn't return, as Ben had done, but was seen about twenty minutes later, being driven off in the back of a car.

The men were marched into a building where they received their uniforms and kit bags.

"Tomorrow, we'll work on your fitness," barked the sergeant. "By the end of the week, you'll know how to use a rifle, what to do when your leg gets blown off and how to dig yourself a foxhole. Now get your uniforms on and go and line up in front of the munitions store."

"Nice chap," laughed Stan, when the sergeant was out of earshot. "What happened about Stubbs?"

"Stubbs said that I am German. I said to the captain that I am a German Jew and I hate Nazis. I said that Stubbs and his father are Nazi sympathisers."

"And the captain let you stay and got rid of him."

"I said that I live here, that I have a job and that I am married, also. Yes. And that I won the boxing championships."

"That'll be it then! You could become the army champion, you know."

"It is a few weeks that I don't train for boxing."

The two men finished putting on their new uniforms.

"Itchy or what!" complained Stan.

They joined the end of the line of uniformed men leaving the dormitory and marched, somewhat haphazardly, over to the munitions store.

"Left, right, left, right, boys. Not left, right, right, left. Go on, once more round the yard. Shambles!"

The marching had improved by the time they lined up in front of the munitions store again.

"At ease."

Ben was a split second behind the others as he hadn't understood the command. The sergeant almost barked something but chose not to, because whilst the men had been putting on their uniforms, he had been in to speak with the captain.

"Get your weapons and come and line up."

Ben felt nervous handling his rifle, even though they hadn't yet been given any bullets.

"You fired a gun before?" asked Stan.

Ben shook his head."

"Rabbit, me. Shotgun though."

"Quiet!" barked the sergeant. "Can't trust you babies with live rounds yet."

For the next half an hour he had the men holding their rifles in several different positions, until he thought they were working in unison.

"At ease!"

The men stood anticipating his next order.

"Lunchtime. I suggest you don't over-eat as we've got some physical exercise planned for you, this afternoon. Dismissed."

"I wonder what the exercise is," mused Stan, as they queued for their meal.

Beef stew and mashed potatoes. Ben only ate a few mouthfuls. It wasn't that he didn't like it, but he took the sergeant seriously. Stan wolfed his down, regardless.

"You will have indigestion," commented Ben.

"Me? Stomach of steel."

Stan was soon to regret his decision, when the captain came out into the yard carrying two pairs of boxing gloves.

"Place your jackets on the ground, men, to make a boxing ring. That's a square, not a round ring. Two-minute rounds. I'll score. Unless you're knocked out. Winner stays in. Linton-House and Drucker. You can be the first."

"Be gentle with me," whispered Stan.

Several of the men were fighters, but Ben was the only boxer in the group. He jabbed away at Stan and won on points.

"I thought you'd have more in you than that, Linton-House."

"Just warming up, Sir."

The next three opponents didn't stand a chance. Ben knocked two of them out and the other reeled and stepped outside the square. The fourth opponent put up a slightly better defence. To his own surprise, Ben won every round he contested. The captain gave an approving nod in Ben's direction.

"As you were, Sergeant."

"Time for a five-mile run," barked the sergeant, setting off towards the gates. "Come on, then. No stragglers. Let's see if you run as well as you can box, Linton-House!"

Ben was glad he had only eaten a small amount of lunch. After two miles, it was beginning to hurt. Some of the men were lagging behind. Ben and Stan were together, still, a few paces behind the sergeant.

"Stitch!" complained Stan, pointing at his abdomen.

"Keep running," Ben encouraged him.

After four miles, Ben was running on sheer willpower, having danced around the makeshift boxing ring for the best part of an hour. The sergeant started to ramp up the speed. Three men went past Ben and Stan, but they kept running, and although the gap increased to about fifty yards, between Ben and Stan and the stragglers, the gap was over a minute. The gates came into view around the next corner. Stan's stitch had worn off, and he mustered a sprint. Ben accelerated in pursuit, and they finished respectably.

"Tonight, you can eat well."

One by one the stragglers came puffing and panting in through the gates. One of them was sick.

"You can clean that up, Smythe!" barked the sergeant.

"Yes, Serge."

Smythe went in search of a shovel, whilst the others went off to the dormitory.

At the end of a week of training, Ben was fitter than he'd been, for a while, and he was confident, all things being equal, he could survive out in the field. Not that anything is equal in a war. Just before lights out, he penned a letter to Betty, telling her he would be leaving for France in the morning, that he loved her more than words could say, and that he hoped their love-making was blessed with a baby. Exhausted from the week of intense activities, Ben experienced his last night of unbroken sleep for several months to come. Early on the Monday morning, the men clambered into three lorries and were transported, on the long and bumpy ride to Southampton, where they joined a throng of khaki-clad men, waiting to board a ship to Dieppe.

Feeling rather nauseous, Ben made his way off the ship, his thoughts overwhelmed by memories of his last disembarkation, and the absence of Saul. A rabble of drunk-looking soldiers tumbled out of a bar, arm in arm with some voluptuous Dieppe girls, and disappeared into an adjacent doorway. Ben stood watching them and was almost knocked over by a speeding bicycle. The rider rang his bell repeatedly and gestured at Ben, exclaiming something Ben didn't quite understand. Stan caught up with him, having just frequented a local tobacconist in search of some cigarettes.

"Do you want one?" he invited Ben.

"No thank you."

Stan lit up a Gauloise and immediately succumbed to a bout of choking.

"Blimey. That's strong," he laughed, once the choking had stopped.

A lorry pulled up in front of them and they climbed aboard. Last to get in, they found themselves sitting opposite each other at the open end. It suited Ben, as it afforded him loads of fresh air. Although an exact destination had not been indicated, Ben understood their general direction to be towards Lille. By the time the vehicle made its first stop, Ben's buttocks were numb. Last in and first out, he jumped to the ground and paced up and down, trying to encourage the flow of blood. The driver poured some water into the radiator and filled up with diesel. There was just enough time for Stan to have a few drags on another cigarette, this time without choking. The men piled back into the lorry.

After another bumpy hour or so, they entered a small town.

"Get yourselves some lunch wherever you can. Half an hour lads," announced the driver.

There was a bakery, a butchers and a bar.

"Bakers?" asked Stan.

"Bread. Yes. And some cold meat, also."

The men had been given a few francs, enough to see them to Lille.

"Bonjour, Messieurs," the assistant in the bakery greeted them cheerily.

"Bonjour," replied Ben. "Deux baguettes s'il vous plait."

He handed over some coins, the woman smiled, and they left.

"Au revoir, Messieurs. Bonne journée."

"Au revoir, bonne journée," reciprocated Ben.

At the butchers, they bought a cured sausage, and went to sit down on the ground by a wall. Stan cut the sausage in two with his army knife, and they chomped and chewed contentedly.

"Do we have time to wash it all down with a beer?" asked Stan, hopefully.

"I think this, also."

And they did have just enough time to down a glass of beer each, before climbing back into the lorry. About a mile down the road, Ben heaved and threw up over the tailgate. Some of the men laughed, and Ben took no offence, but laughed with them. A few minutes later, Stan also vomited out of the back of the lorry.

"The sausage?" they declared in unison.

Ben felt less nauseous for having been sick, and he tried to nod off, to the humming rhythm of the lorry. Every time he started to drift off, a bump in the road disturbed him. Somewhere along the way he must have succeeded in falling asleep, because he was rudely awoken at the next stop by some of the men clambering over him, impatiently.

"I could murder a cup of tea," exclaimed Stan.

"I am happy with a coffee," responded Ben.

They entered the village bar and ordered two coffees, as tea was not on the menu. Stan added three teaspoons of sugar to his, which made Ben smile.

The lorry pulled up in Lille, midway through the afternoon.

"That's as far as I'm taking you," declared the driver. "From here, you'll have to make your own way."

"Thank you," responded Ben.

"Thanks," added Stan.

The men alighted.

"What do we do, now?" mused Ben.

"Someone will know. Scots, Coldstreams, I don't know," responded one of the men. "We'll just have to ask where the Norfolks are stationed. In the meantime, I hear the girls in Lille are good."

"Sorry, Ben. You're hitched," laughed Stan.

"I think we must find a place to stay. Then, we can look for the regiment."

"OK, you go and find us somewhere to stay. We'll go and have some fun," retorted the man who had suggested the girls in Lille were good."

"It's alright, Ben," asserted Stan, "I'll come with you. I can go out later."

They had already lost sight of the others, when they realised nothing had been said about meeting back up again.

"Looks like it's just you and me, then," reflected Stan. "Let's find some place to billet."

"Billet?"

"Stay. Bed and breakfast. Roof over our heads."

Ben nodded and they set off along a random street. As they turned the corner, they almost knocked a British officer off the pavement.

"Steady, lads!" he gasped, recovering his balance.

"Sorry, Sir," apologised Ben, saluting.

Stan saluted too.

"We have just arrived from Blighty, not ten minutes ago. Do you happen to know where we can find the Royal Norfolks?" asked Stan, just as he noticed the Royal Norfolk Regiment insignia on the captain's cap.

"I'd like to think I know where to find my men," laughed the captain. "How fortuitous. Come with me. I'll be returning to Orchies, with two of my men, tomorrow. Our sector is between Maulde and Armentiers, east of here. We've been digging trenches and building blockhouses for months now. Haven't seen a single German, but we're keeping a look out. Just in case Hitler decides to invade Belgium."

"People back home have been calling it a phoney war," reflected Stan, "They're asking why we're bothering to join the army."

"Well, I for one, am exceedingly grateful that you have. The action will start soon enough. Not long ago, a couple of German majors got shot down near Mechelin carrying top secret papers about Hitler's plans. If he thinks he's just going to march into Belgium, he's got another think coming. We're at the ready, for whenever King Leopold asks for our help."

The captain led them to a small hotel, a few streets away.

"Please can you find these men some mattresses?" requested the captain, in French, to a plump lady, of about sixty, dressed all in black.

"How many more?" she replied, throwing up her arms.

The hotel, which normally had rooms for twelve guests, was bursting with British soldiers.

"I know. I will be forever in your debt," added the captain, "And it's good for business."

The woman was satisfied with his response and went to search for some mattresses. Ten minutes later, she returned to the reception.

"I have only the one mattress. Just for tonight, you can share. But you will be in a room with four others."

"I can handle that, as long as you don't kick me, in the night!" agreed Stan.

In the end, Stan sneaked out for the evening, leaving Ben alone on the mattress. It was just after dawn when Stan returned from his amorous adventures, smelling of alcohol and perfume. Lipstick was streaked on his collar. Ben was just waking up.

"You can have the mattress. One hour is left. You can sleep, now."

"I don't need sleep. I need to get washed."

One bathroom, at the end of the landing, served all three rooms on the first floor. It was still early, and Stan had a sink wash, followed by a shave. Ben also had time to wash and shave before some of the other soldiers stirred.

"Might as well go and see if we can get some coffee," suggested Stan.

They went downstairs to the dining room. It was empty, although they could hear a clunking sound from the kitchen. Ben wandered over to the door and peered in to see the woman struggling to light the oven.

"Bonjour, Madame."

"Ah, Monsieur. You are so early," came the stressed response.

"Do you need help?"

The woman burst into tears. Ben felt guilty, wondering what he had said wrong.

"I have not been asked that question for seven months. Not since my husband died. Please."

"What is your name? I am Ben Linton-House."

"Madame Giselle Husson," replied the woman, as Ben took the matches from her.

He got down on his knees in front of the oven. The knob was coming loose, but it looked like he could fix it. By now,

Stan had appeared in the kitchen. Five minutes later, the oven was lit, and a coffee percolator was steaming away on one of the rings. It began to hiss and splutter.

"I will make you both a nice coffee. Then, I will go to the boulangerie."

"I'll go," offered Ben.

"Monsieur is so kind."

She gave him some francs.

"Please bring me ten baguettes."

"Of course."

When he returned with the bread, the tables were laid and Stan was sitting at one of them, drinking coffee. Ben sat opposite. His own coffee was cool enough to drink.

"She was a beauty, Ben," remarked Stan, with reference to his previous evening's encounter.

"I am certain that she is," replied Ben, a wry smile on her face.

"Don't look at me like that! Some of us have to get it where we can."

Ben didn't respond, his thoughts in London, wondering if Betty had conceived.

Mme Husson brought in some bread and jam, and they filled their stomachs, not knowing when lunch might be. They were just finishing when the captain entered the dining room. Ben went to stand up.

"Please. No need to stand on ceremony."

Mme Husson was hovering in the doorway.

"Coffee and bread?" she asked.

"Thank you, Madame. That would be lovely," replied the captain, sitting down at the adjacent table.

They were joined by the two soldiers from the captain's company, who, like Stan, had been out on the town, the night before, and they were feeling a little worse for wear.

"Gentlemen."

"Good morning, Sir," they chorused, saluting.

Half an hour later, Ben and Stan were heading out of the city, squashed into the back of a jeep with one of the two privates.

"What's it like?" asked Stan.

"Like waiting for next Christmas. Not killed any Germans yet, if that's what you mean," replied the private in the back.

"I think everyone is waiting for the Frenchies to make up their minds," added the private in the front seat.

"Whatever the politics of it all, whatever's going on behind closed doors, we'll just sit it out, stiff upper lip, and be ready for when the order comes," insisted the captain.

Nothing more was said on the journey, until they approached a village, where the captain slowed down and parked next to a farm.

"It's far from perfect," observed the captain.

Stan and Ben, along with the two privates, hauled themselves out of the car, stretched and walked over to a barn.

"Look what we found in Lille," joked one of the privates, as they entered the building.

The men cheered.

"You can sleep up there in the hayloft or over there in the stalls," explained a soldier who looked even younger than Ben. "I'm Jim."

"Stan and Ben," replied Stan, pointing at Ben as he named him.

They walked over to one of the stalls, where a vacant pile of straw was still intact. Ben spread the straw across the floor and dropped his pack, claiming the area nearer the opening. Stan flopped down on his patch of straw, tired from the journey and his sleepless night of passion.

That night, Ben hardly slept, he was so cold, drifting off shortly after four and waking again just before six, longing for a hot mug of coffee. An old stove stood in the centre of the barn with a kettle on top. Ben wondered where to get water. When he poked his head out through the door, there was snow on the ground. He spotted a well. Going over to the well, he lowered the bucket, which crashed into the ice. Without considering who he might wake up, he raised the bucket a few feet and let it drop several times, trying to break the ice. Eventually, he pulled up half a bucket of water, which he carried to the kettle. What to light the stove with? He remembered Stan had a cigarette lighter, which he always stuck in his left pocket. Either Stan would be awake, or he ought to be, were Ben's thoughts as he extricated the lighter. Stan groaned, but he hardly stirred. Taking a packet of coffee from his backpack, Ben made two mugs of coffee. Shaking Stan's shoulder, he handed the sleepy, grumpy private, the second mug. They drank their coffee without milk, wondering if the cow, two stalls along, was the usual supply.

Other soldiers, including Jim, gathered around the stove, just as the farmer's wife arrived carrying bread.

"Bonjour, Madame," Ben greeted her.

"Bonjour, Monsieur."

"What's it like here?" inquired Ben, as soon as she had left the barn.

"Boring. We dig. We watch. We drill. We go to the village. We hunt rabbits. And when we get paid, we go to Lille," answered Jim. "And it's freezing!"

"The girls in Lille are something else," laughed another soldier.

"I agree," responded Stan, whistling.

"What do we do about food?" asked Ben, tearing off a chunk of bread.

"The farmer's wife makes a big stew, every day. She loves it when we catch rabbits, otherwise it's chickens," answered the soldier who had laughed.

As if on cue, a chicken rushed into the barn and fled immediately, when it spotted the soldiers. The farmer's wife approached a coop, across the yard, and scattered some grain. Chickens appeared from every opening and dived onto their breakfast.

"Sometimes she gives us eggs. And one of us milks the cow," added Jim. "She makes her own butter and cheese. It's not so bad here, apart from the cold."

"And the boredom," contributed another private.

Over the next few days Ben and Stan learned just how cold and boring life with the Royal Norfolks was. Unusually, with the temperatures they were experiencing, Stan started to sweat, soon realising it was a fever.

"I don't feel so good," he complained to Ben.

"Oh dear."

"Have you got discharge?" inquired Jim, without any embarrassment.

"Bit personal," responded Stan. "Matter of fact, yes."

"Who's been a naughty boy, then," laughed the private who had laughed, before. "You need some Dreadnought ointment."

"You'll have to see the doctor. I've heard they pump your tackle full of disinfectant," Jim observed.

"Bloody hell!" replied Stan.

"Better get yourself some French letters," continued Jim.

"You're loving this, aren't you?" grunted Stan.

Everyone laughed, apart from Stan, who took himself off, reluctantly, to see the medical officer. With antibiotics, he made a full recovery, but the next time he ventured into Lille, he protected himself.

The Germans did march into Belgium. Or rather, their paratroopers jumped into Belgium, at dawn, on 10th May. They were followed by Panzers, infantry and artillery. That evening, the order came for the Royal Norfolks to move up to the River Dyle.

"So, we're finally moving," observed Stan, stubbing out a Gauloise.

"Feels strange," replied Ben.

You could hear shells exploding, over in the French sector. Ben watched as some Stukas, in the distance, dived on their targets, dropping their bombs.

By nightfall, Ben and his company were in position.

"We've got to keep the Germans on the other side of the river, men," came the captain's rallying call.

The fighting was fierce, and both sides sustained casualties, but in the end, Ben's company had to retreat. No one realised, until it was too late, that Hitler had fooled everyone. The German tanks rolled into Sedan, and by all accounts, the French fled. Another order came through to retreat to the River Escaut, but the Germans kept coming, sweeping round behind the British. After a brief lull in the fighting, a counterattack was mounted.

Ben was focused on firing his rifle so didn't notice Stan take a bullet to the chest. Stan never even uttered a cry of pain, as he fell. A few seconds later, Ben turned to his friend, and only then, saw his lifeless stare. The sense of loss was more overwhelming than Ben could have imagined. More even, than the slow realisation that Saul was not coming back. Stan had been a great friend, watching Ben's back, especially when he had started at the grammar school.

Two days after Stan was killed in action, the men were told to go and defend a section of the canal, near Locon. When they reached their position, they found the Germans already there. In the ensuing skirmish, nearly all of Ben's company fell. Ben was lucky to make it out alive, but not without a piece of shrapnel lodging itself in his left knee. At first, the pain was excruciating, but after a tourniquet was applied, Ben started to lose all sensation in his lower leg. The wounded men, either carried or walking, and those still able to fight, retreated to a farm building. Ben loosened the tourniquet. As the blood rushed back into his leg, Ben found the pins and needles almost as painful as the shrapnel wound. Blood started to seep out into his trouser leg, and Ben was forced to tighten the tourniquet again. Whatever Ben had imagined fighting Hitler to be like, this wasn't like any boxing match Ben had experienced, and he started to question his decision to enlist.

Looking out through a crack in the wall, Ben could see a British Army car pull up close by. A man he thought might be a colonel got out. Ben could make out a few words from the conversation and was sure the colonel's accent was Scottish. After some pointing and gesticulating, the colonel got back in the car, and Ben's captain walked round to the opposite side and climbed in as well. The car drove off towards Le Cornet Malo. A while later, the captain returned.

Not long afterwards, a group of soldiers, Royal Scots, came out from some nearby trees, and having been spoken to by the captain, the men threw in their lot with the Royal Norfolks.

"Bastard!" muttered a private, in a broad Glaswegian accent. "The major told us to fall back to headquarters."

Ben's captain set off up the road, and another captain started barking orders.

"Right, men. We will defend this position for as long as we can. All those of you who can still stand, take cover under the hedge, and wait for my command."

Ben hauled himself up and stood, using his rifle as a walking stick. It was a heroic act of stupidity, but in Ben's head, once he was at the hedge, he could still use the weapon to defend their position. Another of the Royal Scots lent Ben his arm.

"I'll help you get to the hedge. After that it's up to you."

"Much appreciated."

Their task seemed futile to Ben, and the fact that no one had made any effort to prevent a man from taking part, who could not walk unassisted, suggested they were unlikely to succeed. Ben reached the hedge.

"Thank you."

"You're welcome."

It was another sleepless night, watching and waiting. No one knew when the Germans would launch their assault. Every hour, Ben loosened the tourniquet, each time with a reduced flow of blood. He needed proper medical attention, but under the circumstances, that was impossible. Ben consoled himself that if he survived, he was unlikely to lose the leg. He just wasn't sure if he'd ever box again. Looking around, he realised he was on the far right of the line. As the trees started to take shape against a lightening sky, the Panzers began to fire. Through the hedge, Ben could see them rolling towards the British.

"Fall back to the farm!" came the captain's order, realising the hedge afforded his men no defence whatsoever.

With the shrapnel in his knee, Ben didn't feel able to cover the distance in time, and in that moment, made a snap decision which probably saved his life. There was a wooded area, about twenty yards over to the right. Throwing his rifle across his back, Ben crawled along the bottom of the hedge, on two elbows and his working knee, reaching the cover of the trees, just as the first Panzer crashed through the hedge. He had every intention of circling round and joining the others, as soon as he was able. In fact, he made it all the way round to the edge of the wood, to a position where he could see the farm. What he didn't know was that the men had retreated even further.

Ben watched as the tanks moved into position, one of them pulling up a few yards away from him. He froze. The moment to cross over the road was gone. Another blessing in disguise. After a short bombardment, the building was demolished. Two men fled, a shot rang out and one of them fell. The other one held his arms high, was soon disarmed by two German soldiers and led away. Ben knew that, somehow, he needed to reach Le Paradis, but it was a long way to crawl, and breaking through the Germans, who were now consolidating their own position, looked impossible. He waited until his immediate surroundings had gone quiet, set his eyes on a target of the corner of the adjacent field, where there was a small building, and set off, crawling along the bottom of the hedge.

As the shelling and gunfire intensified over towards Le Paradis, Ben succeeded in reaching the building at the corner of the field. Crawling in through the door, he flopped onto his back. There was a rustling sound.

"You alright?"

The accent was Scottish.

"I have shrapnel in my knee. I can't walk. What about you?"

"Nothing as heroic as that. I sprained my ankle and got cut off from the others. The name's Scotty, by the way."

"I'm Ben."

"I've got a clean bandage, if you want it."

"Thank you."

Ben loosened the tourniquet and unwound the filthy, bloodied bandage around his knee. The wound looked inflamed.

"That needs proper medical attention."

"I know, but it's impossible."

"Bite down on something. I don't have any surgical spirit, but I'll let you have some of my wee dram."

Ben watched on, a little confused as to what a dram was, as Scotty took out a small flask. After taking a swig, he poured the remaining contents into Ben's wound, which caused him to wince. Ben bit down even harder on the piece of rope he had picked up off the floor.

"Best we can do for antiseptic, for now."

"Thank you. That is very generous of you."

"Your need's greater than mine, although it was a decent malt," laughed Scotty. "I'll let you have a clean bandage, though. We need a plan."

Just as Ben finished applying the clean bandage, there was a loud explosion as a stray shell landed on the building.

"Do you think they've noticed we're here?" mused Ben, as the window, high above them, imploded.

Scotty didn't respond. Ben looked across to see a shard of glass lodged in the side of Scotty's neck.

"I'm a goner. Take care, Ben," rasped Scotty, as he bled out.

At first, Ben didn't notice that another piece of broken window had pierced his left boot, because he was too busy searching Scotty's pockets for a letter home. He took both a letter and the empty whisky flask. Manoeuvring himself back across the floor, the shard in his boot caught on the uneven mud, and he felt it, keenly. Undoing the laces, Ben was relieved to discover the damage was only superficial, although made worse by disturbing the glass. Ripping off a cuff from Scotty's shirt, apologising as he did so, Ben packed the cloth in between the cut and the neck of his boot, re-tying the laces tightly. Over towards Le Paradis, the firing appeared to have stopped.

About thirty minutes later Ben heard several bursts of machine gun fire. Then, only an eerie silence. He couldn't make up his mind what to do next. There was another clump of trees further along the road towards Le Paradis, and he felt sure he would find the remaining Royal Norfolks there. Checking the coast was clear, Ben crawled towards the trees. From his new position, he could see some British soldiers take cover in a farm building, but they were just too far away for him to tell whether they were Norfolks or Scots. The shelling started again, and the roof caved in. Ben looked on, as a small group of about twenty soldiers came out waving a white flag. They stood waiting as a Panzer clunked and squeaked to a halt in front of the building, and the German soldiers marching behind the tank disarmed them. Hardly able to believe his eyes, Ben watched, helplessly, as they were lined up in front of the building and mowed down by machine gun fire.

Just to the side of the building was a ploughed area and several German soldiers dug a grave, waist-deep, into which the dead British soldiers were thrown. After the soil was backfilled over the corpses, the soldiers even created furrows to make it look like nothing had happened. Ben wretched. All that came out was bile and water as he hadn't eaten in thirty-six hours. The tank continued down the road followed by the soldiers, and a plume of black smoke rose from the ruined building.

Ben waited about twenty minutes before crawling over to the building, hoping to find something to eat. He found the remains of a bonfire consisting of backpacks, almost completely incinerated. Whatever the Germans were trying to hide, they had missed a cap, flung behind a pile of hay. The badge informed Ben that these men were Royal Scots. He still felt sick, but on noticing a half-eaten pack of biscuits, also nestling in the hay, forced himself to eat them. Re-energised, he returned to the cover of the woodland to work out his next move. It must have been about fifty miles to Dunkirk, and he was unable to walk. Nor was he certain that the French would help, if they thought he spoke with a German accent, even though he was in a British Army uniform. Somehow, he needed to make it back to England, back to Betty, to tell what he had seen, and to get his knee sorted out. That was when he saw a car, parked at the side of the road, and an idea popped into his head.

If he stuck his left boot onto the butt of his rifle, he could manhandle the clutch, whilst still being able to work the brake and accelerator with his good leg. Not that he had any practical experience of driving, even though he had watched what Bill or Joe did when they had driven him around. Surely, it wasn't that difficult to drive, but what to do about his uniform? If he got stopped in a British uniform, driving a French car, a stolen French car, with a German accent, what could happen? What if he ran into the Germans? And how much petrol was in the tank? His throbbing knee reminded him that he still needed medical attention. In the end, as his brain was bouncing around the myriad questions, he succumbed to exhaustion, his back against a fallen bough. It was just starting to get light when he awoke.

Hearing movement in the trees, he was instantly on his guard. He took hold of his rifle and slowly drew it into a firing position. Through the trees stumbled a young man in British Army uniform, his left arm in a sling.

"Psssst," gestured Ben, feeling it was safe enough to reveal his own presence.

The soldier froze.

"Over here," aspirated Ben, as loudly as he good, without using his voice box.

The soldier spotted Ben and approached, lowering himself to the ground and leaning back against the bough.

"Dougal MacDonald, Royal Scots. Dougie to my friends."

"Ben Linton-House, Royal Norfolks. What happened to you?"

"Glass. Empty farmhouse over there," he responded, pointing. "Shells were coming thick and fast. I was in the attic when the skylight took a hit. Shards of glass everywhere. Lucky the one that landed in my arm didn't sever an artery. Long story short, the others retreated to a barn, leaving me behind. I think they forgot I was up there. The Germans turned their attention to the barn. I don't know what happened. The firing stopped. Then there was some machine gun fire. I was trying to bandage my arm and tie a sling with one hand and my teeth. When I did leave the farmhouse, there was no sign of the others."

Ben worked out that he must have visited the farm building before Dougie. Perhaps the smouldering bonfire had done its job, by the time Dougie entered.

"I'm sorry. I think I saw what happened. Your comrades were killed in cold blood after they surrendered. They are buried in a shallow grave. I'm sorry."

Dougie sat staring into the distance.

"What about you?" he inquired after a moment.

"We were trying to hold the hedge, near the crossroads. I was already wounded. Shrapnel in my knee. My company retreated to a farm. I crawled into the trees. I did not think I could reach the farm. I cannot walk. I arrived at a building. I took cover with a young Scottish soldier. When a window broke, a large piece fell on his neck, and he died. I was lucky. A small piece cut my leg. The same leg as the shrapnel."

"What was his name?"

"Scotty."

"That's helpful!"

"Wait. I have his letter'" added Ben, reaching into his pocket and taking out the letter. "Scot Cameron. Did you know him?"

"No. Must be a different company."

"There are people from every company together, now."

"You sound German," remarked Dougie.

"I am Jewish. From Karlsruhe. I came to England just after the Night of Breaking Glass. I hate the Nazis. I fight with the British. I married an English girl. England is my home."

"You don't look old enough to be married."

"I am eighteen. War is war. I fell in love. Her name is Betty. Her parents said we can be married because the war started."

"I have a girl in Dumfries. If I make it home alive, I'll ask her to marry me."

"We have to try to make it home alive. We have to tell people what happened to your comrades."

"How are we going to get home now? The Germans are between us and the sea."

"Can you drive? I saw a car in the road."

"Where are we going to drive to?"

"West along the sea. Or we could go south."

"South?" exclaimed Dougie. "Do you know how far south we'd have to drive to reach a ship?"

"I think we must try to survive. I prefer it that I am not in a prison camp. I think it is too dangerous to surrender."

"After what you've told me, I agree. Do you speak French?"

"A little. And you?"

"Only a few words the girls like," joked Dougie. "We'll drive south and find ourselves some friendly French people. If we meet any Germans along the way, we'll have to play it by ear. Agreed?"

"Agreed. When do we leave?"

"Now. While it's quiet. Hopefully, we'll be driving away from the fighting. Show me where the car is."

"Less than one hundred yards. I hope there is some petrol."

"Let's see if we can get you on your feet. At least, on one foot. You can use me as a crutch. On my good arm."

Dougie stood and pulled Ben onto his good foot. Ben put his arm round Dougie's neck and hopped. On reaching the car they realised it had been hit and the front wheel was turned inwards on the axle."

"This is going nowhere fast," observed Dougie.

"No."

"Maybe there's a tractor in one of these farms," suggested Dougie. "Come on."

Together, they hopped along the road, past the farm where the Royal Scots had been slaughtered.

"Do you wish to stop?" asked Ben.

"No. I believe you. I'm not about to dig them up."

They continued up the road, until they reached the next farm, where a tractor sat in the yard.

"Shall we ask to borrow it?" pondered Ben.

"What are our options? Steal it and be shot in the back by an angry farmer? Ask to borrow it and be captured? Commandeer it, in the name of the British Army?"

"Perhaps we must go and look for the farmer?"

"Alright. But if there's a problem, we'll have to shoot to kill."

Ben shrugged.

"Wait here, by the tractor. I'll go and look," insisted Dougie.

Ben lowered himself to the ground and leant against the rear wheel, whilst Dougie strode across to the farmhouse and knocked on the door. By the gesticulating and demonstration of turning a wheel, with his good arm, and Dougie pointing towards the tractor, Ben concluded that Dougie was overcoming the language barrier. It might have been better if he had accompanied Dougie to the farmhouse, although to Ben's relief, the next thing he saw was Dougie take the farmer's hand and shake it warmly, turn and walk back over to the tractor.

"I think he was happy to help."

"I think this, also," returned Ben, smiling.

They were just climbing on board when the farmer came rushing towards them with a sack in one hand, some clothes under his arm, and a jerry can in the other.

"Du pain. Du vin," he itemised the contents, pushing the sack into Ben's hands, wedging the can between seat and wheel arch.

"Merci beaucoup," said Ben, taking hold of the sack and placing it at his feet, against the other wheel arch.

The farmer held up a jacket with a rip in the side, a pair of oil-stained trousers and a well-worn jumper, with frayed cuffs.

"It is all I have spare. Remove your uniforms and get rid of these," he suggested, pointing at Ben's belt and pouches.

"Thanks," responded Dougie, taking the clothes and handing Ben the jumper. "I'll have the jacket and trousers."

Ben removed Dougie's sling and helped him take off his jacket. After handing the farmer their jackets, they undid their belts, removing the pouches. Dougie took his water bottle and shook it in front of the farmer, who pointed at a pump, to which Dougie pointed at his wounded arm and shrugged. The farmer nodded sympathetically, put the jackets on the floor, took the bottle and went over to the pump.

"Put some bullets in the jacket pockets," instructed Dougie, as the farmer returned. "We should only take one rifle. I can't use mine properly, anyhow."

After a bit of a struggle, Ben succeeded in removing his gaiters. Dougie was struggling with just the one good arm. Ben undid Dougie's gaiters and laces so he could change his trousers. It was a bit of an ungainly process, but he managed to remove one pair and pull on the other. Ben re-tied his bootlaces for him, as the farmer stood with his arms piled high.

"The packs. We should ditch the packs too. Is there anything in yours you need?"

Ben shook his head and hauling himself up, retrieved his pack from the tractor. Dougie's was on the ground. He opened it, fumbled around inside, paused, and closed the pack again, without taking anything out.

"Thank you. Thank you so much," he repeated, piling the two packs onto the farmer's already overloaded arms, and resting his rifle on top.

The farmer just grinned, lowered his chin onto the rifle and turned back towards the farmhouse.

Ben was scotched between the seat and the mudguard, unable to sit. Dougie had the seat, so he could drive. He hadn't replaced the sling but had no strength in the wounded arm.

"We might have to drive this thing as a double-act," joked Dougie. "My legs, your other hand."

Using only his good arm, Dougie started up the engine and turned the wheel. As they exited the yard, Ben waved at the farmer, who was standing in his doorway. He nodded in response, and the two men headed south along the road.

"How far do you think we can go?" asked Ben.

"Thirty miles, maybe. If we're lucky. Arras."

"There was fighting at Arras. There may still be Germans. We must drive along the small roads. From village to village. Like we are farm workers."

"You're probably right."

"That farmer was friendly. Perhaps other farmers will be friendly?"

Dougie turned down the next road on his right, took the next left, and continued taking alternate turns to right and left, until they came to a village. Thankfully, they hadn't heard any shelling or gunfire, since setting off, although it was difficult to hear anything above the tractor engine. Dougie brought the tractor to a halt in the gateway to a field.

"Why do we stop here?" asked Ben.

"We can eat and fill up the fuel tank."

"Good idea."

"It'll also give us a chance to watch what's going on, in the distance. See any smoke. Listen for shelling."

Ben pulled the cork from the bottle, which was already half empty, and tore the bread in two.

"We don't know when we'll next eat. Better to fill up now, I think," reflected Dougie, taking his half of the bread.

They chewed and swigged without a word. Once all the bread and wine were consumed, Dougie jumped down from the seat and managed to pour the contents of the jerry can into the fuel tank, with just his good arm. He was strong, but like the bottle, the can was only half full. They drove off, and Dougie continued taking right and left turns, until they reached another village.

"How much further can we drive with the diesel?"

"Not far."

"We can try to get some more."

"I don't speak French, remember. You'll have to come too. In case I need to explain why I need it."

Dougie helped Ben down from the tractor and grabbed the jerry can.

"I think we must leave the rifle behind the hedge." suggested Ben.

Dougie thought for a few seconds and nodded. He put the can on the ground. Taking the rifle, he clambered over the gate, and placed it under the hedge. As he climbed back over the gate, he stood on the third bar, his shins pressed against the second, and for a few seconds, scanned the horizon.

"I saw smoke over towards Dunkirk, at least I think it was that way," he reported, once back at Ben's side.

"I just hope they make it back. Otherwise, it will be for nothing," reflected Ben.

"Come on. Use me as your support, again," he encouraged Ben, picking up the jerry can, before Ben leant on him.

They walked towards the village, knocking at the first door they came to. A curtain twitched and a face appeared at the edge of the window. Seconds later, the door opened, and a man in his thirties, maybe forties, grabbed Ben's arm and dragged him inside. The sudden movement caught Ben off his guard, and he lost his balance, unable to bear weight on his left leg. Thankfully, he was able to fall into an armchair. Dougie hesitated, so the man pulled him across the threshold, by the sleeve on his wounded arm.

"Aaaaagh!" he gasped, as the man immediately closed and bolted the front door.

"I am François. You cannot go into the village. The Germans, they are in the mairie."

"I am Ben, and this is Dougie. Thank you."

"You spoke English," responded Dougie, smiling and putting the can on the floor.

"How did you know that we are British?" inquired Ben.

"You still have army shirts and boots. And your trousers."

"Is it that obvious?" joked Dougie."

François laughed too.

"I speak a little English. Yes. Now, sit down, please. How do you come here?"

"We were between Le Cornet Malo and Le Paradis when we lost touch with both our companies. A farmer gave us these clothes and his tractor. Ben, here, is badly injured."

"It seems to me that you are injured also."

By now, a lady, of similar age to François, had joined them.

"I present to you my wife, Amélie."

"Pleased to meet you," responded Ben. "I am Ben. This is Dougie."

"Would you like food? Water?" asked François. "Amelie, she does not speak English."

"Thank you," replied Dougie. "We have left the tractor in a gateway, just up the road. There's a rifle hidden behind the hedge, as well."

François turned to Amélie and spoke in French. Ben understood what he said.

"Stay here. Do not leave this house. It is not safe. I will go," insisted François, disappearing into the kitchen.

Ben and Dougie could hear a door open and close.

"Do you speak French?" asked Amélie, in French.

"A little," replied Ben, in French. "We are very grateful to you."

"What else can we do?" she replied, throwing up her arms.

Twenty minutes later, François returned, bringing with him, the rifle and accompanied by a second man.

"This is Armand Blanchet. He is a doctor."

"Ben. Dougie," responded Dougie, extending his hand.

"Let me look at your arm," responded Armand, in English, shaking Dougie's hand and extending his own towards Ben, who shook it, warmly.

"Please, take off your shirt," instructed the doctor.

Unwinding the bandage, the doctor looked closely at the cut. The wound was deep and slightly inflamed around the edges.

"How did you do this?" asked Armand.

"A piece of window-glass fell on me."

"It needs the stitches. You need the penicillin," declared the doctor, and turning to Ben, added, "Now we must look at your leg. This will not be easy."

Amélie left the room.

"You must take off the trousers."

Seated in the armchair, Ben untied his laces, removed his boots and undid his belt, pushing the trousers down as far as his knees, but unable to lower them any further. Seeing him struggle, the doctor completed the manoeuvre for him. There was blood on Ben's sock, which caught Armand's attention.

"You have two wounds," he observed, carefully removing Ben's sock.

"Glass. From another window," Ben explained, with a wry smile.

"It is infected. Let me see your knee."

On removing the bandage, his face changed to a concerned frown.

"How did this happen?"

"Shrapnel," replied Ben. "How bad is it?"

"It is bad enough. This too, it is infected."

"Can you do anything?"

"I can do many things. What we cannot do is take you to the hospital. If I do not remove this shrapnel, you can lose your leg."

"Can you take it out?"

"I think I must to look for it. I think also it will hurt you."

"Never mind the pain."

"Amélie," called François. Bring in the eau de vie, please."

Amélie came in carrying a bottle and two glasses, which she filled and offered to Ben and Dougie.

"Bottoms up!" laughed Dougie, ironically, downing his glass in one gulp.

Ben followed suit, without the 'Bottoms up'. Amélie refilled their glasses.

"Again, messieurs."

Ben was not enamoured of the flavour, but he knew the effect would be to dull what he anticipated would be excruciating pain. They downed a second glass. Amélie refilled their glasses and returned to the kitchen. She came back with a wooden spoon, a bowl of warm water and some towels. François laid out a sheet on the floor and placed a cushion at one end, ushering Ben to lie down. As Ben stood, he felt dizzy, and stumbled. François caught him and lowered him to the ground.

"Perhaps you do not need the spoon. Perhaps you will sleep," he laughed, patting the side of Ben's face with brotherly affection.

Ben groaned and settled back into the cushion.

"Bite on this," Armand instructed him, handing him the wooden spoon.

By the time Armand had laid out his equipment and washed his hands, Ben was sleeping. Armand poured surgical spirit over the wound, but Ben hardly groaned. This gave the doctor hope that he might not feel the incision. Armand felt around the edge and rested his thumb over a slight bulge, to the lower end of the wound. Taking his scalpel, he made a slit, about one inch long and half an inch deep. Placing a thumb on each side of the wound he massaged the flesh. Puss squirted out, landing on his shirt, but he continued to manoeuvre the piece of metal until a corner appeared above the incision. Taking some tweezers, he pulled it slowly out, and carried on manipulating the flesh until all the puss was removed. He flooded the wound with surgical spirit. Ben groaned again but didn't show any further signs of being conscious. Armand took a needle and some suture, stitched the incision, and unwrapping a clean bandage, wound it neatly round Ben's leg. He turned his attention to the foot. After checking there were no foreign bodies in the wound, he poured in some surgical spirit and made two stitches. Taking another clean bandage, he covered the wound.

"When he wakes, give to him the penicillin. Now, Monsieur Dougie. It is your turn."

"I think I might need the shhpoon," laughed Dougie.

As the doctor washed his hands again, Dougie leant back in his chair and bit down on the handle of the wooden spoon. His eyes watered, as Armand poured surgical spirit on the cut. The doctor pressed the sides of the wound, but was satisfied that there was no puss, yet. He took another needle and made four stitches. Dougie bit so hard on the spoon, he felt a tooth crack. Another swab with surgical spirit, and the job was done. The doctor bandaged his arm, and Dougie released the spoon.

"I think I need a dentist now! Thank you."

"You are welcome. You also, must take the penicillin. Stay here this week and I will come, and I will check that everything is clean."

The doctor cleared away his things, gave both François and Amélie a hug, and left by the back door.

"More eau de vie?" offered Amélie.

"Yes. Thank you. Thank you for everything."

"You are welcome, my friend," responded François.

After his fourth glass, Dougie drifted off to sleep. Ben was still sleeping, oblivious to the surgical experience that had just taken place. Amélie covered them both with blankets and went to prepare the evening meal.

Amélie bathed their wounds every day for the next week, and when Armand arrived to check on their progress, he was relieved.

"I was concerned," he admitted, "but I think now that you will get well. Stay one more week, and then my friends will try to find you passage home."

"We are so grateful," responded Ben.

"The French army may have been overcome, but there are many of us who will never give up. Even if we must fight our war in secret," declared François.

The conversation continued in French, between Francois and Armand, and Ben understood enough to discover that the German army had swept across the north of France and was closing off the coast. Many of the British forces had been rescued, but not without a remarkable demonstration of heroism from hundreds of civilian boats that had crossed the Channel to ferry more than three hundred thousand soldiers back home. The French army had fallen back. There were still British forces further to the west, beyond the Somme. Ordinary French people were fleeing their towns and villages everywhere. Only a few stayed, like the doctor and François and Amélie. No one quite knew what was going to happen. Hitler was already pushing south, and Paris was in his sights.

By the time the doctor returned the following week, to remove the stitches, Rouen had fallen, and the British had retreated over the Seine. Paris was now an open city.

"I think it is not so easy to find for you a safe route," reflected François, that evening, over another of Amélie's delicious casseroles. "Your air force is trying to defend the front line. The army is trying to leave France, from the west. I think we must try to make a way to St Nazaire. Tomorrow, we will go. We will try to arrive at the Somme River. From there, friends with a boat will take you as far as they can."

"We are grateful for anything that you can do," responded Ben.

The following evening, Armand joined them for their meal. He brought bandages, surgical spirit, and a small bottle of cognac.

"This we drink, now," he laughed.

Amélie joined them as they raised their glasses.

"To France and to your safety," toasted François.

"And to victory!" added Dougie, hopefully.

"What time do you leave?" asked Armand.

"Eleven o'clock. The night comes very late," answered François.

While they were talking, a man entered through the back door.

"This is Jean-Luc," François introduced him, after hugs had been shared. "He is like us. He brings for you two pistols."

Jean-Luc reached into his jacket pockets and pulled out two small guns, handed them to Dougie and Ben, and retrieved some bullets from his inside pocket. Almost as suddenly as he had appeared, he disappeared back through the kitchen. Armand tried to pour another glass of cognac for everyone, but Ben refused.

"You saw what happens when I drink!" he laughed. "But I have a small flask, if I may," he added, taking Scotty's flask from his jacket pocket.

Armand filled it.

"Ben, I want to check your knee. It is good to see you walking."

"Now that there is no infection, it heals well. I don't think that I can run, but I can stand and walk."

"We will take two nights, perhaps three, I think," observed François.

Armand replaced the bandage, applying the new one in such a way that it provided extra support, above and below Ben's knee.

"How does this feel?"

"Good, thank you," replied Ben, pacing back and forth.

He could feel the wound, but without a piece of metal embedded in his knee, he no longer felt stabbing pain. Just a dull ache.

Ben and Dougie had been given clean clothing each, during the week. No more khaki trousers and prickly shirts. François had even found them overcoats. He handed each of them a black woollen hat.

"Are you ready?" he asked.

Ben and Dougie nodded. They gave Amélie and Armand a hug and followed François out of the back door.

It took a few minutes for their eyes to grow accustomed to the dark, but soon they were walking confidently along the edges of the fields. Ben was able to walk surprisingly quickly, although he suspected once he stopped, the knee might seize up. They only walked in the lanes when they had to. Once, on hearing a car approaching in the distance, the three dived under the hedge, scrambling through the stems. As it passed, they could tell it was a German army car.

"Phew! That was close," remarked Dougie.

"We must be careful," reflected François. "Perhaps it is better to stay in the fields. I think perhaps we follow the Germans."

They continued on their nocturnal hike until the first light of dawn peeped over the horizon.

"If we cannot find a barn within thirty minutes, we must sleep under the trees," insisted François.

No suitable accommodation was found, so they diverted to a small wood and took refuge in the undergrowth.

"I will watch the first hour. You both try to sleep."

Ben was soon asleep. Dougie took a while longer. The sound of shelling could be heard further west.

When François woke Ben, his leg was throbbing, hurting from the exertion of their long walk. He hoped if it was just sore from bearing weight too soon but feared Armand had missed a piece of shrapnel. François settled down to sleep and Ben surveyed the surrounding fields. As he sat, he thought about Betty and whether she was pregnant. How was she coping? And others filled his mind. Would Simon join the army? What was Max doing now? Saul was lucky to escape these horrors. What was he doing these days?

After two hours, he woke Dougie.

"Your turn."

Dougie was tired and grumpy. Ben must have woken him from a deep sleep-cycle. François was breathing deeply.

"If he starts snoring, I'll kick him," laughed Dougie.

"Goodnight, again," smiled Ben, curling up on the ground.

Having fallen into a bad dream, with bombs exploding and panes of glass crashing to the floor all around him, he woke up sweating.

"You alright?" inquired Dougie.

"Just a bad dream. Thank you."

Ben tried to settle again but gave up, deciding to keep Dougie company.

"What's she like, your wife?"

"Betty? She is clever, beautiful. She wants to be a teacher, one day. She wants a baby first. We tried, before I left. I have received no letters."

"That's tough. My Isla is the cutest woman in the whole of Scotland. What I wouldn't give to be making a baby with her, right now."

"We must keep the hope that there is a future for us all. And François and Amélie."

"Do you think we can find a way through? The Germans are north, south, east and west of us."

"I'm sure that François knows where we are going."

François stirred.

"Your ears burning?" laughed Dougie.

François touched his ear, looking bemused.

"It's a saying. We were mentioning your name."

"What were you saying?"

"That we hope there is a future for all of us," responded Ben.

"It's going to be a long day," reflected Dougie.

"I have bread and sausage in my bag," announced François. "Are you hungry?"

"Always," joked Dougie.

François pulled a greaseproof-paper parcel from his bag and unwrapped it to reveal six slices of bread and some slices of saucisson. He offered them to the others.

"Why did you and the doctor stay behind?" asked Dougie.

"Armand must stay. He's a doctor. Amélie and me? We want to fight. We do not yet know how."

"Helping us is a very good way to fight," Dougie encouraged him.

"Thank you."

"Wait. How come you're not in the army?"

"I am four years too old."

No one said anything else for a while, and the silence was only broken when a farm truck drove along the road, a stone's throw from where they were sheltering.

"Can you still drive through the German army?" asked Ben.

"I do not know. Perhaps they focus on the French and British soldiers, and not on civilians."

"Why don't we drive, then?" suggested Dougie.

"When we arrive at La Chausée-Tirancourt, my friend he has a truck. Perhaps he will drive you."

Ben lay back down on the ground and closed his eyes. The unmistakable scream of a diving Stuka could be heard, followed by an explosion, somewhere in the direction where the truck was heading.

"Maybe it is not so safe to drive," reflected Ben.

"I hate Stukas," responded Dougie.

Eventually, it grew dark enough to continue their journey. Ben's biggest fear was that they would stumble upon some German soldiers in their foxholes. It was hard to see more than a few paces ahead. Luck was on their side and shortly before daylight, they reached the outskirts of La Chaussée-Tirancourt. To François' horror, the Germans had reached there first. Several days previously, in fact. The house where they were due to rendez-vous with his contact was a pile of rubble.

"Wait here. I must go to find out what has happened. Hide in the ruins."

Ben and Dougie did as Francois had instructed.

Half an hour later, François returned, his face downcast, carrying a loaf of bread.

"My friend, he was killed. I cannot go with you any further. I am sorry."

"We are sorry that you have lost your friend," responded Ben.

"At the bottom of this hill is the river. There is a boat tied up at the bank. Be careful of the current. Tonight, you cross. Keep on. The Germans are on this side of the Seine. The British and the French are on the other side. Now I go. I am French. It does not matter if they stop me."

He handed Ben the bread.

"This is for you."

"Thank you for everything," responded Ben.

François gave them each a hug and left them to fend for themselves.

When darkness fell, Ben and Dougie walked down through a field to the Somme River, its banks wooded. Picking their way through the trees, they came to a rowing boat, tied to an overhanging bough.

"We could end up two hundred yards down-river," observed Dougie.

"As long as we can land, it does not matter."

The oars were lying in the bottom of the boat.

"We'll decide what's the best way to paddle when we feel the currents," suggested Dougie.

"I think this also."

Climbing in, Ben untied the rope and they pushed out into the river, where they felt the currents gently manipulating the boat. Dougie took an oar and held it over the side to create a bit of a rudder, and the boat began to move towards the opposite bank.

"Take the other oar," whispered Dougie, pointing at the bows, "and row from that side.

Five minutes later, the bows passed under a curtain of leaves. Ben caught hold of a branch, pulling the boat towards the bank, where they tied the rope to a tree.

One of the items Dougie had retrieved from his pouches, back at the farm, was a compass. He took it from his pocket, turned it towards magnetic north and pointed to west-south-west.

"I think we need to go in that direction."

They soon reached an abandoned farm where a bicycle was leaning against the wall.

"What do you think about me giving you a croggy?"

"A what?"

"A croggy. I pedal, you sit on the saddle. Even if we only go a mile or so, it's faster than walking. If anything comes along the road, we throw the bike over the hedge and hide."

"OK," replied Ben taking hold of the bicycle and sitting astride the saddle, his feet on the ground like stabilisers.

Dougie bent his leg to lift it over the crossbar.

"Would have been better if I'd got on first," he laughed.

He launched the bicycle forwards, with one foot and started to pedal. Just as with the tractor, he took right and left turns along the lanes.

After about half an hour, he started to tire, from not sitting in the saddle.

"You can't pedal with your knee, can you?"

Ben shook his head.

"Alright. Five-minute breather and then we'll see how much further I can go."

Ben got off allowing Dougie space to swing his leg back over, and they sat, strategically, in the gateway to a field.

When Dougie felt refreshed, they continued west-south-west. Faced with a steeper-than-usual hill, Dougie braked.

"We'll have to push it up this one."

"OK," agreed Ben, climbing off again.

At the top, they got back on the bicycle.

"You'd better hang onto me. This is going to be fun."

Dougie freewheeled for about a mile, before having to pedal again.

By dawn, they had made it halfway to Rouen. Having spotted a suitable barn in which to sleep, they covered both themselves and the bicycle with straw. Ben took the first watch.

When night came to provide them with cover, they set off on the bicycle, once more. Dougie's muscles were fatigued from the previous day's cycling and they had to make several stops for him to rest. After cycling for some five hours, he insisted they should stop.

"We must be close to Rouen now. There could be Germans anywhere. Without a map, we don't know how close we are to the river. It's probably best if we find a safe place to hide, and get our bearings, once it gets light," proposed Dougie."

"I think this, also."

The two men made their way over to a small cattle shed, in the middle of a field, where they settled down in the corner, behind a trough. There was no straw, this time, to hide the bicycle or themselves. Shortly after daylight, the shelling started, in the distance.

"We are close to the river, I think," reflected Ben.

High up in the sky, they could see two aircraft, fighters heading east.

"That must be the British," commented Dougie, identifying the silhouettes.

Suddenly, two other planes engaged the British fighters, and a dogfight was played out over Ben and Dougie's heads.

"Hurricanes and Messerschmitts, I believe," remarked Dougie.

One of the Messerschmitts took a hit and spiralled down to earth, a plume of smoke, trailing from his tail. After a few more manoeuvres, one of the Hurricanes was hit, but not before the other Messerschmitt exploded in the air. The second Hurricane turned back towards the river, whilst the one that had been hit started to fall and spin.

"Do you think the pilot is alive?" asked Ben.

Dougie shrugged. The two men watched as the Hurricane spiralled towards the ground. To their relief, a few hundred feet before impact, a parachute appeared in the sky. The Hurricane crashed into the earth several fields away, but the pilot floated down into the corner of the adjacent field.

"Do we help?" suggested Ben.

"We wait. The Germans will be looking for the pilot."

Ten minutes later, they watched the pilot come trotting towards the barn. Once inside, he sat down against the wall. Ben and Dougie peered out from behind the trough. Ben could hardly believe his eyes.

"Max? Is that you?"

Max was startled and grabbed his pistol.

Ben stood up, followed immediately by Dougie.

"Max Sparks. You have joined the RAF?"

"Ben? What the hell are you doing here?"

The two men hugged.

"This is Dougie. We were at Le Cornet Malo. Somehow we survived."

"I didn't know you'd joined up."

"I didn't know you had," laughed Ben, in response.

They heard voices across the field. Peeping through a crack, Dougie could see three German soldiers walking across the field.

"There's no time to reminisce, gentlemen. Max, take off your clothes. Don't argue. Ben here is Jewish. They'll shoot him. I might survive in a prisoner of war camp. We'll swap clothes. Quick. Jacket, shirt, trousers, boots."

He was already removing his own jacket and shirt. As Max removed his, Dougie untied his laces and pushed off his boots with his feet whilst unbuckling his belt. As Max removed his boots and trousers, Dougie was putting on Max's shirt and jacket.

"Hurry."

Finally, Max removed his trousers and Dougie was able to finish impersonating an RAF fighter pilot.

"Be a good father," he mumbled at Ben, squeezing his shoulder and walking out of the barn with his hands held high.

The soldiers were only about twenty yards from the barn when Dougie surrendered. Satisfied that they were only searching for one pilot, they pointed their guns at him and gestured that he should walk in front of them, back across the field. Ben watched through the crack until they reached the gate.

"I think now it is safe."

"It's good to see you. What did he mean by 'Be a good father'?"

"I married Betty. It is possible that she is pregnant."

"Then we must make it back to Blighty, somehow. I'm pretty sure the Germans will have crossed the Seine by now. Maybe we can get across while they're still advancing on the British."

"We only travel at night."

"Yes. You're right. We should stay here until nightfall."

"That was incredible."

"If we make it back, I'm recommending him for a medal."

"I'll keep first watch," offered Ben.

"Thanks."

Max couldn't sleep. It was less adrenalin and more a tune forming in his head. He hummed a few notes.

"I do not know that song."

"You won't. It's an original. I've taken to writing music."

"I am proud for you. How far is it to the river?"

"Depends. The Seine meanders a lot in these parts. We should avoid Rouen. Maybe fifteen miles or so. Let me watch if you can sleep."

"Thanks. I am hungry, not tired. My knee had shrapnel. I cannot walk very fast."

"Alright. We'll see how far we can get and try to find some food along the way. How did you get your knee fixed?"

"Dougie and I, we were lucky. We arrived in a village, we knocked on a door, and a French couple helped us. They had a friend who is a doctor. After some eau de vie I was asleep. Max, I have to tell you something. Stan was killed."

Max didn't say anything but stared ahead at the wall.

"You know that we joined the army together? We were at the front. Shot in the chest."

"He was a good man and a good friend."

"I know this, also."

At nightfall, Max and Ben checked their bearings and set off towards the Seine. After they had walked a couple of miles, it was necessary to cross a lane, but when Max peered out from behind the hedge, to see if the coast was clear, he pulled back, instantly.

"Germans," he mouthed at Ben, holding up two fingers, and tracing a car, followed by making a steering wheel gesture.

Slowly, he peeped round the hedge to take another look. The two soldiers were in a Kübelwagen, parked against the verge. One of them was sitting, the other was leaning over the side. After a minute, Max concluded the one who was leaning over the edge was sleeping in a rather strange position.

"They're not moving," he whispered, pulling back.

"It is a strange place to park at night."

"I know. Do you think they're dead?"

Both men had pistols, which they held ready to fire, and crept along the lane towards the vehicle. Still, the Germans remained motionless. When Ben and Max reached the Kübelwagen, it became immediately obvious that the men were dead.

"It's possible they were hit from the air," surmised Max. "Stray bullets."

"Can you drive?" asked Ben.

"What? You mean, drive this?"

"Yes. We can have a disguise. Overcoats, on the top of our clothes. Their trousers on the top of ours. Their boots and helmets. We can reach the Seine."

"Do you reckon?"

"Why not?"

"Alright. We'll do it at first light."

The two men retreated behind the hedge and waited for the first signs of dawn. Ben actually fell asleep, but Max was happy to keep watch. As soon as a thin band of light appeared on the horizon, they undressed the two German soldiers and laid them down behind the hedge. The trousers Max put on were a bit of a tight fit over his own and Ben's boots were a little sloppy.

"We'll take our own boots in the car," proposed Max. "Grab the guns, too."

There was a map in the car, which Max opened up.

"We'll aim for Le Pont de l'Arche," he announced. "We can dump the car and the uniforms and swim across, when it gets dark, tonight."

Dressed as German soldiers, Max and Ben set off in the stolen Kübelwagen, with Max driving.

"If they catch us, we are dead, for certain," remarked Ben.

"Then we'd better not get caught," replied Max, winking at Ben.

Not having encountered any Germans, they pulled up at the edge of Pont de l'Arche and surveyed the situation.

"We destroyed the bridge, but the Germans put up a temporary one. I think the fighting may have moved across the river by now."

"I hope this, also."

"We've come this far. Dressed like this, in a German vehicle, we could just drive straight across the river, you know. No one's going to stop us."

Ben thought for a few seconds.

"We can try this," he responded.

"At least if we get stopped, you can do the talking."

Max pulled off and followed the streets to where the start of the temporary bridge lay. Ben held his submachine gun at the ready, on his lap. A handful of German soldiers were milling around the entrance to the bridge. Max saluted and kept on driving. Ben followed suit, and the German soldiers saluted and waved them across. As soon as they were over the river, and out of sight, Max turned south and accelerated.

"Listen. The Germans have taken all the Channel ports and there's a good chance they've taken the Atlantic ports too. If we're ever going to make it home alive, we need to head south, to the Mediterranean. I've no idea how much fuel we have, but I'm going to head for Orleans, and cross the Loire, if we can. As soon as we run out of fuel, we'll dump the car and change back into our normal clothes. Maybe try and find some friendly civilians."

Ben nodded. For the first time, he felt in his pockets, and pulled out a quarter-eaten bar of chocolate.

"I liked this chocolate in Karlsruhe," confessed Ben, breaking the chocolate into two and giving Max the slightly larger half.

"Cheers."

They soon passed Evreux and Dreux. Their next target was Chartres. The Germans had occupied the airfield, and dressed as German soldiers in a German army car, it was straightforward enough for Max to keep driving. Whenever they passed German soldiers, they saluted, and no one seemed concerned. Shortly before they reached Gidy, the Kübelwagen ran out of fuel and choked to a standstill. The two men removed their overcoats, helmets, jackboots and trousers, put on their own boots, dumped the vehicle and crossed a field to take cover under some trees. As they sat on the ground, they caught each other's glance and burst out laughing.

"We've been lucky, so far. Let's see if we're lucky enough for some hospitality in the village," suggested Max. "Come on. And let me do the talking. Your accent is still a little German."

No one answered the door at the first two houses they tried, although Ben did notice the curtains twitch in the second one. At the third house, the door opened slowly to reveal an octogenarian, his face and hands tanned and wrinkled from outdoor work.

"Bonjour, Monsieur. We need your help, please," said Max, in French.

"What do you want?"

"Some bread, if you can spare it. And somewhere to stay a couple of nights."

"You are not French."

"We are British. I am a pilot. He is a soldier. We are trying to get back to England, but the Germans are everywhere along the coast."

"France is falling. France cannot win this war," he exclaimed, throwing up his hands. "I cannot go on. I must go on. To lose your son is too much to bear. I have another son in a prisoner of war camp, I don't know where. I have only one son left. When he returns from the fields, he will know what to do. Come in, please."

"I am so sorry for your loss. Thank you."

Max and Ben entered the house.

"My name is Max. This is Ben."

"I am Claude Chevalier. What happened to you?"

"Ben was at Le Cornet Malo. He was injured. Some civilians helped him get better. I was flying over the Seine and was shot down. We met by chance."

"Please, sit down. I will get you bread and coffee. I have very little. Olivier is hunting for rabbits."

Ben and Max sat at the table. It would be several days before they came to understand that 'hunting for rabbits' meant finding ways to resist the occupation. Claude brought them some fresh coffee, saucisson and some not so fresh baguette. They had almost finished eating when Olivier came in carrying a dead rabbit.

"Olivier, these men need our help."

"I'm Max and this is Ben. I am a pilot, and he is a soldier. We want to get back to England, but the Germans are everywhere."

"You are a long way south," replied Olivier, a little suspicious.

"We found a German army vehicle, with two dead soldiers, so we dressed as Germans and drove as far as the petrol took us. It's up the road."

"Are you mad?" exclaimed Olivier. "If the Germans find it, they will come asking questions.

"What could we do? We ran out of fuel. We just wanted to reach a sea-port."

"You are a long way from the sea," laughed Olivier. "Wait here."

He left the house and returned almost an hour later, looking more relaxed than when he'd left.

"I have taken the car and parked it in the barn at the Osiers' farm. It will be safe there. We will strip it down and use the engine to repair a French car. You can stay here until we know it will be a safe to move you. This will not be easy. Montpellier is over six hundred kilometres and La Rochelle over three hundred. Perhaps you can stay and fight."

"Thank you."

"Thank you so much," added Ben, wondering what Olivier meant by staying to fight, when the French army was on the verge of defeat.

"Do you know how to skin a rabbit?" asked Olivier.

Ben shook his head.

"I have never needed to," responded Max.

"Then I will show you. Come."

Ben and Max followed Olivier into the kitchen. The whole experience made Ben want to throw up, but he felt it was necessary to persevere.

"Do you kill a lot of rabbits?" he inquired.

"Lots. Every time I go out, I try to bring home a rabbit. Food is scarce. Why do you not speak French with an English accent, like Max?"

"I am a Jew. From Karlsruhe. I left after the Night of Broken Glass. Believe me when I say that I hate the Nazis as much as you do. I settled in England. I fell in love and married an English girl. My life is in England. I have been fighting for the British."

"Then we must become brothers in arms. I have lost one brother and one brother is in a prisoner-of-war camp. Do you have brothers?"

Max shook his head.

"My brother is in America. He got on the wrong ship at Rotterdam. I sent a letter. There was no reply. I hope one day we will find each other again."

"I hope that you will," Olivier encouraged him.

The next two weeks were a time of confusion and concern for Ben and Max's new French friends. France had fallen. The Germans occupied most of the north. An armistice had been signed allowing a puppet government to be set up in Vichy. Worse still, from Ben and Max's perspective, German law was established in France, which meant the same policies that applied to the Jews in Germany would also now be applied in France.

"We must get you some new papers," announced Olivier at breakfast one morning. "When I go hunting for rabbits, I will try to make it happen. We have friends in the city who can do this."

"Thank you," responded Ben, pondering how Olivier would hunt for rabbits in Orléans.

Later that afternoon, when Olivier returned, he brought with him two new sets of identity papers and a bottle of cognac.

"Tonight, we will have a secret meeting," he explained, holding up the bottle. "You will understand."

A German administration had been established throughout occupied France, and everyone needed papers, but the newness of it all created a useful window of opportunity for anyone needing a new identity. Olivier handed over the papers. Max Sparks had become Max Augustin and Ben had yet another name change, becoming Ben Manon.

From eight o'clock onwards, people started to arrive at Claude and Olivier's house, entering unannounced, through both front and back doors. When everyone who was expected had arrived, Olivier introduced Max and Ben, as friends who had come to join the fight. It soon transpired, that they were in the inaugural meeting of a fledgling resistance movement. The plan was to disrupt the German administration in whatever way possible, by disabling vehicles, breaking electricity generators, and low-level sabotage. It was also decided that they would support any individuals, mostly Jewish or Roma, who found themselves in danger of deportation. It was during the meeting that Ben came to understand 'hunting rabbits' meant carrying out some sort of resistance activity. Whenever possible, you tried to bag a real rabbit as well, in order to allay suspicion. He had no idea when he would return to England, but the thought of a being part of a secret war against the Nazis appealed to him, even excited him.

November brought newspaper reports of a concentrated bombing campaign over London. Ben was desperate to hear news of Betty, but since he had stepped foot in France, no letter had ever reached him. He tried not to worry and tried to focus on his resistance roll. Olivier had become a trusted friend, but it soon became clear, that knowing who your friends were, was becoming increasingly blurred. Whilst some amongst the civilian population joined the resistance movement, others chose to collaborate with the German occupiers.

Several months passed, and another tragedy landed in the lap of the Chevalier family, with Claude's fatal accident. He had been crossing the road, out to fetch bread from the bakery, when a man on a bicycle ran into him. His awkward fall broke his hip and at eighty-four years old, his chances of recovery were slim. Three days later he passed away.

"If I ever get my hands on Herve Linne," hissed Olivier, the evening of the funeral, when he was several glasses of cognac the worse for wear.

Olivier had lost a brother, had no idea when he might see is other brother again, and now his father was dead. Ben thought his pain must be unbearable.

"Do you know what makes this so hard?" inquired Olivier, somewhat rhetorically. "The man who did this is a collaborator."

"His day of judgment will come," Max offered, by way of consolation.

Olivier said nothing and stumbled off to bed.

The resistance movement around Gidy was achieving a measure of success. Its proximity to Orleans, and relative anonymity, allowed members of the group to go hunting for rabbits on a regular basis. The Germans were using Orléans as a rail hub, and it was easy to find a spot along the railway line and position an exploding device on the track. As they always planted the devices at different points, the Germans were never able to cover the length of the line, and only a few were identified. The damage to trains was limited, but the engineers were forever having to replace sections of mangled rail.

One evening, Olivier returned home with some disturbing news.

"The Germans are taking Jews to an internment camp about fifty kilometres from here, at Pithiviers. We are going to try and stop one of the trains and release some of the prisoners. It will involve killing the guards, of course. Will you help?"

"I cannot see us getting back to the British army anytime soon, so yes," replied Max.

"How can I refuse?" added Ben

"Excellent! There are eight who have been chosen to carry out the mission, including you. The train is due to leave Orleans in three days. We will be joined by Jean-Marc, Philippe, Serge, Matthieu and Bernadette."

Ben's gut was making him uncomfortable about Bernadette. It wasn't that she was a woman. She was new to the group and there was something about the way she had first introduced herself that didn't ring true. Ben had gone with Olivier to meet her, two weeks previously, in a café on the outskirts of Orléans. Ben was not normally suspicious of people, but Bernadette had said she could not read, and he was sure he caught her reading something in the newspaper on the table, upside-down.

"I feel terrible to say this, but I think that Bernadette can read. I do not trust her."

"What do you want me to do?" replied Olivier, taken aback by Ben's comments. "Are you suggesting she is an informer?"

"If she is an informer, we must move away from her. We need to test her when we meet to plan the rescue."

"Agreed," responded Olivier, after a pause.

The meeting was to take place at the church in a nearby village. Since the movement had become official, they always met in a different venue, with the address being dropped into letterboxes the day before. If Ben was right about Bernadette, the Germans would be waiting for them at the church.

"Stay here," he instructed Ben and Max, as they entered the village. "I am going to go and see if there's a German welcoming party. Wait ten minutes. Then come to the church."

He disappeared into the night. Ten minutes later, Ben and Max joined him in the church, where Jean-Marc, Matthieu and Bernadette, were already there. When Philippe and Serge arrived, Olivier made an announcement.

"It is not safe to meet here. We must go to the presbytery. Follow me."

He led them out of the back of the church, round to the priest's house. Olivier was simply being cautious. He had also arranged a test for Bernadette. He deliberately uncovered a list of false names and addresses, with comments next to each entry, and watched for Bernadette's reaction. During the next ten minutes, she made definite attempts to read them across the table. Olivier found himself facing a difficult decision, but he had come prepared. If Bernadette shared the plans they were in the process of formulating, the Germans would either arrest them or kill them as soon as they set out on their mission. The good news was that up to this point, Bernadette had only met Ben and himself. Unless she had followed them home, she didn't know where they, or any of the others lived, and only knew their first names. Even though he was inclined to share Ben's suspicions, he didn't want to accuse Bernadette falsely.

"We will arrive, independently, where the train enters the forest, at six o'clock in the morning. All the trains slow down a little, in case there are trees on the line. The forest will provide cover for us and for any passengers who escape. As the train passes, Jean-Marc and Philippe will shoot the guards at the front of the train. Serge will take the engine driver. Max, Ben and I will shoot the guards at the rear of the train and climb on. Matthieu and Bernadette will jump onto the train from each side, as it passes. We will all open the doors. Serge will make the driver stop the train, long enough for the passengers to escape. If the driver is still alive, he will drive an empty train towards Pithiviers. If he is dead, Serge will drive the train a little further along the track, leaving it running as he jumps off. Any questions?"

No one said anything.

"Good. We will rendez-vous in two days' time in the forest."

As the others started to leave, Olivier approached Bernadette.

"I will walk with you," he suggested. "I want to get to know you, a little better."

He had no intention of getting to know her better, but he wanted to make sure she didn't follow them. Ben and Max made their own way home.

It was five o'clock in the morning when he arrived home, with a dead rabbit in his hand. Ben and Max had waited up, although they had both drifted off to sleep in their armchairs and woke when Olivier closed the front door.

"Was it a good night?" smiled Max. winking.

"Nothing like that. I have been to everyone's house, apart from Bernadette's, with a change of plan. Hopefully, if she's an informer, she will lead the Germans to the forest. If she's not an informer, and when we don't turn up, she will just think we abandoned the mission."

"So, what is the new plan?" inquired Ben.

"Before the train leaves the city, we put an obstacle on the line. There is a section which passes through some warehouses near a small spur of track. We will push an empty coal truck onto the line and Serge and Matthieu, in their coal covered overalls, will be attempting to push it back onto the spur, when the train approaches. As the train slows, Serge and Matthieu will approach the engine to distract the driver, long enough for Jean-Marc and Philippe to take out the guards at the front, with knives. Serge or Matthieu will then kill the driver. You and I will do the same to the guards at the rear. We cannot fire shots as it will alert people to the incident. While Serge and Matthieu go back and move the coal truck, the rest of us will open the doors. The passengers will disperse amongst the buildings. Where they go after that is up to them. We will conceal the soldiers in the warehouse. Same as before with driving the train."

"And Bernadette knows nothing of this?" confirmed Ben.

"Nothing at all."

On the morning of the rescue mission, Ben, Max and Olivier got up at four o'clock. After a breakfast of coffee and bread, which Ben forced himself to consume, they made their way into Orléans to meet the others at the warehouse next to the spur of track. Hardly anyone was in the streets. Certainly, there were no Germans visible, not that that didn't mean collaborators and informers weren't out and about. In the event, two warehousemen had arrived early, but they were sympathetic to the resistance cause and joined Serge and Matthieu, in pushing the coal truck onto the line.

The others concealed themselves behind various barrels and wooden crates. Ben could hear the puffing of the train along the tracks, and he started to sweat. This was unlike the previous rabbit-hunting expeditions, which had taken place at night. Neither had he killed anyone with a knife before. The driver had no option but to slow down. The workmen threw up their arms and shouted, making a show of apologetically trying to move the coal truck out of the way, and Serge and Matthieu approached the engine. As Serge was climbing up, Jean-Marc and Philippe ran over to the train and overpowered the two guards at the front, before they realised what was happening. At the same time, Olivier and Max, leaped onto the back carriage, just ahead of Ben. They had killed the guards, almost before Ben was in reach, much to his relief. He didn't mind causing death by acts of sabotage. It was killing an individual that he shunned. All the doors were opened allowing the surprised passengers to flee. They poured out of the wagons, some giving thanks, others turning round, disorientated, trying to work out the best direction in which to run. The doors were closed again, and Serge, Jean-Marc and Philippe all stayed on the empty train, until it was far enough from the outskirts of the city to jump off.

The mission was a success, although Ben wondered how much of a difference it would make in the long-term. Surely, the Germans would just round up the Jews again, and guard the train better next time? He was not wrong. A few days later, whilst Max was out hunting rabbits on his own, Ben accompanied Olivier on an errand in Orléans. As they approached the cathedral, it was obvious from the commotion, that something unusual was happening. Hovering on the edge of a small crowd, they could see a number of civilians being lined up in front of a wall, with their hands bound. Ben counted twenty-four. A German official, standing under a Nazi flag, read out a notice. Twelve of the prisoners were Jews. The other twelve were French. At the end of the line stood Bernadette. Hoping she hadn't already noticed his presence, Oliver took a step back, behind the woman in front of him, so Bernadette would not be able to see him and blow his cover. The twenty-four were all hostages, taken in reprisal for the train rescue. It was meant to be a warning against further acts of resistance. One by one, a scarf was tied over their eyes. Five German soldiers line up with their submachine guns at the ready, the command to fire was given, and the hostages were sprayed with bullets, until none was standing. Ben wanted to be sick. Olivier put a hand on his shoulder and gestured they should leave the scene.

"Did we do more harm than good?" mused Ben, aloud, once they were out of earshot of the crowd.

"We're in a war. We have to keep fighting. What would be the consequences if we did nothing?"

"We will never know if Bernadette was an informer. They may have killed her because the empty train passed through the forest."

"Surely she must have realised something was wrong when the rest of us didn't appear. Maybe the Germans were already there, and she couldn't escape."

No more was said, for a while, as they made their way towards the port, where a barge was being unloaded into wagons.

"Where does the coal go?" asked, Ben, breaking the silence.

"As far as the sea, I think."

"Which port?"

"Nantes, maybe. Why?"

"I think it is time that Max and I try to go back to England."

"What are you thinking?"

"I was thinking about the coal truck, when we stopped the train. We could hide under the coal."

"How will you leave Nantes? It is controlled by the Germans. I think it is better that you go south. Go to Tours, Poitiers, Angouleme, Bordeaux and down to Bayonne. Try to cross the border into Spain. I will help you."

"Thank you."

Ben was beginning to wonder if Olivier had forgotten all about their conversation. Two weeks had elapsed since he had mentioned the idea of travelling south. Out of the blue, on his return from a rabbit-hunting expedition, Olivier spoke of the plan.

"I have been talking to friends who work on the railways. In five days, you are going to join them working on the track. I have got for you a pass to travel free from Orléans to Tours. At Tours, you will go with my friends along the track and work. I do not know what work you will do. It doesn't matter. There are several freight trains moving between Tours and Bordeaux. My friends will know which one to climb on board. When you arrive in Bordeaux, you jump off the train, and when it is passed, you do some more work on the railway track. You will be able to walk along the track to the line which goes to Bayonne and do the same thing as before. If you are lucky, the freight train does not stop in the stations. This time, my friends will stay on the track when you get on the train. At Bayonne, you must find your own way."

"Sounds simple enough," commented Max.

Between the announcement and the departure, Ben and Max took part in two more acts of sabotage. One of them took out a generator and the other cut some telephone wires. It was true, Ben found enjoyment and purpose in these acts of resistance, especially where no actual killing was involved, but the hope which had now been rekindled of seeing Betty again, of discovering if he was a father, was stronger.

It was October 1941 when the day of departure finally arrived. Olivier led them to the railway sidings where his friends were checking the track. He exchanged hugs with all four of the men.

"This is Ben and Max."

"Pleased to meet you and thank you for your help."

"Thank you for all your help. Maybe we will see each other again, on the other side of victory," said Olivier. "We will miss your support."

Max held out his hand to shake Olivier's, but Olivier refused it, hugging him instead, followed by Ben. Olivier turned and walked back down the track, whilst the men walked towards the station where they got on the next train to Tours.

Halfway to Tours, a German guard came through the carriage door. Ben waited nervously, trying desperately not to let his anxiety show. One of the railway workers held up a sheet of paper to the guard who read it, counted the six men with his head, handed back the paper and continued along the carriage.

"Papers, please."

The railwayman with the paper winked at Ben, who now relaxed. Even when the guard walked back through the carriage, Ben felt less nervous than before.

At Tours, the men held back to let the other passengers pass in front of them and followed them off the train. They walked along the platform, beyond the engine, and jumped down onto the tracks, where they seemed to know exactly which line went to Bordeaux. As they made the pretence of checking rivets, a passenger train approached them. The six men stepped back from the track to let it pass and returned to their duties. The next train which rattled along the tracks towards them was a freight train.

"Are you ready?" asked the leader, as they stepped back from the tracks.

But the men let it pass and started work again. Twenty minutes later, another passenger train rumbled past. They all stepped back to let it pass. After another forty minutes, a second freight train clunked and squeaked towards them. It was only travelling at walking pace.

"Get ready," instructed the leader.

As the guard's van passed them, they started to jog along after it, catching hold of it and pulling themselves up. Ben and Max followed suit.

"Why this train?" asked Ben, curious to know why they hadn't caught the first one.

"No guard," smiled the leader. "I'm Antoine, by the way. These are Pierre, Paul and Thierry."

"Happy to make your acquaintance," responded Ben.

Max nodded in acknowledgement.

The men sat down on the floor, and Thierry took out a packet of Gauloises which he offered around. Neither Ben nor Max smoked, but the Frenchmen all did, and the guard's van soon filled with smoke. Ben found it uncomfortable. Leaning over towards the door he opened it to let some air in and the smoke out.

"Apologies," mumbled Thierry.

The smokers stubbed out their Gauloises and threw the butts through the open door.

As the train neared Angoulême it decelerated and came to a premature halt alongside the signal box.

"What's going on?" asked Pierre.

There were several short bursts of machine gun fire further towards the station. Antoine crawled over to the doorway and edged his way out far enough to peep round either side of the guard's van.

"I can see German soldiers on that side of the train. Something is happening in the station, but I can't see anything."

"What do we do now?" inquired Pierre.

"Stay still, for now," replied Antoine.

A few minutes and more bursts of gunfire later, Antoine poked his head out of the guard's van again. When he came back in, his expression was one of mild panic.

"Three German soldiers heading this way. We might just have time, under the cover of the wagons, to reach the signal box. Quick."

Paul pulled two crossbows from his tool bag and handed one to Antoine. One by one, the men jumped down onto the tracks and ran towards the signal box, before the signalman had a chance to realise what was happening. As Antoine entered the box, he fired his crossbow. When Ben arrived in the signal box, a few paces behind, he saw the signalman lying dead in the corner, a bolt in his heart.

"Do you think they saw us" he asked.

"I don't know," responded Antoine. "We will know, soon enough."

Hardly had they reached the shelter of the signal box than two civilians climbed the steps. On reaching the door, they saw the railwaymen, with Ben and Max. Luckily, Antoine spoke before they fired their weapons.

"Comrades?"

"Who are you?" responded one of the civilians.

"We were heading south on this train, to help these two English combatants. What are you doing?"

"We were trying to take out a munitions train."

Before he could expand on his explanation, two short burst of machine gun fire shattered the windows. Ben instinctively covered his head with his arms. One of the shards landed in Pierre's leg. Another flew across the room and caught Thierry in the face. When the glass had settled, Ben looked down to see blood flowing from his finger. Somehow, a shard of glass had sliced the nail from the middle finger on Ben's right hand. Pulling a handkerchief from his pocket, he bound it tightly, trying to stop the pain as much as the blood. Max tried to help Thierry and Paul tended to Pierre.

"Throw out your weapons and surrender," shouted one of the soldiers, outside.

Up to this point, there was nothing to indicate to the Germans that any more than two men were concealed in the signal box, although they may have been wondering what had happened to the signalman.

"Don't shoot!" called out one of the resistance fighters. We are coming out."

They held their hands up as they exited the signal box and climbed slowly down the steps.

"And the signalman?" Ben heard one of the soldiers ask.

"We let him run for cover," lied one of the resistance fighters, to protect the railwaymen.

There was a short burst of gunfire followed by the sound of jackboots on gravel. When the scrunching of footsteps had receded into the distance, Antoine peered out through the window. The two resistance fighters were lying dead on the ground. The freight train was starting to move, again. The problem for the railwaymen was that they might easily be seen exiting the signal box. If they stayed, someone was bound to come to replace the signalman. Thierry and Pierre needed medical attention, but they were able to walk, albeit slowly, for Pierre. Antoine made the decision to try and reach the train.

"We must get Max and Ben away from here. Paul, go with them to the train. We will take our chances here."

"Thank you." replied Ben, as they slipped out of the signal box, down the steps and ran across the tracks to the guard's van.

Ben was hardly able to grip with his right hand and slipped, but Max caught his sleeve and hauled him in. The three of them sat down on the floor and waited for the train to pass through the station. Halfway along the platform, a German soldier jumped onto the guard's van. Miraculously, he didn't look inside but watched along the platform. Paul slowly raised his crossbow and aimed it at chest height, should the soldier decide to come in. To everyone's relief, the soldier jumped off again, at the far end of the platform, and the train picked up speed, leaving the three men to contemplate what had just happened.

"How bad is your injury?" inquired Max, as they passed beyond the outskirts of the city.

"I think I've lost nail and some of the tip of my finger."

"We must monitor it, to make sure it doesn't get infected," commented Paul.

"Thankfully, I am left-handed."

Paul rummaged around in the tool bag which they had left in the guard's van during the incident and pulled out some bread and saucisson.

"It's not much, but we can share it," he offered.

"Thank you," replied Ben and Max, in unison.

"If we reach Bordeaux, it may now be difficult to make out we are working on the track. I think we should get off when we pass through the sidings and hide in a disused carriage until after dark."

"A good idea," agreed Ben.

But they never reached Bordeaux. For reasons which completely escaped them, as the city came into view, the train started to bear east, in the direction of Toulouse. Was it intended? Was it another act of the resistance movement? There was no way of knowing.

The train slowed down, to cross over the demarcation line into Vichy France, and accelerated again. Outside, it was starting to get dark. Ben had discovered a loose knot in the wood which he had knocked out to create a peephole. Time passed and the train decelerated again, this time as it approached Toulouse, not that the men knew where they were, until the train rumbled through the station, and Ben saw the name plates passing by. Once more, the train picked up speed.

After a while, Max fell asleep. Paul was trying, desperately, to stay awake. Ben was in pain and wiled away the time by imagining his homecoming. He decided to peer out through his peephole once more. Sitting back, he rubbed his eyes, and looked again.

"You are not going to believe this but I am certain that I can see the sea."

"Seriously," retorted Paul, standing and stepping over to the door. "You're correct. It can only be the Mediterranean."

Ben shook Max's arm.

"Wake up Max. We have reached the Mediterranean."

Max groaned and woke from his slumber, a little disorientated.

"How the hell did we get here?"

"I think we are perhaps arriving in Sète," suggested Paul.

His suggestion was confirmed as the train passed through the station. It continued to decelerate, and came to a standstill in the sidings, not far from the oil refinery.

"Gentlemen, I think this is where we must go our separate ways. I feel a sabotage coming on. I need to find some comrades. Be careful, this is free France, but even though it is not occupied, there are many informers who support the Vichy government. They do not like the British. Trust no one."

He shook their hands and slipped away across the sidings under cover of night.

BREAKING POINT

For a few moments, Ben and Max remained sitting in the guard's van.

"What do you want to do?"

"We can't stay here forever," replied Max. "If this is Vichy France, that means the Germans don't control the port. Perhaps we can find a ship."

"Where will we go? Not to England, from here."

"Wherever the ship goes," laughed Max. "Gibraltar. North Africa. Malta."

"Shall we go down to the docks tonight, while it is still dark?"

"Makes sense. We can find somewhere to hide tonight and explore in the morning."

"OK by me. What day is it, today?"

"Wednesday, I think."

After double-checking the coast was clear, they started out towards the docks. With few clouds and some moonlight, they could see where they were going, and arrived unscathed, just after nine o'clock. Although the streets were largely empty, rowdy laughter emanated from a bar, close to the waterfront.

"I could murder a beer," whispered Max, smiling.

A man and woman tumbled out of the door and staggered along the street with their arms wrapped round each other. They were followed out of the door by a group of men, one of whom was carrying a football, which he proceeded to practise keepie-uppies with, eventually kicking it to one of the others. Too late to hide, the man who now had possession of the ball, kicked it over to where Ben and Max were standing. Ben couldn't help himself and kicked it back.

"You like football? You come to watch us on Saturday? FC Sète. We're going to win the cup."

The footballers wandered off chanting 'We're going to win the cup', all the while.

"If we are still here on Saturday, we must go to watch. Try to be normal, so no one recognises us."

"Have you forgotten we're to trust no one? They'd soon tell we weren't French as soon as we opened our mouths, and don't forget, you speak both French and English with a German accent, even if it's improving."

"I think it will not be so easy to simply find a ship. Perhaps we must try to make friends."

Max wasn't convinced, but he sensed that Ben simply wanted to do something normal, which for Ben meant something sporty.

"We'll see," proposed Max, after a brief pause for thought. "Now, let's go find somewhere to sleep."

There was a warehouse which backed onto the docks, and although closed, the doors weren't locked. Max and Ben entered. It smelt fishy, mainly because it was a store for all kinds of fishing equipment. There were nets, crates, barrels, lobster traps, packing cases, ropes and baskets. After walking up and down, they settled on a narrow gap, between some piles of rope and some packing cases. It was difficult for Ben to use his right hand, so Max dragged over a folded net for them to lie on.

"We'll get used to the smell," laughed Max.

"I think this, also. Goodnight."

"Night."

They were woken at four o'clock in the morning, when some men came in to collect nets. There was no time to hide, and Max and Ben's makeshift bed was suddenly bathed in lanternlight.

"Eh. What are you doing here?"

"We need your help," replied Max, in French. "We arrived here yesterday on a train. Can you help us, please?"

"You are English?

There was no point in lying.

"Yes. Can you help us, please?"

"How can we help you, Messieurs? We are going to sea. Do you want to come with us?"

Ben was highly uncertain. What if they threw them overboard, once out at sea? Then he realised they were just as likely to be shot, if they stayed.

"Of course, we do," responded Max, before Ben had a chance to say anything.

"I cannot do much," protested Ben. "I have hurt my hand, badly."

"Let me take a look," insisted the man who must be the captain.

Ben held out his hand. With unexpected gentleness, the captain removed Ben's bandage.

"Aye, aye, aye!" he exclaimed, on seeing the bloodied mess that was now Ben's finger. "I will get you some clean bandages. We will fill a bucket with sea water, and you can spend the first hour with your hand in it. Antiseptic. I will give you some morphine too."

The band of seamen, with the two new recruits, walked along the docks to where some small trawlers were moored.

"Welcome aboard the 'Etoile du Midi'," announced the captain, as they stepped across the gangplank.

One of the men let down a bucket on a rope and pulled it up full of sea water.

"Not from here, Michel. It is full of oil and possibly sewage. When we get out to sea."

"Of course, Captain," replied the man.

"This is my boat. And this is my crew. Michel, Fabrice and Jean. I am Nicolas."

"Ben and Max," Ben introduced them, pointing at Max.

"Ben, can you manage an oil can? Everything that is metal and moves, especially around the winch. Max, go and help Fabrice, down below, with the engine. When you and Jean have fixed the nets, please fetch the water, Michel."

Nicolas took his place in the cabin, behind the wheel. The engine spluttered into action, Jean untied the ropes and threw them onto the boat whilst Michel coiled them up. As soon as Jean came back on board, slowly, but surely, the little fishing boat started to cut its watery way out to sea. When they were about a mile out, Michel filled the bucket and handed it to Ben, who lowered his hand into the brine. It stung like crazy at first, until he grew used to it. Eventually, it started to feel quite soothing.

The trawler continued its south-easterly course for an hour, whereupon Nicolas came out of the cabin, leaving Max at the wheel.

"Show me your hand, Ben."

Ben withdrew his white and wrinkled hand from the bucket. It looked and felt a whole lot better. You must do this every day, my friend. Now, let me bandage it again."

Ben held out his hand for Nicolas to bandage, somewhat expertly, it had to be said.

"Morphine injection?"

"I am not sure I need this now. It feels much better. Do not waste it."

"Your choice. Can you boil a kettle with one hand?"

"I can certainly try. You might have to light the stove."

"Good man. Please make us all a coffee."

As Ben went below deck to the galley, Nicolas, Jean, and Michel lowered the nets. The kettle boiled and Ben made coffee, and when everything was running smoothly, Nicholas gave permission for them to have their break. Michel popped below to call Fabrice and Max.

"We trawl for about three hours," announced Nicolas, glancing at the clock.

"Did you bring cake, Jean?" asked Fabrice.

"Of course. It is a plum cake that my beloved Gabrielle made for us, this time," he replied, removing a tin from his bag, and opening it. The cake had been pre-sliced into four."

"I think we need to cut it into eight, don't you?" laughed Fabrice.

"How did you end up here?" inquired Nicolas, when they all had their coffee and cake.

Ben swallowed.

"I was with the British army near Arras. I got injured with a piece of shrapnel in my knee. Because I couldn't retreat, I was got separated from my company. I think that they were all killed. Some wonderful French people looked after me. One of them was a doctor. He operated on my knee. No anaesthetic. Just eau de vie," he laughed. "I arrived in Rouen and met Max. He flew a Hurricane and he got shot down. We stole a German car and drove to Orléans. Almost. There, a member of the resistance movement looked after us. Eventually, we took a train. We planned to go to Bordeaux, but the train diverted. That is how we came to Sète."

"But you do not sound English," came the observation Ben had grown used to expecting.

"No. I am Jewish, from Karlsruhe. I escaped on a children-train and reached England. I fell in love and married an English girl. I hate the Nazis and I think of myself as British. My home is in London. My future is in England."

"You know it is dangerous to be Jewish in France these days?"

"Yes."

"I am Jewish," blurted out Fabrice. "Up to now, we are lucky in Sète. We go fishing. We make love to the women. We are free."

"Fabrice is correct," agreed Nicolas. "Out at sea, no one bothers us."

"How far do you go to catch fish?" asked Max.

"It depends on the weather. On the time of year. We will continue heading south-east, today, until the net is full. Then we will go back to Sète and sell our catch."

"How do you know when the net is full?"

"We don't, really."

"Do you have to guess when or where to find the fish?"

"No. Sometimes the other animals give us a clue. Birds overhead. Leaping tuna. That kind of thing. Otherwise, it is just luck and patience."

"Do you ever return with the empty net?"

"There is always something in the net. But yes, every so often, we do not find a shoal."

"Do you read the newspapers? Or listen to the radio? What is happening in the war? Do you know?" asked Ben, changing the subject.

"I know that Mussolini occupies the far east of France," answered Jean. "I have heard that Hitler has bombed London every night between September last year and May this year. I am sorry. You said you live in London."

"And I think that the Germans are attacking Malta," added Michel.

"I often wonder whether we will come upon a convoy out of Gibraltar," remarked Nicolas.

"Do you mean that the British in Gibraltar try to supply the British on Malta?" clarified Ben.

"Yes," responded Michel. "The British may also be in North Africa."

"In France," interjected Jean, "they are deporting Jews and anyone who disagrees with Hitler. And the Spanish are sitting on the fence. I think Hitler has designs on Russia, too."

"Wow! Thank you for the news report," replied Ben, acknowledging them all.

"Surely you don't want to go back and fight?" reflected Nicolas.

Up to this point, Ben had never really considered the question. It was true, rabbit-hunting with Olivier had been a different sort of fighting, but it was still fighting. Was it not desertion, if he didn't try to get back to the army? Getting home to London seemed improbable but shouldn't he and Max at least try to go to Gibraltar or Malta or North Africa. Ben hated the Nazis, but he hated the horrors of fighting on the frontline more. He did the washing up, with one hand, and went up on deck to watch.

"Let's get the crates ready," instructed Nicolas, after almost three hours. "We gut the fish on board. Can you help, Ben?"

"I'll do what I can, with one hand" he replied, lifting a crate with his left hand.

Jean started to winch in the net.

"It's heavy!" announced Michel as he and Fabrice started to pull it in.

As it was lifted from the surface of the water, it became obvious that it was not bursting with fish. Instead, a large black metal sphere could be seen, its spikes caught in the net.

"My God!" exclaimed Michel.

"It's a mine," declared Jean, fearfully.

Nicolas and Fabrice moved over to the side.

"How did that get here?"

By now, Max and Ben had also come over to the side of the boat where the mine was dangling precariously.

"Perhaps it drifted here from the south, where the convoys run between Gibraltar and Malta," suggested Ben.

"What do you want us to do?" asked Jean.

"We'll have to let the net go," concluded Nicolas. "Just cut the ropes as I increase our speed. We don't want it drifting into the boat."

Nicolas went into the cabin and opened the throttle. Jean cut the ropes and the mine plunged back into the Mediterranean.

That evening, as they docked, without a catch, Nicolas was surprisingly positive.

"We'll just have to get another net. I'm happy to be alive. I don't think we need to worry too much about going out to sea again. I think that was a few hundred miles off course."

It was decided that Ben and Max should stay with Nicolas, on his narrowboat, moored on one of the several canals that traversed Sète. Although he lived alone, the boat had eight berths, so there was plenty of room for guests, even if each berth was not so roomy. He had a small wood-burning stove which had burnt to embers during the day. Nicolas fetched some fresh firewood to stoke it up again and took an old cast iron casserole dish from the oven.

"Tonight, we have fish," he announced, grabbing a rather stained oven-glove, and removing the lid.

"Excellent," replied Max.

"It is fish, most nights," Nicolas added, laughing.

He removed half a baguette from a cloth bag and sat it on the table next to a half-empty bottle of wine.

"We will be on rations, tonight. I did not expect to have guests. Tomorrow I will cook for three."

"It is much appreciated," responded Ben, wondering whether Nicolas had ever been married.

They tucked into their meal. It was tasty, although Ben had to spit out several fishbones. As soon as the washing up was finished, the three men turned in for the night. Ben's bunk was hard and narrow, but he fell asleep within minutes.

No more mines had been netted, and on the Friday, they had happened upon a nice shoal of sea bass which more than made up for the wasted day with the mine.

"Tomorrow is Saturday. We don't go fishing," Nicolas informed them.

"On the day we arrived, we met some footballers. They were coming out of the bar. They said we must go to watch a match. Can we go this afternoon?" asked Ben, hopefully.

"Of course. I go to all the home games," replied Nicolas. "You will be surprised to know that FC Sète have an English manager. Elie Rous."

"Really?"

"He used to manage Racing Paris."

Thirty minutes before kick-off, they left for the ground and managed to find a place to stand, just behind the benches. The players were out on the field, kicking a ball around, but there was no referee.

"Where's the referee?" Max asked Ben, in a low voice.

"I don't know."

On hearing the English voices, Elie Rous looked up from his notebook.

"Hello. Welcome to chaos," he laughed, speaking in French and walking the few paces over to them, so he didn't have to shout. "You are not from round here, I think. Don't worry. I won't say anything. The referee has sprained his ankle on the way to the game. We are trying to find a replacement."

"I can referee," offered Ben, without considering his lack of kit.

"Wait here. I will go and ask the opposing manager."

Rous strode, purposefully, to the other bench. After a brief conversation, he came jogging back to Ben.

"We gratefully accept your offer. Would you like to borrow some kit?"

"If you have some."

"Come with me."

Rous led Ben to the changing room where he handed him a pair of shorts.

"Put these on," he instructed, fumbling around amongst the boots, and gathering some size tens and some size elevens.

"These look about right. I will get you some spare socks. I have a whistle in my bag."

Ben put on the shorts, socks and size tens.

"These are good. Thanks."

"No. Thank you. We were stymied."

Ben was a little nervous. He had refereed several informal games, but never a proper football match. It turned out he was quite good at it, allowing the game to flow, being both stern and fair. Thankfully, there were no difficult decisions, the game ended in a two-all draw, and he hadn't needed to engage in discussion with any of the players. Officially, Ben probably shouldn't have been refereeing the game, but both managers had agreed it was better than postponing the match, and if anyone questioned his qualifications, they would sort it out.

"Come with us to the bar. I would like to buy you and your friends a drink this evening," Rous invited him, when they were leaving the changing room.. "Nine o'clock. The bar at the docks."

"Thank you," responded Ben.

Rous shook Ben's hand and walked off.

"You're full of surprises," remarked Max, when Ben caught up with him and Nicolas, after the match.

"It seemed like the right thing to do. The manager has invited the three of us to join with the team in the bar at nine o'clock. He wants to buy all of us a drink."

"I'm not going to refuse a drink from one of the best managers in France," laughed Nicolas.

"That's settled, then," responded Max.

In fact, Ben, Max and Nicolas watched every home game and nearly always joined the FC Sète players and their manager in the bar afterwards. There was cause for great celebration, at the end of the season, with FC Sète winning the French Cup. Ben loved being involved in something sporty. Life had become fun, almost normal, if you ignored the secret police and the puppet government and stayed out of trouble. The days were filled with fishing trips, and Ben had become adept at mending nets, splicing ropes and repairing a diesel engine. His finger had healed over, and although he would never regrow a nail, his stump no longer impeded holding and carrying things.

The 1942-43 football season had begun, and the Allied forces had invaded North Africa, which caused the French Navy to scuttle their own fleet in Toulon, some might say, courageous, others foolhardy. Hitler's response was to disregard the armistice agreement and march into Vichy

France. It was a bit of a shock to the system, for Nicolas, Ben and Max, when the next time they frequented the bar on the docks, they found German soldiers drinking there.

"We cannot turn round and walk out," whispered Nicolas. "Try and act normal."

The three men sat at a table near to two German officers, Ben with his back towards them. He realised if he could hear them, then the officers could hear what he, Max and Nicolas said.

"Don't say anything," he mouthed at Max.

A waitress approached.

"Bonsoir, Messieurs."

"Bonsoir, Mademoiselle," Nicolas returned the greeting, robustly.

"Bonsoir," aspirated Ben.

Max nodded his greeting. Nicolas ordered a bottle of wine and three glasses, pulled a pack of playing cards from his pocket, and laid the cards out to play clock patience, even though there were three of them, because he realised that they couldn't discuss what game to play. A few moves in, both Max and Ben joined in. It was all perfectly normal, considering they had never once played cards in that bar. But 'normal' was about to become something altogether different.

For a start, the Germans adopted a policy of providing for their own needs first. Supposedly, they paid for the fish they bought in bulk from the market, but the franc was so devalued, they may as well have paid in pebbles. Nicolas became angry with the way a hard day's fishing brought in little income, now. However, the one huge advantage was that, as food producers, fishermen were deemed necessary to the occupation, so when hostages started to be taken, the fishermen were left alone. Funnily enough, most of the fishermen known to Nicolas, were members of the resistance movement.

Several weeks passed, and the two German officers came into the bar again. They were shown to the adjacent table to Ben, Max and Nicolas, and served with a bottle of vintage red wine. The proprietor even treated them to his own crystal glasses.

"Good evening, Hauptmann Brecht, Oberleutnant Fischer. I hope you have a pleasant evening. We have music for you," the proprietor greeted them.

Unusually, entertainment had been laid on, with a woman from the local operatic society being brought in to sing some Wagner. Ben had an innate distaste for Wagner's music. It was all a front, pretending to welcome the occupying army, in order to curry favour. For once, no card games were played, as Ben, Max and Nicolas could simply listen to the music.

During a short break in the entertainment, Ben found he could understand what the German officers were saying. It caused him more pain than he cared to admit. They were discussing their military careers, before being drafted into the invasion of France.

"Do you remember that night, back in 1938? The one where all over Germany, we turned on the Jews. I broke so many windows in Karlsruhe."

"Yes, I do. It was so satisfying to see the vermin rounded up and sent off to the camps."

The opera singer resumed her performance, and the two officers raised their glasses to her, downing the contents in one go. As she sang the closing note, her voice crescendoed. Whether it was helped by the acoustics of the bar, or the fact that there was a slight flaw in the crystal, suddenly, one of the now empty glasses caught the frequency of the diva's voice and shattered. The officers cheered, finding the whole experienced hilarious.

"It's like Kristellnacht again," joked Oberleutnant Fischer.

Everything has its breaking point, as does every person, and tonight, Ben felt he may have reached his. Their taking ownership for the actions of the Night of Broken Glass was bad enough, but now, this jibe was more than he could bear. He wanted to pick up the broken glass and ram it into their faces. Nicolas could see Ben's face had changed but didn't ask why.

"Come on. Probably best to leave now," he insisted, looking Ben in the eye.

Drinking up their wine, they acknowledged the German officers, out of necessity, and left the bar.

"I really hate sharing the bar with German soldiers," remarked Nicolas, as they walked along the canal to his narrowboat.

"I could hear what they were discussing. It is possible they threw bricks into my home on the Night of Broken Glass. They spoke of Karlsruhe. What was worse was hearing them gloat about how they sent the Jews to the camps. Perhaps my parents were included."

"No wonder your face changed," responded Nicolas. "I can understand if you want to kill them, but my friend, if you do, the Germans will take ten hostages and execute them. We must focus on the cause."

"I shall not forget either the names or the faces. Hauptmann Brecht and Oberleutnant Fischer."

Up to that point, apart from Nicolas and his crew, Elie Rous and a handful of the FC Sète footballers, no one had noticed that Max and Ben were British, let alone Jewish. They still had their false papers from being in occupied France. No one had bothered them, perhaps because they were fishermen.

"I have noticed that people are being stopped more often and asked for their papers. It isn't just by the Germans, it's also by our own French officials," pondered Nicolas, one evening during their meal. "It is possible that I can get you some new papers, to prove you work for me, but if you ever have to speak, people will know you are not French, and if the Germans hear you speak, they may well send you to a prisoner-of-war camp."

"Whatever you think is best," conceded Max.

"What I think best is that we get you your papers, we carry on as normal, drinking in the bar, and you join with my friends in their acts of resistance."

"You have friends in the resistance movement?" replied Ben, a little surprised.

"I do. And fish can be very useful for passing messages around. What could be more normal than buying fish at the market. When you get home, you find a piece of paper folded up in the mouth of a fish."

Nicolas winked at them.

"When we were in Orléans, Olivier called it hunting for rabbits. So here, it is buying and selling fish!"

The three men burst out laughing.

"Excellent!" said Nicolas, when he had caught his breath. "I will get your papers sorted and we'll go to the fish market."

So Ben and Max once again became part of the resistance movement.

The third Thursday night, in February 1943, Nicolas returned to the narrowboat with a bag of fresh Red Mullet. There was a message in the mouth of one of the fish.

"Tomorrow, we have a meeting in the warehouse."

The warehouse, where Ben and Max had spent their first night in Sète, was a communal space where people gathered and gossiped. Anyone who fished used the place, but so too did the wider community, either because they had a genuine need to return crates or some other item from the market, or because they fabricated a need to be there, so they could communicate with other members of the resistance movement. With so many people coming and going, it provided an element of legitimacy to any small meeting.

Nicolas, Ben and Max arrived early, and Nicolas had them tidying the nets and ropes into random piles. Four men, unknown to Ben, wandered over to the nets, followed by Fabrice and Michel. It wasn't until the meeting started that Ben realised why the nets were positioned as they were. They had been set out to form a plan of the oil refinery. The ropes were laid out like pipes and the rolls of nets were the tanks. The plan was to break through the perimeter fence and place explosives along some of the connecting pipes. It was scheduled for the early hours of the following Sunday morning. As soon as the discussions were complete, the nets and ropes were moved into different piles.

That day, on board Nicolas' boat, the crew continued to talk about the plans. Ben discovered that the reason Jean didn't take part in acts of sabotage was because he and Gabrielle's job within the resistance movement was equally important, and potentially more dangerous. Their hospitality extended further than making cakes for Nicolas' crew. They were hiding two Jews in their house.

During Saturday evening, Nicolas offered Ben and Max two cups of strong coffee, to keep them alert during the mission. At two o'clock, they left the narrowboat to go and rendez-vous with the other saboteurs. Ben was handed some wire cutters and instructed to make a hole in the perimeter fence on the south side. He would be accompanied by Fabrice, Michel and one of the unfamiliar men from the meeting, who was introduced as Guillaume. Max was to go with Nicolas to the west side, along with two others. They would run detonator wires back to the perimeter fence, with each group set to detonate the explosives at exactly half-past three. Each group would make their own way home. After synchronising their watches, Nicolas' group disappeared into the night.

It was ten past three, and the security guards had just finished their hourly tour of the site. Ben, Michel, Fabrice and Guillaume came out from their cover, and Ben cut the bottom wires in the fence. They crawled through the gap and placed the explosives, which Guillaume was carrying in a canvas bag, on three separate pipes. Attaching the detonators, they ran the wires, about sixty feet, back through the fence to where they had previously been hidden. Guillaume was staring intently at his watch and Ben had his hands on the handle, nervously waiting to detonate the explosives.

"Ten, nine, eight, seven, six, five, four, three, two, one, zero."

Ben pressed the handle, and the darkness was briefly illuminated by several not-quite-simultaneous explosions. If rain had been forecast, the sound might have passed for thunder, the illumination for lightning. As soon as the initial burst of light subsided, the four men ran in the direction of the canal, and once on the towpath, jogged along until they reached the port, where they split up. Ben was back at the narrowboat before Max and Nicolas.

By six o'clock, they had still not returned, and Ben was starting to get more than a little concerned. Various scenarios were dancing around his head, including one where the Germans or secret police might notice the boat hadn't left port that morning. So soon after an act of sabotage, it wouldn't take much for two and two to make four. Ben decided to go and take the boat out himself. He made his way to the docks only to find Nicolas and Max already on the boat, preparing for the day's fishing.

"You didn't return to the narrowboat. I was worried. I thought it is better to take the boat out, as usual."

"Good idea. In the end, I just thought it was safer to come straight here."

Just at that moment, Fabrice, Michel and Jean arrived.

One week later, whilst Nicolas and his crew were out at sea, the Germans rounded up a dozen hostages. A car was driven around the town ferrying an officer with a loudhailer who read a notice.

"If the perpetrators of the sabotage at the refinery do not come forward by midday tomorrow, twelve hostages will be shot."

The first Ben, Max and Nicolas knew of it, was when Jean came knocking on the hatch of the narrowboat, not half an hour after they had all gone home for the night. Nicolas peeped out of one of the portholes and saw Jean there, so let him in.

"What's the matter?" inquired Nicolas, seeing the panic on Jean's face.

"They've taken Gabrielle's mother hostage."

"What do you mean?"

"The Germans took twelve hostages today, and if the culprits of the explosion at the refinery are not handed over, by midday tomorrow, the hostages will be shot. Gabrielle was out shopping with her mother, and they arrested her, completely at random.

"This is terrible," observed Ben.

"What are we going to do?" asked Jean, with desperation in his voice.

"Let me think," stalled Nicolas. "Does she know about the Jews in your attic?"

"I don't think so."

"Would she tell them if she did?" continued Nicolas.

"Of course not."

"How can you be so sure?" Nicolas pressed him.

"Because she wouldn't. I know her."

"Jean. I don't think there is anything we can do."

"What about rescue?" suggested Jean, clutching at straws, knowing in his heart of hearts that Nicolas was right.

"Apart from anything else, she was with Gabrielle, when she was arrested. If we rescue her, they will most likely come and take Gabrielle. And possibly, you as well. I'm sorry. Truly, I am."

Jean said nothing.

"Go home. Hold Gabrielle tightly. Don't come to work tomorrow. Keep her at home. Don't let her see her mother being murdered," Nicolas tried to offer Jean what comfort he could.

"Was it you?" asked Jean, just as he was about to leave.

"Would it make it any easier, if it was?"

Jean didn't reply but turned and left the narrowboat.

"Would it make a difference?" asked Ben, once he was sure Jean had gone home.

"These are desperate times. Loyalty is being tested to breaking point."

The day after the hostages were executed, Jean's home was raided. The Jews they were harbouring were shot during the raid and Jean and Gabrielle arrested and taken away to be tortured for information. When Jean didn't turn up for work, Nicolas made a spur-of-the-moment decision.

"Today, we will not return home. We have fuel and we have the sail. We won't fish today because we won't be able to take the catch to market. We can set our course south-westerly, for Gibraltar, or south-easterly for Malta. The Mediterranean is very large. If we are lucky, we will either find a convoy of British ships or we will reach our destination. We cannot risk staying in Sète, now."

"Whatever you decide," responded Ben. "When I read the newspaper, two weeks ago, there were stories of British ships that were attacked and sunk. There is a battle in the air and on the sea."

"We will be a fishing boat that lost its way!" laughed Nicolas. "What can they do to us? You have fought for the French. Now it is time for us to fight for the British. Fabrice and Michel, you don't have to come, if you don't want to. I'm sure you will find a new crew."

"I will come with you," replied Michel.

"My grandmother is English. Perhaps they will let me join the air force," added Fabrice, laughing. "I have always wanted to fly."

"So, is it to be Gibraltar or Malta. Shall we vote?" proposed Nicolas. "Hands up for Gibraltar."

Fabrice raised his hand.

"Hands up for Malta."

Michel and Max raised their hands.

"I really don't mind," commented Ben.

"Malta it is, then," confirmed Nicolas.

He went into the cabin and consulted his map and compass as the others untied the ropes. The little fishing boat chugged out of Sète for the last time, with the crew arranging the nets, until they were out of sight from the shore. As there was no need to prepare for the usual catch of fish, the men sat down on deck. Michel tried to nap. Fabrice stood up and went to join Nicolas, in the cabin.

"I will find them, you know. One day."

"Who?" responded Max.

"Those two German officers from the bar. I will find them, and I will kill them."

Without the regular tasks to perform, the day became mind-numbingly boring.

"We will have to do some fishing, in order to have something to eat," remarked Michel, having woken from his nap.

"Nicolas," called Ben. "How long will we be at sea? We need to catch fish to eat."

"Who knows. Two weeks, perhaps. It depends if we meet any British ships, or worse enemy vessels. Perhaps the wind will be against us. Lower the net, for as long as it takes to catch today's lunch and evening meal."

The men dropped the net over the side but didn't wait for the net to become full. When it was raised, Michel and Fabrice removed around fifty fish from it.

"We have no bread. We will have to fill up on fish," reflected Fabrice.

"If we had planned this trip, I would have brought flour and oil, to make bread," reflected Nicolas.

"It's a good job we already eat fish, most days!" laughed Max.

"I'll cook," volunteered Ben.

"First we must gut the fish," Michel pointed out.

As they started to throw the entrails overboard, a group of hungry seagulls appeared over them, as if by magic, circling and squawking. Every time one of the men tossed a piece of fish into the sea, at least three gulls dived on it, with only one successful. Several aerial fights had taken place, by the time all the fish were gutted.

They sailed through the night, taking it in turns to stay awake. When Ben wasn't at the wheel, he couldn't sleep, but lay on deck gazing at the night-sky, trying to decide which were stars and which were planets. He wished Betty could be there with him. Was there a toddler, asleep in their room? Had the family survived the bombing? Were the Fields safe? Had Simon and Matty volunteered? What was Walter Stubbs doing now? Prison? He replayed the conversation between the two German officers in the bar. And what about Saul? In the end, he went to the galley and boiled the kettle to make some coffee.

Ten days had passed, and the fishing boat was now entirely reliant on wind power. When the sail caught the wind, they sped along, but when there was only a little wind, they hardly made any progress at all. Ben, Max, Fabrice and Michel were on deck, tidying the net, when Max spotted a dogfight, a couple of miles to the south.

"Look over there!"

"We must be near one of the convoys. That or the coast," surmised Ben.

As they watched, one of the planes started to plummet towards the sea.

"I wish we were near enough to see which plane just got shot down," commented Max.

Ben stared at the horizon. He felt sure he could make out the silhouettes of at least four ships.

"Over there. Can you see the ships?"

"Three miles, maybe," responded Max. "If they are heading east, we can track them."

"Let's just hope their presence hasn't attracted the attention of German submarines," remarked Fabrice.

Ben went into the cabin.

"Nicolas, we have seen a dogfight and some ships on the horizon, to the south. Can we increase our speed and try to reach them? If they are British, we can ask to board one of them. If they are German or Italian, we can just alter our course and pretend to carry on fishing. What do you think?"

"We can try to get close, but I don't think we can reach them," Nicolas replied. "As for fishing, it is unlikely a boat would fish using the sails."

After a few minutes, it was clear that the ships were heading east. What was not so evident was whether the fishing boat could travel fast enough to reach the ships before they passed out of sight. The Etoile du Midi was navigating the hypotenuse of a giant triangle, which meant they had to travel further than the convey, which was already moving faster.

"To be honest, I think, now, it is better to follow at a distance," reflected Nicolas. "After all, we don't know, at this point, if they are going to Malta or Sicily or even Tunisia. We will see. We have come so far in our little boat.

Let's stick to our course. We will pick up the trail of the ships when they are already ahead by a distance, and then we will most likely lose sight of them."

No one disagreed with him.

After three days and nights, Nicolas' map and navigation equipment told him they had passed Tunisia and Sicily, and he felt more confident that the convoy was British.

"I think the convoy is going to Malta," he announced during their breakfast of fish.

Just as they were finishing their meal, a Spitfire flew low overhead.

"Spitfire!" declared Max.

They watched the plane circle round, in the distance, and a few minutes later, it buzzed their boat again. Max stood and waved his arms, wildly, at which point Ben joined him, followed by Fabrice and Michel.

"Do you think he saw us?" asked Ben.

Max shrugged his shoulders.

An hour went by, and to everyone's amazement, one of the ships could be seen, heading in the direction of the fishing boat. As it came alongside, overshadowing them, a sailor with a loudhailer called out to them, in fractured French, "Do you need assistance? Have you run out of fuel?"

"Shall I answer in English?" interjected Max.

"Please do."

"We could use some help," shouted Max. "We have come from Sète. We are trying to get to Malta. We have no diesel."

"You are British?"

"Two British and three French."

"The waters around Malta are dangerous. Mines, U-boats, attacks from the air. Will you come on board? We can attach a line to the vessel."

Max translated for Nicolas, who nodded. A rope ladder was lowered over the side of the destroyer, and two sailors went to find a rope, the end of which they lowered to the fishing boat. Michel secured the rope and the five men clambered up the ladder, one by one, with Nicolas bringing up the rear. The two sailors allowed the fishing boat to drift a few feet away from the destroyer and walked back to the stern, where they tied the rope fast. Nicolas, Fabrice, Michel, Max and Ben were led to the canteen where two sailors stood guard until the captain arrived.

"At ease, gentlemen. I don't think these men are hostile. What are you doing this far south-east of France in a fishing boat?"

"Trying to reach Malta, Sir," answered Max. "I am Max Sparks, 17 Squadron, RAF, shot down over France and this is Ben Linton-House, Royal Norfolks, injured in Normandy. We met by chance when I was shot down. We were unable to break through the advancing German forces and travel north, to the coast, so we travelled south, supported by several civilians. These men are fishermen, Nicolas, Fabrice and Michel. I don't know their surnames. They have been fighting with the resistance movement, until the Germans captured a close friend, and it was too dangerous to stay in Sète. They want to fight with the British, if possible."

"All in good time. I assume you have only forged French papers?"

"Yes, sir. I'm afraid so."

"I understood that the Royal Norfolks were slaughtered at Le Paradis. Only two survivors."

"I do not know what happened, sir," replied Ben. "I took some shrapnel in my knee. I could not retreat to the farm fast enough, because of my injured leg. I crawled into some trees. I waited for a chance to get to my company. I never saw them. I heard machine guns. I did see another group, Scots, who were executed."

"You do not sound British," observed the captain, suspiciously.

"I am Jewish, from Karlsruhe. I came to England in the children-train. I finished school in London. I married a girl in London. My future is in London. I will fight against the Nazis."

"We will have to check this out, of course. I'm afraid not much of London is left standing. There's not much of Malta left standing either, to be honest. Now, please, eat and drink something. Please tell your friends we will process them when we get to Malta."

The captain saluted them, and Max and Ben returned the salute. It felt strange, saluting an officer, after all this time, and even stranger, to finally eat some bread and meat again, after two weeks of a diet whose only variety lay in the type of fish they cooked.

By now, the destroyer was back amongst the convoy. Although accompanied at all times, by the two sailors who had been assigned guard duty, the fishermen were allowed up on deck. Nicolas was keen to check on his boat, so they wandered to the stern. Suddenly, the fishing boat exploded. As the fragments of wood fell back into the sea, Michel had the presence of mind to cut the rope, with the knife he always carried, concealed in his boot. Nicolas was in a state of shock. The two guards were desperately trying to usher Ben, Max, Fabrice, Michel and Nicolas off the deck, as depth-chargers were dropped over the side.

"That was close," commented Ben, once they were all inside. "Sorry about your boat, Nicolas."

"It's OK. What if we had been torpedoed alone at sea, not on board a British destroyer."

Fabrice offered round his packet of Gauloises. Exceptionally, Ben accepted one and immediately regretted it, choking on his first drag. The others laughed, and when he had stopped coughing and spluttering, he joined in the laughter. The commotion outside lasted around thirty minutes. Once it had died down, the captain came to find them.

"I am sorry about your boat, but also immensely appreciative. It is quite possible, that had your boat not been tethered to the stern, we might have taken a direct hit."

Ben translated for Nicolas.

"You are welcome," responded Nicolas.

The following day, Ben leant against the bulwark, watching Malta expand into his field of vision. They docked in Valetta, shortly before lunch. As Ben saw the damage caused to buildings by months of bombardments, he feared what London might look like. Perhaps, once in the garrison in Malta, he might be able to get word to Betty. As soon as the ship was made fast, they were escorted to the underground British headquarters, where Max and Ben were split up from Nicolas, Fabrice and Michel. It was a cause of sadness to Ben, that he never saw them again, and no one would provide any information as to their whereabouts. He hoped, for Fabrice's sake, that he was allowed to join the RAF. In the end, he had to say goodbye to Max, too, as soon as clearance had been given, because he returned to active duty flying Hurricanes. Ben was drafted into the tunnel corps, but not before he he'd had a chance to send a message to London.

"Long story. Safe in Malta. Do we have a child? Your loving husband."

There was so much that he wanted to say, but brevity was required. He scribbled the message down, along with the address.

Later that week, he was called back to the communications room, where he was ushered into an office. A captain, whom he didn't recognise, was sat at the desk, his face revealing nothing. Ben saluted him.

"We have received word from London, and it's not good, I'm afraid. Have a seat, please."

Ben felt the blood drain from his face, as he sat on the edge of the chair.

"Mrs Elizabeth Linton-House, along with three-month-old Roger Linton-House were killed when a bomb landed on the house. Mr Joseph and Mrs Anna Draper were also killed in the blast. I am truly sorry for your loss."

"Thank you," mumbled Ben, trying to take in the loss of his beloved Betty and the son he never knew he had. "Roger. I never knew I had a son. I mean, we tried, but then I left to join the Norfolks."

"Sadly, that is the experience of many young men. I can tell you that they are buried in Barking Cemetery. You are off duty for the rest of the day."

Ben nodded, stood up, his knees like jelly, saluted the captain again, and left the room. He had never felt so alone. Even as he hid in the woods at Le Cornet Malo, he had held onto the hope of returning home one day. Now, there was nothing left to return to.

He walked along the corridors and made his way out into the sunlight, squinting, his eyes hurting from holding back the tears. Along the road was a bar, where he bought a bottle of wine, which he asked them to open. Back out in the street, he took a swallow, chose right, for no particular reason, and kept walking, taking swigs from the bottle as he went along. He had walked perhaps two miles, when he sat down on a rock, looking out to sea. It crossed his mind, he probably shouldn't be there, but he cared not one iota, if he got killed. This time, Ben really had reached his breaking point. Downing the last of the wine, he hurled the bottle onto the adjacent rocks, smashing it into a hundred tiny shards. The sound of glass shattering triggered echoes of grief that he had held inside for too long, and he sobbed until there were no tears left to cry.

A jeep pulled up alongside him.

"Come on, mate. Let's get you back."

Ben looked up at the driver. Somewhere, in his hazy recollection, he felt sure the face was familiar, but as he tried to stand, the effect of the wine, combined with exhaustion and dehydration, caused Ben to pass out, banging his head on the ground and knocking himself out. The compassionate driver got out of the jeep, lifted Ben onto his shoulder and dumped him unceremoniously into the rear seat.

"I'm Corporal Field, by the way. Simon, to my mates," the driver introduced himself, knowing his passenger was unlikely to hear. "You don't half look like someone I used to know in London."

FLAWLESS

Ben's return home was traumatic to say the least. Having arrived at Charing Cross station, he caught two buses to the East End, without any hint of a smile, his packed kitbag over his shoulder. He wasn't even sure what he expected to find, as he walked down the street to the house where he and Betty had started their married life together.

There was nothing to be seen, the bulldozers having long since flattened the rubble, although the Anderson shelter still stood defiantly at the bottom of the back garden. An unruly Buddleia dominated the front garden. It had been hardly two feet tall, when Ben had last seen it. Now, at the end of the war, he walked towards where the house had once stood, picturing the day he first knocked on the door, replaying in his memory, the first time he set eyes on Betty. Where was Ruth? There had been no mention of Ruth being killed by the bomb. Ben walked across the rubble, as if walking down the hallway, into the dining room. He continued through to the kitchen and out of the back door.

Curious to know what an Anderson shelter felt like, he carried on walking down the garden. Bending low to enter it, he sat down on the bench. It was cramped. A steel box, under the opposite bench, caught his eye, and he leant across to pick it up. Opening the lid, his heart was broken. Inside was a photograph of Betty holding their newly born Roger. Ben's eyes filled with tears. Too small to see much detail, it was his only link to the son he had never known. Taking out his wallet, he slid it into one of the slots. Foresight had been a strength of Betty's, and closer inspection of the tin revealed their marriage certificate and one hundred pounds. These too, Ben folded into his wallet.

Recognising there was no longer anything there for him, he walked the short distance to the Fields' house, except that too, simply wasn't there. Had Bill and Dorothy survived? What about Simon, Matty and Jessica? What had happened to them? It occurred to Ben, that the local priest might know, so he went to find the vicarage. The priest did know, and it was the worst of news. Realising Ben's plight, the priest offered Ben a spare room.

The following day, Ben travelled to the cemetery, where he found all the graves, and having satisfied his curiosity, resolved never to return. In time, the good memories would remain, and hopefully, the bad memories would become blurred. Thankfully, Ben hadn't been there to experience the bombs and deaths first-hand, although it was little consolation.

As the days and weeks had passed, Ben found himself a job repairing shop blinds, something practical. 'Stumpy" was something of a hindrance, when holding small screws, but he got by. He re-connected with Max, one evening, in the pub, both having survived the enduring hostilities in the Mediterranean. Ben had been held back from the invasion of Sicily and Max had shot down several enemy planes in dogfights. Unfortunately, the day after finding Ben drunk and distraught, Simon had been deployed to Tunisia, where he stepped on a mine and was killed.

It was on one of their Saturday evenings in the pub that they hatched their plan to travel to South Africa and start a new life, and on 2nd January 1947, Ben and Max found themselves leaning against the railings on the deck of the Roxburgh Castle, as she sailed out of Southampton, her destination Cape Town. Seagulls squawked overhead, and Ben caught himself wondering what had become of Nicolas, Fabrice and Michel.

Max and Ben were not the only passengers hoping to start a new life in South Africa. When eventually, the ship docked, they joined the throng being processed by the immigration services. A momentary pang of regret came over Ben, and he questioned his choice of emigrating to South Africa over the United States. He should have persuaded Max, not that there seemed to be any way of dampening Max's enthusiasm for the southern hemisphere. What was Saul up to? Had he tasted combat when the Americans joined the war? Perhaps he had also experienced Normandy. Had he survived the war?

Although Cape Town had much to offer the new arrivals, Max and Ben's destination was further towards the interior, at a town called Kimberley, built on the profits of the diamond mine, and after a night in a cheap hostel, they boarded a train bound for Pretoria.

It was the middle of summer in South Africa, and Ben's shirt was soaked in sweat. Outside, the dry, reddened landscape passed by, relentlessly. Sensibly, they had filled their flasks with water. Ben remembered his antics with the water bucket, on the children-train, nearly a decade before. Whenever the train pulled into a station, white families got into the front of the train whilst black people boarded towards the rear. It was black people who acted as porters, wheeling overloaded sack barrows along the platform, and black people who worked on the tracks, standing back with their shovels to let the train pass.

Eventually, the train pulled into Kimberley station, where Max and Ben alighted. Immediately, they found themselves swallowed up in a river of mostly black people who, like Max and Ben, were flooding into the cities in search of work. Max and Ben's plan was simply to present themselves at the De Beers offices, although their top priority was finding somewhere to stay.

"Let's go and ask in the newsagents," suggested Ben. "They might sell maps of the city, also."

"Good idea."

A bell attached to the doorframe announced their entrance into the shop.

"Good day," the shopkeeper greeted them in Afrikaans.

"Good day," replied Max, before Ben could speak. "We are English. Can you offer us any assistance in finding accommodation?"

"I can sell you a map," came the enterprising reply. "I will show you some places to stay, on the map."

The shopkeeper grabbed a map, unfolded it on the counter and proceeded to point to various locations, writing down the names and addresses of three possible hotels, on the corner of some brown wrapping paper. He tore off the addresses and handed them to Max.

"Good luck,"

"Thanks," replied Max.

Ben handed over a South African pound note, and the shopkeeper gave Ben some coins. Map in hand, Ben and Max set off in search of some temporary accommodation. Once they found employment, their intention was to move into a more permanent residence.

"Sorry about cutting in," apologised Max, as they walked along the street. "It would be strange, with your accent, if you didn't speak Afrikaans. Didn't want you to have to explain."

"It's fine, really."

Ben's grasp of the English language had come on leaps and bounds since he first arrived in Harwich, but every so often, his intonation and pronunciation revealed his roots.

The first of the three suggestions proved fruitful. Their room was clean and colonial. A black maid brought them towels. At the evening meal, Ben couldn't help noticing that the food was served by a black waitress.

"Have you noticed that it's only black people who do the jobs like waitress and porter and maid?" he asked tentatively, over dessert.

"No, but now you come to mention it. That's colonial history for you."

Ben made a point of making eye contact with the waitress, as they got up to leave, and mouthed 'Thank you' to her. She smiled back at him.

"I shall not be treating black people like a colonial," insisted Ben, as the two men returned to their room.

"In this country, I'm not sure you'll have a lot of choice," replied Max. "White people are the bosses."

"That doesn't mean I have to treat them like a boss," responded Ben.

Both men fell straight to sleep that evening.

Ben was awake early, washed and shaved ready for breakfast, hopeful for the day's visit to the De Beers' office. Max was slow to carry out his morning routine.

"Sorry. I think all the travelling has caught up with me," he reflected. "Ready in ten."

Breakfast was poached eggs on toast, orange juice and coffee. A different waitress was serving. Like the first one, she was black, and Ben made a point of thanking her.

A middle-aged couple at the next table looked disapprovingly at him and spoke to each other in Afrikaans.

After a brief return to their room to retrieve the map, Max and Ben set off for the De Beers office, where they arrived at shortly after nine o'clock.

"Good morning. Is it possible we can speak with someone about a job? We arrived from England this week, looking to start a new life," explained Max.

"Have a seat, please, gentlemen," responded the receptionist, leaving her station and disappearing into the open door a few paces behind the desk.

She was followed back out by a man, in his forties, sporting a moustache. Ben noticed his hair was almost completely grey, but the moustache and eyebrows were still a deep shade of brown, and he tried desperately not to show his amusement.

"Good morning. I am Conrad Pieters. How may I help?"

The deep brown moustache wriggled with each word.

"We were hoping there might be some jobs available. We've come from England."

"You're not the first. It seems that after the war, many Europeans are coming to our beautiful South Africa in search of a new life. What skills do you have?"

"I am practical. I enjoy carpentry. After the war, I repaired shop blinds for a living," replied Ben.

"I'm good with words and numbers," responded Max.

"Hmmmm."

Conrad Pieters looked them up and down and paused for a moment in thought.

"I'm not sure that you can have the same roles, but if you're prepared to work in different parts of the company,

I think there may be a position in accounts for you and we always need people with expertise to keep the natives in hand, especially in the sorting and processing area. Fill out an application form and I'll give you a tour of the site. Miss Bickley, sort these gentlemen out a couple of application forms, will you. Excuse me a moment. I'll be back out shortly."

Conrad Pieters went back to his desk, whilst the receptionist furnished Ben and Max with application forms and pens.

"Our address is currently a hotel. We will find something more permanent when we have jobs," remarked Ben.

"That's perfectly fine," replied Miss Bickley. "I don't suppose anyone will read them. If Mr Pieters says you can have a job, you can have a job."

Ben and Max completed their forms and handed them to the receptionist, just as Conrad Pieters came back out.

"Right. Come with me. It's a short drive out to the mine."

"Thank you," responded Ben.

"Very kind of you," added Max.

They followed Conrad Pieters to his car. Ben climbed into the rear seat leaving Max to sit next to Conrad Pieters. Although only a short journey, by the time they arrived at the mine, the heat was already verging on the intolerable and Ben was sweating again.

"We'll begun down below. You'd better put these on," he added, handing them hard hats.

A team of miners was about to enter the lift. The black men were laughing and joking, in a language unfamiliar to Ben, whilst the lone white man looked on.

"Hold the lift!" called Conrad Pieters.

The white man recognised him.

"Mr Pieters," he mumbled.

Conrad Pieters acknowledged him with a nod. An awkward silence descended on the previously jovial group, all the way to the bottom of the lift shaft.

"This is the main tunnel. As you can see, the wagons filled with blue ground are transported from the face to here where they are emptied into buckets and sent up on pulleys. It takes an awful lot of earth to find just a few diamonds."

"But sometimes you get lucky and find one like the Cullinan," responded Ben, smiling.

"You've done your homework," Conrad Pieters encouraged him.

The miners from the lift had already begun to chat again, as they walked along the passageway. Conrad Pieters pointed after them.

"We'll follow them to the face."

As they walked after the miners, Conrad Pieters noticed how Ben was observing the pipes and cables.

"We have an entire team who check over every inch. Their job never ends. They just go back to the beginning."

After a couple of minutes, the miners up ahead turned into a side-tunnel. On reaching the intersection, Conrad Pieters, Max and Ben took the same tunnel. A muffled blast reached their ears and the floor beneath their feet vibrated momentarily.

"That'll be the dynamite."

As soon as the vibration stopped, three men came out of a recess and walked back round the corner towards the face.

"It's a shame we weren't here five minutes sooner," remarked Conrad Pieters. "You would have seen them drilling holes for the sticks of dynamite. As soon as the fuses are lit, the men take cover. Now it's a case of shovelling the blue ground into the carts and loading the wagons. We don't have time to hang about for the next blast."

They walked back to the lift shaft and stood watching some blue ground being transferred to the pulleys. As they were watching, another group of miners came along the main tunnel, their shift over, ready to return to the surface. The foreman opened the gate and stood back to allow Conrad Pieters, Ben and Max to enter first.

"These men will be checked, before they leave the mine," explained Conrad Pieters, as the lift ascended. "We run a strict security operation here."

At the surface, they watched the buckets of earth being transferred to conveyor belts.

"I'll take you to watch the sorting process, now."

The earth passed along several belts, where the soil was washed away, and the diamonds separated from other small stones by vibration.

"You see, here. The belt is greased. The diamonds stick to the grease. At the moment, they just look like safety glass, when you've had a car accident. My favourite part in the process is in the next area."

Conrad Pieters led Ben and Max into the grading room, where the uncut diamonds were measured and sorted.

"These men are deciding which pieces are good enough to be cut. Not all of them will make it into jewellery. Most will be used in industry for cutting and drilling. Some will go to Johannesburg, but most of them will go to the diamond markets in Europe. Did you know that only a diamond can cut a diamond?"

"I learn something new every day," responded Max. "That's really interesting."

Ben knew, but kept his knowledge to himself, modestly.

"So, Mr Linton-House. Would you like to be part of the tunnel maintenance team or up here amongst the conveyor belts?"

"I spent a long time maintaining the tunnels in Malta, during the last months of the war. I think I'd like to work on the surface, with the conveyor belts. If that's possible."

"Excellent. Tomorrow, you can start your first shift. If you come to the office, there's a shuttle bus to and from the mine. Mr Sparks. You'll be based at the office. Obviously, we'll set you on, on a trial basis, and after three months, if everyone is happy, we'll make you permanent. If you'd like to accompany me back to the office, we'll let you have a look at the terms and conditions."

"Thank you," responded Ben.

"I'm looking forward to working for such a prestigious company," answered Max. "Thank you for the opportunity."

The following morning, Ben and Max walked to the De Beers office where Max went inside to start as a clerk in the accounts department, and Ben caught the bus to the mine. There was one other white employee, who made a beeline for the empty seat next to Ben.

"Hello. I've not seen you before. Are you new here?"

"Yes. I am Ben Linton-House. New to the company. New to South Africa."

"Peter Nettles. Been here about a year. Foreman of one of the maintenance teams in the tunnels. Where will you be working?"

"I think I will be maintaining the belts and machines where they wash the diamonds and get rid of the earth."

Behind them, the black workers were nattering away in Zulu. Some of the talk appeared serious in nature, but the rest of the time it was all smiles and laughter.

"Do you speak Afrikaans?" Ben asked Peter, when they had got out of the bus.

"A little. You said you're new to South Africa. You have a slight accent. Do you speak Afrikaans?"

"No. I travelled from Germany to England before the war, after the persecution began. I fought for the British. I married, and lost a beautiful girl because of German bombs. I changed my name from Lindenheim to Linton-House."

"So, you're Jewish, then?"

"Yes."

"Me too."

"What about their language?" continued Ben, nodding towards the group of black workers who were heading for the lift.

"Which language? Zulu? Xhosa? There are many Bantu languages. They were speaking Zulu. And yes, I have picked up a few words here and there. I can tell you they were thanking Mr Mandela for starting the congress youth league."

"Who's Mr Mandela?"

"Nelson Mandela? He's a member of the African National Congress. I think he may become their leader one day. Better run. Can't have them arriving before me. Perhaps, see you later, if not, tomorrow morning?"

"Yes. It will be a pleasure. Wait. What's 'Hello' and 'Thank you' in Zulu?"

"'Sawubona' and 'Ngiyabonga'."

"'Sawubonga'. 'Enggayabongo'."

"'Sawubona'. 'Sawubona'. 'Ngiyabonga'. 'A'. 'Ngiyabonga'."

Ben made up his mind to buy a book and learn Zulu. He went into the machine shop, approached the small, partitioned office in the corner, and knocked on the door. The man inside beckoned him in.

"Good morning. My name is Ben Linton-House, and I am starting work here today."

"Good morning to you, too. I'm expecting you. I'm Eric Dean, Works Manager," replied the man, holding out his hand. "What experience do you have."

"Maintenance of shop blinds. Carpentry. General repairs."

"I'll show you the set-up and introduce you to your team. Follow me."

Ben followed Dean out of the office.

"Here's the store where you'll find all the cleaning materials, oil and grease, along with the equipment," indicated Dean, opening the door. "You'll be responsible for keeping an inventory, otherwise things go walkabout, if you catch my drift."

Dean closed the door and walked towards a second door, which he opened.

"In here, you'll find some of the basic spare parts. Replacement nuts and bolts, and the like. Along with the tools, which, as you can see, we keep on a shadow-board. If anything breaks that can't be repaired from here, you come and tell me, and we order it in."

Closing the door to the store, he led Ben to an area where there was a concentration of junction boxes, switches and levers.

"This is a really important part of the building. If anything goes wrong, you shut off the electricity. Every machine has a stop button, but for repairs, we shut it down here.

Over there, is where you turn off the water supply. Right, I'll introduce you to the team, and then we'll go back into the office, and you can look at the diagrams and I'll talk you through the processes."

Dean shut down the electricity, and all of the belts came to a halt. The men looked up.

"I would like to introduce Mr Linton-House to you. He is your new boss. Carry on."

He switched the electricity back on and the men got back to work. Ben noticed how they were all black. Back in the office, Dean laid out a large plan on the desk.

"It's up to you, how you organise your routine, but this is the order the machines and belts run in, and these are the weak points. At least, these are the places where there is most wear and tear, and where we find ourselves replacing parts often. Spend some time today, watching each of the machines. I'm sure you'll pick it up very quickly. Remember, you do the telling and they do the doing. If you catch my drift."

It was the second time Ben had been asked if he caught Dean's drift, and both times, it was derogatory.

"There'll be a half hour break at twelve. I'll catch up with you then. Good luck."

"Thanks," responded Ben, walking out of the office.

He made his way to the first machine.

"Sawubona. What's your name?"

The worker appeared surprised to have been asked.

"Samuel Malembe, Mister."

"Well Samuel. What do you do here and does this machine work as it should?"

Samuel was tongue-tied and pointed in several directions.

"Very good machine, Mister."

"Ngiyabonga," responded Ben, fairly confident, without directions from Samuel, that he could see how the machine worked.

He continued around all the machines, affirming each worker and familiarising himself with the machinery. The parts which needed greasing were fairly logical. He continued to wander round the machine shop throughout the morning, watching the men at work. In the afternoon, he took an inventory of the stores. At the end of the shift, the workers needed no instructions to clean down and grease their machines. Ben noticed two of them crawling under their machines to carry out the task. In many ways, Ben was frustrated not to be doing much practical maintenance, but he reminded himself that it was a job, which meant money in his pocket.

Ben and Max caught up with each other back at the hotel.

"How was your day?" asked Ben, first.

"I learnt a lot about the history of the company. Did you know they have a complete monopoly on the diamond trade?"

"I did not know this."

"How was the maintenance?"

"It was OK. I did a lot of watching. I met another English man on the bus. He told me how to say 'Hello' and 'Thank you'. His name is Peter Nettles. He works in the tunnels. He's Jewish."

"Interesting. Maybe we can all go out for a drink sometime. And talking of drinks, I've asked Miss Bickley to go for a drink with me."

"That was quick," laughed Ben, suddenly remembering his own pain.

The following morning, Ben sat next to Peter again.

"Which regiment were you in?" asked Peter.

"Royal Norfolks. You?"

"Royal Artillery. In Africa. Where were you?"

"Normandy and Malta."

Ben had spent the last eighteen months burying his experiences. He didn't like describing what it he had seen at Le Cornet Malo. He couldn't unsee it and he felt guilty for surviving.

"My friend, Max, would like to know if you'd like to go out for a drink with us sometime. To be honest, we don't know where there is a good place to have a drink."

"My pleasure. How about this Saturday?"

"I think this is good. Max has asked the receptionist to go for a drink with him. I don't know when. But I will say 'yes'."

"That's sorted, then."

Behind them, the black workers were chattering away. Peter strained his ear to listen.

"I think one of them said the Royal Family is coming to visit."

"To visit South Africa or to visit the mine?"

"The mine, I think. Sometime in April. They also mentioned the African National Congress."

"Is that bad?"

"Well, the ANC doesn't exactly support the British Empire. I think they said a word like 'demonstration' but I'm not sure."

"They wouldn't demonstrate at the mine, I'm sure. They would lose their jobs, I think."

"True. But nationally, I think there is an increasingly strong movement for African independence."

"Have you ever seen the king?"

"Yes. In London. Have you?"

"No."

"He struugled to speak in public."

The bus pulled into the mine and the black workers waited for Peter and Ben to alight first. Ben wasn't sure he would ever get used to the inequalities, finding himself on the side of the colonial oppressor, when he had once been persecuted by the Nazis.

Saturday arrived and Peter had given Ben the address of a jazz club. Max and Miss Bickley, Joan when she wasn't at work, had agreed to come along as well, rather than go somewhere else. At eight o'clock, Ben and Max were waiting at the jazz club. Joan appeared from the left, just as Peter was approaching from the right. Not working in the main office, although Peter had once met Joan, and found her stunningly attractive, he hadn't had the same opportunity as Max to get to know her. Max sensed a connection the moment they were all at the point of introductions.

"Miss Bickley," Peter greeted her, holding out his hand.

"Of course, reflected Max, "You already know each other."

"If you call 'Please connect me to Mr Pieters' getting to know each other," remarked Joan.

"I'm Peter, by the way," he introduced himself, extending his hand to Max, as well.

Max shook his hand.

"Well now the introductions have been made, shall we go and enjoy drinks and jazz," suggested Ben.

They entered the club and were shown to a table.

"Everyone happy with cocktails?" inquired Peter.

Ben wasn't sure he'd ever had a cocktail.

"Why not?" responded Joan, giggling.

"Gin or whiskey?" added Peter.

"You order," suggested Ben.

"Four coolers, please," ordered Peter, when the waiter returned.

"Very good, sir."

"I love coolers," enthused Joan.

Ben didn't want to show his ignorance. Max was already starting to feel outclassed by Peter.

"So do I," fibbed Max.

The waiter returned with the drinks.

"To starting new lives!" toasted Peter, raising his glass to Max and Ben.

"To South Africa," responded Ben.

"New lives in South Africa," returned Joan."

"New lives in South Africa," repeated Max.

The band, who had been playing softly in the background, started a lively number and Max stood up, holding his hand out to Joan.

"May I have the pleasure?"

Joan giggled again, rose from her chair and took his hand.

"I'll just have to wait my turn," chuckled Peter, as the two were out of earshot. "What about you? Are you looking for female company? Sorry, stupid me! I forgot."

"It's OK, really. Not ready yet. You like her?"

"She's a corker."

It was approaching ten o'clock, and the band leader announced a competition.

"We love to play for you, but we also love to hear talented musicians."

The room erupted in ironic laughter.

"So, are there any brave souls out there who would like to play the piano. You play the melody, and we'll improvise."

At first, no one volunteered.

"I can't believe there's nobody here who plays the piano," pressed the band leader.

Max sensed an opportunity to impress Joan.

"I'll have a go," he offered, standing.

Everyone clapped as he walked over to the piano. Ben was a little surprised.

Max stretched his fingers, clicked his knuckles and started to play Cole Porter's *Begin the Beguine*. The band picked up the tune and started to accompany him. At the end, Max stood and bowed, looking towards Joan, to see if she was applauding enthusiastically.

"Bravo!" declared the band leader. "You can come and join the band!"

Another man got up and made his way to the piano. Peter ordered another round of cocktails.

"When did you learn to play the piano?" asked Ben. "I mean, I don't remember that you did play at school."

"I not only play. I write music. Trouble is, I'm not very good with the lyrics."

"We should do this again," suggested Peter, mainly because he wanted to see more of Joan.

"Yes, we must," replied Joan.

"Now then, let's get you home safely, Miss Bickley," laughed Max. "I'll call a taxi."

"Thank you," responded Joan.

"Which side of town do you live on?" inquired Peter.

"East."

"So do I," announced Peter. "Why don't we share the taxi. You two live near the office, don't you?"

There was nothing Max could do. It would have been churlish and illogical to refuse Peter's offer.

"Indeed. See you on Monday, Joan. Goodnight."

"Goodnight, Max. Goodnight, Ben."

"See you on the bus, Ben. Splendid evening.?

Max watched his chances of a relationship with Joan drive off into the night.

"I thought the music might have clinched it, but I'm pretty sure she only has eyes for Peter. Part of me wishes I'd not suggested going for a drink with him."

"I'm sorry."

"It's not your fault. They'll be another girl."

"So, you are giving up? Just like that?"

"I know when I'm beaten. No hard feelings. Nice cocktails."

"Yes. I had never had one before."

"Me neither."

"But you said you had."

"I know. Rough justice. I lied," laughed Max.

The two men reached their hotel.

By the team the week beginning 14th April came around, Peter and Joan had become an item. There were no hard feelings on Max's part and the three men and Joan continued to meet up regularly at the jazz bar. Max brought along a different woman on two different occasions, but nothing crystalised into a relationship. Ben still wasn't ready for a romantic attachment and had started to process his thoughts and feelings into lyrics, with the intention of offering them to Max, so that he could compose the tunes. Sometimes, Ben would go for a walk in the countryside surrounding Kimberley, to feel the open space and release his creativity from its urban constraints, but he nearly always returned to the same themes of confusion and loss and shattered dreams.

All week a tangible excitement could be felt around the mine. King George VI was due to visit at the end of the week, with the two princesses, Elizabeth and Margaret. Ben never really understood the Commonwealth, but he was excited to see the king and when Friday arrived, the workers were brought up to the surface, to form a guard of honour with the men who worked in the machine shop, to welcome the royal family before they were taken off to see the Big Hole. Originally, the diamonds had been mined above ground, digging an ever-deepening hole that was over seven hundred feet deep. Eventually, it had been left to the elements and had filled with water, forming a dazzling blue-green lake. Now the diamonds were mined underground, a much more dangerous affair.

It was the first time Ben and Max had actually seen Ernest Oppenheimer. With a name like Oppenheimer, Ben thought he must have been born in Germany or Austria. Perhaps, like Ben, Peter and Max, he was Jewish, and like the Draper family, his forebears had made a move out of Germany back in the nineteenth century. Ben was at the front of the white workers. The black workers were in a different group, a few feet away. As the royal party made their way through the workers, King George approached the blacks, whilst Queen Elizabeth and the two princesses came over to talk to the white workers. Ben couldn't help noticing how attractive Princess Elizabeth was. He was just about to say something to her, when a group of children, in Zulu attire, started to perform a traditional dance, and the princesses turned away to watch. As the dancing stopped, the royal party was led away to see the Big Hole, and the workers returned to their duties. It had been an enjoyable and welcome break, but there were still four hours left of the working day.

When he wasn't writing lyrics, Ben had been spending his free time studying the Zulu language. He was now able to bid his team 'Good morning', ask them if they were well, and say 'Goodbye' at the end of the working day. It was not easy for them to interact with him, but he sensed their appreciation. Curious to understand their struggle, Ben read the weekly newspaper, but it was the white paper, and so conveniently quiet, or calculatingly biased with regards to any articles about the ANC. He hoped, over time, to understand something of the conversations between the workers, especially when travelling on the bus.

It was autumn, in the southern hemisphere, and the leaves were starting to change colour. Night seemed to fall much faster than in Europe. One minute the sun was there, and the next, pitch blackness. Ben looked up at the stars, as he walked from the office to the hotel, for the penultimate time. He and Max had found a small furnished house to rent, with two bedrooms, kitchen, bathroom and lounge. He would have to walk ten minutes further to the office in order to catch the bus, but Ben didn't mind. The exercise kept him fit, and he hardly experienced any discomfort from his former shrapnel wound, and only when he broke into a run for whatever reason.

One such reason was the first morning in the new house when he slightly miscalculated the time it would take to reach the bus, or perhaps it was early. In any case, Ben had to sprint about a hundred yards and his knee hurt for the rest of the day, as his job mostly involved walking around the machine shop.

"You have hurt your leg?" inquired Samuel, in Zulu, as Ben approached his machine.

"Old wound. I run to bus. New pain," replied Ben, in Zulu. "You oil the machine, please."

Samuel's face beamed. Ben had no idea if it was because he was trying to speak Zulu, demonstrating care and identity, or whether he had made a mistake with his language. He smiled back and continued on his rounds.

After the end of the war, Ben's shrapnel wound had been assessed and he was paid a small pension, paid into a bank account in London. In his head, Ben calculated the approximate amount that might have accumulated. At present, he had no idea whether he would remain in South Africa for one year or ten years, but either way, it would become a useful little nest egg. Here, his wages were more than sufficient, and moving into the rented house would save him and Max some money each month. Max had suggested they use the surplus to hire a housekeeper, to cook and clean for them. At first, Ben had rejected the idea, as he didn't want to become too colonial in his outlook, but it was customary to have one, it created employment, and it would give him an opportunity to practise his Zulu, so he had agreed. Ben resolved to treat the housekeeper with the same respect he afforded his team at work. Today, Max would be placing an advert in the local paper.

When winter gave way to spring, Zobhule had been working as Ben and Max's housekeeper for just over three months. She lived up to her name. With her high cheek bones and flawless complexion, she was indeed beautiful. Ben found himself not just attracted to her but wanting to be with her, something he knew was socially unacceptable. Ben wasn't concerned about how Max might react, but he was concerned about the wider community and keeping his job. He was not consciously a rebel, but he knew it would be playing with fire. Under the pretext of practising his Zulu, Ben found himself spending more and more time with Zobhule. He learnt words to praise her with, for the work she accomplished, and soon, he developed a vocabulary of more personal compliments.

At first, he sensed an element of confusion in Zobhule and, knowing he was in a position of power, sought to reassure her. Thankfully, Zobhule spoke enough English to allow Ben to explain his intentions.

"I know what it's like to be mistreated. It is not my intention. I know we cannot date, officially, but I want to be with you. I promise you will not lose your job because of it. I will be a gentleman."

"Mister Ben is very kind."

"Is there a man in your life? Are you promised to someone?"

"No, Mister Ben."

"I am twenty-five years old. I married when I was seventeen. It was the start of war. When I was away fighting, my wife and our baby died. The house was bombed. I think I am ready to be with another woman. You are twenty-two and very beautiful. I want to get to know you. We don't have to do anything physical. Not if you don't want to."

"But we cannot be seen together, Mister Ben."

"Then we will be together in secret."

Zobhule was folding the laundry and Ben was leaning against the doorframe. As she approached him, carrying the basket of folded laundry, he refused to move out of the way.

"Just one kiss and you may pass!" he laughed.

She held the basket out to the side and leant towards Ben, who kissed her on the cheek, holding his lips against her skin for several seconds, allowing her scent to fill his nostrils.

"You may pass," he laughed, again, pulling back and stepping aside.

Zobhule came to the house on Saturdays, Tuesdays and Thursdays. On Saturdays, she arrived at seven in the morning and left at four. Saturday was usually laundry day, as the linen had time to dry outside. On Tuesdays and Thursdays, she was trusted to do her housekeeping while Ben and Max were at work and was hardly ever still at the house when they came home. At the next opportunity, on a Saturday, Ben had a gift for her.

Waiting until she was in the kitchen, cleaning the cooker, he handed her a small carved bee which he had whittled from a piece of deadwood, picked up on one of his walks in the countryside.

"I made this for you," he explained, as he handed it to her.

"I don't know what to say, Mister Ben. Thank you."

"Will you take a walk with me tomorrow afternoon. We can meet near the woods. Just before you reach the farmstead, about a mile from here," suggested Ben, pointing west. Keep walking until you hear my voice."

"Mr Ben is very mysterious."

"Two o'clock."

"And what if people see us?"

"If there are people around, I won't call to you. If you go past the farmstead, you will know it's not safe, so you can turn back."

The following afternoon, Ben left for one of his regular jaunts, leaving Max to compose music at the old upright piano they had acquired shortly after moving in. Reaching the woods at about ten minutes to two, he stood behind a mature tree, whose species he didn't recognise. His love of carpentry meant he was familiar with the characteristics of many types of wood, but the indigenous trees of South Africa were new to him. At this time of year, the leaves were only just starting to bud, so the cover provided by the trees was not as dense as it would have been in summer. Ben had wandered these paths many times and rarely met anyone, so he was not too concerned that he would be seen with Zobhule. Peering out from behind his tree he watched Zobhule walking along the road, and when she was within earshot, he called out to her in English.

"Beautiful one!"

She looked towards the voice and Ben moved to the side, so he was visible. A quick look over her shoulder and she stepped off the road. As soon as she was close enough, Ben grabbed her hand and pulled her towards him, folding her in his arms, so their faces were a few inches apart.

"Kiss me," he invited her, in Zulu.

Zobhule allowed herself to be kissed, still a little shy. She felt safe in his embrace, and not a little strange, to be pressed against his torso. Sensing her nervousness, Ben released her from the embrace but kept hold of her hand, starting to walk deeper into the woods. When the road was no longer in sight, he beckoned Zobhule to sit down at the foot of a stout tree.

"What tree is this?" he asked.

"A marula," I think.

"Tell me about your life, Zobhule."

"I grew up here. My father works at the mine, like so many of our men. My mother sews. I have three brothers. One works at the mine. The others are still at school."

"Where at the mine does your father work?"

"He puts the dynamite in place. Where do you work, Mister Ben? It is very dangerous."

"Amongst the conveyor belts where the earth is washed and graded to separate the diamonds. I have a team of men. I oversee the maintenance."

"There is talk of a white man who is kind to his men, who speaks our language. Is that you Mister Ben?"

"It might be," he teased her.

"Why are you in South Africa, Mister Ben."

"A new start. A new life. My old life was sad."

"Is Mr Ben's new life happy?"

"It is now I have met my beautiful one. That is what your name means, isn't it?"

"Zobhule? Yes, Mister Ben. I am beautiful one."

Ben pulled her towards him and started to kiss her face.

"I cannot become pregnant, Mister Ben."

"Then I will be careful."

Ben started to undo Zobhule's blue seersucker blouse. She wasn't wearing a bra and he paused for a moment to survey the polished mahogany contours of her chest. She truly was beautiful. He untied the band of her indigo-printed, shwe-shwe skirt and peeled it away from her body. Undoing the top button of his own shirt, he pulled it off over his head and started to kiss her from the abdomen up to her lips. She moaned gently and right there, under the marula tree, Ben made love to his beautiful one. For a moment he felt lost, remembering his wedding night with Betty. In a split second, the lostness turned to curiosity, realising there had been no sudden twinge of pain as he penetrated her, as there had been for Betty, his only other partner of intimacy. After seven years of abstinence, his body ached for the ecstasy he had once experienced, but in honour of his promise to be careful, he focused on the build-up of hormones and withdrew from her before it was too late.

"I am not the first for my beautiful one?" he observed as he lay down beside her.

"That is true, Mister Ben. But the first time was not done with love."

Ben wondered if she meant rape or whether she had been involved in a cultural, tribal ceremony of celebrating puberty, amongst the adolescents of her community. How many had there been? Ben felt an inexplicable jealousy.

"And was this time with love?" he inquired, stroking her cheek with the side of his index finger.

"Yes, Mister Ben. It was."

"How can you call me 'Mister Ben', when we have just shared such intimacy? It was with love, for me too, not with power."

"People must not know we share this love. I must always call you 'Mister Ben."

He kissed her gently and affectionately, as if to prove his point.

"We must get dressed, Mister Ben."

"Yes. You go first. I will wait before I walk back into town."

As Ben watched Zobhule walking off into the distance, from the cover of the same tree he had hidden behind earlier, he found himself already impatient to see her at the house, on Tuesday. He decided to write a song for her, at least, to pen the words of a song. If he asked Max to write music for his lyric, he might have to explain how he had suddenly found his romantic muse again. Just before heading home, he noticed a branch lying on the ground, its dark wooded core visible where it had broken away from the trunk of a nearby tree, another species Ben didn't recognise. Picking it up, he resolved to carve it into a slender female sculpture. As Max was used to Ben returning from his wanderings with random natural objects, there would be no immediate need to explain his tryst.

On Tuesday afternoon, Ben grew impatient for the bus to arrive, to ferry him back into town, desperate for Zobhule to be at the house, when he got home, just to steal a smile and maybe a kiss. Glancing around at the men from the mine, he scanned their features, looking for traits that were similar to Zobhule's, wondering which, if any, was her father. He turned away, not wishing to appear rude. To his frustration, Peter was talking to another white man, as they exited the lift, and their departure was delayed.

"How's it going with you and Joan?"

"Splendidly! You should try it," he teased Ben.

He was laughing with, not at Ben. Ben laughed too, with the laughter of a man who has a secret love. Unfortunately, by the time he reached home, Zobhule had left for the day, but had left a casserole in the oven and set the table. Max was already there

"I have to go back to the club for a band practice. Apologies."

Since his performance of *Begin the Beguine*, Max had been standing in regularly for the pianist. Ben cleared away the meal and did the washing up, leaving them to dry in the air.

Not long after they had moved in, Ben had built a veranda, with the permission of the landlord, who could see the benefits. At one end stood Ben's work bench. He took the vice and bolted it to the bench, and getting out his mallet and chisels, he tightened his recently discovered piece of dark wood into the jaws and started to shape it. There was no need for a sketch to work from. As he chipped away at it, he simply retraced the contours of Zobhule's figure, in his head. Also, as he chiselled away at the wood, he started to mull over the words of his song for Zobhule. For now, he hadn't decided whether to call it 'Marula' or 'My beautiful one'.

When Max returned from his band practice, Ben had chiselled away enough wood to see how tall the sculpture would be, or rather long, as Ben's intention was to create the form of a woman lying on her side, one knee, slightly bent in front of the other leg, head resting on her hand.

"What are you making?" inquired Max, coming out onto the veranda.

"A Zulu woman. Lying on her side."

"You mean Zobhule? It's obvious there's a spark between you."

"It is socially unacceptable."

"So, what. What happens behind closed doors stays behind closed doors. I admit, it would be difficult to take her to the jazz club with you, but it's not like she doesn't come here three times a week."

"Then you would be OK with this?"

"It's your life."

On the Thursday, Zobhule was still at the house when Ben arrived home. He walked into the kitchen, pulled Zobhule into his arms and smothered her with kisses.

"Mister Ben is very happy!"

"We don't have to hide in the woods. Max asked me if there is something between us. He won't tell anyone. Come to my room."

"Now, Mister Ben?"

"Yes. Behind closed doors. In my bed."

"But I cannot, this week, Mister Ben. It is my week."

Ben was a little disappointed but understood perfectly.

"Stay and eat with us," he insisted. "Max will be fine about it. You can eat some of the casserole that you have cooked for us.

"I will lay the table, Mister Ben."

"No. You will sit in the armchair and rest. You are not at work now. You are my guest."

He kissed her, gently pushed her into the cushions and went to find the plates and cutlery, setting three places at the table. Max came through the door and saw Zobhule and the table.

"I hope you don't mind. I have invited Zobhule to stay."

"Mind? I'm delighted for you."

"Mister Max is very kind. How was your day at the office?"

"Same old, same old. I think they are about to recruit some more staff in order to blast a new tunnel. Two new teams. Do you have friends or family who need a job?"

"I will ask, Mister Max. Thank you."

As weeks turned to months, Zobhule's monthly period became a welcome sign that he had been careful enough. She had started to come round on Sundays, until her father complained that it was unfair to make her work on Sundays, so she started to visit on Mondays, instead. Never to work. She would relax and read or sew until Ben returned from the mine. He would shower, they would make love, and she would leave. Ben was frustrated not to be able to show her off at the jazz club, but he was in love and inexplicably hopeful. The sculpture was finished too, and on Zobhule's last working day before Christmas, he presented it to her.

"Mister Ben is so clever," she declared, as she unwrapped the figurine. "She is beautiful."

"She is beautiful because she is like you."

"Thank you, Mister Ben. I do not have a gift for Mister Ben."

"You are my gift."

"I will see Mister Ben next week. On Tuesday."

"Not for work. Just to see me. You must take holidays. No more working until Saturday next week."

They kissed longingly.

"Happy Christmas, Mister Ben."

"Happy Christmas, my beautiful one."

Christmas for Max and Ben was strange. They had not pulled crackers in such heat before, and although it hardly ever snowed in London, at Christmas, short-sleeved shirts and melting in the heat were not usually associated with the time of the year. As his Christmas gift to Max, Ben had sculpted a key fob, out of an offcut from the dark wood, engraving it with Max's initials. A few weeks before, Max had arrived home in a bright red, second-hand Plymouth. He had been saving up for it since they started work with De Beers.

"This means a lot. Thank you, my friend."

Max handed Ben a small brick-sized parcel. Ben was surprised by how heavy it was for the size, and his curiosity was piqued. Tearing off the paper revealed a rectangular carpenter's stone, in a box, the kind you oil and sharpen chisels on.

"I noticed how worn down yours is," explained Max. "You do a lot of woodwork, and I wanted to get you something practical, but I know precious little about tools."

"This is great. Thank you."

They sat down to a simple roast chicken meal, cooked by Ben, followed by a small plum pudding which Zobhule had made a few weeks before. Ben was relieved that the tin had been sufficiently airtight for it not to go mouldy. They drowned it in custard.

"About Zobhule. She's a great cook by the way. Now I've got the car, I think it would be perfectly acceptable for two white men to take their housekeeper out in the back of a car. We can explore further afield. I can leave the two of you to your privacy and just meet up back at the car. Apart from anything else, being stuck in the house all summer is a shame. What do you think?"

"I think you are a gentleman and a friend," responded Ben, warmly.

"That's settled then. Once a month on the Saturday, we'll drive out somewhere."

"Thank you."

"Did you say she's coming over on Tuesday?"

"Yes."

"Then let's go out somewhere on Tuesday."

Ben couldn't wait to tell Zobhule of the plan, and when she arrived on the Tuesday morning, Ben could hardly contain his excitement. Zobhule always entered through the back door, as a housekeeper might. He embraced her, took her hand, and led her through to the sitting room.

"Max has a surprise for you," he announced.

"Hello, Mister Max."

"Hello, Zobhule. How would you like to accompany us on a drive into the hills?"

Zobhule looked at Ben.

"It's OK. You can sit in the back. When we get where we are going, Max will go and write music and we can go for a walk."

Zobhule's face softened into a beaming smile.

"I love this idea, Mister Max."

"Then if you're ready, we'll head out in ten minutes."

Half an hour later, they had packed up some bread, cheese, fruit and bottles of beer for a picnic, and the red Plymouth was rolling towards to hills, with Zobhule in the back seat and Ben in the passenger seat. Every so often, he would look back at his beautiful one and grin, with both affection and anticipation of making love to her outdoors. Having turned off the main road, they were now following a track into the hills, where Max pulled over to the side, at a suitable spot, and parked the car.

"If you go off in that direction, I'll wander around over there. I'm feeling inspired to write some music. Shall we have our picnic at twelve-thirty?"

"Yes. See you at lunchtime."

Ben grabbed Zobhule's hand, and they ran off, unafraid of prying eyes.

"I am hot and sweaty, Mister Ben," protested Zobhule, slowing to a standstill.

"I'm sorry. We'll walk. See, let's aim for those rocks," he suggested, pointing about two hundred yards ahead.

Before continuing, they stood admiring the vista. Max's white shirt could be seen moving away from them in the distance. Ben pulled Zobhule towards him and kissed her.

"Come. Not much further."

They walked, hand in hand, until they reached the rocky outcrop where Ben spread out the picnic blanket that he had snatched from the car. He was just unfolding a wayward corner when he remembered he always withdrew.

"Just for our top halves. My knees and your backside will just have to get dirty."

They both knelt on the blanket and got undressed. As they embraced, they found their torsos sticking together from their sweat. The moment Zobhule lay down, her bottom turned red from the dust gluing itself to her skin. Ben's knees were the same. After they had made passionate love, Ben's knees had left two indents in the dry earth. He laughed at his knees, brushing them off with a handkerchief.

"Turn round. I'll clean off your back."

Zobhule turned round to allow Ben to brush off what dust he could.

"Now, I want to make love to you all over again," he laughed.

"Mister Ben is too passionate," giggled Zobhule. "We must go and find Mister Max."

Ben didn't argue. He shook off the picnic blanket, folded it and rolled it up against his legs. They returned to the car, hand in hand, where they set out the picnic, as Max could be seen walking back towards the car.

The trips out continued until autumn started to give way to winter, when Ben and Zobhule needed to keep their clothes on, and on this, the last of these excursions, for several weeks, the first of two life-changing events occurred.

"I think I prefer the bedroom now it is too cold, Mister Ben," she remarked.

"I think this also. Can you wait a minute, please? I just need to go behind the rocks, before going home," apologised Ben.

He trotted off beyond the rocks to find a suitable spot. As he stood relieving himself against the outcrop, his gaze landed on a small pile of what looked like broken glass, where the rock rose out from the reddened earth. His first thought was indignation, that someone else had been to their rocks, and carelessly, left behind the remains of a bottle. On closer inspection, he realised these were uncut diamonds. Crouching down beside them, he scooped them up in his cupped hands, blew off the dust and deposited them in his trouser pocket. He trotted back to Zobhule.

"I think Mister Ben was lost," she joked.

"Sorry, he responded," not mentioning his discovery.

On the way home, they dropped Zobhule in the centre of town, something they did occasionally, to create the impression, the excursions were strictly business. Back at the house, Ben got out a map and spread it on the table.

"What are you looking for?" asked Max.

"I am looking to see who has claim on the land. Is it mining territory?"

"Why? Are you afraid that we have been trespassing?"

"No. Today, when I went behind the rocks to relieve myself, I found these," he explained, pulling the uncut diamonds from his trouser pocket.

"Good grief! I see why you want to know. Do you think there are more where those came from?"

"It is possible."

"You do realise you'll never be able to sell those here in South Africa? Not without losing your job."

"I know."

"What do you want to do about it?"

"Shall we go back, next weekend, and look for others?"

"Let me look at the map," responded Max, moving across to the table. "We were here, and here, and here."

"There are lines around here and here. This is the De Beers' mine."

"I imagine the tunnels underground extend along here and here and somewhere around here," suggested Max, tracing his finger across the map.

"So, how can we find out who owns the land where our rocks are?"

"I think the town hall or the library. There are maps at the office of what De Beers owns, but not who owns the land that they don't mine."

"I think we must look for more, before we start to ask questions about land."

"I agree."

Over the next few weeks, Ben and Max drove out to the rocks without Zobhule, to search for diamonds. Ben even took his mallet and one of his old chisels, to chip away at the foot of the rock where he found the diamonds. Each hit of mallet on chisel echoed around the rocks and he became nervous that someone might be alerted to their presence. The red Plymouth wasn't exactly inconspicuous. He stopped using the mallet, and instead, used both hands on the handle, to dig away at the earth. Nothing. He had hoped to find evidence of a vein, he gave up, disappointed.

"Either there's a really deep vein, another kimberlite funnel, or you discovered someone's stash," laughed Max, as they drove home from their sixth trip.

"I will give you half of what I found," offered Ben.

"That's not necessary. You found them before I got involved."

"But you are my oldest friend. We have lived through life and death experiences together."

"I can't see how we're going to find any more, without buying the land and setting up a mine, and I'm pretty sure we don't have the financial backing to do that. The moment we start sniffing around the banks, you can be sure De Beers will get wind of it, and step in."

"I think you are right."

Ben wrapped the uncut diamonds in the torn off sleeve of an old shirt and concealed them under the tools in his toolbox. One day, he felt sure he and Max would return to England, and then he would sell them.

Not many days later, the second of the life-changing events took place. Ben arrived at the mine, one Wednesday morning in June, to find an ambulance and two fire engines, parked by the lift shaft. There was no sound of machinery, and his team were standing outside the building, watching the activities over by the headstocks.

"Do you know what has happened?" he asked Samuel.

"An explosion."

"Is anyone hurt? Or dead?" asked Ben, concerned.

"I don't know. They are bringing people up to the surface. There is an ambulance."

It would be three hours until operations above ground started again, and three days, before the safety checks had been concluded and the mine deemed safe to resume operations in the tunnels. There had been one death and one serious injury caused directly by the explosion. Others experienced concussion and trauma.

That evening, when Ben arrived home from work, he discovered a tearful Zobhule in the kitchen.

"What is the matter, my beautiful one?"

He held her in his arms.

"I cannot stay here, Mister Ben."

"That's ridiculous. Why not?"

"My father. He has lost his legs. The explosion at the mine."

"I am so sorry, Zobhule."

"He cannot work now. I must find another job to support my family."

Ben was stunned into silence by her statement.

"I wish I could marry you. Rescue you from all this."

"But who would support my mother and father, Mister Ben?"

"Will we still see each other?"

"I don't know. Perhaps sometimes at the weekend. My heart is sad, Mister Ben."

"My heart is, also, my beautiful one."

"Now I have to go. Tell Mister Max, goodbye."

Zobhule allowed herself to be embraced, unable to reciprocate the passion, with her heart breaking.

"Thank you Zobhule. I will try to find a way."

As Ben watched her walk down the path, his heart was breaking too. What if he were to give Zobhule the uncut diamonds? That would only make things worse. The authorities would assume they came from the mine. He poured a whiskey and flopped onto the sofa. Max came through the door.

"What's the matter? You look like you're sick."

"Sick in the heart. It was Zobhule's father in the explosion. He lost both his legs. She has just told me she must leave us to get another job, so she can support her family."

"Oh Ben, my friend. I am sorry. How will you still see each other if she cannot work for us?"

"Exactly. I don't know."

"I'll sort out our meal."

"I'm not hungry."

"Well, at least keep me company."

Max set two places and fried some eggs, enough for them both.

"I'll eat yours if you don't," conceded Max, placing both plates on the table.

Ben joined him at the table and after toying with his eggs, reluctantly started to eat them.

"Good man. Now, I have found out today, that the death in the explosion was the foreman. But no one is really sure if he was struck by a rock launched by the dynamite, or by the hand of one of the workers. It's well-known that there are some strong supporters of the ANC working at the mine."

"What will they do?"

"I think there's an investigation going on. They'll certainly have to get a new foreman."

The two men finished their eggs, and Ben cleared away the plates. Having downed a second glass of whiskey, he went to bed early.

After a couple of weeks, activities returned to normal at the mine. Peter stayed overnight at Joan's house, more and more frequently.

"I'm thinking of asking Joan to marry me," he announced to Ben, one morning on the bus.

"Wow. That's fast! I remember how my wedding to Betty was brought forward, but that was because there was a war going on. Are you sure?"

"Never been surer. If she says 'Yes', will you be my best man?"

"Of course."

"Top man."

A few days later, on the Monday morning, Peter took his seat on the bus next to Ben.

"She said, 'Yes'."

"Congratulations!"

"Thank you. Now you will have to organise a bachelor party for me. Make it at the jazz club, will you?"

"Of course. Would you like me to tell Max that you are going to marry Joan?"

"Surely, he doesn't still hold a flame for her. Anyway, I have a feeling he will know soon enough," laughed Peter. "Joan can't wait to tell the whole office."

"I am very pleased for you. really, I am."

Ben acted jovially, but inside he was aching for Zobhule.

"There's a couple of men from the tunnel teams I want to invite. The new foreman is an interesting chap. Dieter Graf. He's from Switzerland."

"I shall look forward to meeting him. When is the wedding? I mean, when will the bachelor party take place?"

"We are hoping it can be the first Saturday in November, but I have to check that the church is available?"

"She's not Jewish, then?"

"No."

That evening, Ben did talk to Max about the impending wedding of Peter to Joan. He wanted to ask Max if the band would play, and how much they might charge for the occasion. It was a week before Peter could confirm the date and another week before Max could come back to Ben with the band's response. Not only were the band delighted to perform, but they had insisted Max play. There was, of course, a third confirmation required, and that was the availability of the jazz club.

The day after Max's confirmation, Ben took himself off to the jazz club after work and asked to speak with the manager. It was all sorted for the last Saturday in October, and the manager asked only that the wedding drinks were purchased from the club. The bachelor party would be accommodated in the side room, with access into the main room where the dance floor was. That way, the bachelor party had some privacy, but could benefit from the music and the dance floor, whilst the jazz club didn't lose out on other paying customers.

Before leaving, even though he knew it would make him late for the evening meal, without letting Max know, Ben bought a half-pint of beer and sat at a table in the corner. Suddenly, the sound of glasses smashing broke his peace. He had noticed over the years, that whenever he heard the sound of glass breaking, not only did it bring him out in a cold sweat, but it also evoked painful memories of the night in Karlsruhe, the horrors of Normandy and the face of Hauptmann Brecht in the bar, when the opera singer shattered his wine glass.

"Everything alright?" he called over to the manager.

"No injuries, but lots of broken glass to clear up. I dropped a tray of glasses."

Ben finished his beer and left. As he walked home, a lyric began to take shape in his head.

'When glass breaks, I think of you, and
My heart aches to reason why, when
All it takes to make me cry,
Is that you never made it through.'

He couldn't decide if that would be a verse, a chorus or even a bridge, but it was a start.

It was the evening of the bachelor party. Max had gone early to rehearse with the band, and Ben was wrapping the pewter tankard he had bought for Peter, engraved with 'Caught and bowled! 30th October 1948'. Peter played for the company cricket team, always bought a copy of *Wisden's Almanack*, and he'd clearly been bowled over by Joan. Ben hoped he would appreciate the humour. Washed, shaved, and the parcel wrapped, he set off for the jazz club.

Peter was already there when Ben arrived.

"That's a little something for you," said Ben, handing over the gift. "A little something to mark the occasion."

"Thank you," responded Peter. "Shall I open it now or save it for later."

"You can open it now, if you want."

Peter removed the string and folded back the paper to reveal a box.

"I'm intrigued," he smiled,

The lid fit snugly, and it took some effort to slide it upwards and remove it. His eyes lit up when he saw the tankard.

"Very amusing. I love it. Thank you. Now, let me buy you a drink."

"Tonight, you are not supposed to buy any drinks."

"I know, but while there's no one else here, let me by my best friend a drink."

"If you insist. I'll have a gin sling. Thank you."

"Bartender. Two gin slings, if you please."

"I'll bring them over to you, sir."

The band had taken up their positions and started to play. Before Ben and Peter went and sat at a table in the side room, Max acknowledged Ben and carried on tinkling the ivories. Ben realised that with Max playing in the band, the only other person he knew was Peter. It was Peter who had handed out invitations to various friends and colleagues. Although he didn't know their names, several of the guests seemed familiar to Ben. There were twelve included in the bachelor party, split across three small round tables. Peter introduced Ben to Henry Stevens, from the supplies team, and Martin Wolf, from one of the tunnel teams, who both got up to move between tables and mingle with the others.

Looking across at the other tables Ben thought he recognised two of the men but couldn't quite place them.

"Do you know who the men on the third table are?" he asked Henry and Martin, who had returned to their seats.

"The one on the left is Dieter Graf, one of the new tunnel foremen. No idea who the other one is," replied Martin. "He's from Switzerland."

That was when Ben identified a few words of German coming from the table where Dieter was sitting. Suddenly, to his shock, the familiarity found its explanation, even though these two men were no longer in uniform. Ben was sitting a stone's throw from Hauptmann Brecht and Oberleutnant Fischer.

They may well have been in Switzerland, immediately prior to travelling to South Africa, but it was as clear as crystal to Ben, that these two former officers had blood on their hands and had fled after the war, once the hunt for Nazis began. He thought he was going to be sick. Did they recognise him? In Sète, where they may have noticed him stand up and leave, he had been far more focused on them than they were likely to have been on him, surely. Everything inside Ben resisted being introduced to them, let alone having to shake their hands. Thankfully, Ben didn't have to work alongside these murderers, but he also recognised the very real possibility of being able to exact his revenge on them.

Just as he was contemplating justice for his family, Jean's family in Sète, and countless members of the Jewish community, Peter started banging an ashtray on the table. There was a break in the music, and Max had come over to join them.

"Gentlemen. Thank you so much for joining me in my end-of-bachelorhood celebrations. Thank you to my good friend Ben for organising us. For obvious reasons, my lovely wife-to-be is not here with us, but I'm sure those of you who know her will realise how deliriously happy I am to be taking her as my wife next Saturday. You are all invited to be present at the exchanging of our vows at St Andrews

Presbyterian Church at two o'clock. Now enjoy the rest of the evening."

The others applauded him.

"Have you got time for a drink, Max? asked Peter

"Some iced tea would be great. I still need to play the rest of the session. I have ten minutes, perhaps."

"Sit yourself down next to Ben and I'll be right back."

Peter nipped to the bar.

"Have you been introduced, yet?" inquired Ben.

Max shook his head.

"Go and say 'Hello' to the two men on the far table and tell me later if they look familiar to you. Say nothing of your past. Don't linger but move onto the middle table as soon as you can and come back here," instructed Ben, making sure his back was to the two ex-officers, and he was speaking quietly.

Max knew Ben well enough to take the hint, and although he was a little confused, he did as Ben had said. By the time he had made his introductions, Peter had returned carrying an iced tea, and Max sat down to drink it.

"Thank you."

"You're most welcome. Enjoying the music."

Max looked Ben in the eyes, nodded deliberately, and downed his glass in one.

"Speak later. Must dash."

Ex-Hauptmann Brecht and Ex-Oberleutnant Fischer were the first to leave, followed by everyone apart from Peter and Ben.

"Bit of a random question, I know, but do you know of any Nazi war criminals who have been arrested in South Africa, since the war?"

"That is a random question. I can't say I have. Should I ask why?"

"What would you do if you met one? I mean, would you go to the police?"

"I don't know my friend."

They shared another gin sling and Ben put Peter in a taxi home. Max was helping the other members of the band to pack up, so Ben waited for him.

"Joost, over there, will give us a lift."

"Great. I think Peter enjoyed himself."

"I'm sure he did. We need to talk, I think."

Ben nodded.

"Can I help?" he asked Joost.

"Thank you. Can you carry that trumpet case for me, please?"

"Certainly."

Ben picked up the case and went over to the bar to thank the manager.

"Thank you. I think our man had a great celebration. I think the club was busy, also?"

"It was. Win-win, if you ask me. I'm glad for your friend. Is he marrying the gorgeous lady he's been coming in here with?"

"I hope so," laughed Ben, following Joost and Max out.

Nothing was said during the journey.

"Thank you, Joost. See you next week."

"Bye," added Ben, shifting across the rear seat and getting out of the driver's side, after Max.

"Sleep well, my friends," replied Joost through the open window, as he pulled off.

"Do you want a whiskey?" asked Max, once they were inside.

"I think I need one. So, do you think it's them?"

"Ninety-nine percent certain. Do you think they recognise us?"

"I hope not."

"What are you going to do?"

"Honestly, I have no idea. I could report them, but it would be difficult to prove my account. If I am to arrange some sort of accident for them, I will need to get to know them. I could ask the ANC supporters to help. Just like the other foreman was struck in the head."

"Ben. Have you thought this through?"

"I never thought I would have this chance. I don't want to lose it."

"Sleep on it. Think it through properly, my friend."

"I know. You are right, of course."

Ben finished his whiskey and went to bed. He started to imagine various scenarios involving accidents, and at some point, he fell into a troubled sleep. At three-thirty he woke with a start, as a trapdoor opened in his dreams, and the bodies of Ex-Hauptmann Brecht and Ex-Oberleutnant Fischer fell through it. He stumbled to the kitchen, poured a glass of water, went to the bathroom, and returned to bed. Sometime in the next few days, he would find out how many, if any, Nazi war criminals had been tracked down to South Africa and arrested. In the morning, he rewarded himself with a lie-in.

"Do you want to go for a drive?" offered Max, midway through the morning.

"Can do. Why not?"

"Ready in half an hour?"

"Yes."

Half an hour later, Max and Ben set off across town in the red Plymouth.

"Let's go somewhere we've not been," suggested Max.

"Alright," responded Ben, half-heartedly.

As they were driving through one of the poorer suburbs, Ben spotted Zobhule standing outside a church, talking to a tall, slim, young-looking, black man. To add to Ben's feelings of depression, he watched the man place his arm round Zobhule's shoulders and walk her off along the pavement. Pangs of jealousy erupted within Ben. He wasn't angry, because his anger was now channelled into revenge on Ex-Hauptmann Brecht and Ex-Oberleutnant Fischer. It was more a sense of longing, almost of homesickness, that he felt. Saying nothing to Max, Ben wondered if he too had noticed Zobhule.

"Do you know how or where I could buy a hand-gun?"

"That's a bit drastic. In any case. How would you get away with murder?"

"What do you suggest, then?"

"I can't believe I'm even suggesting this. It is better to arrange an accident, at the mine. The inquiry into the death of that foreman during the explosion remains an open verdict."

"Do we know where the former lieutenant works. Does he work at the mine also, do you know?"

"I haven't seen any payroll details for him, but that doesn't mean he doesn't."

"If he's changed his name, though, like Brecht, how would you know?"

"Good point. I'll check for other new names. You should ask your friend Samuel, or Peter. He's more likely to know who works underground. Have you dismissed the idea of reporting them to the authorities?"

"How would I prove their identity?"

"I'm sure I read something in the newspaper about a man called Wiesenthal in Austria. I think he set up an organisation to track Nazis and former SS members. I don't remember the name. It was last year, sometime. I doubt we still have the newspaper."

"But all we've got on him is a conversation I overheard of him boasting about the Night of Broken Glass and sending Jews off to a work camp. That and the hostages who were executed in Sète."

"At least let's write to the organisation and ask what to do. I doubt the former officers are going anywhere, if they're certain of their anonymity here. It might take several weeks to receive any kind of response, but do you really want blood on your hands."

"I already have blood on my hands."

"Defending yourself during war is not the same as cold-blooded murder, Ben."

Ben didn't answer. In his imagination, he set out a fleece, a bit like Gideon. If he could find the newspaper, he would take it as a sign and write to Wiesenthal's organisation. Now, he was impatient to get back and start searching.

No sooner had they arrived back at the house than Ben began hunting for old newspapers. Zobhule used to pile them up and use them to wrap up scraps and bones, before placing them in the rubbish. In the few cold weeks in winter, they also used them, screwed up, under the kindling and coal, to start a fire. Ben went into the pantry and took out the pile of old newspapers from under the sink. Turning the pile upside-down, he checked the dates. Working his way through the 1947 issues took some time, but eventually he came to an article about Wiesenthal and the Historical Centre for Jewish Documentation in Linz, Austria.

"Max!" he called. "I've found it. The article about Wiesenthal."

"That's really good news. No address, I take it."

"I'm certain that a letter to Simon Wiesenthal, Historical Centre for Jewish Documentation, Linz, Austria will reach him."

"Better write that letter, then."

Ben took some notepaper and an envelope and sat down at the table. Having written his address and the date, he began. 'Dear Sir. My name is Benjamin Linton-House. I served in the Royal Norfolk Regiment as part of the British Expeditionary Force until France was occupied. I escaped with my life. I could not reach the Channel or the Atlantic. Instead, I went south and ended up in Sète. One day, after the Germans had entered Vichy France, I was in a bar and sat next to two German officers. They boasted about their involvement in the Night of Broken Glass, in Karlsruhe, where I lived with my family, until I escaped to England with the Children Transport. They also spoke, with some joy, about rounding up my people and sending them to the work camps. The two officers were Hauptmann Brecht and Oberleutnant Fischer. They also played their part in hostage executions in Sète. After reaching Malta, I served until the end of the war. In 1947 I came to South Africa where I work for De Beers, in Kimberley. I recently had the unfortunate experience of discovering the two former officers in Kimberley. Hauptmann Brecht works in the mine and has changed his name to Dieter Graf. He says he is from Switzerland. I do not know where former Oberleutnant Fischer works or if he has changed his name. I trust you will be able to use this information to bring justice. Yours faithfully, Benjamin Linton-House.'

"Will you read it? Tell me what you think, please."

Max cast his eyes over the letter.

"Seems fine to me. Would you like me to take it to the post office on my way to work, tomorrow?"

"Thank you."

Ben folded the letter, slipped it into the envelope, and wrote the limited address on the front.

"There you go. Let me know how much it costs."

"Don't be ridiculous. It's as much my justice as it is yours. Well, of course, it wasn't my family, but it is my people, our people, we are talking about."

Ben nodded.

That evening, as Ben walked through the door, Max was ill at ease.

"We have a problem, I think."

"What do you mean?"

"This morning, I took the letter to the post office, paid for the stamp and handed the letter to the clerk. Just as she was placing it in a wire basket, sitting on the shelves behind her, Ex-Oberleutnant Fischer, or whatever his name is now, came out of the backroom and took the wire basket. He must work in the sorting room. He will see the address and either open it or throw it straight in the bin. It is possible he didn't see me hand it over. There were three clerks and several customers, but if he recognised me, he may have asked who brought the letter in. If he opens it, they will know you recognised them and have sent the letter."

"Oh no! That's a disaster. I knew I should have taken matters into my own hands. What shall we do?"

"Move to somewhere else, somewhere much bigger, like Pretoria or Johannesburg or Cape Town. Leave South Africa and return to Blighty."

"Or I could deal with them myself, before they have a chance to react. I could blackmail them to lure them into a meeting by the Big Hole and arrange a terrible accident."

"If you're sure that's what you want to do. I can't stop you."

"I'm sure."

"You wouldn't rather just walk away? We've got the uncut diamonds to sell. We could start again, somewhere."

The following day, when Ben sat next to Peter, on the bus, he handed him an envelope.

"Please would you give this to Dieter Graf, if you see him?"

"I don't see him every day, but I'll do my best. Did you two hit it off at my bachelor do."

"I wouldn't call it that. I just need to get a message to him."

The message read, 'Dear Hauptmann Brecht. Meet me at the Big Hole, at ten o'clock on Sunday evening. Bring Oberleutnant Fischer with you. I want £1000 or I will tell the authorities who you are.' He didn't sign the letter.

Ben's plan was to arrive at the big hole at around nine o'clock, with his saw. He would saw through the railings, leaving less than half an inch on the uprights and crossbars. He would stand leaning against the safe section, inviting the former officers to stand next to him. When they were close enough, he would try to get them to lean on the weakened section, talking as they looked into the hole. He was sure they would fall to their deaths, and it would look like a tragic accident.

Sunday evening arrived.

"Max. I know you don't agree with this, but it's something I have to do. If anything happens, you've been the best friend a man could want. I think my plan will work, but just in case it doesn't, the uncut diamonds are yours. They're in the bottom of my toolbox."

"At least let me give you a lift."

Ben paused for a moment.

"I insist."

"Alright. Thank you. But the car must be gone by nine-thirty."

"Of course. Whatever you say."

They got into the red Plymouth and Max drove them out to The Big Hole, where he dropped Ben off. Nothing more was said. As Ben set out for the railings, Max drove the car a hundred yards round the track, out of sight, and positioned himself behind a tree to listen and watch.

At five minutes to ten, a car could be heard crunching its way along the approach road. As soon as it was past, whilst the engine was still running and the wheels still scrunching, he got into his Plymouth, and reversed it back into the approach road, without his lights on. He got out, left the door on the latch, and moved forwards to where he could see what was happening.

The two former officers parked their car several yards away from the viewing point and got out. Ex-Oberleutnant Fischer had been driving. Ex-Hauptmann Brecht went to the boot and took out a luger, out of sight of Ben, and concealed it in his pocket. Ben was leaning with his back to the railings. The two former officers approached him.

"Good evening gentlemen," Ben greeted them, in German.

"How did you think you would get away with this, Benjamin Linton-House? Jew. I don't remember you," hissed Ex-Hauptmann Brecht. "There were so many."

"I was in the bar, in Sète," continued Ben, in German, "when you admitted to your part in the Kristallnacht and deportation of my people. My parents."

"It appears you, too, have changed your name," Ex-Oberleutnant Fischer taunted him, taking out the letter to the Historical Centre of Jewish Records.

"Yes. But only to serve my new country and fight against the Nazis. Not to hide in plain sight. I am not ashamed of my past. I came here for a fresh start. Not to escape crimes against humanity."

"Well, since you are so sure we have committed crimes against humanity, how would you like to witness one more," Ex-Hauptmann Brecht mocked him, taking out the luger. "How about you jump over the railings. We like to see vermin drowned. Especially, Jewish vermin."

At first sight of the luger being drawn, without any hesitation, Max sprinted to the car, started the engine, switched on the headlights, and drove as fast as he could towards the former officers. As he drove, his mind started to process how he was going to stop in time. There were seconds to make up his mind, otherwise the Plymouth would crash through the railings, and he would plummet to his own death. Thankfully, the headlights and sound of the speeding vehicle distracted, and momentarily blinded, Ex-Hauptmann Brecht, just long enough for Ben to step away. Max slammed on the breaks and skidded to a gravelly halt. By some miracle, the front bumper collided with the former officers' legs with enough impact to send them flying through the broken section of railings and bring the Plymouth to a halt with only two feet to spare.

He got out of the car, shaking, and peered over the edge, although it was too dark to see anything. It was unlikely that they had survived the impact on the water below, and even if they had, it would have been impossible for them to swim or climb the cliff face. Ben approached the car.

"Thank you. You could have died."

"So could you. What were you thinking?"

"I wasn't thinking with my head. I was thinking with my heart. I am eternally grateful that you were thinking with your head. Now, let's go home."

"I don't know about you, but I think it's time we went home-home. Back to England. I think I can carve out a career in song-writing. I'll need to collaborate with a lyric-writer, of course. You've got the uncut diamonds to fall back on."

"It's true, this new start hasn't exactly been positive. Let's go to Cape Town. I'll sell the uncut diamonds and we can take the next ship back to England. In fact, the sooner the better."

"Better resign from our jobs then. Say we're going travelling. Might look obvious, though, so soon after the accident."

"I didn't sign the message asking them to meet me."

"But you signed the letter to Wiesenthal's organisation. What if they find that?"

"Ex-Oberleutnant Fischer had it with him. With a bit of luck, the ink will have dissolved by the time they find the bodies. Hopefully, they'll have sunk without trace. It was too dark to see."

"If the police connect you, we'll explain everything. Let's just leave tomorrow. I'll say I was sick. Something we both ate. You can say the same thing. I'll drive us to Cape Town and sell the Plymouth at the first garage that will take it."

Early in the morning, shortly after six, they packed their belongings into a trunk and their clothes into two cases. Max penned a short note to the landlord and wrote a cheque for two months' rent, urging him to keep or sell the piano. Ben wrote a short letter to Peter. They loaded the Plymouth, and set off for Cape Town, stopping once to post the letters, and once to fill up with fuel, before leaving Kimberley.

The journey was long, dusty and tiring. They stopped five times, for food, fuel and drinks. Just before five o'clock in the evening, they reached their destination, parking up at the same hostel they had stayed at when they arrived in South Africa, all those months before.

In the morning, they went out to get breakfast.

"Shall we sort out our passage home, first? We need to leave the trunk somewhere at the docks before I sell the car. We'll never carry it from the hostel."

"I think this, also."

"It makes me smile. Even after all this time, when you'd hardly know now, that English wasn't your first language, you still say 'I think this, also'!"

"I know," laughed Ben. "It's habit."

They went down to the docks and asked about the ships due to sail for England. A cargo ship was leaving the following morning, which the helpful harbourmaster pointed out to them. Ben and Max found the captain and on asking if they could work their passage, found him to be appreciative and understanding. He also agreed for them to load their trunk on board immediately. They were to return on board at seven in the evening.

Next on their agenda, having carried the trunk to the ship and stowed it in what would be their cabin, were the car and the uncut diamonds. Max went in search of a garage, and Ben a jeweller. He was nervous, because of the syndicate.

"Good morning," he greeted the jeweller, in the first shop he came to.

"How can I help?"

"I'm looking for somewhere to sell some uncut diamonds I found."

The thought of word getting back to De Beers, along with his sudden departure from Kimberley, caused Ben to feel even more guilty than he already was.

"And where did you find these uncut diamonds?"

"In some hills in the Northern Cape."

"Whose land?"

"No one's land. It was up in the hills."

"Let me take a look."

Ben removed the cotton parcel from his trouser pocket and unrolled it to reveal nine uncut diamonds of varying sizes. The jeweller picked up his loupe in one hand and one of the uncut diamonds in the other. Carefully, he examined each and every one.

"You say you found these in the hills?"

"Yes."

"Well, I'm sorry to disappoint you, but I think you have found some well-weathered, broken glass."

Ben's heart sank.

"I don't understand."

"Look," explained the jeweller, picking up a small piece. "If this were an uncut diamond, you would be able to see tiny faults, flaws. But these are flawless. Look for yourself."

Ben took the loupe and the uncut diamond from the jeweller. He was sure he could see the tiniest of faults.

"Are you certain."

"Look again, please."

The jeweller took another look.

"Honestly, it's flawless, and I'm afraid, worthless."

The jeweller folded the material around the broken glass and handed it back to Ben.

"Keep them. Dispose of them for me, please," insisted Ben, finding it hard to hide his disappointment.

He left the jeweller frustrated, as well as disappointed. What he didn't see, as he walked away from the counter, was the jeweller smiling, and pocketing the parcel.

Ben caught up with Max, back at the hostel.

"Any joy?"

"The jeweller said the uncut diamonds were just well-weathered, broken glass. Worthless."

"You took his word for it?"

"He explained that diamonds are flawed, and glass is flawless. He gave me his loupe to check. I thought I saw a tiny flaw, but the jeweller looked again and still insisted they were worth nothing. What about you?"

"I managed to sell my car. Reasonable price. We should go back to the jeweller. Did we ever see anyone in the hills? What are the odds of someone breaking a bottle, up there?"

"I asked him to dispose of them," responded Ben, shrugging.

"No! Take me to the jeweller. No time to lose."

Ben led the way. On reaching the shop, the closed sign was hanging in the door, and it was all locked up.

"It's not even lunchtime. I think you were conned."

"We could wait until he comes back."

"It'll be your word against his. Do you really want to involve the police?"

"I suppose it's only money. I'll have my war pension saved up in the bank."

"I'll buy you lunch," smiled Max.

That evening, they boarded the cargo ship and joined the makeshift crew for the four-week voyage to England. Ben's elbow was itching. It had been for a couple of days, on and off, but he had ignored it. He rolled up his sleeve to see the skin flaking. He thought he should get it checked out, when they reached London.

WHEN GLASS BREAKS

Ben and Max arrived back in London, shortly before Christmas 1948. On the voyage, in between shifts working on maintenance of the engines, Ben penned the rest of his song. He couldn't wait to show it to Max and hoped his friend might fit the lyrics to a tune.

They agreed to share a flat, until such time as one or other of them might find himself in a committed relationship. Ben paid three months' rent in advance, from the war pension payments which had accumulated in his bank account. The flat was in Ladbroke Grove and consisted of one large room, a small kitchen and a bathroom with toilet. Utilising his carpentry skills, Ben made shelves and wardrobes to partition off two bedrooms at one end of the main room, to afford each of them some privacy. Max also bought an upright piano with some of the proceeds from the red Plymouth. It was a comedy worthy of Laurel and Hardy, manoeuvring it into the first-floor flat.

Max decorated the main room with tinsel and placed a small, artificial tree on top of the piano. The two men invited the neighbours for a Christmas drink, an older lady from the top floor, a middle-aged couple from the ground floor, and an artist from the basement.

The evening was spent drinking port and making small talk, although Max was interested to get to know the artist better, already wondering if some sort of collaboration might be possible, producing a musical.

"I quite like that Raymond chap," commented Max, after the guests had gone. "He visualises things well. Maybe we could produce something together."

"I've written a lyric," responded Ben. "I was hoping you could write the tune. It's called 'When glass breaks.'"

"Excellent. Let's see it then."

Ben went to his room and came back with the sheet of paper on which he'd scribbled the words:

I kissed your smile
To words of 'Mozel Tov!'
We danced a while
And celebrated love
But you were gone too soon
Now look down from above
Once I found gladness in the sound breaking glass

I held your arm
And watched you slip away
You looked so calm
There were no words to say
But there's no healing balm

To let you fight another day
So, I saw sadness in the sound of breaking glass

When glass breaks, I think of you, and
My heart aches to reason why, when
All it takes to make me cry,
Is that you never made it through.

You who caused pain
It's time to pay the price
To meet again
The sword will fall within a trice
All the days I remain
My heart is only filled with ice
Now I feel coldness in the sound of breaking glass

Max was pacing up and down, mumbling the lyric under his breath. Every so often he hummed a few notes. Sitting down on the piano stool, he began to pick out a tune.

"Bah, bah, bah, bah …. Bah, ba, ba, ba, ba, bah …."

He scribbled the notes on a page of manuscript paper.

"How's this? 'I kissed your smile, To words of 'Mozel Tov!' We danced a while. And celebrated love. But you were gone too soon. Now look down from above. Once I found gladness in the sound breaking glass.' What do you think?"

"I love it."

"The bridge might be a bit trickier. I'll try and finish it in the morning. Goodnight."

"Goodnight. And thank you."

In fact, Max woke at four in the morning and got up to capture the bridge which had come to him in his sleep.

"It's finished!" he enthused, when Ben surfaced for breakfast.

Max sang the whole song whilst Ben made coffees for them both.

"Brilliant."

"I'll produce a professional-looking manuscript, get it copyrighted, and see if I can find a record producer. You've got a gift, Ben. Any more lyrics percolating?"

"Maybe. Can you just put my name as Ben House, please?"

Ben had never finished the song inspired by Zobhule.

In between Christmas and New Year, Ben made an appointment with a doctor, to look at his elbows. By now, the left elbow had a pink, flaky patch, about the diameter of a cricket ball, while the right elbow sported a slightly smaller patch. There was also a small patch forming on his left knee. The doctor examined the patches.

"I believe you have a mild case of psoriasis. I'll prescribe you some cream for it, but first, can you tell me a little bit about your circumstances, please?"

Ben looked quizzically at him.

"Now or up to now? Is this due to damp or a change in diet?"

"There is a link between what is going on for you emotionally. Stress can cause a physical reaction in your body. It starts to fight with itself. I was wondering if you had experienced any stressful circumstances recently."

Ben began to chuckle.

"Any stressful circumstances apart from leaving my home in Germany after the Night of Broken Glass, getting separated from my brother, fighting on the frontline in Normandy, losing my family in the Blitz, assisting the French Resistance, travelling to South Africa and back?"

He omitted the part in South Africa that heralded his return to England.

"I see. But the patches are only recent?"

"Yes. I first noticed one on my arm, just before leaving Cape Town, a few weeks ago. It's been getting worse."

"We'd better monitor it. Keep a diary of when it flares up, any stress triggers, where it flares up, and when it disappears. Hopefully, this lot will disappear with the cream and your body will form a new skin. Come back and see me in six months. It doesn't look very nice but it's not infectious. If the cream doesn't help within the next two weeks, make another appointment and we'll try something else."

The doctor scribbled a prescription and handed it to Ben.

"Thank you. Bye."

"Bye, Mr Linton-House."

The cream was a success, and to Ben's relief, after a few weeks, the scales had cleared up.

He had started repairing blinds again and had bought a small van to transport his ladders and equipment. A few weeks into his self-employment, a young boy on a bicycle hurtled across the road, at the lights. Ben jammed on the breaks. Whether it reminded him of the red Plymouth, by The Big Hole, or whether it was the shock of having nearly run down a child, a few days later, the psoriasis came back. This time it was both elbows, both knees and his scalp. It was virtually impossible to apply the cream to his scalp, in spite of the hint of premature balding. Not wanting to bother the doctor again, so soon, Ben went to the local pharmacy and asked the chemist what might help, and left with a bottle of tar shampoo. Again, a few weeks later, his body healed itself, until the next time. Ben had three flare-ups throughout 1949, all fairly similar in extent.

During the year, Max copyrighted *When Glass Breaks* and sent it to several of his contacts in the music industry. It was starting to be performed by amateur and professional musicians in various clubs across London. Just before Christmas, Max also succeeded in getting a recording made. It was produced as a forty-five, with another of his own songs on the B-side. He had kept the record secret, until Ben unwrapped his Christmas present.

"You had a record made!"

"Yes. Only recently, mind. Play it. I think it sounds great."

Ben placed the record on the gramophone. Listening to it caused a mix of emotions to well up inside him.

"Some of the best compositions rise like the phoenix from the ashes of adversity," Max attempted to encourage him.

"I know, my friend."

Max was now making an acceptable income as a songwriter, and with his war pension, a few shillings in royalties, and his blind-repairing business, Ben was comfortable too. The psoriasis was annoying, but manageable. At the check-up in June 1949, the doctor had told him to come back in a year's time, but to continue with the diary. His annual appointment was due this week, and armed with his diary, he set off for the surgery.

"Good afternoon, Mr Linton-House. How is your psoriasis?"

"About the same. Flaring up every four months or so."

"How would you like to take part in a trial for a new treatment at the Middlesex?"

"What does it involve?"

"You take a drug. That's the trial part. And then spend two minutes under a sun lamp. Once a week for six weeks and then once a month, as a booster. You're already keeping a diary. I think they want to see if the treatment can prevent flare-ups."

"How long does it go on for?"

"Eighteen months."

"Is it dangerous?"

"No trial is guaranteed. That's why it's a trial, but the drug and the treatment have been tested extensively on mice."

"Do mice get psoriasis?"

"Very amusing, Mr Linton-House."

"Alright, then. I'll give it a go."

"Jolly good. I'll have them send you a letter."

"See you in six months?"

The doctor paused.

"The Middlesex will be monitoring you. Let's wait and see what happens."

"Thank you. Bye."

"Goodbye, Mr Linton-House."

Ben started the trial psoriasis treatment in September 1949. He popped over to the hospital at the end of a working day. For the first seven months, the new drug and the ultraviolet light seemed to be having a positive effect as Ben experienced no flare-ups.

No one mentioned any changes to the length of time he would spend under the sun lamp, so Ben was more than a little surprised when, on his next visit, he was left for fifteen minutes.

"Was there a reason for the increase in time under the sun lamp?" he asked, when a nurse came to switch off the light.

"Err, I'm not sure," she stuttered with embarrassment. "I think it might have been an oversight. I'm sorry."

Ben didn't think too much more about it, although three days later, he started squinting in the early spring sunlight. His work was mostly outdoors, so it was hard to avoid the sun. Blinds protect shop windows from direct sunlight, but if you're working on one of them, it is unlikely that you will be underneath it. By the end of the day, he had developed quite a headache, and just made it home before retching into the toilet. That evening, he went to bed early, without eating his evening meal, worried that he might have to miss appointments tomorrow.

Although by morning, he was not feeling sick, he still had the headache, but went to work anyway. The headaches continued for three days. When it came to his April visit to the Middlesex Hospital, he had different answers to the regular pre-treatment questionnaire.

"And have you experienced any headaches since your last visit?"

"Yes. A few days after my last trip. I also found I was squinting in the sunlight a lot more than I would usually."

The nurse noted everything down.

"And have you felt nauseous or vomited?"

"Yes. When the headaches first started."

"I see from your notes that, on your last visit, you were left under ultraviolet light for thirteen minutes longer than prescribed. Is that correct?"

"Yes."

"I am going to stay here throughout the two-minute dose, this time, Mr Linton-House."

She handed him the tablet to swallow and settled him under the sun lamp. Hardly had the lamp been switched on than Ben felt violently sick.

"Stop!"

The nurse switched off the lamp.

"I'm going to be sick."

She handed him a receptacle. There was little more than bile, because lunch had been several hours previously, and he was on his way home after work.

"Wait here, please."

The nurse left the room and came back accompanied by a registrar who took Ben's temperature and listened to his heart.

"I think you might have become over-sensitive to ultraviolet light, Mr Linton-House. I think it is best that we discontinue the trial."

"That's a shame," responded Ben, putting his shirt and trousers back on. "I haven't had a flare-up since the start."

"Yes. It's looking like a successful treatment. I'm sorry."

Ben tied his shoelaces, picked up his jacket and left the hospital, thinking it would be the last time he crossed the threshold. As he feared, two months after he finished the trial, he experienced another flare-up. Not having used the cream for nearly ten months, he made an appointment with the doctor. It was for eight o'clock in the morning.

"Good morning," the doctor greeted him, cheerily. "Have a seat. Tell me all about the trial. They were kind enough to send me a copy of your notes."

"There's not a lot to tell. It was working really quite well, until someone left me under the sun lamp too long. Now, it turns out, I'm over-sensitive to ultraviolet light, so I couldn't carry on. As you can see, the psoriasis has returned. Could I have another prescription for the cream, please?"

"Certainly. I'm really sorry to hear about the trial."

He wrote out another prescription.

"Thank you. Bye."

"Goodbye, Mr Linton-House. Come and see me in six months, if not before."

Ben went off to work.

Over the next six months, he had another flare-up. This time, it was slightly worse, with the psoriasis spreading to his lower back and buttocks. As usual, the cream helped, and the flare-up cleared. Unexpectedly, however, he was to find himself back in hospital, but not the Middlesex.

It was 9th January 1951, just after nine o'clock in the morning. Although only butchers seemed to use their blinds in winter, as even winter sun on meat was not acceptable, most proprietors benefitted from the winter months to have their blinds maintained. Whilst Ben disliked working outdoors in the winter, he was grateful for the regular income. This morning, there was a frost on the pavements. Having rested his ladder against the wall, Ben climbed up to inspect the mechanism. Just as he stepped on the sixth rung, the bottom of the ladder slipped on the frosty flagstone. Somehow, Ben had the presence of mind to leap from the falling ladder, but his weaker knee, the one resulting in his war pension, was unprepared for the landing, gave way, and caused him to fall heavily against the door frame. Meanwhile, the ladder, in slow motion, slid away from the wall, its top colliding with the widow glass, shattering it. Ben sat there, shaking. The butcher, who fortunately, had not yet filled the window display, came out.

"Are you alright?"

Ben stared at him, aware of an intense pain in his right wrist. In his head, his own personal cinemascope of Normandy was flickering by.

"Are you alright?" repeated the butcher.

Ben looked at him.

"I'm sorry. I'll pay for the damage."

"Yes. But are you alright? You seem far from alright. Can you stand?"

Ben tried to haul himself up. He winced. The butcher placed his arm under Ben's left armpit and pulled him up.

"Come inside and sit down. I'll call an ambulance. Don't worry about your van or tools or ladder. They can stay here, for now. I'll make you a strong cup of tea."

While Ben waited for the ambulance, drinking his tea, the butcher started to sweep up the glass. It took twenty minutes for the ambulance to arrive. Ben handed the butcher the key to his van and was helped into the back of the ambulance.

"I'll see you when I see you," smiled the butcher.

"Thank you and I'm sorry."

"Che sera sera."

It was a ten-minute ride to St George's Hospital.

After an initial examination, the doctor on duty determined Ben may have broken his arm. He was wheeled off to be x-rayed, which confirmed the fractured ulna. Ben was put in plaster and admitted onto an orthopaedic ward.

With a dose of morphine in his system, Ben slept soundly from early afternoon through to four-twenty in the morning.

"Could I have something to eat, please?" he asked the rather attractive nurse, when she came on her round.

"I can get you some toast, if you hang on a few minutes," she replied, without any impatience.

As she smiled at him, Ben noticed she had a central tooth, rather than the two front teeth most people present. He thought she was sweet. He was the last but one on her round, and as promised, she went to the kitchen and made some toast. None of the three other patients on the ward was awake.

"There you are. Only butter, I'm afraid."

"Thank you, Nurse Norton."

To Ben's great pleasure, she came and said goodbye, at the end of her shift.

"Wait. When are you next on shift?" he asked, as she turned to walk away.

"Tonight, and tomorrow night. Then I'm off for three days."

"Have a good day's rest," laughed Ben.

He watched her walk back to the nurses' station, put on her cape, and leave with the second nurse, who had spent most of the latter part of their shift cleaning bedpans and sterilising equipment.

During the morning, Ben borrowed a newspaper and wiled away the hours. Two of the other patients were discharged. Just Ben and a man with a broken leg remained. The man was stuck in bed, his leg suspended from a pulley. After he had been to the toilet, Ben went and sat down next to him.

"Hello. I'm Ben. Broken arm."

"I'm Frank. Builder. Or was until recently. Broken leg."

"I repair shop blinds. The ladder slipped. I was lucky to get away with a broken arm."

"Looks like you're limping, too."

"Oh, that. War wound. Shrapnel in the knee. It didn't like me landing on it when I fell."

"Where did you get it?"

"Normandy. 1940."

"Dunkirk?"

"Almost. I was with the Royal Norfolks. We didn't make it back to Dunkirk."

"Then you have my heart-felt thanks. I was one of the lucky ones. Came back on a fishing boat. How did you get back?"

"Long story. Went south. Got medical attention through some resistance fighters. Ended up on the Mediterranean coast. Made it as far as Malta. On a fishing boat, also. Served out the last few months of the war on the island repairing tunnels."

"Did you find it hard? Coming back here, after the war, I mean."

"To be honest, I went to South Africa, to escape the memories?"

"Why did you come back, then?"

"That's another long story. Maybe for another day."

Frank didn't press him for the story.

"Family?" asked Frank, changing the subject.

"Lost them in the Blitz. You?"

"Lost them in the Blitz, as well. Those Germans have got a lot to answer for."

"Not all Germans. Just the Nazis. Hitler. The officers who committed crimes against humanity. Most ordinary

Germans were caught up in it all. They were as scared as we were."

"If you say so."

"Chat later."

Ben went back to his bed. His arm was hurting him, and he was tired from waking so early. Lowering himself into the pillow, he closed his eyes and tried to picture Nurse Norton. After a quarter of an hour or so he dozed off, only to be woken when the latest dose of medication was due.

"Sorry to wake you Mr Linton-House. You need your painkillers."

"It's fine, really."

Nurse Butterworth was older and rather more stern-looking than Nurse Norton, and Ben thought it wise not to protest. She handed him two tablets and a glass of water, which he swallowed obediently. Nurse Butterworth moved on to Frank's bed.

It was soon lunchtime. Fish pie. Ben was unsure of the type of fish, and also quite nervous of finding a bone, but he cleared his plate without incident. Dessert was tinned fruit and evaporated milk. He returned to reading the newspaper and decided to do the crossword, which he completed with ease. Somehow, he had a head for cryptic clues. Having done the crossword, he got out of bed and wandered over to the nurses' station.

"Excuse me, Nurse Butterworth. Might I have a sheet of paper and a pencil?"

"I'm sorry, but I don't have any spare paper."

The second nurse on shift, Nurse Rudd, shrugged her shoulders and winked at Ben, from Nurse Butterworth's blind-spot. Ben appreciated her solidarity, although she was not as cute as Nurse Norton. He returned to his bed, frustrated and a little miffed. It wouldn't have hurt to give him a page from the pad the nurses used to make notes on. He was just processing his annoyance, when in walked Max.

"I thought I'd find you here," laughed Max.

"Hello, my friend. I'm afraid they're keeping me in for the week, at least."

"I've brought you some toffees. Oh, and your writing pad."

"You must have read my mind."

"I know you like toffees."

"No. The writing pad. I just asked the nurse for a sheet of paper, and she refused. I'm going to compile a crossword."

"Yes. She does look a bit stern."

"You should see the nurse who's on nights this week. Cute."

Max looked at Ben with a here-we-go-again sort of look. They both burst out laughing. Ben got out of bed and took the toffees over to Frank.

"Want a toffee? This is my friend, Max. Max, meet Frank. Frank thinks all Germans have a lot to answer for."

"I take it you didn't tell him."

"Tell me what?" inquired Frank.

"That I'm German."

"How can you be German" You said you fought in Normandy, on our side."

"I am Jewish. I escaped Germany before the war, after the Night of Broken Glass. I hate some Germans as much as you do."

"No offence meant."

"None taken. I married an English girl. London was my home. London is my home."

Max couldn't stay for long, and it was time for him to go.

"Can't stop. On my way to a meeting. Do you want me to collect your van?"

"That would be helpful. Actually, can you settle up with the butcher, for the broken window, and I'll pay you back?"

"Of course."

"Thank you."

Ben wrote down the address of the butcher's shop in the bottom-right corner of the writing pad and tore it off.

"I'll pop in tomorrow, if I'm passing."

"Bye."

"Bye."

Ben started drawing a blank crossword. He wasn't quite sure whether the blanks were added before or after the clues, but he did know the crossword was meant to be symmetrical. Having created a grid, he inserted various words, until it was complete, apart from fourteen across. He had ended up with needing to find a nine-letter word, with the third letter an 'o', and the third from last letter a 'u'. Some tweaking might be necessary. The fun part was compiling the clues, which came easily to Ben, even though English was not his first language. He paused briefly to eat his jam sandwiches, at teatime. Jam sandwiches always reminded him of the children-train.

About two thirds of the way through the clues, Ben heard the ward door open. Looking up, he felt his heart skip a beat, as Nurse Norton arrived for her night shift. She came through the door with another nurse. They exchanged smiles with Ben. The second nurse, Nurse Clarke, came over to check the charts and replenish cups with water. Ben was disappointed it wasn't Nurse Norton, who he could see attending to paperwork at the nurses' station. He told himself to be patient.

At almost three o'clock in the morning, Ben woke. He could see Nurse Clarke's head at the nurses' station, but Nurse Norton was nowhere to be seen. Suddenly the sound of breaking glass could be heard from the utility room. Nurse Clarke rushed over to find out what had been dropped. Ben realised he was shaking. Frank was looking confused, having been startled out of deep sleep.

"It's alright, Frank. Probably, just a glass jar being dropped. You can rest easy. You're safe," Ben reassured him, getting out of bed and making his way to the utility room, without slippers.

"I'm sorry. I've woken you," apologised Nurse Norton.

The floor was spattered with clear liquid and shards of glass.

"Don't come any closer."

"Oh, yes," he replied, looking down at his feet. "Are you alright?"

"I'm fine, but Matron is going to be furious. I just smashed a bottle of ether."

"Is Matron an even sterner version of Nurse Butterworth?" inquired Ben.

Nurses Norton and Clarke burst out laughing.

"I'll go and put the kettle on and make us a cup of tea, shall I?" offered Ben.

"Thank you," responded Nurse Clarke.

"You can stick some bread under the grill as well, if you like." added Nurse Norton.

"I'll shout if I need another arm!"

Fifteen minutes later, the ether and glass had been cleaned up, and Ben found himself drinking tea and eating toast with Nurses Norton and Clarke. He would have preferred it to only have been Nurse Norton, but at least Frank had fallen back to sleep.

"Am I allowed to know your first names?"

"Ooooh. Not sure about that," laughed Nurse Norton.

"She's Gail and I'm Rosemary," Nurse Clarke contradicted her colleague.

"I'm Ben to my friends."

"Are we your friends, then?" joked Gail.

Ben wanted to pursue the relationship after he was discharged, but he didn't want Rosemary tagging along.

"When I've left, I shall have to come back and bring you a jar of marmalade or something."

"Buttered toast not good enough for you?" giggled Rosemary.

"Butterworth toast," retorted Ben.

The three of them fell about laughing.

"Stop it," pleaded Gail. "My sides hurt."

Rosemary started to choke on a crumb. Gail thumped her on the back. She drank some tea and the choking subsided.

"Do either of you do crosswords?" asked Ben, randomly.

Rosemary shook her head.

"I do," answered Gail. "Why?"

"I'm compiling a crossword and I need a nine-letter word with the third letter 'O' and the third from last letter 'U'. Until I get the word, there's no clue.

"Procedure," announced Gail, after a few moments thought.

"Wow. I'm impressed," reflected Ben. "Thank you. Would you like to do my crossword? You obviously know the answer to fourteen across."

"I'd love to do your crossword. May I take it home with me?"

Ben glowed on the inside. Not only did he have something in common with Gail, and helpfully, not with Rosemary, but he had made a connection which could be prolonged.

"I'd better go back to bed and let you get on with your work. Thank you for the tea and toast."

"Thank you for making it," responded Gail.

Ben climbed back into bed and realised he was too excited to sleep. Perhaps Max was right, with his 'here-we-go-again look'. Maybe here Ben did go again. Betty, Zobhule and now Gail.

Ben stayed in hospital for ten days. To his frustration, after Gail's third night shift, he didn't see her for four days and nights, when to his surprise, she woke him just before breakfast.

"Hello, Gail."

"Nurse Norton, when I'm on duty, if you don't mind."

Rather than feeling ticked off, Ben took her remark as an invitation to spend time with her when she was off duty.

"Am I allowed to inquire if you found my crossword a challenge, Nurse Norton?"

"I very much enjoyed it. I do like a good cryptic clue," replied Gail, as she checked Ben's notes. "I believe today is the day when they remove your plaster and take another x-ray, to see if you're on the mend. If it's healing, they'll put another plaster on and send you home. I'll check what time the porter is due."

"Thank you. What shifts are you on this time?"

"Two long days."

Ben tried not to stare at Gail as she went about her work. An idea popped into his head. Taking his pen and writing paper, he designed a simple crossword. The across clues made the words, PATIENT, INVITATION, AFTER WORK and PICTURE HOUSE. The down clues spelt BEN, NURSE NORTON, LEICESTER SQUARE, EMPIRE and TOMORROW. He had just completed it when the porter came to take him to have his plaster removed. It was something of a relief to have the old plaster cut off. Ben had been dying to scratch his arm. The x-ray showed a measure of healing, and a new cast was applied. When he returned to the ward, there were three new patients, and Gail was kept busy. To Ben's disappointment, it was the second nurse, another new face, Nurse Wilson, who came to give him his medication.

Just before Gail's shift ended, when Nurse Wilson was at the far end of the ward, Ben made a point of going over to the nurses' station.

"Tonight's crossword," he whispered, placing the folded-up paper on the desk in front of her.

"Thank you."

"I'll be discharged in the morning, so it's important to do it this evening."

He looked at her with soulful eyes.

"Alright."

"Have a good evening, Nurse Norton," he said, audibly, turning to walk away.

He went over to Frank's bed and dealt the cards for a game of cribbage.

"She's alright, that Nurse Norton."

"Yes, she is," responded Ben, hoping Frank was not his competition.

"Fifteen two, fifteen four, a pair's six, and one for His Nibs," counted Frank.

Frank won the first game, Ben the second.

"Shall we play a conqueror?" asked Ben.

"Go on, then. Deal them."

Nurses Butterworth and Clarke had arrived on shift.

"No extra cups of tea, tonight," chuckled Ben.

"I wonder what she's like when she's off duty."

"Why? Do you fancy your chances?" Ben ribbed him.

"Very funny."

Ben yawned.

"I think I'll call it a night."

"Goodnight."

"Goodnight. I meant to say, I'm getting discharged in the morning."

"Lucky you. Another three weeks of being stuck on my back. At least, then, I'll get to move about on crutches. Then I can wander over to the nurses' station at all hours of the day or night."

"I thought you were asleep."

"It's a skill of mine!" laughed Frank. "I can look like I'm asleep when I'm awake and sleep looking like I'm wide awake."

The two men burst out laughing.

"Quiet!" called Nurse Butterworth.

"Ooops," responded Frank, quietly. "Better get to bed before she decides to make you stay another week."

"Can she do that?"

"I wouldn't want to test her."

Ben returned to his bed. A few minutes later it was lights out.

He was awake, bright and early, not wanting to miss a moment of his final morning in Gail's presence, unless, of course, she accepted his invitation. She smiled briefly at him as she passed his bed, heading directly for the handover with Nurses Butterworth and Clarke. Nurse Wilson rushed onto the ward a few minutes after Gail, much to Nurse Butterworth's disapproval.

"Late, again!" she remarked.

"Sorry Nurse Butterworth. It's the buses."

Ben watched as Nurses Butterworth and Clarke left the ward and immediately jumped out of bed to cross to the nurses' station. Nurse Wilson picked up a clipboard and went to the utility room.

"How did you get on with the crossword?"

"I enjoyed completing it."

"And?"

Gail made him wait an inordinate amount of time before sliding her own piece of folded paper across the desk. He lifted the corner slightly and recognised his own crossword, now filled in, but with an additional line of vacant boxes. He smiled and returned to his bed, where he started to decipher her clue. '10 across: Mixing pure ales causes joy.' It was an anagram of 'pure ales'. Ben smiled and wrote 'PLEASU-E across the 'R' in 'NORTON'. Looking up at Gail, who had been watching him, he grinned. The breakfast trolley arrived.

After a bowl of porridge and a cup of tea, Ben packed his bag, with his good arm, and went over to Frank's bed.

"Final session of crib, before I leave?"

"Why not?"

Ben won two games and Frank one. They were just finishing up when Max appeared on the ward.

"That's me out of here. Nice meeting you. Good luck with your leg."

"Thanks. And you with your arm. Back at work soon, hopefully."

Ben extended his good arm towards Frank, who shook his hand, warmly. Max was standing by the nurses, station. A sudden surge of jealousy ripped through Ben's body. Grabbing his bag, he joined Max.

"Thank you, Nurse Wilson. Nurse Norton."

Next time, be more careful when mixing your drinks," bantered Gail.

It was a cryptic in-joke, just between them. Quick as a flash, he responded.

"Sometimes, you can't stop yourself falling."

"Goodbye, Mr Linton-House," said the nurses, in unison.

"Bye. And again, thank you."

Max nodded, and the two men left.

"Thanks for coming to fetch me. I won't be driving just yet."

"You're welcome. Cute nurse."

"Which one?"

"What do you mean, 'Which one'? Nurse Norton, of course."

"I know. I'm taking her to the cinema, tonight."

"I knew it. Here we go again," sighed Max.

"A man has to do what a man has to do."

"I really hope it works out for you, this time, my friend."

"Thank you."

Ben was spruced and waiting outside the cinema at ten minutes to eight, on tenterhooks, his arm in a clean, new sling, courtesy of Max's first aid skills. Without any idea which direction Gail would appear from, he scanned the square, back and forth, only to discover she had crept up behind him.

"Hello," she announced.

Ben nearly jumped out of his skin.

"Hello," he responded, when he had restored an element of calm. "How was the rest of your shift?"

"Frank tried to chat me up."

"You rebuffed him, of course?"

Gail laughed.

"Have you read any reviews of *The Blue Lamp*?" inquired Ben.

"No. Have you?"

"Me neither."

"We'd better go in and decide for ourselves."

They entered the American-styled theatre and Ben bought two tickets. An usherette directed them to their seats in the vast auditorium.

"Wow! What an organ," enthused Gail.

"Wurlitzer, I believe. Have you not been here before?"

"No."

"Well, I am glad to have introduced you."

They removed their coats and took their seats.

"How long have you been a nurse?"

"Eighteen months."

"What made you become a nurse?"

"I would have liked to be a doctor, but my parents had to move, just after I took my School Certificate, so I never took my Higher School Certificate. I became a nurse instead. My mother was a nurse."

"What does your father do?"

"He manages the farm on Osea Island. It's in the Blackwater Estuary."

"Isn't that Major Allnatt's island?"

"Yes."

"He's very wealthy."

"Yes, he is. What do you do?"

"I repair blinds. That's how I ended up like this," explained Ben, holding up his sling-wrapped arm. "I fell off my ladder."

Their conversation was interrupted by loud music. The lights dimmed, and images started to flicker onto the screen.

During the film, Ben considered putting his arm round Gail, but refrained, thinking it was too soon, and not wanting to frighten her off.

"That was good. Very enjoyable," reflected Ben, at the end.

"Yes, Jack Warner was really good as PC Dixon. They should make a television series."

"I think this, also. They do a good job, don't they? The police, I mean."

"Yes, they do."

Ben felt a tinge of embarrassment, remembering what Max had said about his phrase, 'I think this, also' and resolved to try and include 'as well' rather than 'also' when he agreed with people. As soon as the closing credits had finished, everyone stood for the national anthem.

"There's no rush," remarked Gail, as she put on her coat.

Ben took this as a positive sign.

"Where do you live? May I walk you home?"

"Paddington, but it's fine, honestly. I take the bus everywhere."

"May I take you out again?" asked Ben, struggling with his coat.

"Let me help you with that. One more week in plaster?"

"Probably. Then some physiotherapy."

Gail helped Ben manoeuvre the coat over his broken arm.

"I'm not buttoning it up for you," she laughed.

"Thank you."

Ben smiled, enjoying the attention and the closeness of Gail even more. He did up the top button with one hand.

"How about we go for a walk in Hyde Park, next week? I'm off on Friday and Saturday."

"Two o'clock. Let's meet at Speakers' Corner."

"Yes, let's."

"Thank you, Gail. See you next Saturday. Have a good week. Stay out of Nurse Butterworth's bad books!"

Gail laughed.

"Perhaps you can compile another crossword for me to do?"

"I'd like that."

"Bye, Ben."

"Bye."

It was too soon to kiss her, as well. Gail walked off across the square and Ben went into the tube station. As the train rumbled beneath London, he replayed their conversation in his head. Her central front tooth was quirky and her way of being easy-going. She can't have been more than about nineteen or twenty. Ben would be twenty-nine in May. Was ten years too big an age-gap? Would he tell her of his past? Of his Jewishness? What about his psoriasis? Would it disgust her? After all, she was a nurse. He started to doubt himself, but then found reassurance recalling that she had readily suggested a walk in the park, not to mention the crossword. When he arrived back at the flat, Max was still up.

"How did it go?"

"Well, I think. We're going to the park next Saturday. And she asked me to compile another crossword for her to do."

"I'm pleased for you, my friend."

"Her parents live on Osea Island."

"That's near Mersea, right?"

"Yes. They don't own it. Her father manages the farm."

"Goodnight, Ben. I only stayed up to see how things turned out."

"Thank you. Goodnight. I can't sleep. I might start on the crossword."

Ben took a pen and his writing pad and started to design a new grid. Somehow, the clues flowed more easily than they had ever done before. Was Gail his crossword muse? He had never imagined he would find a girl who was a fan of cryptic crosswords. Perhaps it was a sign that this time, things would work out. It was gone midnight, when he finally went to bed, and at half past six, when he woke up, he was itching again. The psoriasis was back.

By the time he was due to meet up with Gail at Speakers'
Corner, the flare-up had spread across both elbows,
both buttocks and both knees. It was also on his scalp,
although possibly not visible to the untrained eye. He
rubbed cream on his elbows, knees and buttocks and
washed his hair with the tar-based shampoo. Having
shaved, he splashed on Old Spice, in the hope it would mask
the smell of the tar.

"Hello. How has your week been? I've compiled another
crossword for you."

"Thank you. It's been much the same as usual. Frank is
on crutches now, so he keeps coming over to the nurses'
station. I should tell him I'm not available. I thought you
were getting the plaster removed?"

"This coming Tuesday."

"That's good news."

Ben thought Gail being unavailable to Frank might also be good news. They started walking, without any fixed destination.

"Do you have brothers and sisters?" he asked.

"Me, no. I'm an only child. What about you?"

"They were all killed in the war."

Wise or unwise, Ben had made the decision to conceal his Jewish heritage, and the debacle in Rotterdam, when he and Saul were separated.

"I'm sorry to hear that. Parents?"

"Also lost. Do your parents enjoy life on Osea Island?"

"My father gets very stressed in the run up to harvest time. It's mostly wheat and barley. My mother nags him a lot. But, yes, the surroundings are lovely. The only way on and off the island, other than by boat, of course, is a tidal causeway for a few hours a day. The salt-water plays havoc with the car chassis."

"Perhaps we can go there one day. When you're ready for them to meet me, that is."

As they neared the Serpentine, a flock of Canada geese were harassing some coots.

"I'm never sure if they are coots or moorhens," laughed Gail.

"I think that coots have white foreheads and moorhens have orange bills."

"Are you interested in birds?"

"Not really. I mean I like them. I only know the difference because I asked the same question, a few years ago."

"Winter always makes the pond look sad," observed Gail.

"Unless it freezes, and the trees are covered in frost. Then it's not quite so sad."

"I just don't enjoy winter much."

"It's a damp cold, isn't it? Goes right into your bones."

"Yes. Our flat is not very warm."

"You said 'our' flat?"

"Yes. You met Rosemary. Nurse Clarke. We share a flat."

"I share a flat with Max, my oldest school friend. He writes music. I wrote a song lyric which he put to music."

"Ooooh. What's it called?"

"*When Glass Breaks*."

Ben suddenly realised it was too close to the truth. What if she knew it or went away and looked it up, and then asked him what inspired it?

"Have you written any other lyrics?"

"None that have made it into the public arena. Have you always enjoyed cryptic crosswords?"

"I started when I was about sixteen. I picked up my father's newspaper. He hadn't attempted the crossword, so I tried it. Somehow, things just clicked into place. Have you noticed how hard it is to get into the mind of the compiler, into their thought processes, sometimes?"

"And was it hard to get inside my thought processes?"

"Not at all?"

Although the air was cold, walking round the park was making Ben feel quite warm and the sweat, under his coat, was causing the psoriasis on his buttocks to itch. He was desperately trying to avoid scratching, and every so often, he tried to ease the itching by pressing his hand against his back, but it simply wasn't as effective as a good old scratch. Gail had noticed.

"Have you hurt your back?"

"No. I seem to have developed psoriasis."

The truth allowed him to scratch.

"I thought I could pick up the unmistakable aroma of tar-based shampoo."

She was a nurse! There was no hiding anything medical from Gail.

"Yes. Elbows, knees, buttocks and scalp. I think the stress of my recent accident brought on the latest flare-up."

"And how often does it flare up?"

"Maybe three times a year."

They had reached the far end of the Serpentine and were now heading back towards their starting point.

"Would you like to go and get a cup of tea, or a drink?" asked Ben, hoping to prolong the encounter.

"That would be lovely."

"Tea or beer?"

"I quite fancy a half of Guinness."

"Pub it is, then."

"We could go to the Gloucester Arms."

"Is that your local?"

"I wouldn't say I go there all that often, but it isn't far from my flat."

"Then, we will go to the Gloucester Arms. Lead the way."

As they walked towards the exit, Ben took hold of Gail's hand and was relieved that she didn't snatch it away. He let go just before they reached the pub.

"I'll get these," insisted Gail. "At least, let me give you half a crown. You can go to the bar. I'll save you a seat."

She pulled her purse from her coat pocket and took out a coin. On entering the pub, they found it quite busy. In fact, there were no free tables.

"Do you mind standing at the bar?" inquired Ben.

"Why don't you come to my flat and we'll have a cup of tea instead."

"If you would like to?"

"Yes. Rosemary made a cake this morning."

"I'm persuaded," laughed Ben.

Walking through the door to the flat, Ben realised what Gail meant about it being cold. It wasn't until they moved from the hallway to the living room that he felt the effect of a small, portable radiator.

"Look who I bumped into," Gail joked.

Rosemary knew that Gail had gone to meet up with Ben. Afterall, it was their second date.

"I told him you had made a cake. Shall we have tea and cake?"

"I'll put the kettle on," offered Rosemary, helpfully.

"Make yourself at home," added Gail, following Rosemary into the kitchen and coming back out with some plates, cups and saucers on a tray.

Rosemary came back out, a few seconds later, bringing a cake tin and a milk jug.

"Do you take sugar?"

"Please."

She went back into the kitchen for sugar and a knife to cut the cake with. The kettle started to whistle.

"I'll go," said Gail, jumping up.

She brought a knitted-cosy-clad teapot back into the living room.

"Strainer!" burst out Gail and Rosemary, in unison.

"I'll get it," insisted Gail.

Finally, the three of them were sitting at the table drinking tea and eating cake. Ben was a little frustrated to share his time with Rosemary, but as best friends go, she seemed happy for Gail. It amused him that they probably talked about him when he wasn't there.

After Ben and Gail had been in a relationship for about six months, she suggested it was time for him to meet her parents on the island. For his part, he was curious to see Osea. July 1st was the first off-shift weekend day on Gail's rota and her next shift would be on Monday night. Ben picked her up at eight o'clock in the morning.

"Sorry it has to be my work van. You're looking lovely in that blouse, by the way."

Gail was wearing a multicoloured, floral, cotton blouse with a cotton skirt which matched the mid blue in the blouse. The seat was dusty but didn't appear to have any oil stains on it.

"Wait. I'll nip back in and get a towel."

"Alright."

Returning with an old towel, she draped it over the seat and got in.

"I'm nervous," admitted Ben, as they drove off.

"Don't be. Oh, my mother smokes in the house."

"People smoke. I smoke the occasional roll-up myself."

"I've been thinking about all the crosswords you compile for me to do. Have you thought about contacting a newspaper?"

I think London's catered for, but yes. Perhaps one day. It's just nice to compile them for you. I love that we have cryptic crosswords in common."

"Me too."

It took about two hours to reach the causeway. The tide had only just started to go out, but the seaweed-strewn, compacted shingle track was visible. Another vehicle was at the start, on the opposite side.

"There's a passing place. We can go, too."

"Thank you."

Ben drove in second gear. He could feel the tyres crunching on the shingle and losing a little bit of traction every time they drove across patches of seaweed.

"How often do your parents make this journey?"

"Two or three times a week. It depends on whether my father needs parts for the farm machinery."

They reached the passing place and pulled in to wait for the other vehicle.

"I bet the owner doesn't drive a Bentley across here," laughed Ben.

"I don't think he visits much. He seems happy to let my father handle the affairs of the farm."

The other car passed, its driver acknowledging Ben and Gail with a slight raising of his fingers from the steering wheel, and they continued on their way.

"Now just keep on this track, through what they call the village, past the tractor house, to the opposite shore. My parents live in the Captain's House."

"Village?"

"It's just a handful of houses and what they call the Old Home, which was once a sanitorium."

They reached the village.

"I see what you mean."

"Not much further. Keep going, and where the road turns sharp-left, the driveway to the Captain's House is on the right."

Ben pulled into the driveway, also shingles, and hearing them arrive, Eileen came out to greet them.

"Hello, Mummy."

Gail kissed Eileen on the cheek. Ben walked over and extended his hand.

"This is Ben."

"Hello, Ben."

Eileen shook his hand and turned to walk back inside. Gail caught Ben's eye and they followed Eileen into the hallway.

"Your father is just over at the mine-store. He'll be here shortly. I'll make us coffee."

The mine-store was actually the grain-store, having been used during the war to store munitions. The name had stuck. Keith was checking the moving parts, making sure the conveyor belt and hoppers were in good working order, ready to receive the harvest in a few weeks' time. He worked seven days a week, although on Sundays, usually only for a couple of hours. He could take time off when he needed to, around key points in the agricultural cycle, and worked hard, the rest of the time. Gail had a sneaking suspicion, though, that he chose to work seven days a week to avoid Eileen's nagging.

Whether there was much love left in the marriage, Gail was uncertain. She wasn't even sure if there had been love at the start. There had definitely been passion, because Gail had been born seven months after the wedding, and as far as she was aware, she had not been born prematurely.

"Can I do anything to help, Mummy?"

"Why don't you show Ben round the house and garden. I'll call you when the coffee is ready."

"Alright."

Gail led Ben back out of the kitchen and into the hallway.

"Living room. Dining room. Both have French windows onto the garden, but my parents don't tend to use them. There are three spare bedrooms on this floor and the bathroom. It's there if you need it."

She led Ben up the stairs. The Captain's House was a dormer bungalow, and Keith and Eileen's room looked out across the front garden to the sea.

"There's a secret room."

"A secret room?"

"Through this door."

Gail opened a small door, up a couple of wooden steps into what might have been intended as an ensuite, but had no plumbing installed. A cast-iron single bedstead half-filled the room. In the other half of the room was a chest of drawers, wardrobe and wooden chair.

"Who sleeps here?" asked Ben.

"I have no idea. I have never asked."

Gail closed the door.

"Let's go out into the garden."

They went back downstairs and out into a utility room.

"We call this the Back Room. And beyond this, is the Very Back Room, commonly known as the Very, for short."

The Very led out through the back door into the back garden. Keith grew flowers that could be cut and brought inside, like Dahlias, Chrysanthemums, Goldenrod, and Gladioli. Beyond the flower garden was a small vegetable garden. When he wasn't working on the farm, Keith would be working on his flowers and vegetables. Gail and Ben made their way round the side of the house to the front garden which was mainly laid to lawn. Crossing the lawn, Gail showed Ben the broken concrete steps down onto the beach.

"We don't use these, for obvious reasons. But over here ….," she continued, walking to the other end of the lawn, "….. over here, we have the good steps. I should have told you to bring your swimming trunks. Next time."

"I did bring them."

"Good thinking. I always keep a spare bathing suit here. Perhaps we can swim this afternoon."

"I'd like that."

Just then "Coffeeeeee!" could be heard from the kitchen window.

Ben and Gail went back inside, and as they sat down at the kitchen table, Ben felt an immediate anxiety, as he had no idea what to talk to Eileen about. He sipped at his coffee. It was bitter and there was no sugar bowl in sight.

"Help yourself to a biscuit," Eileen encouraged him.

A plate of malted milk biscuits languished in the centre of the table.

368

"Thank you," responded Ben, reaching for one of his least favourite biscuit options and dunked it in his coffee.

Immediately, the hot liquid reclaimed the squidgy bottom third, too weak and heavy to remain attached to the biscuit. Unfortunately, the demise caused a slight splash of coffee onto the white tablecloth. Eileen's expression noted the stain with silent irritation. Ben kicked himself, and to his relief, Keith appeared at the door.

"Hello, Ben. Is your arm better now?"

"Yes, thank you. Nice to meet you," responded Ben, rising from his seat.

"Goodness me, no need to stand on ceremony."

"How long until the harvest?"

"Four to six weeks depending on the weather we get between now and then. You work with your hands, don't you?"

"Yes. I repair and maintain shop blinds."

"Ben also compiles cryptic crosswords, Daddy."

"Not to earn a living though?" queried Eileen.

"Just a hobby," replied Ben.

There was a brief, uncomfortable silence, partly because Gail had already told her parents about Ben's family.

"We're thinking of going swimming after lunch," announced Gail.

"Good for you," Keith encouraged them. "I think I'll get some more lettuce sown. Do you garden, Ben?"

"I live in a flat without a garden," replied Ben, adding, "At the moment."

"Do you collect brass?" inquired Ben of Eileen. "I saw a lot of it, as Gail was showing me round your house."

"Yes. It seems like a constant round of cleaning and polishing, but yes, I like to pick up new items, if I see them when we go on holiday."

"Which is your favourite piece?" Ben pressed her, gaining confidence from her initial response.

"Possibly, the candle-snuffer. And maybe the doorknockers."

"Ah. I will have to take a closer look when we leave. I didn't notice before because the door was already open."

"Ben, I don't want to benefit from free advice, but I'd value your opinion," interjected Keith, "with you being an engineer."

"How can I help?"

"Follow me."

Keith stood up. Ben looked across at Gail, who nodded, got up and followed Keith out. When they were outside, standing in front of the garage, Keith surprised Ben.

"I don't really have a question. I just thought we were safer out here," he laughed.

"Thank you," responded to Ben. "It was already a little awkward, even before I splashed coffee on the tablecloth. Actually, now we're out here on our own, can I ask if you would be happy if I asked Gail to marry me."

"I'd be delighted. I trust my daughter's judgement."

"Thank you. As soon as I have put aside enough for the deposit on a place of our own, I will propose."

"Don't worry. It will be our secret, until then. Do you fish?" added Keith, changing the subject.

"I have done."

"Well next time you come we will have to go fishing. I've landed a good few plaice from the beach."

"That would be my pleasure."

"Good."

"Where do you get your farming supplies from? And the machinery?"

"Mostly from Chelmsford. I try to keep spares of parts which are more likely to need replacing, because of the tides. You can't just go and get something. Still, it's a small price to pay for the surroundings. That and the rust!"

"It is rather idyllic here. In a British-weather, river-estuary, kind of way."

Keith pointed at the wheel arches on his Morris Minor.

"It's less than two years old."

"Can you put something on to protect the chassis and bodywork from the sea? I have a product that I always spray on the metal parts of the blinds I work on?"

"I would have to buy an awful lot of the product and drive the car over the inspection pit two or three times a week to apply it. I think I'll just resign myself to a fast turnover of second-hand cars."

There was no questioning Keith's hard work on the farm, but one of the things Eileen nagged him about was his lack of proactivity on other fronts. The truth was, Keith was simply too exhausted to put the same energies into anything outside of work.

"I'll take you out in the motor-boat too, sometime."

"I shall look forward to it."

"Come on. Better get back to the ladies."

They both chuckled and went indoors, where Eileen was making pastry for a mince beef and onion pie, and Gail was peeling potatoes. Once the vegetables and pie were cooking, Gail and Ben retreated to the sitting room and between them, completed the crossword in last week's newspaper, which they found still stuffed in the rack. Ben answered the final clue just as lunch was being served.

Conversation was limited, but no one minded as they were hungry. Dessert was a steamed jam pudding with custard, which Ben enjoyed far more than the meat pie.

As soon as their meal had gone down, Gail and Ben got changed into their swimming things, borrowed two towels from Eileen's airing cupboard, and set off for the beach. It was quite a walk from the concrete steps to the water's edge, although the advantage of the sea so far way out was that they passed beyond the pebbly part of the beach to a strip of sand. Gail was looking at Ben's physique. She had not been called on to give him a bed-bath, at the beginning of his stay in St George's, which was perhaps a good thing. He ran straight into the sea, splashed around, and swam out about twenty-five yards, before turning and swimming back. For her part, Gail waded slowly into the water, until it was waist-height, ducked down, and swam along the shore. They enjoyed their swimming for half an hour or so, at which point Gail got out and wrapped her towel round her shoulders. Ben felt obliged to come ashore too, not wanting to leave Gail standing around waiting, and possibly, shivering.

"That was fun," he declared, towelling himself off.

"The salt-water is probably better for your psoriasis than it is for the car," laughed Gail.

Ben had a momentary panic that Gail had heard his conversation with Keith, until he remembered they had talked about the rust.

"When do we need to start back?"

"Definitely no later than four o'clock.

They walked briskly back to the house and got changed back into their regular clothes, Gail taking the opportunity for a lightning-quick bath.

"What time are you thinking of heading back?" inquired Eileen.

"By four o'clock," replied Ben.

"I'll make a pot of tea and there's a fruit cake."

"That would be lovely. Thank you. I noticed a piano in the dining room and a stereogram in the lounge. Do you play the piano?"

"Gail plays the piano. I'm afraid I don't. Do you play?"

"No. What kind of music do you listen to?"

"Musicals. And I love Paul Robeson's voice."

"I wrote a song lyric, and my friend wrote the music. It gets played around the clubs."

Ben had made an instant decision to blow his own trumpet to Eileen.

"What's it called?"

"When Glass Breaks."

"Sing me the chorus or the first verse."

Ben instantly regretted his boast because he was no singer. Nevertheless, he sang the first verse, his voice shaking.

"Not bad. What inspired the words?"

"Listening to people's stories from the war," responded Ben, concealing the truth.

Cake and tea were served in the lounge. Eileen had put on a Paul Robeson record in the background. Keith came in from planting his lettuce. The cake was particularly good.

"Delicious cake," commented Ben, on swallowing his final mouthful.

"Thank you," responded Eileen, declining to offer a second slice.

"Is this Paul Robeson?"

"It is."

Ben nodded his approval.

"Right. Time for us to go," announced Gail.

Ben made a point of noticing the doorknocker, on the way out. It was a brass lion's head.

"Very nice," he remarked.

Keith and Eileen waved them off.

"Well done. It's always awkward. I don't mean I've taken home many men. Just that my mother can be difficult."

"I'm just glad you chose to introduce me. Your father is great. He has already invited me to go out in the motor-boat and to fish from the beach."

"Oh, good."

It was half-past six when Ben dropped Gail off at her flat.

"See you next Friday evening?"

"Yes. I think it's off-duty. What about cine-variety at the Empire?"

"Good choice."

They kissed briefly. Ben had appreciated watching Gail in her swimsuit, and would have loved to be intimate with her, but this had not even been mentioned in six months. He may well have to wait until they were married.

Unusually, Gail had both Christmas Day and Boxing Day off shift, and Ben had been invited to spend Christmas on the island. It made sense for them to travel down together. Ben wondered which bedroom he would be given. It was unlikely he would be in the same room as Gail.

On the second Saturday before Christmas, he went Christmas shopping on Portobello Road. He bought a tin of shortbread for Eileen. For Keith he found a shop selling fishing tackle and purchased a nice orange and green sea-use float. Max was a man who seemed to need very little. In the end, Ben settled on a fountain pen. Having discovered Gail's favourite brand of lipstick, on one of his many visits to her bathroom, he bought a deep pink one and a brighter red one, which he would add to with some antique jewellery from the market.

Gail wore clip-on earrings, when she wasn't on duty. Ben thought some pearls might be neutrally acceptable. As he was browsing, he noticed a rather fetching ring. Genuine gold, at least the hallmark suggested as much, it contained a row of five tiny pearls and three quarter-carat rubies. It was decided, if he could afford it, he would ask Gail to marry him, on the island, at Christmas. The antique ring also happened to go beautifully with the earrings, so he would give her the earrings as a present, almost as a teaser, find a reason to go down to the beach, and propose to her there. If she refused him, he would simply drive home as soon as the tide allowed.

He needn't have worried. Early on Christmas morning, he picked Gail up from her flat and drove them to catch the start of the tide. On arriving at the Captain's House, he realised he had completely forgotten to write Christmas cards for them. No doubt, Eileen would find it irritating.

"I meant to say, don't have any breakfast," mentioned Gail, as they pulled into the drive.

"Never mind. I'm sure I'll have room."

"We always have grapefruit followed by scrambled eggs, on Christmas morning. That way, it soaks up the sherry that accompanies the opening of presents."

They didn't knock. Eileen was in the kitchen, flustered, stuffing the turkey. Keith was in the Very, sharpening the carving knife. There was no need to sharpen the knife in the Very, but it was safer than remaining in the kitchen whilst Eileen was stressed.

"Happy Christmas!"

Eileen was wearing a full-length apron, which although clean when she had put it on, was now smeared with grease and breadcrumbs.

"Happy Christmas. I'll hug you shortly, as soon as the turkey is in the oven."

"Can I do anything to help?" inquired Gail.

"Perhaps if you opened the tinned grapefruit and put it into bowls, that would give me time to sort the turkey. We'll have breakfast in here. As soon as I've cleared the table, we can lay it."

By now Keith had appeared with the freshly sharpened carving knife.

"Happy Christmas."

"Happy Christmas," replied Ben and Gail, in unison.

He placed the carving knife in its case, gave Gail a hug and shook Ben's hand. Eileen removed one of the shelves in the oven and positioned the turkey on the remaining shelf. Having wiped the table, she removed her poultry-stained apron and replaced it with a clean one. As soon as she had made the scrambled eggs and toast, she switched on the oven. Four hours ought to do it. Eileen served the scrambled eggs on toast and wolfed down her own grapefruit, playing catch-up with the scrambled eggs on toast.

"We'll do the washing up," insisted Gail.

She washed and Ben dried, whilst Eileen went into the dining room to switch on the Christmas tree lights and pour sherry. The tree was always a six-foot one, and you could bet your bottom dollar that the lights would fail at least twice during the twelve days of the season. It was always set up in the dining room, rather than the sitting room, because the floor was wood, and the tree always shed its needles everywhere. Ben, Keith and Gail joined Eileen around the tree and the gift distribution began.

Gail had bought her mother an LP of the soundtrack to *Annie Get Your Gun* and had knitted a pair of gloves for her father. Both voiced their heartfelt appreciation. Feeling slightly nervous, Ben handed Keith and Eileen their gifts. He hardly knew them, so it was hard to buy something personal. As luck would have it, shortbread was Eileen's favourite, and her face broke into a rare smile. Keith absolutely loved his fishing float. They had bought a bottle of whiskey for Ben. It was time for Gail and Ben to exchange gifts. Gail had been busy with her knitting because she gave Ben a hand-made scarf, which he loved. She was happy with the lipstick and immediately swapped the pearl earrings for the ones she had been wearing. Finally, Gail unwrapped her present from Eileen and Keith. It was an electric hand mixer. Beyond excited, she jumped up and gave each of them a hug. Eileen gathered up all the wrapping paper and flattened it to form a pile. She would recycle what was worth keeping for next year. Ben couldn't help noticing that Keith and Eileen didn't exchange gifts. Perhaps things were a little squeezed, financially?

"Shall we go for a Christmas morning walk on the beach," Ben suggested to Gail.

"Yes. Let's."

They put on their coats and Ben wrapped his new scarf round his neck.

"We won't be long," Gail reassured Eileen.

Crossing the lawn, they went down the concrete steps and walked along the line of dried seaweed marking high tide, in the direction of the pier. Glancing around, Ben couldn't see anyone else, so he knelt on his non-shrapnel-wounded knee.

"Gail Norton, will you marry me?"

Although she had hoped for a while that he might ask, nothing had quite prepared her for the shock of him actually asking. For a second or two she looked at him in stunned silence. A loan seagull squawked overhead, enough to draw her out of her shock.

"Yes, of course I will"

"That's a relief. You had me worried there."

"I'm sorry. It came as a huge surprise."

Ben fumbled in his coat pocket and brought out the ring.

"You'd better have this, then."

"Oh, my goodness! It's lovely. And it goes with the earrings."

"I hope it fits," he pondered, pushing it onto her finger.

It was a little tight, but then they had been walking and plenty of blood was circulating in her fingers.

"I can always get it enlarged."

"Come on. Time to go back and break the news to your parents."

They walked back, Ben holding her right hand, and Gail continually holding up her left hand to survey the ring.

"Guess what," announced Gail, once they were back in the warm.

Eileen stared at them.

"Do I get a clue?"

Gail held up her hand to show Eileen the ring, whose reaction was polite support. Keith had gone up to the Village to give the regular farmworkers each a bottle of sherry and entered the kitchen about three minutes after Gail and Ben.

"Look!"

"Oh my! Congratulations," enthused Keith. "We'll have to have another glass of sherry to celebrate."

The wedding was planned for 19th July. A distinctly quiet
event, only Keith, Eileen, Rosemary as Maid of Honour and
Max as Best Man attended the service. Ben was quite glad
for the lack of trappings and guests. His psoriasis was
starting to flare up again and he just wanted to get the
honeymoon underway. He and Gail had planned three days
in a quaint little hotel in the Cotswolds, in Boughton-on-the-
Water, a stone's throw from the village that Gail had been
evacuated to for nine months during the Blitz. She wanted to
visit, for nostalgia's sake, which caused Ben some anxiety.
He had no desire to talk about his wartime experiences, and
reciprocal probing questions were bound to come up, if he
asked Gail about hers. Apart from anything else, he had
chosen to conceal from his wife, a huge chunk of his past
life, of who he was. He had already had to fabricate his
provenance, stating that his father was Claude Edgar Linton-
House, surgeon deceased. The lie would be forever recorded

in the marriage certificate, but it was unlikely that anyone would bother to check.

Ten days prior to his wedding, Ben had moved out of the flat he shared with Max, to a flat in Upper Norwood. Ben was confident he would find new customers in the area. As a married nurse, Gail would have to leave the profession, so being on the doorstep of the hospital no longer mattered. He had done his best to make the flat welcoming. There was one bedroom, into which Ben and Max had man-handled a metal-framed double bed. Max had paid Ben what they agreed was a fair price for the furniture in their flat in Ladbroke Grove and Ben had used the proceeds to furnish, albeit sparsely, his new marital home. Gail could add her quirkiness once they had settled in together.

The train was due to leave Paddington at two in the afternoon, which left barely two hours after the service, to sign the register, have photographs taken, read the telegrams, drink a toast and cut the cake, before rushing to the train station. Ben had booked the church hall for a simplified wedding breakfast, provided by some of Max's music connections, for which Max insisted on paying.

If the register had proved tricky, negotiating the telegrams was fraught. Peter and Joan, who were now living in Radlett, repeated Ben's cricket greeting from the bachelor party.

"But you don't play cricket?" observed Gail, a little confused.

"Just an in joke."

Gail smiled, happy with his response.

"Maybe we should meet up with them, we we come back from our honeymoon," she suggested.

"Maybe."

Ben knew he couldn't avoid such a logical social occasion forever and resolved to contact Peter, asking him to keep the Jewish heritage and wartime experiences out of any conversation. They could talk about working at the mine in South Africa, but nothing else about his past.

Max had also insisted that the short journey to the terminus would be in the Jaguar he had borrowed from a friend. Ben appreciated the effort his best friend had put into what they both knew was Ben's second wedding. Max had tied some empty tin cans to the rear bumper. The friend had requested that nothing be stuck or tied to the bodywork, but Max felt there was no harm in a few pieces of metal attached to the bumper by three-foot lengths of string. Once the cake was cut, Mr and Mrs Linton-House left the church hall under a shower of confetti and climbed into the rear seat of the borrowed Jaguar. As Max drove away, the tin cans made a terrible racket, so as soon as they were round the corner and out of sight from the waving loved ones, Max stopped, jumped out and untied the strings. Spotting a dustbin a few paces along the pavement, he unceremoniously dumped the tin cans, and continued chauffeuring Ben and Gail to Paddington Station. Their suitcases were already in the boot, courtesy of Max and Rosemary's foresight.

As the train trundled through the Oxfordshire countryside, Ben struggled to keep his mind from drifting into memories of his wedding to Betty. Neither could he avoid a sharp pang of regret that Saul had missed both his weddings. Was Saul married now? When they reached Moreton-in-Marsh they had to alight and catch a bus to Boughton-on-the-Water. As Gail had worn a blue and white matching floral skirt and blouse, there had been no need to get changed, and apart from the remnants of some confetti in her hair, it was not obvious that they were on honeymoon.

"Oooooh," exclaimed the hotel proprietor. "If I had known you was honeymooners, I'd have put flowers in your room."

"It's absolutely fine. We're just glad to have arrived safely," responded Gail.

"Breakfast is at eight o'clock, not that you two lovebirds will be up, I shouldn't imagine."

She handed them a key, attached to a wooden fob.

"Room six, at the end of the landing on the first floor."

"Thank you," replied Ben, taking the key.

Gail and Ben went up to their room. They were hardly across the threshold when each let out the laughter they had been holding back. Once their mirth had subsided, Gail's stomach began to rumble.

"Oh dear. Are you hungry?"

"Well, I haven't eaten much all day. I was too nervous for breakfast and only had a small portion of pork pie and some salad in the church hall. We never got to eat any of the cake, either."

"Do you want to ask the proprietor if there is something to eat?"

"Could we? It's a long time until breakfast."

Ben was attracted to Gail, but he didn't feel the same passion he had felt for Betty or Zobhule, so a delay before their nuptials hardly caused frustration.

"Yes. Let's go and ask."

They went back down to the reception where the proprietor was surprised to see them.

"Is the room not to your liking? Or the mattress lumpy?"

"We are both hungry. Is it possible to eat here?" inquired Ben

"I could make you a bacon sandwich."

"That would be just perfect," responded Gail.

"Come through to the dining room and sit yourselves down."

They followed the proprietor into a small dining room, with six tables, all neatly laid, ready for breakfast.

"There you are. Can I get you something to drink? There's some nice homemade ginger beer in the pantry or I can make you a cup of tea."

"The ginger beer sounds exciting," enthused Gail.

"Yes, I'll have ginger beer too," added Ben.

The proprietor disappeared through a door into the kitchen and returned a couple of minutes later with a bottle and two glasses. Releasing the metal clasp, she unstopped the bottle and just caught the fizzing overspill in one of the glasses, before it flowed down the side of the bottle onto the clean tablecloth. After filling both their glasses, she went back into the kitchen to cook some bacon.

"It's a good few years since I've been to Boughton-on-the-Water," reflected Gail.

"Do you remember much of it?"

"Not really. I remember cycling down a hill. Lower Slaughter was the village. I wonder if Mr and Mrs Jones are still there."

"Is that who you stayed with?"

"Yes."

"It can't be more than a couple of miles away. Why don't we walk there tomorrow? I'm sure the proprietor will pack us up a picnic. Us being honeymooners," added Ben, winking at Gail.

"Stop it!" whispered Gail. "She's probably listening."

The unmistakable aroma of bacon frying wafted into the dining room. Gail breathed in deeply.

"Mmmmmmm."

The proprietor reappeared in the dining room carrying two plates, each bearing doorstep-sized white-bread sandwiches.

"I didn't know if you wanted any brown sauce?"

"No thank you," answered Gail.

"Yes please," replied Ben. "I promise I won't spill it on the tablecloth."

The proprietor looked at him in a way that suggested she knew he was reading her thoughts.

"I'll go and get you some."

"Don't wait for me," insisted Ben, mainly because if Gail was eating, there was no chance of her asking where he was during the war.

"Ginger beer is a good accompaniment to bacon, I think," commented Gail, halfway through her sandwich, as she reached for her glass.

"It is very good."

"Do you think she might give me the recipe?"

"You can ask?"

"I'll ask before we leave, but not tonight."

"That did the trick," reflected Ben as he stood up.

"Yes. No more rumbling stomach."

On hearing them moving their chairs, the proprietor returned.

"Thank you for taking the trouble," said Gail, appreciatively.

"You're welcome. You need your strength."

The bathroom was shared, but helpfully, was the door next to Gail and Ben's room. Gail grabbed her spongebag and towel and went back out to freshen up and use the facilities. Rosemary had once told her of her experiences with a boyfriend, and Gail, who was still a virgin, was nervous about her wedding night. While Ben was using the bathroom, she got changed into a nightdress and climbed into the bed to wait for him.

"Well Mrs Linton-House," he smiled, as he closed the door.

He climbed into the bed beside her. They kissed.

"I don't think we need this, do you," he laughed, pulling her nightdress off over her head and caressing her chest.

As he moved on top of her, she put her arms round him, and sliding her hands down his back to his buttocks, flinched involuntarily. His psoriasis was obvious to her touch.

"It's alright. It just took me by surprise," explained Gail, trying to reassure him.

She pulled him towards her. The consummation of their marriage was unspectacular. Pleasurable for Gail, given that she hadn't really known what to expect, but without the rush of tingling which Rosemary had described.

They slept in until eight o'clock and took it in turns to use the bathroom. Downstairs, they discovered that breakfast was porridge or toast and marmalade, but not both.

"Toast, I think," said Gail.

"Agreed."

"Is there any possibility that we could have our lunch as sandwiches, to take on a picnic?" inquired Ben, hopefully, when the proprietor came over to their table.

"It will be my pleasure, you being honeymooners," responded the proprietor, checking them over for signs that they had enjoyed each other, the previous evening.

It was just after nine when they left for their walk, with Ben sporting the small canvas knapsack in which the proprietor had packed their picnic. It took them about three quarters of an hour to arrive in the village.

"I think the house was the other end," suggested Gail.

They continued up the road until Gail stopped in front of a gate.

"I'm certain this is it."

"Are you sure you want to knock on the door?"

"Yes. Very sure."

Gail opened the gate and approached the faded green door, pulling on the doorbell, and sensing the butterflies congregating in her stomach. Ben stood a couple of paces behind her. A curtain twitched. Gail could hear someone coming.

"Good morning. Can I help you?" asked a neatly dressed, petite lady, possibly in her sixties, peeping out through the half-opened door.

"I was wondering if Mr and Mrs Jones still lived here."

"I'm sorry, my dear. I've been living here for about six years, now."

"Sorry to have troubled you?"

"No trouble. Wait! Are you that little girl that stayed here during the war?"

"Yes," replied Gail, her disappointment giving way to a sense of curious affirmation.

"I thought as much. I used to help deliver prescriptions for the doctor. Wasn't there another little girl in the village?

German Jew. One of the children who came over on the boats?"

"Yes. Sometimes we played together. Her name was Ruth, I believe. She was evacuated from London."

Ben strained to hold back his excitement at the news that, somehow, Ruth might still have been alive, and marvelled at the coincidence. However, she was part of his complicated past, and he had resolved to keep that part of his life secret.

"I think Mr and Mrs Jones moved to Cheltenham, but I'm not sure."

"Thank you," responded Gail.

She and Ben left, closing the gate behind them.

"Good luck," called the woman.

"Have you done everything you wanted to? I'm sorry Mr and Mrs Jones don't live here anymore."

"There was a huge copper beech tree in a field near here that I used to climb. Maybe we could find it and have our picnic underneath."

"Which direction?"

"That way, I think," replied Gail, pointing back along the road. "Across a field. We used to hurdle the five-bar gate."

"Well, let's see if we can find the field and the gate."

"I'm probably not going to hurdle the gate," giggled Gail.

They did find the gate, and the copper beech tree across the field, although it was two fields, and the second one had cows grazing. The sun was beating down, and Ben and Gail were glad of the shade. Thankfully, the cows were enjoying the shade in another corner, and didn't seem interested in their latest guests. As Gail unpacked their picnic, Ben remembered his first time with Zobhule, under the marula tree. He wondered if Gail was open to making love under a tree. The picnic was an unexciting collection of cheese sandwiches and fruit cake, but at least the proprietor had provided a bottle of ginger beer. Unfortunately, the ginger beer had been jiggling up and down in the knapsack as they walked, and when Ben released the stopper, half the contents of the bottle erupted out of the top like Vesuvius and rained down on the neatly laid out picnic. A brief pause and both Ben and Gail burst out laughing.

"Soggy sandwiches it is, then," remarked Gail.

"I think the ginger beer goes well with the cheese," laughed Ben, after taking a bite.

"I hope the tablecloth doesn't stain."

When the debris of their picnic had been consumed, Ben shuffled towards Gail, on his bottom. Gazing into her eyes, he started to undo the buttons on her blouse. To his relief, she didn't resist.

"Let's go round to the other side of the trunk. I'm pretty sure no one can see us. After all, we are in the second field from the road, and there's a hedge in between. I'm sure the cows won't mind. We can lie on my jumper."

He took Gail's hand and led her to the other side of the tree where he pulled her into his arms and started kissing her. When she was in her bra and knickers, he started caressing her body and to her own surprise, she began to relax. This time the event was not a complete unknown to her, and she was not as nervous as on her wedding night. Also, now that Ben had seen her naked, she was less self-conscious and more passionate. For his part, Ben took more time to satisfy her needs, and Gail's experience was much more like Rosemary had described. In the heat of the moment, they hadn't noticed their bovine audience approaching, and sat up to find a semi-circle of curious Friesians watching them.

"Just stay calm. I don't think they will hurt us."

Reaching slowly for their clothes, Ben handed Gail's to her. Once they had their clothes on, the cows seem to lose interest, and one by one, they turned and wandered off.

"Time to wander back to Boughton-on-the-Water," declared Gail, taking hold of Ben's hand.

Back at the hotel, the proprietor didn't seem unduly upset by the ginger beer accident. Tired out from their walk, both Gail and Ben decided to attempt a nap, with the intention of going for a drink in the evening. Ben was soon snoring, but Gail lay awake, replaying her wartime memories and wondering what had become of Ruth. She also found herself pondering why Ben was circumcised. Was he Jewish or had he simply undergone a medical procedure? She just wasn't sure if it was appropriate to ask.

The evening meal was a lamb stew with dumplings, followed by trifle. This time, another, somewhat older couple were present, sitting at the opposite side of the dining room. The two couples acknowledged each other, but conversation was avoided. Ben and Gail finished their meal and left to find a local pub.

Just as they were emptying their first glass of beer, the couple from the hotel walked in. The only empty chairs were at Ben and Gail's table.

"Would you mind, terribly?"

"Be our guest," replied Gail.

It was hard not to engage in conversation with them, and even harder to continue their own.

"How long are you staying in the village?" inquired Ben.

"Just tonight and tomorrow," replied the man. "Jeremy and Yvonne, by the way."

"Gail and Ben," replied Gail, noticing that Yvonne was not wearing a wedding ring. "We're on our honeymoon."

"Oh, I do apologise. If we had known we would have given you more space," apologized Yvonne.

"It's quite alright," responded Gail. "Anyway, where would you have sat? Are you on holiday?"

Jeremy and Yvonne's faces coloured with embarrassment.

"Just a weekend away," answered Yvonne.

"Do you come here often?" asked Ben, feeling naughty, having sensed Jeremey and Yvonne might be sharing an extra-marital liaison.

"About once a month, if we're lucky," Jeremy played along, sensing Ben had rumbled them. "Can we buy you a drink, to celebrate?"

"Thank you," replied Ben.

"Another half of bitter?"

"Yes. Thank you."

Jeremy went to the bar and returned with four halves of bitter.

"What do you do, when you're not on honeymoon?" inquired Jeremy.

"I repair blinds and Gail was a nurse, but had to give up, now we're married. What about you?"

"I edit a local newspaper and Yvonne is our receptionist."

There was no reason for an editor not to be married to the receptionist, especially if it was a small family business, but Jeremy appeared to have acknowledged their affair.

"Ben compiles really rather brilliant cryptic crosswords," announced Gail. "Does your newspaper have a crossword?"

"No, it doesn't, but I can quite see how it might be good for business. Why don't I give you the address of the newspaper? You can send me a sample, for which I'll send you a cheque. If the customers like it, we'll set up an arrangement. How does that sound?"

"It sounds perfect. Thank you," responded Ben.

Jeremy raised his glass.

"To honeymoons and crosswords!"

The others joined in the toast.

When all but Gail's glass was empty, Ben offered to buy the next round.

"Our shout."

"No, thank you. We're heading off, now," Jeremy replied, scribbling the newspaper's address on the back of an old shopping list that was languishing in his pocket. "Don't forget. Send me one of your crosswords."

"Thank you," responded Ben, taking the piece of torn-off paper.

"Bye," said Jeremy and Yvonne, in unison.

"Bye."

"Drive safely," added Gail. "Bye."

Jeremy and Yvonne left. The pub had quietened down a little, and other tables were now available.

"Would you like another drink?" asked Ben.

"No. Let's go back to the hotel. I'm tired. Probably from all the excitement and nervous energy of the last few days."

Ben took their four glasses and placed them on the end of the bar. The bartender acknowledged him with a nod of the head and picked up the glasses in one hand with three fingers and a thumb. Unfortunately, his grip failed him and two of the glasses fell to the floor. Lightning reactions allowed him to save the two between index finger and thumb. Ben was halfway across the bar when the glasses reached the stone floor, and shattered. He froze. Gail noticed. Certain he would talk about it, in his own time, Gail simply picked up both their coats from the backs of the chairs and approached him.

"It's alright. Here's your coat."

Almost mechanically, Ben put his arms in the sleeves, whilst images of Normandy flashed through his mind. Gail took his hand and towed him to the door. Once outside, although remaining taciturn, he changed hands and walked alongside Gail, back to the hotel.

"I know you don't want to talk about it, but did the breaking glasses bring up your experiences during the war."

Ben nodded.

"Let's try and get some sleep," advised Gail, adding, "I probably, won't need much encouragement."

A few minutes later they were both under the covers, where they kissed but didn't make love. Gail was asleep within minutes. Ben lay staring at the ceiling, his head replaying the traumas of the Night of Broken Glass, of Normandy, of the car crash in Kimberley. Eventually, he drifted off to sleep. When he woke up, his entire back, knees, elbows, sides and scalp had flared up with the psoriasis. Gail watched him getting dressed.

"Can we go home today, please," he pleaded. "I know it's our honeymoon. I'm so sorry."

"You can't help it. Your body is reacting to what's going on in your thoughts. Yes. We can go home today."

"We'll pay the proprietor for the three nights we booked. We'll just tell her that I'm ill. She'll understand."

"She'll probably think we honeymooners have had a fight," observed Gail, trying to lighten the mood.

Ben smiled.

"Did you bring any of your ointment?"

"Yes. There's a jar in my bag."

"Would you like me to help you with your back."

"That's very kind of you. Thank you."

After Gail had applied ointment to the parts of Ben's back that he was unable to reach, he completed the task. There was no way of stopping it from scaling and being shed, but the ointment helped prevent the skin from cracking.

Downstairs in the reception, the proprietor was surprised to see them appear with their bags.

"I thought you were staying three nights. You haven't even had breakfast, this morning."

"We were going to stay three nights. I'm sorry, but I am not well. We will pay you for all three nights. I think the early bus to Moreton-in-Marsh leaves in half an hour."

"I hope it wasn't the food."

"No. It wasn't the food."

Ben counted out the money owed and handed it to the proprietor.

"I don't suppose you could scribble down the ginger beer recipe for me?" inquired Gail, hopefully.

Being paid for the extra night caused the proprietor to feel an element of empathy with Gail.

"I can do better than that. I'll give you a small bottle. You need a plant to get each batch going."

Gail looked slightly bemused.

"It contains live yeast. That's what gives it the fizz. If you add a small amount of the matured batch to the ingredients of the next batch it gets the process started."

Gail smiled, and the proprietor went off to the kitchen. She came back three minutes later with a piece of paper and a small bottle of ginger beer.

"There's the recipe. Now, when you get back home, don't open the bottle until it's had a chance to settle. Otherwise, it'll explode over you again."

All three of them laughed.

"Thank you," said Gail.

"Have a good journey. If it's a girl, you can call her Muriel, after me."

"Muriel. That's a nice name," responded Gail graciously, hoping it would be a while before she fell pregnant. "Goodbye Muriel."

"Goodbye, Mr and Mrs Linton-House."

"Bye."

Ben picked up both their bags, so Gail opened the door for them, and they walked the short distance to the bus stop. They were back in Upper Norwood by four o'clock, where Ben made the traditional, chivalrous gesture of carrying Gail over the threshold into their new marital home. Disappointingly, due to the flare-up, it would be three months before they made love again.

SHATTERED

In June of 1961, after years of disappointment, and one heart-breaking miscarriage at four months, two years previously, Gail finally gave birth to a healthy baby boy. They named him Owen. Their attempts at starting a family had been hindered by Gail's gynaecological challenges and Ben's psoriasis, which by now, spread across ninety percent of his skin, every three to four months. He could hardly expect Gail to make love when he was in that condition. The psoriasis was so bad, he had two lengthy stays in hospital, although there was very little they could do after the debacle with the sun lamp. His blind-repair business had folded, as customers were left disappointed by his inability to work during the flare-ups. Ben and Gail had been surviving on the income from his crosswords, which now featured in two local newspapers, including Jeremy's, and his war pension. Gail had managed to secure some part time clerical work at the British Consulate but had to leave when Owen was due.

The family income was topped up by social security payments, due to Ben's illness, and twenty months after the gift of Owen, along came Helen, with her brandy-glass jawline and cute brown eyes. Ben and Gail always tried to be considerate of their neighbours, and no one had ever complained about Owen, but when Helen had just turned six months, the landlord informed them of complaints about babies crying in the night and screaming during the day. Helen could only recall one episode of toothache with Owen, and another of colic with Helen. Ben protested, convinced the complaint was more about his unemployed status, his broken-down van parked outside, or his appearance during a psoriasis flare-up, but their landlord was adamant, and they were given three months to find somewhere else to live.

Looking back on his life, Ben reflected that he had benefited from a number of seemingly lucky interventions and finding Moat Cottage was no exception. Jeremy had sent word, with his latest cheque, that a colleague in Chatham might be interested in Ben's crosswords. Two weeks after notice to leave the flat, Ben travelled to meet the editor, and while waiting at the train station, to return home, he was browsing a discarded copy of the Kent Messenger. His appointment with the Chatham editor was fruitless, although a gesture of paying his expenses was made. Out of curiosity, Ben started to scan the classifieds, where he came upon an advert for a two-bedroomed cottage to let, in a village near Maidstone. Most importantly, the wording stated that a family would be welcome. Ben made an instant decision to take a train to Maidstone from Chatham, to telephone the landlord, and visit the property, immediately, if possible. To his horror, once he arrived in Maidstone and called the landlord, he discovered that Collier Street was still a bus ride away, and the service was only hourly. The landlord, realising Ben was utilising public transport had factored in the journey time, but Ben was worried about getting home for the night. Although desperate to provide for his family, he located the bus station and travelled to the village to meet the landlord at Moat Cottage.

The first thing Ben noticed, from the road, was an Anderson shelter in the garden. Thoughts of his return to London and the house he and Betty started their marriage in came flooding back to him.

Frederick Sawyer was a tall, gangly farmer, with a strange lump on his wrist. He was checking the size of the apples in the adjacent orchard and saw Ben enter the front gate. As the father of two under-fives himself, Frederick was delighted to offer Ben and Gail the tenancy. He even offered to drive Ben back to Maidstone, where he reassured him, it was just as easy to get a train from Maidstone as from Chatham.

When Ben arrived back at the flat, after nine o'clock, Gail was worried sick.

"Where on earth have you been?"

"Well, I didn't get a new crossword contract, but I've found us somewhere to live."

"Really?"

"How would you like to bring our children up in a village, surrounded by apple orchards?"

Gail looked bemused.

"I saw an advert in a newspaper, when I was at the station in Chatham, ready to come home. It stated that families were welcome, so what could I do other than go and see it. I took the train to Maidstone, telephoned the landlord, and then caught a bus to the village. The landlord is a farmer, with two children of similar ages to Owen and Helen. We can move in next week if we want to. No deposit needed."

Gail's eyes welled up with tears of relief.

"Perhaps at the end of the month. If we could get your van fixed, we would be able to move our stuff."

"A new gear box isn't cheap."

"Perhaps you could find one in a scrapyard. As long as we can do two or three trips between here and Maidstone. It doesn't matter if it dies after that."

"I'll search for one tomorrow and see what it costs."

The following day, Ben visited three scrap dealers, and to his surprise, the third one seemed keen to exchange Ben's van, for an Escort van that had just come in, even with the broken gear box.

"It's simple economics, mate. I can make twice as much money doing yours up and selling it. You need me and I need you. In fact, I'll tell you what we'll do. We'll hook this one to the truck, and you can ride with me. When we get to yours, we'll swap them over."

"Can I have a look and have a quick drive? I just need it to move house, about thirty-five miles away."

"Alright," agreed the scrap dealer, grabbing the keys from the counter. "Take us round the block."

Ben reversed the van out of its parking spot, with the scrap dealer in the passenger seat, and drove a mile up the road before taking three right turns and a left and returning along the same road. Although Ben had noticed a fair bit of rust on the dark-green bodywork, there was nothing to indicate it was about to break down. Nevertheless, Ben was still a little suspicious, but the scrap dealer was right in his observation. Ben needed him. He was in no position to do up his own van.

"Seriously. This is a rust-bucket, but the engine's good."

"It's a deal," declared Ben.

"Well, it's almost a deal. I do still need to see your van. But yes, I think we're onto something here."

The scrap dealer hoisted up the front of the Escort van with the hook of his pick-up truck, Ben got in, and they drove back across to Upper Norwood.

"She's in good condition, to look at. A bit dusty. How long has she been like this?"

"Just over a year."

"I bet the neighbours will be pleased to see the back of her. Just the gear box, you say."

"As far as I know."

"You've got yourself a deal, then," announced the scrap dealer, holding out his hand.

"Deal," responded Ben, shaking his hand.

The scrap dealer lowered the Escort van to the ground and released the hook, while Ben went up to the flat to find the key and logbook. When he arrived back on the street, the scrap dealer was just reversing the pick-up truck up to his van.

"There you are."

"Thanking you. And here's the key and paperwork for the Escort."

Ben stood watching as the pickup drove off.

"We have a new van?" he announced, going back up to the flat.

"What do you mean, we have a new van? How can we afford a new van?"

"We can't. The scrap dealer had just taken possession of an Escort van and could see that once he does up my van, he can make a load of money from it. Far more than he'd get for the Escort van, which has really rusty bodywork. He suggested we swap. It's not like we need it for more than moving house and visiting your parents, and I'm sure they understand our situation and would come and fetch you and bring you home again, if needed."

"Owen. Helen. Do you want to come and see daddy's new van?"

Helen was still a babe-in-arms, so had no choice in the matter, but Owen understood what a van was. His eyes lit up. Ben scooped him up and the four of them went down to see the Escort van.

"We'll work out how to transport the children. I think most of our furniture can be unscrewed and piled up. Maybe three trips should do it."

"I'm just so relieved. Now you've found a van, maybe we should just call Mr Sawyer and move."

"Yes. I will go and telephone him now."

A few days later, Ben drove Gail and the children to Collier Street. Lisa Sawyer was there waiting for them. She had put fresh cut flowers in a vase on the window ledge and baked a cake.

"Hello. I'm Lisa. I'm so glad you are able to move here. Why don't you come and spend the day with us while Ben moves your belongings? It's ridiculous trying to entertain two young children, until your furniture arrives. And, please, it's Lisa and Frederick."

"Thank you," responded Ben. "We thought it was safer to move the children before having the door open all the time and shifting heavy objects. Your kind offer makes it so much easier."

"Yes. Thank you so much," added Gail.

"We live a quarter of a mile along the road. We can walk. What are your children's names?"

"This is Helen and that's Owen."

"Shall I hold Owen's hand? I think someone is going to be very excited to play with you. We have a four-year-old and one who is almost two."

"See you later," said Ben, getting back into the van.

"Bye."

"Is the cottage not needed for a farm worker?" inquired Gail, as they walked along the road.

"We have a worker who lives over the road from you and another who lives next door to you. With Frederick doing much of the work himself, there is no need. It's been empty for a year. We're glad to have someone living there, finally. You'll have to let us know immediately, if there are any problems with the gas cooker, the chimney, or the hot-water cylinder. Obviously, moving forward those things will be your responsibility to maintain, but we want to make sure the place is in good working order at the start. The electricity is on a metre. It'll be wonderful for Owen and Helen to grow up around the farm, although Frederick will give you a list of the places which are completely out of bounds. Only for safety's sake."

At just shy of two and a half, walking was slow-going with Owen. Lisa stooped down and scooped him up into her arms. As they continued along the verge, he started to play with her hair. Soon, they reached the farmhouse, where Lisa lowered him to the ground and opened the door. Two young children came tearing into the hallway, followed by Frederick, who had been catching up on some paperwork, in his office.

"Hello. I'm Frederick. Has Ben gone off to get your furniture?"

"Yes. Hello. I'm Gail, which of course, you already know, and this is Owen and Helen."

"Well, I'm very pleased to meet you in person. Has my wife told you to let us know if the hot-water cylinder and gas cooker are still working properly?"

"And the chimney not smoking," added Lisa.

"Let's go into the sitting room, where the children can play, and I'll make a cup of tea," suggested Lisa.

"I'll make the tea," offered Frederick.

"Thank you, darling," responded Lisa.

She showed Gail, Owen and Helen into the sitting room, where Gail sat Helen on the floor by her feet, with her back propped up against the settee, and Owen toddled over to investigate Malcolm's box of Matchbox cars.

"Please share nicely, Malcolm," advised Lisa, as she sat Amy on the floor, placing a collection of wooden bricks in front of her.

Frederick brought in a teapot and went back out to fetch the cups and saucers.

"Do excuse me, whilst I go back to my desk."

"Of course," responded Gail. "Lovely to meet you."

Gail and Lisa chatted about babies and children and how they had met their husbands, whilst the children played nicely. Helen needed feeding.

"Please, be my guest," Lisa reassured Gail. "I'll just pop and tell Frederick not to come in for a bit."

When she returned, Lisa sat on the floor next to Amy and coupled up a little wooden train, with engine and three carriages.

"Frederick made it. He's good with wood."

"And Ben!" responded Gail, laughing. "He has made a wooden farm for you know who for you know when."

There were only two weeks until Christmas.

"There are some lovely walks to go on around here, along the lanes. There are some lovely walks across the fields, too, but not so easy with a pushchair."

"Yes. I'm looking forward to exploring."

"And when Owen starts school, it's the other end of the orchard from you."

"I'm not sure I've thought that far ahead," smiled Gail.

"It creeps up on you, believe me," laughed Lisa.

Helen had finished feeding and Gail was burping her on her lap.

"I'm going to go and prepare lunch. Please make yourself at home. I'll pop Amy in her high-chair and Malcolm will do some colouring at the kitchen table. Is there anything you don't eat? It's just sandwiches. I've made you a cottage pie for later, but I wasn't sure how soon you would have a fridge, so I've kept it in ours."

"You are so very kind. I think we eat all the regular sandwich fillings, thank you."

Whilst Lisa made sandwiches, Gail lulled Helen to sleep on the settee. It wasn't until Lisa called them into the kitchen that Gail realised Owen was without his highchair.

"Owen would normally be in a high-chair, too."

"No matter. You can either eat your lunch in the sitting room, or you can surround Helen with cushions and sit at the table with Owen on your lap."

Gail positioned the cushions alongside Helen. She would no doubt wake up and cry before she manoeuvred herself into a position where she could fall off. The sandwiches were a choice of cheese and chutney or ham, cut into quarters, diagonally.

"I added the chutney without thinking, but I didn't put mustard on the ham," apologised Lisa.

"Did you make the chutney?" inquired Gail.

"I did," smiled Lisa.

Gail cut one of the ham sandwiches into tiny triangles for Owen and made a demonstrative point of placing one in her own mouth.

"Mmmmmmm. Yummy."

Owen picked up another of the little sandwiches and bit into it.

"Mmmmmmm," he imitated Gail.

While Gail and the children were eating lunch at the Sawyers' house, Ben and Max arrived at Moat Cottage with the first vanload of furniture, which they unloaded and piled in the living room. Frederick had taken three rounds of cheese and chutney sandwiches, wrapped in grease-proof paper, and left them on the draining board, with a note to say, 'Gail and children having fun. The workers must eat! Hope it's going smoothly.'

"I think we will be alright here, Max. The landlord and his wife are very kind. The children have all this space, not just the garden."

"I will visit once in a while."

"I shall hold you to that promise," laughed Ben.

They gobbled down their sandwiches and got back in the van for the second journey. This time, it would be all the smaller things, which Ben could unload alone, and Max would stay back in London.

At six o'clock in the evening, Ben knocked at the farmhouse door.

"Mission accomplished," he announced, as Lisa opened it.

"Come on in. You must be shattered. I'll make a cup of tea."

"Thank you, but I think we probably need to get to the cottage and start sorting out beds."

Owen had heard Ben's voice and came toddling into the hallway.

"Daaaaddy!"

Ben picked him up and carried him into the sitting room.

"Hello," Gail greeted him.

"Hello. Everything is now at the cottage. Tomorrow I shall put all the furniture back together. I'll do the beds this evening, obviously."

"Lisa has made us a cottage pie for our evening meal, which I can put in the oven."

"Yes, and I'll give you a bottle of milk. There is a village shop about a quarter of a mile further along the road from here, which is also the post office, or another shop half a mile in the other direction from you. Maidstone is for everything else. We have a milkman."

"Thank you so much for all your help and your welcome," reiterated Gail.

Ben put the cottage pie in the back of the van. Gail gathered up coats and children and squeezed all three of them in the passenger seat for the short drive to the cottage.

"I'll check in with you tomorrow evening, otherwise, I'll leave you in peace," promised Frederick, who had come out of his office when Ben knocked on the door. "I forgot to

410

mention, there's some coal in the Anderson shelter. It'll probably last a month. I'll give you the number to call the coal merchant. Help yourself to any pruned or fallen branches in the orchard. I've left an old newspaper, some kindling and a box of matches on top of the coal."

"Thank you," responded Ben, getting in behind the wheel.

"This is it," announced Ben, when they were all inside the cottage. "Our new home. I'll light the fire, if you would like to heat up the cottage pie. Then I'll get started on the beds."

He went outside with his torch and collected the newspaper, kindling and a bucket of coal. Mentally, he started a shopping list, with coal skuttle at the top. Thankfully, there were some iron tongs and a poker lying in the hearth. A fireguard was also essential. Suddenly, the lights went out.

"The metre," laughed Gail. "Do we have some shillings?"

Ben reached into his pocket and brought out a handful of change.

"I have three. I'm sure that will see us through the night, and we can monitor how much we need to feed it and when."

He put a shilling in the metre and the lights came back on, so he added two more.

"Now, where was I?"

"The fire."

Ben screwed up some newspaper and placed it in the grate, covered it with a layer of kindling and balanced some of the coals on top. Striking a match, he set fire to the newspaper in several places and stood back to watch.

Helpfully, the smoke was drawn up the chimney, indicating it was clear. As soon as the kindling was burning, he went and sorted out his toolbox, and began to carry the sections of bed upstairs, where he reassembled the metal double-bedframe, followed by Owen's small wooden bed and Helen's cot. The cottage pie was ready to eat. Owen was strapped into his high-chair and Gail and Ben ate sitting in their two armchairs.

"We've not had stairs inside our home before. I need to make some sort of barrier to stop Owen falling down."

"For tonight, you can rest the back of the wardrobe across the top of the stairs, with a box of books to hold it against the wall."

"Good idea."

Ben and Gail were rudely awoken by a loud crashing sound.

"What on earth was that?"

Ben went to the window but couldn't see anything. He went to the landing window and looked across the front garden to the road. On the other side, he watched the most comical of scenes unfold. There was a long, narrow pond along the opposite side of the road from the cottage. The cottage was situated on a bend, but there was an adverse camber. Ben could see a Citroen 2CV sitting in the pond, having breached the crash-barrier. A man threw open the door and dived into the water, only to find it was hardly two feet deep. Splashing around, he stood up, somewhat disorientated, and waded to the edge. Ben grabbed his dressing-gown and went outside to help, returning shortly, with a miserable-looking, bedraggled Frenchman. Gail found a blanket to wrap round him as he stood shivering in the kitchen.

"We only moved in yesterday," explained Ben, in French, completely forgetting Gail knew nothing of his years in France.

There was a knock at the kitchen door.

"Hello. I'm Charlie Hughes, your next-door neighbour. This happens a lot. I will go and get a tractor to tow the car out."

The Frenchman looked blank.

"He's French," remarked Ben, followed by translating, "The man will pull your car out of the pond with a tractor."

"Thank you," replied the Frenchman, nodding.

"Ben and Gail, by the way."

Charlie went to fetch a tractor and Gail boiled the kettle. By the time, the car was sitting in the layby on the crown of the bend, the Frenchman was drinking a hot cup of black instant coffee. Gail could tell from his expression that it was not to his liking, but it was hot and sweet, and he was both wet and polite.

"Better try the engine," suggested Ben.

They finished their coffees and went over to the parked Citroen. Thankfully, none of the luggage had got wet, and the engine started.

"Thank you. You are a hero," declared the Frenchman, falteringly, in English. "I am Hervé. I go to Maidstone."

"You can get changed in our bathroom," replied Ben, in French.

"Thank you."

The Frenchman grabbed a suitcase and followed Ben back into the cottage where he was shown the bathroom. Once changed, he went on his way, and Gail made breakfast.

It would be the first of many watery crashes over the years the Linton-Houses lived in Collier Street.

"You speak French?" remarked Gail, with surprise.

"School," replied Ben, with a half-truth, shutting down the conversation.

In his head, he told himself to pay more attention in future to references to his past life.

By Christmas, the cottage was ship-shape. The little table-top tree made its annual appearance, with a few lengths of tinsel added to the mantlepiece and doorframes. Gail had got the children into a new routine and was already exploring the lanes, as Lisa had suggested, whilst Ben had started on the garden, digging out vegetable plots. As usual, since Gail left nursing, Christmas would be spent at her parents' house on the island. Ben drove them up, stayed for Christmas Eve, Christmas Day and Boxing Day, before returning home and going back two weeks later to collect them. The excuse was decorating an empty house. The truth was nearer to the difficult relationship he had with his mother-in-law.

Owen loved his wooden farm. Keith and Eileen, now known as Nonny and Gramps, had given him a tricycle. Owen was unable to pedal it, just yet, so Ben found it a great excuse to spend his time on Osea, pushing him around the garden, before returning to Collier Street. Keith was more than happy to take on the responsibility, once he had gone, to help Gail with the grandchildren, and avoid Eileen.

Back at the cottage, Ben busied himself painting the downstairs walls magnolia, which was the cheapest non-white emulsion to buy in bulk. He told himself that one day, he would be more varied with the decoration. Apart from anything else, magnolia went with most of the curtains they had brought down from Upper Norwood, which Gail had hemmed to fit the new windows. All of the woodwork was painted with white gloss. The stress of moving brought on another major flare-up, and by the end of January 1964, Ben was back in hospital, leaving Gail to manage on her own, with two small children. After a month at the Middlesex, he was discharged.

Once the soles of his feet could be walked on again, he got back on with digging the garden, and having turned over all the beds, he started his next project, which was to make some wooden cupboards for the kitchen. To Owen's delight, in the March, Ben also found a second-hand swing, in the Kent Messenger classifieds. The frame needed to be secured into the ground. Gail stitched together a harness on her hand-propelled Singer sewing machine, to fix on the seat so he didn't fall out. Ben hated having the Anderson shelter in the garden, due to it being a constant reminder of Betty, but asking to have it removed would raise too many questions, and it served well as a coal-shed. The other shed was wooden, large enough to keep the garden tools, two adult bicycles and Owen's trike, and a lawnmower. Something else they were required to buy for the first time was a petrol lawn mower, to maintain the grass in what was a satisfyingly large garden. Like the swing, Ben had found it in the Kent Messenger, a second-hand ATCO four-stroke.

Life was good, apart from the flare-ups when Ben found himself in the Middlesex Hospital. At least Max visited him, so they could catch up. Gail learnt how to use and maintain the lawnmower. Weeding and planting successional salad vegetables was something she already knew how to do from her father.

In September of 1964, when he was between flare-ups, Ben happened to wander along the road one Saturday afternoon during a home-game of the village football club. Ben had always had more than a passing interest in football, and did the pools on a weekly basis, but up until now, it hadn't occurred to him to get involved in the village. Walking through the gate into the field where the pitch was located, he approached a man standing on the touchline with a ball at his feet.

"Hello? What's the score?"

"Two-nil to us?"

"Us being Collier Street or are you with the opposition? I'm new here."

"Alan Williams. Village copper and part-time football coach. My boy is playing inside-right."

"Ben Linton-House. Moved into Moat Cottage a few months ago. Love football, but unfortunately, I'm often ill and not up and about. I've driven past the pitch but never seen the team play."

"Can you play?" asked Alan, hopefully, always on the look-out for skill to add to the squad.

"Yes, but I'm bed-ridden three times a year for a few weeks with my illness."

"Why don't you come and practise with us, when you're well?"

"What day and time?"

"Wednesdays after work during the summer and into the season until it gets dark too early. Then we do Sunday afternoons through the winter. We don't have floodlights. The boys commit to going for a run during the week, in their own time. Wednesday, five o'clock, if you're interested."

"Thank you. I'll stay and watch the rest of the match."

Collier Street won three-one. Ben noticed that when the team missed the goal at one end, the ball disappeared into a ditch, and someone had to climb down into the muddy water and retrieve it. Some of the team, including Alan's son, looked to be quite useful with the ball, but mostly, Ben thought he wouldn't be out of his element if he joined the squad for a practice.

"I thought you'd got lost," joked Gail, when Ben finally arrived home.

"Yes. I walked past the football pitch and there was a game on. I stayed to watch. The local policeman coaches the team. He asked me if I want to practise with them. I explained I'm ill a lot, but he didn't seem to mind. I'm thinking of going along this Wednesday, at five o'clock."

"You should. We'll have our tea when you get back. I can feed the children at the normal time."

Wednesday arrived, and Ben took himself off to the training session, with an old pair of football boots, which had seen better days, and his one pair of shorts. He soon realised it was a bad idea. Although he could run on his shrapnel-wounded knee, he was left-footed, as well as left-handed, and the first time he went to kick the ball, he felt a sharp twinge. A few minutes later, whilst dribbling the ball, one of the defenders went in for a fairly innocuous tackle, which left Ben clutching his left knee.

"I'm sorry," apologised the concerned player. "I didn't think I went in hard, at all."

"You didn't. I was stupid to think I could play football again. War wound."

Ben hobbled to the touchline and watched the rest of the practice.

"I think I'm going to have to pass on this," he reflected to Alan, when he came off the pitch, at the end of the session. "I'll still come and watch home-games when I'm free."

"Are you going to be alright getting home?"

"I think so," replied Ben, thinking he had managed far worse.

He limped off down the road, wishing he had gone sooner, before the knee stiffened up.

"What on earth have you done?" asked Gail, when he limped through the door.

"Bad idea. I forgot the war-wound. Can't really kick or tackle and be tackled."

"Oh dear. Will you wash beforehand, or shall I serve the meal?"

"Give me ten minutes to wash, and then perhaps you could apply a crepe bandage for me, before we eat."

"Let me know when you're ready."

Ben went into the bathroom and when he came out, with his dressing-gown on, Gail bandaged his knee for him.

"Thank you. You can serve up while I get dressed."

The next day, he could hardly walk, but he didn't think there was any lasting damage. His knee just needed time to repair itself again. It took four weeks before he could walk properly, and he went along to watch a home-game. It needed a further four weeks before he could ride his bicycle again, and by Christmas, he was able to run and drive, although hardly had he collected Gail and the children from Keith and Eileen's, in the New Year, than he was back in hospital once more.

One afternoon, whilst wiling away the hours, lying on top of his bed, a thought popped into Ben's head. Why didn't he qualify as a football referee? It would enable him to stay involved with football, without having to kick a ball or get tackled, and he would be paid a small fee for each game, plus his expenses. As long as he was able to run on his feet, he could cover up the start and finish of a flare-up with black leggings under his shorts and socks. The shirt was long-sleeved, anyway, and he just might be able to get away with wearing a cap. He felt sure that those players or managers who noticed would be sympathetic, and if he was any good, they would ignore his illness. He only had to try and be healthy between September and May, so hopefully, would only have to manage one flare-up, as long as he wasn't in hospital. By the time he left the Middlesex, this time, he had resolved to explore the referees' qualification. He would worry about the practicalities later.

Back home, he sent a letter to the football association, who sent him a reply explaining what he needed to do and where and when he could take the exam. If he passed, he should register with the association and make inquiries with the local leagues. He was too old now ever to make it to the football league proper, but he still had several years of refereeing locally.

His psoriasis started to flare up again in June, but Ben was well on the way to achieving his referees' qualification, and being ill, did not stop him from memorising the laws of the game. The one challenge was being able to travel to Rochester to sit the exam, which was booked for July 24th. He was cutting it close, because on July 10th he was still at the Middlesex. Only just discharged on 20th July, he made it to Rochester to sit the exam. Three weeks later, a letter arrived in the post. The postman had to knock on the door because the hard-backed foolscap envelope wouldn't fit through the letterbox.

"I wonder if this is your certificate?"

"I don't know if I've passed, yet."

"I know, but if you hadn't passed, they wouldn't send you a certificate."

Gail handed Ben the envelope. Getting out his tiny stainless-steel pocket-knife, he slit the fold, and peeped inside. It contained three copies of his certificate and a letter on headed notepaper. He pulled them out of the envelope, handed Gail the certificates and scanned the letter. 'Congratulations, Mr Linton-House. I am pleased to inform you that you are now a qualified football referee, registered with the Football Association. I would like to add my personal congratulations, because, most unusually, you have achieved 100%. Good luck in your career with the local leagues. I am only sorry that the English football league will be deprived of your skills, due to your age.' His face broke into a smile, and he passed the letter to Gail.

"Well done!"

"I'd better send copies of my certificate to the West Kent Sunday League and the Maidstone and District League."

"I'm going to the post office in the morning, if you have envelopes."

Ben checked in his writing bureau, a dark-stained piece of wooden furniture he had made, to see if there were any envelopes, and set about typing letters of introduction to accompany the copies of his certificate. In the morning, Gail took them and posted them at the post office.

Two weeks later, when his acceptance letter came through from the Maidstone and District League, with the matches he was to referee, he thought it was time to go and buy his kit, along with an elasticated support for his left knee. Gail kindly sewed the badges onto his shirt. The next day, the letter from the West Kent Sunday League also arrived through the letterbox.

The day of his first matched arrived. He swallowed a teaspoon of salt to prevent himself from getting cramp, packed his kit into a small suitcase, and drove to Ditton. As he blew his whistle to start the game, memories of Sète came flooding back and his stomach knotted up, making it hard to run, but he persevered, and after about fifteen minutes, it got easier. At the end of a game, it was customary for each team to give marks for the official's performance, and because Ben was able to anticipate play well, and was fair in his decisions, he received top marks.

Whether it was the salt he ate regularly, or the sense of satisfaction which refereeing gave him, or the fact that life had finally settled down emotionally, Ben couldn't say, but miraculously, he managed to get to the end of April, before he recognised the early signs of a flare-up. His good marks continued all season, and when it was time for the cup final, he was invited to referee the match. Although his body was almost completely scaled up, the skin on his heels was still intact and he was able to run. After a brief visit to each dressing-room to explain his condition, and to reassure everyone he was neither infectious nor contagious, he led the teams out onto the pitch. At the end of the game, Ben received good marks from both teams, in spite of having to award a penalty. Glowing inside, he went forward to receive his referee's medal, which took him back to the boxing championship he won all those years ago. In truth, Ben was really quite competitive, a trait which he would later see had been passed down to Helen.

Two seasons later, and Ben had acquired four more cup final medals. Helen was three and Owen five, when Ben returned once more to the Middlesex Hospital. It was to be the last time. The day he was discharged, Helen ran into the kitchen in a panic.

"What is it?" asked Gail.

"There's a man in the garden."

To Gail's shock, when she went out to see who it was, she was greeted by Ben. His own daughter didn't recognise him. She took some convincing that he was her father, and it caused him to reflect on the amount of time he spent away from home. Gail also spent the day thinking about what to do and arrived at her own conclusion, which she spelt out once the children were in bed.

"There's nothing they can actually do for you at the Middlesex that I can't do here. I'm a trained nurse. Of course, it'll be more work, keeping on top of the scales, but if we ask for a supply of ointment and gauze, you wouldn't have to go into hospital every time you have a flare-up. It's not good for the children to have you away for long periods."

"I know. I was going to ask you what you thought. I'll talk to Dr Reece about it."

Dr Reece lived in Marden, where his practice was based, but he ran a weekly surgery in the village hall. There was a dilapidated brown leather examination couch which was wheeled out of the storeroom and concealed behind canvas screens that had also seen better days. Gail had been there often for the baby clinic, but other than a couple of home visits, Ben hardly had anything to do with Dr Reece. Ben was either fit and well or in the Middlesex Hospital.

"Good morning, Mr Linton-House."

"Good morning, Dr Reece."

"To what do I owe the pleasure, this morning?"

"I don't know if the Middlesex have sent my notes through yet, but I've just had a spell in there, and when I came out, my own daughter didn't recognise me. I, that is Gail and I, were wondering if it was possible to have ointment, painkillers and gauze prescribed, and for her to nurse me at home. She was a nurse when I met her."

"That's not good at all, that your daughter didn't recognise you," reflected Dr Reece, with his soft Ayrshire accent, scanning Ben's notes. "No notes yet from your latest stay, but I can't see any specialist treatment. Are you quite sure about this? Gail will be forever hoovering up after you."

"It's better for Owen and Helen, if I'm at home."

"Then I can't see a problem. Call me when you start getting your next flare-up, and we'll sort out the prescription."

"Thank you, Dr Reece."

"How's the refereeing going?"

"Well. Thank you. Bye."

"Goodbye, Mr Linton-House."

Ben reported the conversation to Gail, and next time his itching skin heralded a flare-up, he made an appointment to see Dr Reece. The following week, when he passed the cottage on his way to the village hall, the doctor dropped off two large boxes, one full of gauze, the other plastic pots of ointment, and some painkillers.

As his flare-up worsened, and Ben retired to bed, Gail did have extra sweeping and hoovering to do, along with taking many hot drinks to Ben, but not a lot changed in her daily routine. The decision proved to be a good one, as although jumping on Daddy when he was poorly was banned, the children got to see Ben every day. For his part, Ben continued to compile crosswords from his bed and started to write a novel.

There was also a useful by-product from treating Ben at home. The empty plastic ointment pots could be turned into sticky-back-plastic-covered string distributors at Christmas. Without a lot of spare cash for presents, each year, resourceful as ever, Gail involved Helen and Owen in craft activities to make presents for Nonny and Gramps, and the two great aunts and great uncles. By covering the pots and making a hole in the lid, a ball of string could be concealed inside, its end threaded through the hole. The following year it was strawberry-shaped pin cushions made from offcuts to a dress Gail made for Helen to wear to parties, and the year after, they made pen pots from the cardboard tubes inside toilet rolls, with the ubiquitous covering of sticky-back-plastic making another appearance. There was no television in the house, but someone had gifted Owen a Blue Peter annual, and Gail was naturally creative. When Helen started school, she constantly pestered Gail to make things at home that they had made in school, and Gail started a collection of scrap materials, with every empty box and plastic pot being added to the empty ointment pots.

Although she enjoyed making things at school, it soon became clear that Helen was finding it hard. The schoolwork was fine, but she was getting picked on by some of the other children. Gail had given Helen elocution lessons, so she spoke with a received pronunciation, rather than the Medway accent, and with a double-barrelled surname, the other children mocked Helen, saying she was posh.

"Helen is very unhappy at school," announced Gail, one day, after the children had gone to bed. "She's being bullied."

"Have you spoken to her teacher?"

"Yes, although I don't know how much difference it will make as she's too scared to name the bullies."

"It's probably a good thing she doesn't, otherwise I might not be able to contain my annoyance with them."

As Ben lay in bed that night, waiting for sleep, he considered an alternative course of action, as a way of helping Helen cope. He remembered the therapeutic contribution Nelson had made to his own wellbeing, when Saul had got on the wrong boat, and he was left to settle at the Fields' house on his own.

In the morning, he made a surprising announcement.

"I've been thinking. Maybe we should get a kitten."

"Oooooh yes, Daddy," exclaimed Helen.

"A kitten?" reflected Owen.

"Yes. A kitten. The Bennetts have four. Shall I fetch one of them?"

Gail was a little surprised, but couldn't see a problem, other than the additional cost of food and possible vet bills, but she also recognised that if Ben had made up his mind, there was no changing it.

"Why not?" she concluded.

As soon as breakfast was finished, the children took themselves off to school, across the orchard and over the style into the playing field, and Ben cycled over to the Bennetts' house with a cardboard box tied to his bicycle rack. Calling in at the post office stores, he purchased a small tin of cat food and a box of kibble, which he hung from his handlebars in a string bag. When he arrived at the Bennetts' house, one of the four kittens had already been collected. The remaining three were all various degrees of ginger and white.

"Is that a boy?" he inquired, pointing at the one with most white.

"Yes," replied Audrey Bennett.

The oldest Bennett boy was in Owen's class, and they generally attended each other's birthday parties, so George and Audrey were not total strangers.

"He'll do nicely."

"I hope you enjoy him."

"Thank you. I hope you find good homes for the other two."

"One of. We'll keep the one that isn't chosen."

Ben popped the kitten into the cardboard box, not unduly concerned for its wellbeing, as the journey back was less than ten minutes.

Gail was waiting impatiently for Ben to return. He leant his bicycle against the back wall of the house and released the reef-knot on a length of the medical gauze he benefitted from during psoriasis flare-ups. Tubular and stretchable, it came on a roll, in its flattened, unstretched form, and was extremely useful for non-medical purposes, like tying items to his bicycle rack. Peeping inside the box, he made kissing noises.

"Welcome to your new home, Tiger."

"Let me see," Gail pressed him before he had even made it across the threshold.

"Close the living room door," he instructed her, pushing the back door shut with his foot.

He placed the box on the floor and gently lifted out the kitten.

"Can we call him Tiger?" he asked, insistently, handing the bundle of fluff to Gail.

Gail cuddled the nervous addition to their family.

"Hello little Tiger. Are you hungry?"

"I bought some wet and dry food. I'll open the tin."

He went back outside to fetch the string bag, with Gail shielding Tiger inside her cardigan to make sure he didn't jump and run out.

"Shall we let him explore in the living room and put his food in there, for now?" suggested Gail.

"Good idea. I'll fill a litter-box with some soil from the garden."

Gail carried Tiger into the living room and Ben brought the food. The fire guard was sitting next to the grate, so he quickly placed it in front of the burning coals. Little Tiger shot straight under Ben's fireside chair, ignoring his food.

By the time Owen and Helen came home for lunch, Tiger had eaten his food and discovered the curtains. Gail waited in the kitchen for when they arrived home and ushered them in, very quietly, through the back door.

"Now, don't start fighting. You can each have a turn at touching the new kitten. We need to make sure we keep the kitchen and stairs doors closed at all times. Remember, he's not a toy and he's still a little timid."

"Yes, Mummy," responded Owen.

"Alright," groaned Helen.

"When you go into the living room, can you please sit down on the floor, carefully and quietly?"

Gail opened the door and the children slipped into the room, where they sat down, Owen on the hearthrug, Helen opposite. Ben was holding Tiger.

"Helen, first."

Helen crept forward on her hands and knees and started to stroke the kitten's head.

"What's its name?"

"His name is Tiger. Now Owen's turn."

"Hello, Tiger," whispered Owen, reaching to stroke the kitten.

"We'll have to keep him indoors for the next two weeks, to get used to us and all the new smells," declared Ben.

Tiger was let out of the house two weeks later under Ben's watchful eye, and for the first few days, only when the children were at school, just in case they frightened the kitten with their enthusiasm. Eventually, Tiger was allowed out on his own.

After he had been going outside a while, Ben or Gail would call him in by tapping a saucer of food. Tiger would come running. About three months after he had gained his freedom, Tiger announced his presence at the back door by knocking over an empty milk bottle, without being summoned by spoon on saucer. Thankfully, the bottle didn't smash. Ben found the whole thing fascinating. He also recognised that it was only breaking glass that seemed to traumatise him still.

"Do you think it was a one-off?" he asked Gail.

"We'll have to wait and see."

It wasn't a one-off, by any means. Tiger had somehow worked out that he would be let in, whenever he knocked over a milk bottle.

Tiger was treated as a full member of the family, always being served a few morsels, on a saucer, of whatever the family were eating at mealtimes. He also received a birthday and Christmas card. One evening, when Tiger was about nine months old, Ben was breaking off a piece of Caramac chocolate, and a tiny fragment dropped to the floor. Tiger rushed over, sniffed at it, and took it into his mouth.

"Did you like that? We'll have to start giving you a little treat at bedtime."

A new family habit was instigated of giving Tiger a minuscule portion of Caramac last thing at night.

He was an adorable cat, friendly with strangers, intelligent and affectionate. By ten o'clock at night, he was always safely at home, either on his own initiative or because he responded to the shaking of the kibble box. Until the night in May, when he didn't come home, that is. Worried sick, Ben went in search of his beloved cat, across the road, to the part of the farm beyond the pond, to the straw barn and pigsty, calling as he went. It was walking back along the road towards the front gate, that Ben came upon Tiger, motionless, lying on the verge, half under the hedge. Ben knew, instantly, that Tiger was dead. During his life, Ben had seen so much pointless death, but this was different. Already unable to see clearly through his tears, Ben picked up Tiger, concealing him in his jacket, and carried him home. He hadn't felt this kind of grief since the cliff top in Malta.

"Go into the living room, please," he insisted, as he walked in through the back door.

Gail went into the living room. He didn't need to explain. Starting to cry herself, at the realisation Tiger was no more, she closed the living room door and sat patiently in her fireside chair. Ben wrapped Tiger in some broadsheets from the previous week's Kent Messenger to make a newspaper shroud, and carried him out into the garden, where he laid him on the ground momentarily, whilst he went to the shed for a spade. The moon gave enough light to see what he was doing. Digging down into the barren flower bed, Ben buried Tiger. His intention was to cover Tiger's grave with a rose bush, but that would have to happen tomorrow, while the children were at school.

After returning the spade to the shed, Ben went indoors, washed his hands and slumped into his armchair.

"Where did you find him?"

"At the side of the road, between the front gate and the farmyard. I don't remember hearing car breaks, so all I can hope is that it was instant, and he didn't suffer."

"Would you like a cup of tea?"

"No, thank you. I think I'm just going to go to bed. We'll tell the children when they come home from school, tomorrow. Otherwise, they will be too upset to go."

"But they'll wonder where he is, when they get up."

"I'll say I let him out early," responded Ben, getting up to go to the bathroom.

It was only a matter of days, before his skin started to show the signs of another flare-up.

As soon as Ben was up and about again, after weeks of lying in his bed thinking about Tiger, he came to a decision that the family needed another cat.

"I miss Tiger. I miss the flash of ginger around the place."

"Shall we get another cat?" suggested Gail.

"I was thinking as much. I'll ask around."

"And we can look in the paper. I'll be fetching this week's tomorrow."

Hardly had Gail arrived back with the latest Kent Messenger than Ben was scanning the pet section of the classifieds. A ginger tom kitten was available in Barming. No telephone number, just an address.

"Barming isn't far. I'll cycle over there."

"What! Now?"

"Yes. I want to be the first. I'll see you later, hopefully with a ginger tom kitten."

"Bye."

Ben set off for Barming, a shoebox tied to his bicycle rack with some gauze. When he arrived at the address, an elderly lady led him to the bottom of an unmaintained garden to a corrugated-iron-roofed pigsty.

"He's a stray. I don't know if he's on his own. Never seen the mother. I thought it best to feed him down here until someone agreed to take him."

"I'll take him."

The lady bent down and picked up a small bundle of ginger fluff, which sat expectantly beside an empty saucer.

"I've got nothing for you, Button, but this nice man here wants to give you a good home."

"Button?"

"Yes. Little ginger Button," she replied, handing the kitten to Ben, who sheltered him inside his jacket.

"I've got a box on my bike. What food have you been feeding him."

"Choosy, mixed with a bit of milk."

"What's the price of Button? It didn't say in the paper."

"Nothing. I just want him to be looked after."

The Linton-Houses were hard up, but Ben could see this old lady was probably worse-off. He reached into his back pocket and pulled out three pound-notes.

"Please, take this. It'll cover the cost of looking after the kitten."

The lady hesitated, but Ben held out his hand firmly.

"Please. You can give it to an animal charity if you don't want it."

In the end, she took the money.

"Thank you. That's very kind."

Ben followed her back up the path, wrapped Button in one of Gail's old cardigans and placed him carefully in the shoebox.

"Thank you. Bye," said Ben, swinging his leg over saddle and shoebox.

"Goodbye."

All the way home, Button miaowed tiny, fearful mews.

"I know. I'm going as fast as I can," Ben reassured him. "We're nearly there."

They were still three miles from the cottage, but the kitten wasn't to know. As they cycled past the Sawyers' house, an articulated Alan Firmin lorry, overtook them, on its way to Marden. Ben thought the thundering monster must have terrified Button and was torn between covering the last few hundred yards as fast as he could or stopping there and then to check on the kitten. He braked steadily, got off, leant the bicycle against the next gate and opened the box. Button was shaking, so Ben picked him up, still wrapped in the cardigan, and squeezed the whole bundle into his jacket. Taking the handlebars, he pushed the bicycle the rest of the way home.

Gail went to meet him at the back door.

"I think he may need to have a few fleas removed. He was living in an old pigsty. He's a stray. Well-fed, by the looks of things, though."

Gail took the bundle from Ben.

"His name is Button, the old lady told me. I gave her three quid. She looked worse off than us."

Gail sat with Button on her lap, teasing out several fleas as she manipulated Button's claggy ginger fur.

"He's going to need regular brushing, once we get rid of these clags."

"He'll be spoiled, just like Tiger was."

And he was. Button grew to love being brushed, something they hadn't needed to do with Tiger. When the adored ginger tom was about seven months old, Ben thought Button was putting on weight.

"Maybe we're feeding him too much. Now he goes outside, he probably catches his own lunch."

"He's also been acting rather strangely this last week. I'm no cat expert, but I don't think he's getting fat. I think our ginger tom may not be a tom."

"What do you mean?"

"I think he, or rather she, is pregnant. Although most gingers are male, just as tortoiseshells are female, you can get female gingers."

Ben felt Button's tummy, gently.

"I think you might be right."

They both burst out laughing.

Three weeks later, Button gave birth to four kittens. As a trained nurse, Gail was unphased by the birthing process. She stayed up all night, checking on Button regularly. All four were ginger, two short-haired and two long-haired. When she got up in the morning, Helen was beside herself with excitement.

"Can we keep one of them?" she enthused, naively.

"And have two cats. Can we afford two cats?" Gail deferred to Ben.

"I think so."

"Alright. Which one shall we keep?"

Helen pointed at one of the short-haired ones.

"That one. Can I name him?"

"Perhaps, as you chose him, Owen should name him."

Helen scowled, and stomped downstairs for breakfast.

"We'd better get an advert into the paper, and the local shops," proposed Ben. "We'd also better get Button spayed."

"Yes, but we'll let her get over this litter first."

Three of the four kittens had gone to their new homes, and Threepence, as Owen had named him, had established himself in the Linton-House home, Ben took Button to Marden, to the vet. They had bought a second-hand cat carrier which was secured to the bicycle rack with gauze threaded through the handle and the grill. Cumbersome but manageable.

"Hello. We have a cat that needs to be spayed. She's recently had kittens. We didn't know she was a 'she', when we got her, otherwise we would have brought her in earlier."

"Let's take a look," replied the vet, taking Button from Ben and placing her on the table.

He examined her with his stethoscope, felt her belly and looked at Ben, with a concerned frown.

"I'm really sorry, but I don't think I can operate."

The blood drained from Ben's face.

"Why not?"

"Has she been outside since having her kittens?"

"Yes. We let her out for a break."

"Well, she's expecting again."

"I see. We'll be more careful next time. Thank you. I'm just relieved she's well. For a moment I thought you meant you couldn't operate because she was ill."

"Perfect cat health. Just pregnant," smiled the vet.

"Oh, and we've also got a boy from her first litter who will need to be neutered very soon."

"Make an appointment to have him neutered before the kittens are born."

"Will do," replied Ben, taking hold of Button.

He rode home to break the news to Gail.

A month later, Button gave birth to seven kittens. Ben found a sheet of hardboard which he placed across the doorway of the enclosed half of the attic, so that Button could come and go in the house, if she wanted. A good mother, she never once left her kittens, using the litter tray and eating food that was brought upstairs to her. After three weeks, Helen went up to the attic every day to play with the kittens.

"No, Helen, we're not going to have any of these," laughed Ben, firmly.

At eight weeks, Ben took Button to the vet.

"We're not taking any chances this time," he joked.

When he went back in the evening, to collect Button, the vet came forward with a suggestion.

"Why don't I come and collect the kittens and look after them for a few days or so, while Button here recovers. I can bring her with me in the car."

"That would be helpful. Thank you."

The vet gave Ben twenty minutes' head-start and then drove to Collier Street, arriving five minutes after him. Gail was in the attic with the kittens.

"Probably, best to keep her away from the kittens, for now. She's still a bit woozy, and they will want to climb all over her," suggested the vet, as he entered the house carrying

Button's cat carrier in his right hand and two empty ones in his left.

"Up the stairs, along the landing and up to the attic. My wife is there with the kittens."

"Thanks," replied the vet, disappearing through the stairs' door.

"Hello," Gail greeted him.

"Good afternoon, Mrs Linton-House. They are rather gorgeous, aren't they?"

Gail smiled.

"How is Button?"

"She'll be fine after some rest and recuperation."

They caught five of the kittens without any trouble at all, but Ginger-Barrel, a long-haired, mini-Button had decided to hide under the chest of drawers, and Jester, whose nose was half ginger and half black, had squeezed between the wall and one of Ben's trunks. Eventually, the vet and Gail outwitted the two escapees, and each carried a carrier down to the living room.

"I'll bring them back on Saturday morning."

"Thank you. Bye."

"I'll carry the second carrier," offered Ben, following the vet out. "Thank you, again."

"You're welcome."

At nine in the morning there was a knock at the back door. Gail was washing up the breakfast dishes and not expecting anyone. She grabbed a hand towel and went to see who it was. Standing on the doorstep, looking a little stressed, was the vet, with a cat carrier full of kittens in his left hand and another in his right.

"Good morning," he greeted her, sheepishly.

"Good morning. Is everything alright?"

"I have a better idea," responded the vet. "How about you look after the kittens, and I take Button?"

Gail couldn't help laughing, and the vet's face broke into a compassionate grin.

"Not a problem. They are a bit of a handful. Come in. Do you have time for a cup of coffee?"

"Thank you, but no, not really. Surgery opens soon."

"I'll go and get Button."

When Gail came back downstairs, she had Button in a cat carrier.

"See you at the weekend. And thank you, again," she said. "I'm assuming you don't need your two carriers until then."

"No. I'll pick them up when I bring Button back. By the way, they've had their breakfast. Bye."

"Bye."

Gail closed the door behind him and picked up the cat carriers, at which point she decided that one at a time was more sensible. Two trips up to the attic later, and all seven kittens were having a mad half hour in their room.

Ben placed an advert in the Kent Messenger, and one by one, the family had to say goodbye to the kittens. Churchill, a long-haired black kitten, was the last to go. Button appeared a little out of sorts for a couple of days.

When Ben was well, he gardened, refereed, did carpentry around the cottage, and in the summer, drove a tractor to help Keith with the harvest on Osea. When he was ill, he stayed in bed, mostly to keep the scales in one room, although he still had to use the bathroom, which was downstairs. Ben thought his hospital visits were a thing of the past, until one day, when he was mowing the grass, he stupidly, managed to run the blade over his foot, slicing off the front of his old leather lace-ups, which had been relegated to gardening, and taking the top off his right big toe. There was more blood than damage, but they felt an ambulance was needed. Gail and Ben didn't have a telephone, so Gail had to walk, briskly, down to the school, where the public phone-box was located. The ambulance arrived and took him to the Kent and Sussex Hospital, where he was stitched up.

As soon as he could walk again, he took Owen across the road to the pond, for his first fishing experience, testing out his new, birthday fishing rod. Such rites of passage were always a poignant mix of both joy and sadness for Ben, as he wondered what it would have been like to share these moments with Roger. He never spoke of his feelings, though.

Only a couple of feet deep, the pond was mostly home to Gudgeon, Roach and Stickleback. There was another much deeper pond further along, on the opposite side of the road, where it was rumoured that Tench and Pike lurked. The surface was permanently covered with duckweed, and it was out of bounds for Owen and Helen. Not so, it appeared, for the cats, who came home on a couple of occasions covered in duckweed.

Ten minutes into their fishing expedition, Owen's float started to bob up and down, and then went under.

"I've got one!" he exclaimed, gleefully, reeling it in.

On the end of his line was a hapless, four-inch Roach. He went to hold it, to take out the hook, but snatched his hand back.

"What's the matter?"

"It feels strange."

"It will do, but if you're going to fish, you'll have to get used to it. Let me show you how to remove the hook on this one. You've got to be careful, because of the barb. Wait! Let me go and get the camera."

Owen stood waiting with his catch dangling in the air, whilst Ben went back over the road to the cottage. He came out with the camera and two digestive biscuits. Placing the biscuits on the top of one of the low, white posts, which supported a single line of black chain, by way of a barrier, Ben wound the film on one frame.

"Smile."

Owen stood proudly holding out the rod in one hand and the line, just above the Roach, in the other. The shutter clicked.

"Right. Have a biscuit and watch."

Owen stood looking on, munching on his Sainsbury's digestive, as Ben took out the hook.

"You can try the next one. We'll put this in the bucket, and put back what we catch, at the end."

Owen loaded a tiny piece of squashed bread onto his hook, whilst Ben ate his biscuit, and cast the line halfway across the pond. Twenty minutes later, he caught a Gudgeon.

"You try this one."

Owen struggled to remove the hook.

"It keeps wriggling," he complained.

Ben took hold of the fish, so Owen could remove the hook.

"It'll come with practice," Ben encouraged him.

When Owen had caught ten fish, they poured the contents of the bucket back in the pond and crossed back over the road to the cottage. It was time for lunch. Cheese sandwiches.

Every year Gail made apple jelly with windfall apples. There were also several pear trees, to aid with pollination, along the edge of the orchard, and Ben usually picked up five or six fallen pears for Helen to make his favourite pear jelly. Ben's sandwiches were cheese and pear jelly. No one else was allowed any of the jars.

Earlier in the year, Frederick Sawyer had replaced the old wooden shed in the garden at Moat Cottage.

After constructing a proper concrete base, he built the new shed from interlocking panels of reinforced concrete. The roof sloped from front to back and was made from corrugated asbestos. About one foot larger than the old shed, in both directions, Ben had fitted some shelves along one side. There was enough space to walk between the bicycles and the shelves. The bottom shelf of two was about five feet off the ground and filled with various boxes and jam jars containing anything from screws to hinges. The fishing floats were kept in a large kilner jar, that had long since lost its lid.

Owen had gobbled down his cheese sandwiches and gone back outside to play, whilst Ben had settled down into his wooden-armed, fireside chair, with a cup of tea sitting on one arm and his pouch of Clan tobacco on the other. Smoking a pipe was a recently acquired habit of his. Having packed the bowl, he was just striking a match to light it, when the simultaneous sounds of a child's scream and of glass smashing interrupted his peace. Ben froze, pipe in right hand, flaming match in his left. Gail, who was in the kitchen, looked out through the window to see Owen sitting in the doorway of the shed, clutching his left wrist, surrounded by fragments of a broken jam-jar. She dropped the dishcloth into the washing-up bowl and rushed out of the back door.

"It's OK, darling. Just let Mummy take a look at your wrist."

Owen was crying and reluctant to let go of his wrist, so Gail gently prized up two of his fingers. Blood had been seeping from a deep laceration, and now the pressure had been released, flowed more abundantly.

"On second thoughts, keep holding it tightly," she suggested, replacing Owen's fingers and holding her own hands around his hand.

A trained nurse, she knew that the glass had missed Owen's artery, which was reassuring.

"Ben!" she called. "Owen's had an accident. We need you out here."

Ben, who was re-living his own trauma, had just been brought back to present reality by the match burning down to his thumb and finger. He dropped it on the hearthrug, thankfully, not causing any damage as the match was now dead.

"Ben! Can you come out here, please!"

Placing his unlit pipe on the arm of the chair, Ben stood up, and went to see what all the fuss was about.

"I think we need to call an ambulance for Owen."

Ben took one look at the shattered glass, the blood on the concrete and Gail's hands, and ran down the road to the phone-box, without changing out of his slippers. When he got back to the cottage, Helen was now outside with Gail and Owen, curious as to the commotion.

"When the ambulance gets here, which of us is going to hospital with Owen?" asked Ben. "We can't take Helen and we can't leave her here alone."

"I'll stay here with Helen. I'm sure you'll be fine."

The ambulance arrived, Owen was bandaged up temporarily, and taken off to the Kent and Sussex Hospital, with Ben on board. In the panic, neither Ben nor Gail had considered how they would travel back from Tunbridge Wells. Either Owen would be admitted, and Ben would need to come home, or Owen would be treated, and they would both need transport. Taxis were expensive, but by bus, they would probably need to change twice, and may miss the last bus out from Maidstone. By train, it would involve a bus into Tonbridge, a train to Marden, and a two-and-a-half-mile walk, although a taxi from Marden was affordable. There was no way of communicating without a telephone.

Fortunately, Frederick Sawyer had been carrying out maintenance in the tractor house and had heard the ambulance arriving. Seeing that it had parked outside Moat Cottage, he had watched from a distance, to see who got in, and on discovering it was Ben and Owen, had wandered round to the cottage to offer help.

"I don't mean to be nosy, but I was in the tractor house and saw the ambulance. Can I be of assistance?"

"Owen had an accident and cut his wrist rather badly on some broken glass."

"That's not good. Would you like Lisa to phone the hospital and ask Ben to call the house, when he knows what's happening? More than happy to drive over and fetch them, or take you over there, if Owen has to stay in hospital. Lisa can watch Helen."

"That is very kind of you. Thank you."

"How did it happen?"

"I'm really not sure. I can understand how he might have knocked the jar off the shelf. I'm less clear about how he then managed to cut himself so deeply in his wrist, on the broken glass. I'm just grateful he missed his artery."

"I'll go and tell Lisa, then."

"Thank you."

Three nervous hours later, having made a sponge cake, with Helen's help, to distract both of them, Gail caught sight of Frederick through the kitchen window. He knocked at the back door.

"Come in," she called, grabbing a hand towel.

Frederick opened the door and stepped inside.

"Me again. They've checked the wound for fragments of glass, cleaned it, bandaged him up, and they're ready to come home. We should be back inside the hour."

"Thank you so much. You will let us pay for the petrol, won't you."

"Don't be silly. I'm sure you'd do exactly the same for us."

Gail knew Frederick was being more than generous, especially as they had sold their van, the previous year.

"Thank you, again."

Frederick left to fetch Ben and Owen.

After it had been in the oven for twenty-five minutes, Gail tested the cake with a thin knitting-needle. It needed another five minutes or so but would be cool enough for the filling by the time Owen and Ben returned. As a former nurse, she anticipated that Owen's lower arm would be heavily bandaged, so it would be difficult for him to carry out his usual activities. Like his father, Owen was left-handed. He was also old enough, now, to be embarrassed by help of a personal nature from his mother. However, Gail's main concern was keeping Helen and Owen apart. They were twenty months apart, and either they played calmly together, or they fought tooth and nail. Gail worried that Helen might try to take advantage of Owen's incapacity. The more she thought about it, the more convinced Gail became that although they were still just about young enough to share a bedroom, it was time to decorate the enclosed half of the attic to create a bedroom for Helen. Removing the cake from the oven, Gail tipped it out of the tins onto a wire cooling-rack and covered it with a muslin, to keep the flies at bay. She fully intended to give Frederick some slices to show their appreciation.

His car pulled up behind the house, at the edge of the orchard, where Ben used to park his van, identifiable by the recovering wheel-tracks worn into the turf. Gail went outside with a Tupperware container of cake, in case Frederick drove off without getting out of the car. He wound down the window, as Ben opened the rear door for Owen to get out.

"Just a small thank-you," announced Gail, handing over the container.

"No problem. Let me know if you need anything else."

"Thank you, Mr Sawyer," said Owen.

"You're welcome," replied Frederick, putting the car into reverse, ready to pull off.

Ben nodded his appreciation at Frederick.

The bandage around Owen's left lower arm was huge, partly to protect the wrist, should a squabbling sibling jump on it, and partly to ensure the edges stayed together long enough for it to heal. Helen laughed at him.

"You can stop that before you've even started," asserted Gail. "We have cake inside. Does it hurt?"

"Not too much," responded Owen.

"They have given him some pain relief. Apparently, the glass missed his artery by an eighth of an inch. He's a lucky boy?"

"What actually happened?" inquired Gail, "I mean, how did you cut yourself?"

"I reached up for the jar, and then I lost my balance, and then the glass hit the wall, and broke."

"Ah. So, it didn't smash when it hit the floor?"

"I think it was both. first against the wall, enough to cut me, and then when it fell to the floor."

"I think maybe we should start putting things you and Helen need to reach for in plastic pots or cardboard boxes."

They went indoors and each consumed a large slice of sponge cake."

"I helped Mummy," declared Helen.

"Well, it tastes delicious," replied Ben.

That evening, when the children were in bed, each parent had a major proposition to make.

"I've been thinking," started Gail.

"So, have I."

"You first, then."

"When I was in the waiting area, I started reading the newspaper. I'm probably not supposed to have defaced it, but I tore out this advert."

Gail read the snippet, silently. The trustees of Yardley Court Preparatory School in Tonbridge were seeking entrants for a competition. The prize was full fees paid until thirteen and then half fees at Tonbridge School. Applicants needed a recommendation from their primary school. They had to live in Kent.

"What are you thinking? Owen?"

"We should ask Mr Morton what he thinks Owen's chances are."

Mr Morton was the headteacher at the village primary school. He understood the family situation and was grateful for Gail's weekly visits to listen to the children read. What

Ben and Gail didn't know was how many other parents had similar aspirations. With five other boys of a similar age to Owen to choose from, it was not a foregone conclusion.

"What have you been thinking about?"

"The children need separate bedrooms. I think the attic room can be emptied and painted for Helen."

"Not Owen?"

"I think Helen needs to feel everything doesn't always go to her brother first. She has hand-me-down clothes. He's older. He's a boy. Take the Yardley Court scholarship. Where are the opportunities for girls?"

"We'll have a look tomorrow and see how much space we can create in the open side of the attic, to tidy things out of the room. We can get a second-hand bed and some furniture. I can sand down any wood and re-varnish it."

"I'm glad you like the idea."

Mr Morton liked Ben's idea too, and Owen was entered for the scholarship competition. He won one of the scholarships. Ben and Gail could not have been prouder and agreed to worry about the other half of the school fees for Tonbridge School, when Owen turned thirteen.

Ben and Gail were well-thought of in the village, although mostly due to Gail's involvement with the school. Ben did what he could, like the disco he organised for the youth club in the village hall, but generally, he was ill or recovering or catching up with all the things he couldn't do when he was in bed. He and Gail hardly ever got invited anywhere as a couple, partly due to his health, but mostly, because Helen and Owen couldn't be trusted to be left on their own for the evening. After so many refusals, people gave up asking them. In all truth, the situation suited Ben, who never liked making polite conversation at the best of times.

During the summer, of 1970, Alan Williams caught up with Ben and asked if he could teach his son, Brian, how to become a referee. Ben agreed, and a first meeting was set up. The children were banned from the living room during the session. Unfortunately, it immediately became obvious that Brian was illiterate. He was embarrassed.

"Don't worry about it. I'll teach you to read, and then we'll tackle the laws of the game. Do your mum and dad know you have trouble reading?"

"I think the teachers said."

"But no one offered to help?"

Brian shook his head. What he didn't realise, was that Brian was dyslexic.

"I was just labelled the naughty kid, which, as you can imagine, is a bit of a problem when your dad's a copper."

"Well, we'll just have to make up for it. You'll need to sit an exam to be a referee. Tell me what you know about the game."

"I play it, so I understand the game. I'm never sure why some refs give a direct free-kick and others an indirect one though. Who decides what 'ungentlemanly conduct' is?"

"Why the sudden interest in refereeing? I thought you loved to play."

"Did my cartilage in. Can't play anymore. Like you, I can run but I can't tackle."

"Right. I'll sort out some stuff for next time. In the meantime, I'm going to write out the alphabet for you, and you can practise making the letters."

Ben grabbed his ruled pad and a pencil and wrote out the alphabet with capitals and lower-case letters.

"Get some grease-proof paper and lay it over the page. Then, start to trace the letters."

"I'll see you tomorrow, then."

"Yes. Thank you."

Brian left with his alphabet and Ben turned his hand to creating a football pitch on the back of a sheet of hardboard, with pipe-cleaners for the goals and half matchsticks for the corner and side flags. They could use tiddlywinks to represent players and a tiny magnet for the ball.

Brian came almost every day. He was a motivated student, but Ben soon understood that what had held Brian back was the way he jumbled the letters. They persevered, and within a few short weeks, Brian was able to read the referees' handbook, enough to improve his knowledge. After all, he would be tested on how he applied the laws of the game, not on how he spelled them. Every week, Ben would write out problems for him to solve, and Brian would come back with his homework completed, something he rarely ever managed at school.

"I think we should book your exam," suggested Ben, one evening. "It'll take six weeks to come through, I shouldn't doubt."

"If you think I'm ready."

"I definitely think you will be, in six weeks. Now, I've got a tough one for you this week. The away-team defender kicks the ball. The home-team attacker runs after it. It's going out, so he picks it up and takes a throw-in. The referee blows his whistle and gives a free-kick to the away-team. Why?"

Brian thought about it for a moment.

"Foul throw?"

"Wouldn't be a free-kick."

"Wait. The ball hasn't gone out when the attacker picks it up. Handball."

"Well done."

Brian was entered for his referee's exam and passed.

"I LOVE THE SOUND OF BREAKING GLASS"

Owen started his new school wearing his new school shoes, his second-hand uniform, and a new school cap. For the first week, Ben rode with him to Marden, and caught the train to Tonbridge. He would spend the day in Tonbridge and catch the train back again with Owen. Once Owen was confident, Ben continued to cycle to and from Marden, but no longer accompanied him on the train. The school was a short walk from the station, so no danger of getting lost. At the Marden end of the journey, Dr Reece had agreed to let the Linton-Houses padlock their bikes at the practice. By half term, Owen was allowed to cycle on his own. The children had friends, two brothers of a similar age, who lived at the far end of the village, and now that Owen was allowed to cycle to their house on his own, as well as round the village, it seemed acceptable for him to make the journey to and from Marden on his own.

One day, in February, he arrived home without his cap. Gail was tidying his clothes ready for the following day. He had two shirts, and she washed the dirty one every night, and hung it in front of the fire to dry.

"Where's your cap?" she asked?

For a moment, Owen didn't say anything.

"Please try not to leave it at school."

"I didn't leave it at school."

"What did you do with it?"

"It came off. I was leaning out of the train window. It's somewhere between Marden and Paddock Wood."

"Do you know how dangerous it is, to lean your head out of a train window?" asked Gail, rhetorically, more concerned about Owen's life than the cap.

There was a strict uniform code, and Owen might receive a detention if he went to school without his cap. As soon as it was getting light, Ben got on his bicycle, rode to Marden station, and walked along the track. Technically, he was trespassing, but he figured if anyone stopped him, he would have an excuse ready. It was possible to hear a train at some considerable distance along the rails, and he could always hide in the undergrowth or climb back over the fence. As it turned out, no trains came along, and he found the cap lying in the middle of the eastbound track, about a mile and a half from Marden. He was waiting on the platform when Owen arrived to catch his train to Tonbridge.

"No more leaning out of train windows," he insisted, handing Owen his slightly grubby cap. "We can wash it tonight."

"Thanks, Daddy."

Ben got on his bicycle and rode home. Cycling kept him fit, and without the van, he cycled to and from the matches, as well as refereeing them. Sometimes, the journey involved a steep incline, Yalding Hill, Hunton Hill and Linton Hill, and even Blue Bell Hill, which was a killer. On dark winter evenings, Ben needed the use of cycle lamps to ride home. His were powered by a dynamo, and it was not unusual for him to pick up so much speed, freewheeling down a long hill, that one or both of the light bulbs would blow.

On one such journey back from Chart Sutton, in the pouring rain, the front lightbulb blew. Protected by a voluminous yellow plastic cycle-cape, and with wet, cold hands, due to his woollen gloves soaking up the rain, he propped up the bike, against the verge, resting on one pedal, and set about changing the bulb. Hindered by 'Stumpy', he dropped his spare bulb, which landed on the tarmac and shattered. Although glass shards always brought flashbacks, for reasons beyond Ben, it was the sound of breaking glass which left him stupefied, something of a relief on this occasion, otherwise he may have ended up with hypothermia. Forcing himself to focus on the task at hand, and resourceful as ever, he decided to dispense with his rear light and place the bulb in his front lamp. Arriving home, he peeled off his wet clothes in the kitchen, whilst Gail ran him a hot bath, where he soaked for an hour.

It was customary for the two football teams to submit a mark, scoring the referee's performance. Somehow, without considering the consequences on Helen's self-worth, Ben had taken to turning it into a joke, at her expense. Having warmed up in the bath he came out and finding Helen reading a book by the fire, he entered into the usual repartee.

"They asked me if I had a daughter called Helen, and I said that I did. 'Right no marks,' they said."

Helen looked at him, searching for affirmation. Of course, Ben generally received good marks, but Helen grew to thinking she wasn't worth anything. Nonetheless, she always looked forward to when her father refereed the factory team matches for Trebor-Sharps, because they presented the officials with a bag of sweets, after the game.

If Ben cycled miles to referee a football match, he was also a familiar sight, riding through the countryside with eight-foot lengths of wood or veneered chipboard, strapped to the side of the bike frame. He had no other choice, once the van was sold. 'Contiboard' was a brand of veneered chipboard, and like biros and hoovers, 'contiboard' became the colloquial nomenclature based on a brand. Whether it was just the Linton-Houses who called it 'contiboard' Ben didn't know. On this occasion, he needed materials to make some simple furniture for Helen's new attic bedroom. The wardrobe would consist of an upright and top, fixed to the wall in the corner of the room, with a curtain at the front. He would make a similar structure, for a desk, but with an extra supporting upright piece, fixed against the wall in the opposite corner. Ben's project required two eight-foot lengths of the board, which he strapped on either side of his bicycle, against the frame and the struts which supported a bike-rack over the rear wheel. There was just enough space to attach it to the front column, between the handlebars and the brake calliper, to allow the wheel to turn. Most of the board extended beyond the front of the bicycle, and his ride home from Maidstone was precarious, especially negotiating the bends in West Farleigh and on

Yalding Hill, because when the handlebars turned, the board remained straight.

As a father, Ben was complicated. He loved his children and was trying to support them, but he was low on patience and didn't suffer fools gladly. He never once raised his hand to either of them, but when he raised his voice, the required response was instant. Gail had also learnt when to let things stand, not that he ever hit her. Ben had two models to follow. His own father had been strict but loving, revelling in the son who was his apprentice carpenter. Then there was Bill Field, who had shown Ben unconditional acceptance and supported him with his boxing, as if Ben were his son.

Owen was not at all sporty, which was the cause of some disappointment to Ben, as he had no reason to stand on the touchline as a proud, cheering father, as Bill would have done. Helen, on the other hand, was a tom-boy, played football as well as any boys in the primary school, but wasn't allowed to represent the school, and when she went off to secondary school, played in the hockey team. It was Helen who was allowed to pick the teams in one of the lines in Ben's weekly football pools entry. She was also practical, like Ben, and from a very young age, took on the role of 'Daddy's little helper'.

Ben had a catchphrase when working on do-it-yourself projects. 'Work clean'. As he sawed and sanded, Helen would sweep up any sawdust and tidy away the offcuts. He paid her pocket money for the duties she carried out as his assistant. When she was old enough to handle a hand-drill, he let her drill some holes, although he knew the locations would be hidden from sight. He also encouraged her to saw lengths of wood, although she often gave up on anything thicker than an inch. Much later, she was allowed to use the electric drill and drill in places that would be visible. At the age of eleven, Helen made a wooden pencil-box, in woodwork lessons at school, with well-sanded bevel-edges and neatly cut joints. Ben glowed with pride.

He taught Helen to play cribbage, which they both enjoyed, being equally competitive. It was something they could do when he was stuck in bed. They played for money, and when Helen lost, Ben offered her the chance of 'double-or-quits', until she owed him more money than she could earn in pocket-money. He let her off the debt, hoping she might learn the lesson not to gamble, something which may have been considered hypocritical, in the light of his weekly flutter on the horses.

When he was mid-flare-up, even his fingertips were affected, either through loss of skin or through being covered in ointment. Helen learnt how to roll his cigarettes for him, with Rizlas and Golden Virginia, hardly an eighth of an inch thick, to make the tobacco last longer.

In spite of the many activities which they enjoyed doing together, which Owen showed no interest in, it was always, 'Helen, go and help Mummy with the dishes', and never Owen.

The decade of the seventies brought many changes for the Linton-Houses. After the unfortunate events on Osea Island, Keith and Eileen had retired to North Wales. No more driving the tractor and trailer for Ben, or so he thought.

When Helen was twelve years old, Frederick Sawyer decided to sell Moat Cottage, and the Linton-House family had to move to social housing in Yalding. Their new house was actually owned by Courage's brewery, but let by the local council, and was about three quarters of a mile from the centre of the village, surrounded by hop gardens. Ben, with Helen's assistance, made 'contiboard' shelves and cupboards for the living room, and some wooden-framed and plywood wall-cupboards for the kitchen.

Outside, he planted dahlias in the flower bed which bordered the lawn, against the concrete path running from the house to the gate. They were all different varieties, yellow, yellow and pink, purple and white, white, red and white, salmon-pink, deep orange and deep red, with half the tubers coming from Keith, and the other half brought as divisions from the cottage. The blooms had always been spectacular, although they were a little sparse for this first flowering in their new situation.

When September arrived and it was time to bring in the hops, Ben found himself entering another flare-up, but was determined to work on the hop-harvest if he could. He wandered down to the farm to ask if there were any tractor-driving jobs, explaining his condition and the need for an opportunity where he could be seated. Ben couldn't be sure if the manager was being desperate for workers or compassionate towards him, but he was taken on as the driver of the tractor which supported the crow's nest. Self-conscious of his beard, rapidly filling with scales, he donned sunglasses, and a canvas hat pulled down over his upturned collar. As they entered the second week, Ben was in agony every time he put pressure on the pedals, but he survived the three weeks of hop-picking.

Apart from Ben and two permanent Courage's farmworkers, most of the hop-pickers were not local. This year, unannounced, a Social Security officer came to check their identities, including Ben's, and he was still claiming sickness benefit. On the penultimate day of hop-picking, the same Social Security officer knocked on the Linton-Houses' door.

"Come in," Gail greeted him.

Ben was sitting in his armchair, looking like Lazarus, with his feet resting on the pouffe, having just finished applying ointment and gauze.

"Mr Linton-House?"

"Guilty as charged. I mean, yes, I'm sorry. I was claiming benefits and I was driving a tractor. But look at me. I was just trying to earn some extra cash for Christmas. No one will employ me when this happens every three or four months."

"I understand, fully. The thing is though, you were still committing fraud. Is this the only thing you do to earn money?"

Having given up refereeing, the previous season, Ben could reply honestly.

"Just this. And only for three weeks in September."

"I'll tell you what I'm going to do. You will receive an official warning, and if it happens again, you risk going to prison. If you pay back the benefits, for the weeks you worked on the tractor, we'll leave it at that."

"That's very understanding of you. Thank you."

The Social Security officer handed Ben a document to sign, which Ben scanned briefly, before scribbling his name at the bottom.

"In practice, what will happen, is that you won't receive the next three weeks' payments, to claw back the money you received when you were working."

"Understood," replied Ben, as the Social Security officer got up to leave.

"If it was up to me, I'd ignore it. To me, you're a hero for putting yourself through this. I can't imagine what it's like to live with that condition. But I'd lose my own job, if I didn't follow things up properly."

"Thank you."

Gail showed him to the door.

"Thank you. Bye."

467

"Goodbye Mrs Linton-House."

Gail went and sat down on the settee.

"Phew," she sighed.

"I think we were lucky. He was a decent man. I'm glad the children weren't here to hear it all, though.

Owen had started at Tonbridge School, and the family made no end of sacrifices, to muster the half fees and season-ticket for the train, so losing the three weeks wages for tractor-driving hurt. They were also trying to save enough money for Owen to go on a school trip to Russia the following Spring, now that he was learning Russian.

It was while Owen was away that Gail had overheard a conversation in the village store about strawberry-picking. Although the Linton-Houses' house was on Courage's land, the opposite side of the road was a different farm, belonging to the Waltons. Although they owned several hop gardens, half of their land were established apple and cherry orchards, and diagonally across from the Linton-Houses' were two large strawberry fields.

Gail went to the office and asked if she could pick strawberries. As the strawberries were coming to an end, she also discovered that they grew runner beans, and she was asked if she wanted to pick them, which took her through the holidays. Strawberries were piece work, paid by the tray, and many of the women were helped by their children, who had come down from London, missing school. Gail and Ben would not allow Owen and Helen to miss school. Bean-picking began at the end of term but was paid by the hour. Beans gave way to hops as the new term started, so Gail stopped working.

Through picking fruit, Gail got to know the farm manager, Donald Vine, and Helen started to baby-sit his two small boys. He understood things were difficult for Ben and Gail, and when Helen was fourteen and Owen sixteen, he suggested they could work for the same hourly rate as Gail, just as long as they picked a sensible number of boxes and worked the same hours. Appreciative of his offer, as soon as they returned from a fortnight in Wales, with Keith and Eileen, the two teenagers accompanied Gail to the bean field, where they worked hard, but were simply not as quick as Gail, who was herself slower than most of the other women. Sometimes she gave one of her boxes to Owen or Helen, in the hope that the other women wouldn't judge them and complain. In any case, their own children picked beans which added to their overall count of boxes, so Gail wasn't lagging behind quite as much as she felt she was. Donald watched them from afar, and was satisfied that the children were working hard, so said nothing about the numbers.

Being paid four weeks' wages was like winning the football pools to Helen. At the end of the first summer, she ordered a stereo record player from Gail's Littlewoods catalogue. Owen asked if his money could be banked as he wanted to add it to the following year's, to buy a motorbike. At the end of his second summer, he bought a Honda 250cc motorbike, and started going to parties, now that he had transport, which was where he acquired some cannabis resin.

Unfortunately for Owen, he left it sitting on top of his bureau, and Ben had to go into his room for the household roll of Sellotape, saw it, and picked it up. Helen was in the living room when Ben came downstairs and saw him place something in one of the empty brass candlesticks on the mantlepiece. After Ben had gone out into the garden, Helen's curiosity got the better of her, and she went over to look in the candlestick. About the size of a rabbit dropping, with a similar appearance and texture, she knew exactly what it was. Owen had shown her some cannabis, a few weeks before, but she had declined his offer to smoke a joint.

Not always the loyal sister, Helen figured there was no way of preventing Owen from being disciplined, but wasting the drugs was pointless, as they weren't cheap. Taking herself off for a walk down the hop garden, she found some rabbit droppings and picked one up in a tissue. When she got back to the house, and with Ben in the bathroom, she swapped the dropping for the cannabis, which she wrapped in a second tissue and kept in her pocket.

About an hour and a half later, Owen arrived home and went straight up to his room.

"Owen!" called Ben. "Can you come downstairs please."

Owen anticipated the worst, because the cannabis was no longer where he had left it. He went downstairs.

"What is this?" inquired Ben, sternly, shaking the dropping out of the candlestick into his hand.

Helen tried not to smirk.

"Cannabis resin."

"Are you completely stupid?"

"It's just cannabis, Daddy. It's not like heroin or cocaine. You can't get addicted."

"I'm still not happy about it. It can lead to something worse."

"Well, I won't allow it to lead to something worse."

"You won't full-stop. I'm throwing this in the Rayburn. I don't want to find you've been buying any more drugs. Are we clear?"

"Perfectly clear."

"Now go to your room."

Owen went up to his bedroom, and Ben disposed of the dropping in the Rayburn fire, topping it up with coke as he did. The Rayburn had to burn all year round, as it supplied their hot water, but Gail only ever used the oven side, a bit like a slow cooker, to make rice pudding or Tuesday rubbish. The latter was a root vegetable and potato casserole, usually with mutton, and occasionally with chicken. Gail would put the casserole in the oven in the morning, go to Maidstone on the bus, for the weekly Tuesday shopping, and it was ready when she came home. As for rice pudding, if it sat for several hours in the oven, by the time it was served it had grown a thick brown skin on top, and underneath was all creamy.

Helen waited for an hour after the reprimand and tapped on Owen's door.

"What do you want?" he asked, clearly irritated.

"There's no need to be nasty. You should be grateful."

"Why?"

"Because what Daddy threw in the Rayburn was a rabbit dropping. This is the cannabis," whispered Helen.

"No way! Why did you do that? I mean thank you," responded Owen, almost unable to keep his voice down.

"Sometimes you have to show solidarity against your parents."

"I owe you one."

"Yes, you do," laughed Helen.

Ben was frustrated at not being able to support his family. He wondered if Saul had become a successful doctor or lawyer in New York. There was no way that Ben could ever afford to go to America to find him. Limiting his stakes severely, Ben tried to increase his income through betting on the horses. If he won, he allowed himself to re-stake half his winnings, the other half going in a box in the wardrobe. Mostly, he was betting with pennies rather than pounds and had to rely on accumulator bets to stand any chance of a decent win. Usually, he placed three ten pence accumulator bets on the ITV Seven, with a couple of other random place bets. Gail knew he gambled but didn't mind too much as she had control of the family finances, and in any case, Ben was using his 'pocket money', the amount he and Gail agreed that each could spend on themselves. He was not the luckiest person on the planet, his horse often finishing fourth when he had a place bet which paid out on first, second or third.

One exceptional moment of luck produced a new colour television, not from gambling, but from winning second prize in a competition for naming a new soft cheese. Their old black and white television constantly needed thumping, to stop the screen from shifting, always at a key moment in the programme. Understandably, Helen was excited about the new, colour television. It was a remote-control model, so Ben decided to have some fun at Helen's expense. Nothing was said, and having switched on manually, the family settled in to watch Coronation Street. Ben was concealing the device between his armchair and the bookcases, on the opposite side of the room from where Helen was seated, and after about five minutes, he changed channels. At first there was no response, so he changed it back again, waited another five minutes and switched channels again.

"Wait. What just happened? Is this remote control?" asked Helen.

"Maybe it was just the signal," replied Ben, returning to the soap opera.

He waited a further few minutes and changed it again. Meanwhile Helen, who now suspected more than ever, that the dark, opaque plastic strip along the bottom of the screen covered the receiver, played along. Nothing more was said, even though Ben changed channels twice more, before the end of the episode, much to Gail's frustration.

In the morning, whilst Ben was still asleep, Helen investigated further, and her suspicions were confirmed. She resolved to play her own practical joke and removed the batteries from the device. When Ben came to switch on the television to watch the ITV Seven, he couldn't change channels.

"Are these what you're looking for?" laughed Helen.

"Rumbled again," responded Ben, laughing too, as Helen handed him the batteries.

"You know you won this television in a competition Daddy? I want to enter a short story competition. Will you read my story, please?"

"Of course. What's it about?"

"Well, the last line has to be, '… and with that, he waved to the crowd'. I've written a sort of science fiction. I mean it's an operation that hasn't happened yet, but I think one day it could. It's called 'The Operation'. I won't spoil it by telling you the plot. It's only a thousand words."

"Alright. I'll read it after I've watched the racing."

Helen ran up to her room and came back with a hand-written page of file paper.

"Here it is."

Ben took it, smiled, placed it on the bookshelves and settled back into his armchair, the Mirror on his lap, his betting slips on the arm of the chair.

By the end of the afternoon, he had just about covered his outlay with two horses that finished second and third in the last two races. Gail liked to watch the wrestling at four o'clock, so Ben took Helen's story and went upstairs to read.

'Nothing unusual ever happened at O'Brien & Sons. The machines were turned on at eight o'clock in the morning and off again at twelve, you had half an hour for lunch, and the machines went on again until five, unless, of course, there was a blockage or an accident. Then the machines would be turned off and Mick O'Brien senior would pace up and down, impatiently, losing money by the minute.

Mick O'Brien junior, his eldest son, had left school at sixteen without any O Levels to his name, and began working at the family business. Metal rods came in by lorry, once a week, and were unloaded into the store. Mick and the other two employees either worked the cutting machine, the drilling machine, or the press, and if they weren't at a machine, they were welding. O'Brien & Sons made industrial cages, and the only variation was the size and shape of the cages.

To relieve boredom, a transistor radio was tuned to Radio One, and played at full volume, although you could hardly hear the music over the machinery. That morning, Mick O'Brien junior was on the cutting machine. In between cutting, he could hear the DJ announce a competition. He would play three songs backwards, and the listener had to send the song titles on a postcard to the BBC studios.

As O'Brien passed a metal rod under the saw blade, he turned to catch the third song being played backwards. What happened next was a blur. All he could remember was a stinging sensation unlike any he had felt before and the sight of blood pouring from his glove.

"Help!" he yelled, thumping the red emergency button with his good hand.

The workshop fell silent, as Chaz and Jonesy came running. Wondering why the machines had been switched off mid-morning, O'Brien senior came out of his office to see Chaz running out of the toilet with the entire roller towel.

"Call an ambulance. Mick's had an accident."

O'Brien senior went back into his office and dialled 999, and then realised he didn't know what had happened. He ran back into the workshop. There was blood all over the cutting machine. His son was lying on the floor, his hand wound round with towel, like a Halloween mummy.

"What the hell have you done?"

"He's going to lose his hand, Mr O'Brien," responded Chaz. "It's about cut through. He missed the fingers and thumb but the blade's done a lot of damage."

Chaz demonstrated where the cut was by pointing to his own hand, but O'Brien senior had already started back to the office. A few minutes later, he returned to his son's side.

"Health and Safety will be all over us. We'll have to shut down for a bit, boys."

O'Brien junior could hardly string three words together. He'd lost a lot of blood and was in a bad way. The ambulance arrived.

"Tidy the workshop and lock up will you, boys. I'm going in the ambulance. I'll let you know when you can come back to work. Don't worry. You'll get your wages."

"Thanks Mr O'Brien," replied Jonesy, 'Hope Mick's going to be OK."

At the hospital, they rushed him into Accident & Emergency, and O'Brien senior was made to wait in the seating area. After what seemed like an eternity, the consultant came and found him.

"Mr O'Brien?"

O'Brien senior nodded.

"I have some good news for you. Your son is being prepped for emergency surgery. The cut was clean. We have a team who have been pioneering a new technique in what we call micro-surgery. They are going to try and re-attach your son's hand. It will mean re-joining tendons, blood vessels and nerves. If it doesn't work, they will have to amputate anyway, but they want a shot at saving your son's hand."

"Right. Yes. Good. Thank you."

"It will be a very long operation. You're welcome to wait here, but I suggest you go home, and we'll let you know when your son comes out of surgery."

"It's OK. I'll wait. Is there somewhere I can get a coffee?"

"Yes. Go back to reception and the cafeteria is beyond."

"Thank you."

Seven cups of coffee later, the neurosurgeon came to find O'Brien senior.

"We think the operation was a complete success. At least, we have attached all the vessels, tendons and nerves and stitched up the flesh. We won't know for certain for a few days whether the hand is viable. If it is, there is still the big question if the nerves will function properly, and even then, your son will need several weeks of rehabilitation and physiotherapy to get the fingers working again. He may never regain a hundred percent control. We just don't know."

"Can I see him?"

"He's on morphine, but you can sit with him. I expect he'll sleep through until the morning. Follow me."

O'Brien senior was led to his son's bedside where he sat waiting for him to wake up.

O'Brien junior recovered well. The surgery team monitored him closely for the first week and decided that the hand did not need to be amputated. He was discharged after three weeks.

The successful, pioneering operation drew a lot of media attention. At first, they spoke mostly with the surgical team, but the day that O'Brien junior was discharged, reporters were waiting for him in front of the hospital, and a small crowd had gathered.

"Mr O'Brien. Do you have anything you would like to say?"

"I just want to offer my heartfelt thanks to the team of surgeons who have saved my hand," he answered, holding up the hand they had operated on. "This hand is nothing short of a miracle. That's all."

And with that he waved to the crowd.'

Ben thought that it wasn't a bad story, although he wondered if the judges would think it was too far-fetched.

"Well done. I think you should send it in," Ben encouraged her when he came downstairs for dinner.

"Thanks, Daddy."

Feeling that his daughter's creative-writing abilities came from him, Ben thought he might give it a try himself. He spent more and more time in his room, occupied by his new interest, which he shared with Helen. First drafts were done by hand, with his spidery, biro script, which unusually, was all in capital letters. It took a while for Helen to grow accustomed to reading it. His first novel was science fiction and recounted the spread of a global pandemic, whose origins were in Africa. Having typed the manuscript on his manual typewriter, which took forever, due to Ben only using his two index fingers on the keys, with every sheet carbon-copied, and every mistake corrected using a special white transfer, he sent off his novel to a publisher, only to have it returned a few weeks later. Five publishers later, and still not accepted, Ben gave up and started writing a children's story, about a bear named Wendy. This little bear had several siblings, Sunday Bear, Monday Bear and Friday Bear, named after the days on which they were born, but her mother couldn't say Wednesday, so 'Wendy Bear' it was. The adventures were entertaining enough, but with Pooh and Paddington already on the market, the first publisher that Ben approached rejected it as unoriginal, as did the second and the third. Ben grew disillusioned.

Remembering that he once wrote song lyrics, Ben sent a letter to Max and invited him to collaborate on a song for the competition to identify the United Kingdom Eurovision entry. Sadly, the song was unsuccessful, which generated a bitter remonstration about contemporary lyrics, none of which Ben considered skilful.

"Songs are rubbish these days. Half of them don't even a rhyme. Rubbish, I tell you. Not like we used to write songs."

His own collection of 45s included songs like Roger Whittaker's *I don't believe in 'If' anymore* and The Everly Brothers' *Cathy's Clown*. Most of his music collection was instrumentals, LPs, very often theme music from films. He also had a collection of crackly 78s, but these were more recorded stories than songs.

When the Sex Pistols brought out *Never Mind the Bollocks*, it caused another opportunity for Owen to clash with his father. Not only did Owen have a bright yellow and pink poster of the album cover on his wall, but he also had a poster showing images of feet in eight different positions, clearly intended to represent a man and a woman having sex under a quilt. They were visible opposite the open door, and even though Ben hardly ever went into Owen's room, since the occasion of the cannabis, he couldn't help noticing the posters.

"You can take those posters down, for a start," he barked.

Owen took them off the wall, reluctantly. It was only a few months later that Ben chose to impose his opinion again. Owen was playing the radio, with his bedroom door open. Nick Lowe could be heard singing, 'I love the sound of breaking glass', and it proved too much for Ben.

"Well, I don't love the sound of breaking glass!" he yelled up the stairs.

Owen turned the volume down, remembering how traumatised his father was when glass shattered.

"Sorry Daddy," he conceded.

Whether Ben had heard his apology was unclear, because he seemed more concerned about the structure of the lyrics, than the content.

"They've got no idea how to write lyrics these days. Total and utter rubbish."

Owen started to spend more and more time at friends, and when he was home, he stayed in his room and made sure he only ever listened to music with headphones on.

For reasons which Ben was unable to fathom, their next-door neighbours decided to buy a pedigree, chocolate-point Burmese, which they named Cadbury. During the day, the cat was shut outside, while Abe and Carol were at work. Needless to say, Cadbury meowed, on and off, all day and every day, and Burmese cats have a whining voice. Button had died a few years before, from kidney failure, having to be put to sleep, and last year, Threepence lost his life to a car, a few yards along the road from the front gate. After three weeks without a cat, after waiting to come out of the other end of another flare-up, Ben had fetched Joey, another ginger kitten. It was never Ben's intention to have a second cat in the house but listening to Cadbury angered Ben.

After four months, he couldn't tolerate the neglect any longer, and when Abe came home from work, Ben marched round to the neighbours' back door.

"Hello. I noticed you got a cat, but you are out all day. As you know, I love cats. I was wondering if you'd sell Cadbury to me. You'll still see him, but he'll be able to come into the house during the day."

"I'll have to talk with the wife."

"Let me know what she says."

Ben was frustrated not to have an instant response, but hopeful Carol might agree. He had to wait until the following day. There was a knock at the door just as the dinner plates were being cleared away. It was Abe.

"Carol says you can take Cadbury off our hands."

"How much did you pay for him?"

"You can have him for fifty quid."

"Wait there," replied Ben, curious if that was the price Abe had paid, but not about to haggle.

He went upstairs and rummaged around in the bottom of his wardrobe, returning downstairs with five ten-pound notes.

"There you go. I'll come and fetch him."

"Carol's got him in the house."

Ben followed Abe round to his kitchen. The house smelt of Tom cat.

"Is he neutered?" inquired Ben.

"No. We was going to breed from him."

Ben managed to control his annoyance. At least Cadbury would now get to experience the affection he deserved. Carol picked up Cadbury by the scruff of his neck and handed him to Ben, who wrapped his cardigan round the cat and held him tight.

"Thank you."

"You're welcome."

Gail and Ben kept Cadbury shut in the house for two weeks, until they felt he had familiarised himself with the sounds and smells of his new home and got used to his new brother. Joey spent the first ten days peering out from under the bed, until he realised that Cadbury was a permanent fixture, whereupon he returned to his regular spot, curled up on the pouffe. After hissing at Cadbury a couple of times he just ignored the interloper.

Now registered with a vet in Wateringbury, Ben made an appointment to have Cadbury neutered, which restricted him to a further two weeks of quarantine. Both cats were spoiled with tinned pilchard. Like the cottage in Collier Street, the house in Yalding benefitted from an open fire, and Cadbury liked nothing better than to stretch out on the hearthrug soaking up the heat.

Hardly had they settled into being a two-cat household again than Joey lost his life to a passing car. The emotional effect on Ben was to bring on an immediate psoriasis flare-up, putting him back in bed. Cadbury joined him on the bed for hours on end. Unfortunately, whenever he ventured into the bedroom, he picked up flakes of dead skin from the floor and trapsed them through the house on his way to the catflap. Gail didn't mind, as Cadbury was good for Ben. Helen, for her part, made a point of trying to spend at least half an hour every day talking to her father.

Gail and Ben had had twin beds since moving to Yalding, and Helen would sit on Gail's bed, chatting. One day, prompted by watching *The Dambusters* on television, the night before, Helen caught Ben off guard, by speaking about the war?

"Daddy. Why do you have a war pension?"

"Because of my knee."

"Yes, but how did your knee get injured?"

"A piece of shrapnel from a Stuka."

"What's shrapnel?"

"A fragment of metal, usually caused by a weapon of some sort."

"Which regiment did you serve with?"

"The Royal Norfolks. Why do you want to bring up the painful past?"

"I wanted to know. Owen's in the CCF isn't he? He wants to be a fighter pilot when he leaves school."

"Any chance you could bring me a cup of tea, please?"

"Of course," responded Helen, knowing that the conversation had been shut down.

She couldn't understand why Ben wouldn't talk about the war. Surely, he was proud of what he'd done. She went downstairs and made him a cup of tea.

The following summer, Helen took her 'O' Levels, which meant she had most of June off school, after her last exam. She was able to pick strawberries, as well as beans. It was also another summer when Ben's heart was broken, not by a woman, but by his own son.

Owen was expelled from school, on his last day there. Apparently, he had been selling pornographic magazines to the other boys. He had found them in a bin, whilst on a Combined Cadet Force camp. One of his runners had been caught, at which point, Owen owned up to his enterprise. After all the sacrifices which the family had made, Ben could hardly look at Owen, and worse was to come.

The day before his eighteenth birthday, Owen went off on his motorcycle and didn't come home. Ben was worried sick, fearing an accident, until the next day when the phone rang, shortly before five in the evening. The Linton-Houses had only recently had a telephone installed.

"Hello, Daddy. It's Owen. I'm just letting you know that I'm not coming home. I'm sorry. I think it's for the best. Tell Mummy I'm sorry. Bye."

Owen had replaced the receiver before Ben even had a chance to reply. Replacing his own receiver, Ben sat motionless, trying to process what Owen had just said. He knew things were bad, but he didn't think they were that bad. Ben had hoped that the distance created by Owen going off to university would ease their strained relationship. Had he been too hard on Owen? Had he and Gail put too much pressure on their son? He went into the kitchen.

"That was Owen. He asked me to tell you he's sorry. He also said he isn't coming home again."

Gail's eyes welled up, and she sat down at the kitchen table.

"At least we know he's safe. Do you think he told Helen?"

"I don't know. We'd better go up and tell her."

Ben led Gail up the stairs and knocked on Helen's door. There was no response. He opened it and went in, followed by Gail, who was crying. Helen was lying on her bed, listening to a record through her headphones. Their entrance startled her.

"Sorry. Didn't mean to make you jump," apologised Gail.

"What on earth has happened? Is it Owen?"

"He has just rung to say that he's left home, for good. We thought you should know."

"I saw him leave, yesterday. I thought he was just going to a party."

"He probably did go to a party. He just isn't coming home from the party. Or ever."

"OK. Thanks for telling me."

"We'll leave you to your music."

For the next few days, the Linton-House household, minus one, was rather subdued. Helen felt like she was walking on eggshells. Gail was dealing with her sense of loss, as well as walking on eggshells. Neither Gail nor Helen quite knew how Ben would react. They fully expected him to blow at any moment, having tried to keep a lid on his emotions. Finally, the volcano erupted, at lunchtime the following Sunday. Gail had made scrambled eggs on toast and the eggs were not as firm as Ben liked them. He threw his fork across the room. Thankfully, it missed Gail's head by a foot, and clanged into the Rayburn. Not enough to quell his rage, he took a swipe at his glass and sent it flying from the table with his forearm. It went flying into the fridge where it shattered. This time, instead of freezing, carried by his anger, Ben stood and stormed off down the garden path, out into the hop garden.

STAINED GLASS

During the next eighteen months, Ben and Gail cleared Owen's bedroom and re-painted it, and Helen and Drew became closer. On the agreement that she was always home before the pubs closed, Ben had agreed to Helen buying a Honda SS50 with her fruit-picking earnings. She was also selected to play for the Kent Under 18 second eleven, which was a huge disappointment to her as she'd played for the Under 16 first team, but in practice, she was always the first-choice substitute and played in all the first team games. Ben spent more and more time in bed, partly due to his flare-ups, although even when he could have dressed and gone downstairs, he seemed reluctant to. He was sinking into a spiral of depression. His successes were past, his failures ever-present. Top of the list was his sense of failure as a parent to Owen.

The hockey season was half over when Ben recovered from his latest flare-up. The Kent U18s were due to play at home, against Hampshire, and Helen was called up to the fist team, again.

"Will you come and watch me play, Daddy?" asked Helen, hopefully, the evening before her match.

"Where is it?"

"Tonbridge School. We're using the school pitches because it's about as close to Hampshire as you can be, when you're in Kent."

The thought of going to Tonbridge caused Ben heartache, but he didn't want to disappoint Helen. After all, she did take after him, with her sporting abilities, something about which he reminded her of often. She hated, the way he seemed be trying to take credit for her sporting successes.

"Yes, of course. I can go over on the moped. What time does the match start?"

"Eleven o'clock. I've got to be there for ten."

"I'll see you there, then."

On matchday, Ben went over to Tonbridge, as promised, and stood on the touchline, waiting for the teams to come out of the changing room. Seeing him, made Helen feel unusually nervous. Twenty minutes into the game, the ball went out to the right wing. Running down the centre of the pitch, Helen tracked the progress of the winger.

"Cross!" she called.

Looking up, the winger hit the ball diagonally into the circle, behind the defender who was coming out to tackle her. Helen ran onto the ball, and with the goalkeeper rushing towards her, connected with the moving ball and smashed it through the goalkeeper's legs, into the goal. As the satisfying sound of ball thwacking wooden backboards echoed across the pitch, Helen jumped up with her arm aloft, looking across at Ben, for approval. He nodded to her, all the while applauding the goal. The game finished one-all. It was the only time Ben watched Helen representing the county, and she had scored.

He didn't wait for Helen to get changed after the match.

"You played well," he encouraged her, when she arrived home.

"Did you play football, as well as referee it?"

Once upon a time. I couldn't really tackle, with my knee."

"Did you do any other sports?"

"I boxed, when I was your age. I won a championship. Then war started. I won an army boxing tournament. I haven't boxed since. Are there any more home matches?"

"No. The last game of the season is away to Berkshire. I really hope I can play for the university."

Helen was due to start at Nottingham, in the autumn, having been given a conditional offer.

"Yes. I really hope I am well enough, come September, to get you to Nottingham. We'll have to hire a car at the start and end of the year. You can come back on the coach and train, in between times."

"If you're not well enough, I'm sure Drew's mum will let him drive me in her car. He drives us places now."

"Of course. I'd still like to be able to be a father dropping his daughter off at university."

"Thank you."

As a father, Ben could be a walking contradiction. A couple of months later, when Helen announced she and Drew were going on a hitch-hiking holiday to the Lake District and Snowdonia, he went all Victorian on her.

"One tent or two?" Ben inquired.

"One. We'll have separate sleeping bags, but why carry two tents?"

"Trollop!" blurted out Ben. "Not my daughter."

Helen was somewhat taken aback. She and Drew weren't even sleeping together, and the decision to take one tent was purely practical. She knew not to argue, though, and went up to her room.

When she told Drew, at the weekend, he surprised Helen in a different way.

"Well, what about if we got engaged? Do you think your dad would be OK about it then? I mean, I want to marry you, not just so we can share a tent."

"Wow. Of course, I'll marry you."

"Let's go to London for the day and we can get you a ring from Oxford Street."

At the end of their exhausting but fruitful excursion, Drew drove Helen home, and went in with her to break the news to Ben and Gail.

"We've got some news for you," announced Helen.

Ben and Gail were watching television, so Ben lowered the volume.

"Helen and I have just got engaged."

"Congratulations!" responded Gail.

"We won't get married until Helen graduates, but we thought we'd get engaged before she goes off to university and I go into the RAF."

"Very good news that is too. By the way, I've been thinking. You're right. It's better to carry only one tent."

That was about as close as Helen was likely to come to an apology, but she knew to quit while she was winning.

Come the start of the university term, Ben was just about well enough to drive, so he hired a Fiat 127, and loaded it with Helen's belongings, two suitcases and a rucksack. Helen placed her hockey stick on top, and Ben closed the boot. She would be living in one of the halls of residence, so no pots and pans were necessary. Gail, however, packed a cardboard box with coffee, tea, sugar and powdered milk, two mugs, two plates, two settings of cutlery and one of those one-mug boilers that you plugged in and placed the element in a mug of water of milk. There was no room in the boot for the box, so Gail squashed it on the floor behind her seat. Drew came too.

Feeling nostalgic, Ben chose to drive into London, out along the Edgeware Road, and up the M1. He was confident driving in the city, although there was a lot more traffic than he had previously experienced as a driver. By the time they reached Toddington Services, everyone was ready to use the toilets. Gail had brought along a flask and some fruit cake, as everything was so expensive at motorway services. After Ben had closed his eyes for twenty minutes, they went on their way.

Helen had been sent directions, which indicated they needed to leave at Junction 25. Counting off the junctions, she grew more and more nervous. For a couple of years now, since Owen had left home, she had felt the weight of her parents' aspirations pass to her shoulders, especially now she was heading off to university. She was also becoming increasingly weepy, as up to this point, her longest time away from home was three weeks with a Belgian family in south-west France. Four hours and five minutes after leaving Yalding, Ben parked the car outside the hall of residence, which he thought looked strangely reminiscent of Colditz. Between the four off them, they carried Helen's things up to her room on the second floor in one trip.

"We'll say goodbye, here," insisted Ben. "Mummy and I will go back down to the car so you and Drew can have five minutes."

"Thank you for driving me," mumbled Helen, her eyes welling up.

Ben stepped forward and gave her a hug.

"You can come home for the weekend at half-term. The time will fly by," Gail encouraged her, holding out her arms for a hug. "I'll write to you every week, and you can always phone us. We'll call you back."

"Come on. Let's give these two some space. Five minutes, Drew."

"Yes, Mr Linton-House."

Ben and Gail turned and went back along the corridor.

"She'll be fine," declared Ben, as he and Gail got in the car. "Especially if she gets to play hockey for the university."

"You know she doesn't make friends easily. I just hope she settles quickly and doesn't find the study too difficult."

Drew came jogging over to the car.

"Thank you," he said, as he got in.

Nothing else was said for the entire journey. Ben was wrapped up in his thoughts at the same time as concentrating on his driving. Gail would have burst into tears if anyone had forced her to chat. Drew was wondering if their relationship would survive. RAF Cranwell was not so far from Nottingham, but he might not get much opportunity to visit.

Ben's flare-ups became more regular, and with Helen away at university, not only did Ben draft in Gail to take his weekly flutter to the bookmakers, but she also learnt how to roll his cigarettes for him. During his second spell in bed that year, he found his thoughts turning to Saul, and he chided himself for going to South Africa, all those years ago, when he had the means to travel to New York in search of his brother. What was he doing now? Had he fought in the Korean War? Where had Saul been when President Kennedy was shot? Ben decided to write a letter to Max, who sometimes went to New York on music business, asking him to search the public records for Saul Lindenheim, next time he was on the other side of the Atlantic.

Max was Ben's oldest and dearest friend. He had married late, too late for his wife, Diana, to have children. Ben should have been Max's best man but was right in the middle of a bad flare-up when the date arrived, and not wanting to embarrass Max, turning up at his wedding scaly and smelly, had declined the honour and sent a telegram instead. Every year, until they each turned eighteen, for birthdays and Christmas, Max sent a card and some money to Owen and Helen. It was a longshot, but if anyone could trace Saul, it was Max. Ben wrote regularly to his friend, and if Ben was going to need Gail to post the letter, it was better addressed to Max than to a Jewish-American organisation or even to a Saul Lindenheim, c/o New York Public Library. Ben surmised that his brother, who had always loved to read books, might well be a member, if he now lived in New York at all. Half hopeful, Ben resolved to cross the bridge of explaining a return letter, as and when he came to it.

The summer vacation, at the end of Helen's first year at university proved traumatic. Drew decided to break off the engagement. He waited until Helen was home and visited her in person to declare his intention. Apologising to Ben and Gail, saying his own parents had split up, and he was axed from flying fighter-jets, so just wanted a clean break. In many ways, Ben felt he understood the sentiment. Helen was inconsolable. After Drew had left, Helen went through the back door and headed off down the hop garden. Realising there was a river at the bottom, and concerned for her state of mind, Ben pulled on his wellingtons and followed at a distance. Reaching the bank, she was nowhere to be seen, and he started to panic.

"Helen! Helen! Daddy's here," he called.

No reply.

"Helen. Are you alright!" he called out, again.

Still no reply.

Helen was concealed under an overhanging bush and had no intention of being found. Ben walked along the bottom of the hop garden and returned to the house.

"Didn't you hear me calling?" he asked, a little irritated, but also relieved Helen came back.

"No," she lied.

"Where did you go?"

"Through the hedge and back round past the sewage-works."

"Will you be OK?"

"What else can I be?"

Gail came in with Helen's Chelsea FC mug and Ben's extra-large cup and saucer.

"I've sugared it," explained Gail, handing the mug to Helen.

"Thanks."

Helen just wanted to go to her room and cry. Ben's feet were sore from walking round the hop garden, mid flare-up.

"I'm going to go and put some ointment on," he announced, levering himself out of the armchair and hobbling across to the stairs.

In the summer of 1985, Helen graduated from Nottingham University, but like every other occasion relating to his children's achievements, with the exception of the Kent Under 18 hockey match against Hampshire, Ben was absent, and Gail attended the ceremony alone. Throughout her schooling, Ben had attempted to hold a conversation with Helen in French every so often. By the time she graduated, he admitted that she probably spoke better French than he did, but somehow claimed her linguistic genes, like her sporting genes, came from his side of the family, much to Helen's annoyance.

At the end of the holidays, just before she was due to leave for a year in French-speaking Switzerland, Helen had a road-to-Damascus conversion to Christianity. Although no longer a practising Jew, but with the indelible memories of his experience of persecution, Ben struggled to accept Helen's new-found faith. The subject was avoided in conversation, and although they still conversed, Helen felt a growing distance from her father. Having struggled to find motivation, until her final year at university, Helen understood Owen's burden to live up to his parents' aspirations.

"Where did you go to school, Daddy?" she inquired, on one occasion.

"Winchester."

"Is that why you wanted Owen to go to Tonbridge."

"There was an opportunity for your brother to get a good education. What parent wouldn't have encouraged their son?"

"But not daughter?"

"Helen, there were no opportunities like that for girls. You know we would have put you forward, if there had been."

"Did you have a brother or sister?"

"A brother who was killed in Africa. Two sisters and my parents were killed in the Blitz. Now, you know I don't like talking about the past."

"Sorry," apologised Helen, getting up to leave.

A letter arrived from Max, in the second post. Helen took it upstairs. Ben was nervous to open it. Unsure what he had been expecting of Max, disappointment started to choke Ben as he read. It turned out there were thirteen Lindenheims registered in the New York area, of which four had the initial 'S'. There was no way of finding where they all resided during the time Max had to spare. He also mentioned five deceased Lindenheims. Ben began to wonder how many cousins he had, who successfully fled Germany before the war, or even how many people shared the name, but weren't related, and had perhaps settled in New York in the previous century. Ben chided himself for having dared to dream. Max's final sentence, however, held the tiniest fragment of hope. Acknowledging the lack of time and attention he had to follow up on his enquiries, Max had placed an advert in the Liederkranz Club, with Ben's name and address.

It seemed a cruel blow, six weeks after receiving Max's letter, that the Linton-Houses had to change their address once more. The farm was being sold, and the houses withdrawn from the local council. Ben and Gail were given only four weeks' notice to leave, and Ben created such a stink, demanding better protection from the local authority, that they were offered a brand-new house on a small estate in Leeds Village, not far from the castle.

Ben was just on the recovering side of a flare-up and could walk. He hired a van, and he and Gail moved themselves. Cadbury was taken over in the second trip, after they had configured the bedroom to look as similar as possible to the bedroom they were vacating. He had food, drink, his litter tray and space to hide under a bed, if necessary. The move required eight trips to and from the new house, and with no time or opportunity to sort and pack properly, they moved a few items which might otherwise have been relegated to the tip. The final trip was completed at just after seven, too late to return the van. Gail insisted on staying behind to clean the old house, despite Ben's remonstrations.

"Why bother. The council should be made to pay to have it cleaned."

"The council will pay to have it cleaned, anyway. At least they won't think we live like pigs, though."

With the furniture gone, Gail was embarrassed by the amount of Ben's scales she discovered against the skirting-board, which had escaped her regular efforts at sweeping under the wardrobe and bed.

"I'll see you back at the new place, then. I don't want to leave Cadbury any longer than I have to."

"Yes. See you shortly."

Ben went off in the van, leaving Gail to finish off. After three quarters of an hour of cleaning, she locked the house and rode over to Leeds on her moped with the hoover sitting between her legs on the step-through footrest, and the broom tied with gauze like a crossbar. She felt safe enough, but if the police had stopped her, they might have disagreed.

The new house in Farmer Close fronted the main road through the village. The garden gate opened onto a parking area, edged by the recreation ground. One of the first do-it-yourself tasks which Ben undertook at the new property was to build a cat-flap in the six-foot wooden gate. Gail thought it was a strange thing to do. After all, cats are very good at climbing, as demonstrated on a regular basis, in the months to come, by Cadbury sunning himself on the roof of the shed and crawling, commando-style, along the fence-panels.

Cadbury took to wandering off, regularly, down to the wood at the bottom of the playing field. At least, that's where Ben assumed the almost daily supply of baby rabbits was coming from, when Cadbury dragged them through the cat-flap in the fence and deposited them on the path.

The house in Leeds was a two-bedroom property. The second bedroom became Helen's but was not decorated according to her tastes. After her year in Lausanne, she started a doctorate in Nottingham. Her rented accommodation was not student-accommodation, so was available all year round. She visited her parents every few weeks, but never really moved back home.

Ben probably spent eight months each year in bed, with his thoughts and Cadbury for company. Gail became involved in village life, painting scenery and making props for the pantomime. She joined a local singing group for mature ladies and went to 'wine and wisdom' events in the village hall.

It was at one of those quizzes that she met Mary and Ronald, who lived in the detached house next to the post office, over the road from Ben and Gail's house. Mary was a freelance writer, mainly documenting history, and Ronald was an amateur painter and sculptor. Although most of their leisure time was consumed with creativity, both were parish councillors.

"Can we invite Mary and Ronald for coffee or a meal as soon as you are well? They live opposite. I met them at a 'wine and wisdom' last month," suggested Gail, when Ben was almost recovered from his latest flare-up.

"If we must. What do we know about them?"

"Two sons, similar ages to Owen and Helen. Retired early. At least, Mary is a freelance writer. Ronald's an artist. They're both on the parish council. I shared a table with them, and we started to chat."

"Did you tell them about Owen?"

"Only that he left home, and we didn't know where he was. Nothing about school."

"Did you tell them about my psoriasis?"

"Yes, of course. They were very sympathetic."

"I don't need pity."

"You might actually like them."

A few more weeks passed, and the invitation was given. Mary and Donald came for a simple lunch of homemade quiche, salad, followed by blackberry and apple crumble and custard. Too late, Gail noticed she was offering pastry and crumble in one meal, and she felt a twinge of embarrassment. It was normal for the Linton-Houses to fill up on foods based around flour, fat and sugar, but it demonstrated a lack of finesse to serve guests both in the same meal.

Ben wasn't one for conversation, but neither, it turned out, was Ronald. They exchanged raised eyebrows as Mary and Gail bantered away. Over the last twenty years or so, Gail had found few opportunities to engage her extensive general knowledge, beyond the horizon of crosswords and quizzes. Ben was genuinely happy for her.

"This crumble is amazing," Ronald encouraged Gail. "Mary never lets me eat pastry and crumble in one meal. She's worried about my heart."

The encouragement backfired, and Gail instantly found herself feeling guilty of a faux pas.

"Which is why this opportunity is an exceptional pleasure," responded Mary, noticing Gail's expression change.

"Thank you," replied Gail. "Who would like coffee?"

Three hands were raised. Gail carried the dishes out to the kitchen and put the kettle on. Mary appeared in the doorway holding the serving dish.

"You needn't have," reflected Gail.

"On the contrary, I shall return for the custard jug. Those two seem to have become allies."

They both laughed.

"Ben, would you be a sculpture subject for me. I would love to model your head."

Ben had chiselled features, sunken cheeks and a long nose that seemed to have grown longer as his flesh receded with age and lost its elasticity.

"I would love too, but you'll have to get the timing right. Between psoriasis flare-ups."

"Perfect."

The coffees were brought in.

"Ben is going to model for me, Darling," announced Ronald.

"I really do hope he keeps his clothes on," laughed Mary.

Ben had to admit this couple were fun to be with.

"Shall we start this week, now that you're well? The whole project will probably take four sittings."

"Of course. Delighted. When would you like me to come over?"

"Tomorrow, if you're free."

"I'm pretty much always free," responded Ben, laughing ironically at his own situation.

"Shall we say eleven?"

"Eleven it is."

The following morning, Ben crossed over the road and sat while Ronald formed some clay into the shape of Ben's head.

"Goodness! Is the back of my head really that shape?" inquired Ben, feigning shock.

"It is now," replied Ronald, quick to pick up on the opportunity for humour.

"Are these all your paintings?" asked Ben, looking round the studio.

"Guilty as charged."

"Have you always painted?"

"I went to art college, if that's what you mean, but it's only since I left the Civil Service that I've had the chance to dabble again."

"I'm impressed."

"Thank you."

Ben was not a religious person and the last time he could remember stepping foot in a church was his marriage to Gail. For him, stained glass belonged in a church, which was why the stained-glass window in Donald's studio door caught his eye. It depicted two roses, one red, the other white.

"And did you make the stained-glass window also?"

"As a matter of fact, I did. There's a story to that window."

"Tell me, please."

I'm not sure if you are aware, but I am from Yorkshire and Mary is from Lancashire, hence the white and red rose. But that's not the story. When we were married, her beloved grandmother gifted us a glass rose bowl. Mary loved it, I not so much. So, when I accidentally knocked it off the sideboard, it caused a bit of a hiccup in our three-and-a-half-year-long, hitherto blissful marriage. Mary didn't speak to me for the rest of the day. When she did, it was to accuse me of breaking it on purpose, on the premise that it was impossible to simply knock it off the sideboard. I knew as soon as I had broken it that I needed to salvage it, due to its sentimental value. Having swept up the fragments, I secretly selected all but the tiniest and turned them into a piece of stained glass with some glass paint and lead. I gave it to

Mary for our fourth wedding anniversary. I'll never forget the look of adoration in her eyes when she unwrapped it. It stood on our dining-room window ledge for the next few years, and when we moved here, finally, it became a window. So, Ben, you can take something broken and turn it into something beautiful. You can mend things and make them even stronger."

"It certainly is beautiful, as is the story," responded Ben, wondering if Donald had the slightest inkling of the broken glass in his life.

"Thank you."

Four weeks later, the sculpture was fired, and Ben and Gail were invited over for the unveiling, along with dinner. Mary was probably one of the kindest and most genuine people Gail and Ben had ever met. Similar in many ways to the Sawyers, they seemed to see beyond the economic circumstances in which the Linton-Houses found themselves. Mary served chicken pie and lattice-topped apple tart, both of which contained pastry. Nothing was said, but everyone knew she was being kind and affirming.

As the eighties drew to a close, Helen introduced her parents to Finn. She had met him at the night shelter where she volunteered, and when he moved into permanent accommodation, they struck up a relationship. Now, he had asked Helen to marry him. Once a semi-professional footballer, Helen hoped Finn would make a connection with her father. It was not to be. Finn's rather dismissive way of talking, and the fact that he had been married and divorced twice, caused Ben concern. Even though Ben was ten years older than Gail, the same age-gap between Finn and Helen bothered him.

He's a nasty piece of work," declared Ben, after Helen and Finn left for Nottingham. "If he lays a finger on her, in anger, I'll kill him."

Gail said nothing. She was more disappointed for Helen than concerned.

"He's not welcome here again, either. If Helen comes to visit, she can leave him at home."

Predictably, Ben did not attend the wedding, in September 1990. It was a simple affair, in a Methodist church, due to Finn's divorced status, with the reception in the upper room of a local pub. The wedding was one of those moments which crystalized the contradictory nature of the Linton-House family. Economically, they were working, if not benefit class. Educationally, they were middle class. The values and aspirations which Ben and Gail had for their children were beyond the reaches of their economic circumstances, and once a life is moulded by poverty, it becomes increasingly difficult to embody middle class mores. Owen had struggled to shake-off his poverty, and Helen, it appeared, had refused to embrace the opportunities her education provided for her.

Ben, however, was not wrong in his appraisal of Finn. Several months into the marriage, Helen was visiting her parents and divulged to Gail that Finn was psychologically abusive towards her. Helen feared giro-day when he received his benefit-check and could go out drinking, heavily. Gail let it slip to Ben, and just before Helen left for Nottingham he spoke to her about it.

"If he hurts you physically, Helen, I will kill him," insisted Ben. "Don't think I'm not serious. I'm very unhappy about the way he talks to you. In fact, if I ever see him again, I won't be answerable for my actions."

Helen had never had an easy relationship with her father, even though he had tried his best. They were too similar in personality. No one could deny that he had tried to make the right decisions, but he was a product of his own traumatic circumstances, and sometimes, his choices were shaped by his own failures. His failures seemed to have piled up, a little like the princess's matrasses on top of the pea, and he had never really addressed his pea, which was being separated from Saul. Everything since then had been an attempt to cover up the pain which that separation had caused him.

In Ben's defence, it is difficult for anyone to recover from the traumas of persecution or the horrors of war, and his psoriasis, as a psycho-somatic illness, may well have stemmed from his experiences under the Nazi regime. It was also true, that his depression may have been a genetic time-bomb, waiting to explode. But underneath it all, was the sense of loss. Ben blamed himself for becoming detached from his brother, when he went back to help Ruth with her teddy-bear.

Certainly, the sound of glass breaking was enough to relive the trauma he had experienced, but it was his failures, to parent his children successfully, to provide for his family, to be published as a writer, which always reminded him of losing Saul. He would have given anything, to see Saul again. He simply didn't know how to make it happen.

LIGHTBULB MOMENTS

If Helen's marriage to Finn wasn't disappointing enough for Ben, his heart was broken once more, by Cadbury being found at the side of the road, under the hedge skirting the recreation ground. The cars drove far too fast through the village, and he didn't stand a chance. Ben spent endless hours punishing himself, trying to work out why Cadbury would have been crossing the road, when his rabbit supply was located in the woods on the same side of the road as Farmer Close. Within the month, Ben had found a lilac-point Burmese advertised in the Kent Messenger and rode over on the moped to fetch him. They named him Misty. Ben didn't want to let him out of the house.

"You can't keep him in forever," Gail challenged Ben.

"I know you're right. I just don't know I can handle any more heartache, but I hate being without a cat."

Misty was given his freedom, and Ben found some joy in his new feline companion. One day, whilst he was browsing the racing results in the Kent Messenger, the telephone rang. Rarely did anyone phone for him so he left it ringing.

"I'm on the toilet!" Gail called down. "Please can you answer that and take a message if needed?"

Ben reached for the phone.

"Hello."

"Hello. Is that Benjamin Linton-House?" inquired the voice at the other end of the line.

"Yes, although I prefer Ben."

"My name is Barrington Haynes, from the British Consulate in Barcelona, Spain. I have your son Owen here with me. He'd like to come home."

For a split second, Ben was stunned.

"Is he there? May I speak to him?"

"Yes, I'll pass him the receiver."

"Hello. Daddy. It's a very long story. I'm sorry for everything. Can I come home?"

"Of course, you can. Do you need Mummy and me to send the fare?"

"Probably. I think the Spanish authorities cleared out my bank account. I've been in prison for the last six years."

"It doesn't matter. Phone us when you know. Can you pass me back to Barrington Haynes?"

"Yes. Thank you. See you soon."

"Hello."

"What happens now?"

"It might take three or four weeks to sort this all out. You should receive a letter in the next few days with bank details and the price of the ticket from Barcelona to Heathrow and train journey to Maidstone. Once the money is received, we'll purchase the tickets, and your son can travel."

"I really can't thank you enough."

"You're welcome. It'll be nice to have a happy ending after all this time."

"Are you a parent, Mr Haynes?"

"Yes. Bye."

"Bye."

Ben could hear the toilet flushing, followed by Gail coming down the stairs.

"Was that for me?"

"Actually, it was for me. Well, both of us. That was the British Consulate in Barcelona. Owen has been in prison and now he is being released. They've asked if we can send the fare home."

Gail sat down on the settee.

"Did you speak to Owen?"

"I did. I hardly recognised his voice. He said he was sorry and asked if he could come home."

"I hope you said yes."

"Of course, I did. Now we have to wait for a letter from them with the bank details so we can transfer the money. How much do you reckon a flight from Barcelona costs? We also have to pay for a train ticket from London to Maidstone."

"When?"

"It may take three or four weeks. I told Owen to let us know when he leaves."

The letter arrived with the bank details and Gail rode her moped into Maidstone to transfer the money at her branch. More time passed and they heard nothing from Owen.

"We should have heard something from Owen, by now, shouldn't we?" asked Gail.

"Do you think that even after all he's done, he would do this just to get some money?"

"Surely, you don't really believe that? In any case, we paid the money to the government, not to Owen."

"I don't know what to believe, anymore."

The phone call from Barcelona had sent Ben into another flare-up. Sometimes he sat downstairs, in his gauzes, pyjamas and dressing-gown, trying to avoid dropping scales everywhere or getting ointment on the chair cover. He rested his feet on the pouffe, on top of an out-of-date Kent Messenger. The days were long, filled with depression, and the gut-wrenching nausea of receding hope consumed him. One evening, Ben was just considering going up to bed when there was a clunk as the garden gate closed on its latch. Gail looked out into the fading light. Owen was walking up the path.

"It's Owen!"

Ben turned and looked out of the window, hardly able to believe his eyes, and now with guilt consuming him for thinking Owen might have cheated them. Gail opened the door to Owen, and hugged him silently, her eyes tearing up. Although he wanted to stand, Ben remained seated. The skin on his heals had fallen off, and his feet were at their most painful.

"I won't get up. Besides, you probably don't want to be hugged by Lazarus."

Instinctively, Owen leant forward to hug his father.

"Let me have a look at you," insisted Ben, surveying the man he had last seen as a teenager.

"I bought you some cognac," remarked Owen, to soften the awkwardness.

"Then we'd better drink some to celebrate," responded Ben.

Gail went to get some glasses from the kitchen.

"Are you hungry? I can make some sandwiches."

"That would be great, thank you, but not just yet. So many questions. So much to tell."

Owen poured them each a drink.

"Cheers!"

"To hope fulfilled," responded Ben, raising his glass. "Before we get into your story, we need to make a phone call to Helen. She got married last year to some lowlife called Finn. Nasty piece of work. She lives in Nottingham."

Ben hardly used the phone, and he certainly didn't know Helen's number off by heart. Having located her in the address book, he dialled. After a few rings, Ben was relieved that it was Helen who answered.

"Hello."

"It's Daddy. There's someone here who wants to speak to you."

Owen took the receiver from Ben, and in a deep, ex-patriot voice, greeted her.

"Hello, Sweetheart. How are you?"

"Are you in the UK?"

"Yes, I'm at Mummy and Daddy's. We've already started the bottle of cognac I bought."

"Stay up. I'm leaving now. I should get to you by one-thirty, two o'clock."

"See you soon."

Ben, Gail and Owen continued to drink cognac, and by the time Helen arrived, there was hardly any left in the bottle. She gave Owen a hug, and then stared at him quizzically.

"Cup of tea?" asked Gail. "There are a couple of cheese sandwiches left in the fridge. I'll go and make the bed up. You can have your old room and Owen can have the settee."

"Yes, please, to tea and sandwiches. Now tell me, where have you been, all this time?"

"I'll save most of the story for tomorrow, as we're all really tired, but in a nutshell, London, Amsterdam, Ottawa, Afghanistan, Spain."

"Wow. I speak Spanish, after a fashion. I studied French with Spanish at Nottingham. Did you go to SSEES, in the end?"

"Yes, but I dropped out at the end of the first year. Tell me, have you ever been to Madrid?" asked Owen.

"As a matter of fact, yes. I was there briefly in the summer of 1984, on my way to Salamanca."

"No way! You were in the Puerta del Sol, weren't you?"

"Yes."

"I saw you. I just didn't recognise you."

Gail appeared with Helen's cup of tea and the leftover sandwiches.

"Thank you," said Helen.

"Helen and I have just discovered we were a few yards apart in Madrid but didn't recognise each other."

"How many languages do you speak?" asked Helen.

"French, Russian, Dutch, Spanish, Catalan, Pashto."

"We're going up to bed," announced Gail.

She helped Ben to his feet and Owen watched as his father hobbled through the door. Helen went upstairs shortly after, and Owen settled down on the settee, with Misty for company.

As Ben lay in bed, waiting for sleep to relieve the pain in his feet, but unwilling to take his regular co-codamol, having consumed so much cognac, he found himself daring to imagine that one day, he might also be reunited with Saul, even after more than fifty years. Maybe miracles did happen in his life. Was it really that long ago?

The Linton-Houses settled into a new routine, with Owen back under their roof. It was difficult at first as there remained a residue of eggshells to tiptoe about on. Able to ride his parents' moped, by Christmas, he had secured a job, so reduced his presence at home considerably, out all day at work, and Friday evenings, socialising with colleagues. Ben worried about Owen riding home on the moped, after an evening in the pub. To add to Ben's worries, Helen announced at Christmas, that Ben and Gail were to become grandparents in June. What should have been joyful news was tainted by the knowledge that fifty percent of the genes were Finn's.

In the New Year, Owen bought a second-hand Suzuki 125, a two-stroke, with a high-pitch engine which Gail described as a demented wasp. She would lie awake on Friday nights listening out for the buzz, which somewhere around half-past eleven could be heard passing through

Langley Heath, along Upper Street, and turning into Farmer Close. Once Gail heard the garden gate closing, she fell asleep.

Owen had started dating a woman with whom he spent most of his weekends, so Ben and Gail saw even less of him. At least, when he was drinking with Teresa, he wasn't riding home on his motorbike. When the relationship was established enough for Teresa to be introduced, Ben was measurably more impressed with Owen's choice of partner than Helen's. Whilst it was an unexpected blessing, having Owen back home, Ben assumed it wouldn't be long before Owen and Teresa either married or moved in together.

One night in May, Ben was woken by an ashen-faced Gail.

"You need to come downstairs. There's a policeman here. I think it's the worst kind of news."

Ben acknowledged her statement with a grunt and sat up. Putting on his dressing-gown over his pyjamas, he followed Gail downstairs. The policeman had sat himself down in Ben's armchair, so Ben sat on the sofa. Gail hovered for a split second and joined him in sitting down.

"I am so, so sorry to have to tell you this, but we believe your son has had a fatal motorcycle accident in Langley Heath."

A lock of shock traversed their faces.

"The ambulance is still at the scene," continued the policeman. "Would you be able to come with me to identify the fatality? I wouldn't normally ask, but given the distance and the time, it seems to be appropriate. I can take you in my car."

"Can you give us a moment to put some clothes on?" Gail mumbled in a daze.

"Of course."

When ill, it was not unusual for Ben to wear his day-clothes over his pyjamas, so he pulled trousers and jumper on without taking them off and retrieved his coat from the walk-in cupboard under the stairs. Gail changed out of her pyjamas into trousers and jumper. The policeman watched quietly as they sat together on the settee, putting on socks and shoes. In silence, they followed the policeman to where his car was parked and were driven the short distance to Langley Heath.

Ben hauled himself out of the vehicle and stood on the road, surrounded by the broken plastic and glass from Owen's front light. The rest of the mangled Suzuki lay on the tarmac. It was clear from the precariously balanced top part of a brick gate post what had happened. The gateway was on a bend in the road, and it didn't look like anyone else was involved. A few yards away, an ambulance was parked, its blue light still flashing.

"He's in the ambulance," the policeman informed them.

Two paramedics stood by the rear doors.

"This way, please," said one of them, opening a door.

Ben looked desperately at Gail.

"I'll do it," insisted Gail.

Ben nodded. Gail climbed up into the ambulance. A few seconds later, she lowered herself back down to the pavement, holding onto the door, her legs like jelly. On seeing the look in her eyes, Ben did something he had hardly ever done throughout their thirty years of marriage. Stepping towards Gail, he put his arms round her.

"It's him," she stammered. "He looks so peaceful."

"My condolences," said the second paramedic, who had stayed outside the ambulance with Ben. "We are pretty sure that he died instantly. He wouldn't have known what was happening and he wouldn't have suffered."

"Thank you," responded Ben, walking Gail back to the car.

"We'll wait until morning to call Helen," suggested Gail.

"Agreed."

"There will be an inquest and we will keep you fully informed," explained the police officer. "Again, I am so, so sorry."

"If there is anything that it's not too late to donate, please will you use it," offered Gail, unsure whether the inquest would make a difference.

"Thank you," said the one who had gone into the ambulance with Gail.

The paramedics drove off, and the policeman took Gail and Ben home.

"Is there anything I can do? Anything you need, right now?"

"No. Thank you. And please will you get rid of the motorbike," requested Ben.

"We will. Take care. I will speak with you again, soon."

"Goodnight," responded Gail, as she closed the front door. "I'll make us some tea."

"Thank you. And thank you for going into the ambulance. I didn't want to see him, not like that. I waited so long for him to come home. At least we had him for one more year."

Ben wasn't quite sure he believed what he was saying. He was angry at the injustice of it all, angry that there was no one else to blame, angry at himself for being a coward and not getting into the ambulance. Misty appeared in the living room, disturbed from his sleep, confused by lights being on, at this hour. Almost as if he sensed something was wrong, he curled up on Ben's lap. Stroking Misty's head had a calming effect on Ben. Gail came in with the tea.

"I don't want anyone other than family at the funeral," he insisted.

"I don't want Helen to travel, in her condition. It'll be hard for her, but we have the baby to think about."

"Yes. We have the baby to think about."

The realisation of his son's death was also a lightbulb moment for Ben. Girl or boy, this grandchild was now the only potential for continuing his family line.

Neither Ben nor Gail slept. In the morning, Gail phoned Helen. Later in the day, she found Teresa's number in Owen's room and broke the news to her. Just before lunch, Gail went over the road to tell Mary and Ronald. While she was gone, Ben drifted off to sleep, with Misty still on his lap. Five minutes after Gail returned home, Mary appeared at the door with some lunch.

"I don't suppose you're very hungry, but I had this in the freezer," she explained, as Gail opened the door to her.

"That is so kind of you. Thank you."

"Do you want something to eat?" she asked Ben, after Mary had left.

"Yes. Life must go on."

When the results of the inquest came through, Owen's death was deemed accidental, brought on by four times the legal limit of alcohol in his bloodstream. The funeral was a simple affair, with the cheapest of hardboard coffins, no flowers and one song from the cassette that was still in

Owen's music centre. There was absolutely no mention of God.

The condolences and sympathy cards had started to drop through the letter box. Ben was overwhelmed by the message from Owen's employer, 'Your son was a rising star. Talented at languages, we had great hopes for him, as we expanded into Europe'. Most of the cards came from extended family and Gail's friends in the village, but there were also cards from friends and colleagues of Owen's that Ben and Gail had never met. Ben realised he hadn't let Max or Peter know and got out a pen and writing-pad.

Owen had died a matter of weeks before his thirty-first birthday. Helen's baby was overdue, and she went into labour the day before what would have been Owen's birthday. Ben and Gail's granddaughter finally put in an appearance at one-thirty on 21st June, the day after Owen's birthday. Two weeks later, Helen drove down from Nottingham to introduce Emily to them. It was an emotional weekend, filled with talk of the uncle-who-might-have-been and new beginnings. Ben held his granddaughter in his arms, frustrated by how much she resembled Finn, hiding his thoughts from Gail and Helen.

Gail had grown used to Ben blowing hot and cold, especially when it came to his relationship with Helen, but even she could not have foreseen his latest outburst.

"No spawn of that idiot, Finn, is ever darkening this door again," he barked, when Helen and Emily had left for Nottingham.

"Is that really fair on either Helen or the baby? The baby is half Helen and a quarter you," Gail challenged him. "Not to mention fair on me."

Ben didn't respond to Gail's argument but took himself off for a walk. Gail went over the road to talk to Mary where a plan was hatched. Mary and Ronald agreed that whenever Helen wanted to visit, she could stay with them, and Gail could come over and spend time with her daughter and granddaughter. The plan was required for Helen's next four trips to Kent, during which time Gail felt guilty for concealing the truth from Ben. Had she known how much of a lie Ben was living, she might not have felt such a burden. To everyone's relief, when Emily was twenty months old, Finn left Helen, and now that he was out of the picture, Ben relented, with a similar lack of logic to his original edict.

Eighteen months later, Helen met Peter, through work. They married after only a short engagement. Ben was experiencing yet another flare-up so did not attend the wedding. Mary and Donald kindly drove Gail to Nottingham.

Not long afterwards, Gail's mother's best friend, an elderly spinster who lived in Chislehurst died. Having always considered Gail the closest thing she had to a daughter Auntie Jackie left her estate to Gail. After four years of residential care was subtracted from the total, Gail inherited just over sixty thousand. She and Ben bought their council house under the right-to-buy scheme and Gail bought a bog-standard Nissan Micra, passing her driving test at the age of sixty-three, at the second attempt. For the first time in their lives, they had a few thousand in a savings account, no longer having to worry about the boiler breaking or the cat needing and emergency operation.

Gail was able to drive to Nottingham, nervously, to see Helen, Peter and Emily, who also visited regularly. In 1997, Emily gained a baby brother, Mike, who didn't experience any of the antagonism from Ben that Emily had suffered. With nearly five years between them, Emily was a doting older sister, and watching them together brought back memories of Rotterdam and Saul. Ben had run out of options for tracing his brother, and now feared he would die without ever being reunited. He was seventy-five, Saul seventy-seven, if he was still alive.

Not long after he had turned seventy-six, one afternoon, Ben went into the kitchen to make a glass of squash. As he stood at the sink, he started feeling strange, and his legs went from under him. The glass smashed on the tiles. Hearing the crash, Gail came into the kitchen to find Ben slumped against the cupboards, surrounded by shards of glass, with a vacant look in his eyes.

"Ben. Can you hear me?"

Ben groaned.

"Talk to me Ben. I need to know if you can speak."

"I'm OK," he pronounced slowly.

"You're not OK. I'm going to call an ambulance."

She went into the living room and made the call. When she returned to the kitchen, Ben was still sitting against the cupboards.

"I can't get up."

"And I can't lift you. I'll go and get a blanket, whilst we wait for the ambulance."

She went upstairs to the airing cupboard and came back with an old, red, cellular, hospital blanket and a pillow. Having made Ben comfortable, she boiled the kettle.

When the ambulance arrived, one of the paramedics recognised Ben and Gail, having attended Owen's accident.

"How are you getting on?" he asked, kindly.

"We were doing quite well, thank you, until this happened. I think my husband may have had a stroke."

The second paramedic gave Ben an injection and they positioned him on a stretcher.

"Would you like to come in the ambulance with us?"

"No. I'll follow you shortly, in my car, otherwise I'll not be able to get home again afterwards."

"Very good. Take care, now."

The paramedics carried Ben out. Gail fed Misty, ate a slice of marmalade on toast as she didn't know how long she would be at the hospital, and packed a bag for Ben which contained pyjamas, his writing pad, a book of crosswords, some pens, and some toiletries.

She arrived to find Ben already on one of the wards. He had indeed experienced a mild stroke, but there didn't appear to be any lasting damage, so he would be kept in overnight for observation and, all things being equal, discharged in the morning.

The ministroke turned out to be the first of three that would blight Ben over the next two-and-a-half years. Fortunately, neither the first nor second was severe enough to leave him without movement down one side. His second, however, seemed to affect his mental faculties, and Gail discovered a side to Ben she never knew. Her first inkling of his labilities caused Gail some amusement. Ben suddenly acquired a taste for garlic. In all their years of marriage, whenever Gail cooked with garlic, for example, if she made a spaghetti bolognaise, she had to remove a portion for Ben before adding in the garlic. On the rare occasions when she forgot, he would become inordinately angry. A few weeks after his second stroke, she forgot, but instead of getting angry, he remarked on how tasty it was. In fact, now, it seemed, he couldn't get enough garlic.

A second impact of Ben's strokes was that some day-care was organised, twice a week at a local centre. All those years that Gail had nursed Ben through his psoriasis, without any respite care, and now, she had four hours, twice a week, without having to worry about Ben. For someone who was solitary and sullen, and normally shunned social interaction, Ben also developed a surprisingly gregarious side to his personality. He loved going to the day centre, and by all accounts, they loved having him.

The third, and slightly more troubling result of having two strokes, was that Ben started to lose his ability to manage his memories.

"Where is my son, Roger?" he asked Gail, one morning, quite out of the blue.

"Your son was called Owen, and he died in a motorcycle accident. Don't you remember?"

"No, my son, Roger."

Gail was at a loss. Something of a lightbulb moment, she started to consider there was more to Ben's life than even she could have imagined. Was there another Linton-House somewhere in the world? Was he in contact with them? Even so, she resisted the urge to quiz him.

Her suspicions were increased, about six months later, when just after the minibus transport had collected Ben to take him to the day centre, the post arrived. One of the letters was hand-written, but not the script Gail had come to recognise as either Max's or Peter's. She wanted to open it, curious to discover what other parts of Ben's life had been kept hidden from her, but she stopped herself.

"There's a letter for you," she announced, when Ben arrived home. "I don't think it's from either Max or Peter, though."

Ben took the envelope from the letter-rack and slide his finger under the flap. As he scanned the letter, Gail could see he was shocked.

"Everything alright?"

"Everything's fine."

"You don't look fine."

"I am quite fine. Thank you."

Ben was in no mood to share, so Gail left him to his thoughts. Ben replaced the letter in the envelope, folded it in half, and wriggling to one side, placed it in his trouser pocket, making a mental note not to leave it there. When Gail ran herself a bath that evening, he took out the letter and read it a second time, still in a state of incredulity. A man named Jacob Drucker was trying to contact Benjamin Linton-House (formerly Lindenheim) on behalf of his brother Saul. Please could Benjamin get in touch via the address above as Saul would be visiting the UK, very soon. This was now the second time Ben's eyes had scanned the document and he still couldn't quite believe what he was reading.

Writing a response would be the easy part. The challenge would be meeting with Saul without Gail knowing, and the entire house of cards Ben had constructed coming tumbling down. His only sensible option was to make the day centre their meeting place, which restricted his availability to Tuesdays and Fridays. Ben resolved to write his reply and ask one of the care assistants at the day centre to post it for him. Gail was still enjoying her soak in the bath, so he took the Basildon Bond writing pad from Gail's drawer and worded his response. 'I am Benjamin Linton-House. Please tell my brother Saul I am well and happy to meet him. As I have no transport of my own these days, I would ask that we meet at The Oaks, Heath Road, Coxheath, Maidstone. I can be available on Tuesdays and Fridays. Relying on your discretion.' He signed it, folded it, placed it in an envelope, copied the address from Jacob Drucker's letter, and slipped it into the zipped, breast pocket of his coat. Three days later, when he asked Lindsay if she could buy a stamp and post the letter for him, she was delighted to help.

The next three weeks were almost as difficult as the wait between sending money to the British Consulate and Owen arriving home. The address in the letter was in London, Ben wondered whether Jacob Drucker would phone Saul or write to him, in which case, how long did the post take to reach the States. His feelings swung from joyful anticipation to fear.

On his next visit to The Oaks Ben arrived to be greeted by Lindsay waving an envelope at him.

"You have a letter, Mr Linton-House. From America."

Her curiosity was as obvious as her excitement.

"Thank you. How many times do I have to tell you, you can call me 'Ben' and not 'Mr Linton-House'?" he laughed, taking the letter from her.

Now he wanted some privacy to read it, but he was already being ushered into the main room for a cup of coffee and the monthly quiz. He folded the envelope and put it in his trouser pocket. He had waited this long, so another few hours couldn't hurt.

With the quiz and lunch and a walk round the gardens, Ben didn't get a chance to read his letter. Lindsay insisted on sitting Ben on the swing.

"Hold on! I'll push you," she laughed, giving him a gentle nudge forward.

Joanna, another of the care assistants, approached with a camera.

"Smile, Ben," she encouraged him, pressing the shutter.

The letter was still in his pocket, when Ben was dropped off at home, so he went to the bathroom, before removing his coat, under the pretext of being desperate. Even though he had agreed not to lock the bathroom door since his second stroke, Ben slid the bolt across. Sitting on the toilet, he took off his coat, threw it on the floor and removed the letter from his trouser pocket. His hands were shaking as he prized open the flap. He started reading, 'My dear brother Ben. It makes me so happy to know that you are alive and well, and twice as happy to find that you want to meet up. I have longed to see you since our lives became unravelled in Rotterdam, but the circumstances have not permitted it. Finally, I have been able to trace you. It was a surprise to hear you had changed your name, but I imagine a lot of our people did something similar on settling in the United

Kingdom. I shall be visiting London in the week beginning 10th January. I will travel to Maidstone on the 14th and meet you at The Oaks. I can hardly wait. Your brother Saul.'

What struck Ben most was Saul's suggestion that he might not have wanted to meet. Why would Saul think he wouldn't want to meet? Placing the letter back in the envelope and returning it to his pocket, Ben flushed the toilet, washed his hands, and made his way downstairs, carrying his coat.

"Have you had a good time at the day centre?"

"Yes. One of the care assistants was taking photos today. Hopefully, I'll have a nice one of me sitting on a swing, to collect next week."

"Lovely. Would you like a cup of tea??"

"If you're making one. Thank you."

Whilst Gail pottered in the kitchen, Ben hid the letter from Saul amongst his papers in a tatty old cardboard document wallet that resided between the books on the shelves next to his armchair. The document wallet contained old football pools selections, betting slips, newspaper articles, crosswords torn out from the newspaper and random loose pieces of paper with creative scribbles. It was unlikely that Gail would discover Saul's letter.

"Has Helen said what the children would like for Christmas yet?" he asked with calculated randomness, when Gail brought in his tea.

"Not yet. She said she would let us know by the end of November."

On 12th January 2000 Ben had his third stroke. Unlike the previous two, this one was more severe, causing some loss of movement down his right side and rendering speech difficult. He was rushed to the Maidstone Hospital in an ambulance. Before following in her car, Gail called The Oaks to tell them not to send the minibus and that it would probably be a while before Ben returned to the day centre.

Conscious throughout, Ben was terrified. In all the fighting he had experienced, even when ex-Hauptmann Brecht and ex-Oberleutnant Fischer cornered him at The Big Hole, he had never been this helpless, and not being able to speak caused feelings of complete powerlessness. At the hospital, they ran various tests and ascertained that he could understand what they were saying and nod or shake his head to communicate. No one thought to ask if he could write. He was catheterised, given some medication and admitted him to a general ward. Gail arrived.

"Hello. How are you feeling?"

Ben produced a few guttural noises, pointed at his mouth with his left hand and shook his head.

"You can't speak?"

Ben shook his head.

"Your left side is still alright. Can you write?"

Ben smiled as Gail opened her bag and took out a pen and some paper, which she placed on Ben's bedspread. He grasped the pen and started to scrawl with his usual capital letters, 'HELLO. BAD THIS TIME. TELL THE OAKS.'

Helen was reading the upside-down writing.

"I have. I told them you had had a stroke and it might be a while until you go back to the centre. I'll call Helen later. What has the consultant said? How long are you likely to be in here?"

Ben scribbled 'THANK YOU' and 'I DON'T KNOW' on the paper.

"It's possible that your speaking will come back. Time will tell," offered Gail, hopefully. "I've brought your pyjamas, toiletries, crossword book and writing things again."

Ben smiled and pointed at the 'THANK YOU' he had written.

"Are you thirsty? Shall I poor you some water?"

Ben nodded and Gail obliged, handing him the beaker. He immediately poured the water down his chin.

"Oh dear," reflected Gail, jumping up, grabbing a tissue from the box on Ben's bedside table and mopping his face for him.

"Like going to the dentist?" inquired Gail, supportively. "I'll tell the nurse."

Ben wrote 'I'LL GET USED TO IT. PRACTICE.'

"Can you swallow your saliva?"

Ben attempted to muster up enough saliva to swallow. It was a challenge, but not impossible.

"Better get a spout for the beaker. Just until you can manage. I'll come back tomorrow. Is there anything else you need?"

What Ben needed was to not be in hospital, and to be present at the day centre on Friday. The whole thing was just one gigantic, unfair mess. He couldn't even let Saul know because he didn't know where he was staying. He couldn't tell Gail. Feelings of frustration, nausea, anger and sadness started to overwhelm Ben, in no particular order. The consultant approached him.

"Good morning, Mr Linton-House. We are going to monitor you for a few days and carry out further tests. As of this afternoon, a speech and language therapist will start working with you. We're going to see how much of the impact of your stroke we can reverse. I don't want to give you false hopes, but I can promise you that we will try our very best."

Ben smiled a lopsided smile and wrote 'THANK YOU' on his paper.

"You can write? Why did no one pick up on this before?"

Ben wrote 'LEFT-HANDED?'

Neither the registrar nor the nurse, who were accompanying the consultant on his rounds, attempted to offer a defence for the rhetorical question and were clearly embarrassed.

"Is there anything else you need?"

Ben wrote 'SPOUT' and pointed at the beaker.

"I'll get one for you," interjected the nurse, without waiting for the consultant.

"Very good. I'll be back tomorrow."

Ben smiled as he nodded in acknowledgment.

The nurse brought Ben a spout and attached it to the beaker, staying to watch that he could swallow safely. Ben succeeded in downing half a beaker of water, sip by sip. He was thirsty and held up the empty container for a refill, smiling as he did.

"Hopefully, the catheter is temporary. One of the tests they will do."

Ben nodded.

"The buzzer's there if you need anything."

Ben pointed at 'THANK YOU' and smiled again. Momentarily, he was back in St George's Hospital, in his memories, with Nurse Norton at his bedside. Nurse Moss walked off across the ward to tend to another patient.

As Ben lay there watching the activities going on around him, he grasped the one shard of light in this otherwise dark episode. If Saul arrived at The Oaks, they would tell him where Ben was, surely. All was not completely lost. Ben also took comfort from the circumstances which forced him to make their rendez-vous at the day centre rather than at a train station, or some other impersonal location. Closing his eyes, he drifted into a light sleep.

At twenty-past eleven, on Friday 14th January 2000, an elderly gentleman, not dissimilar to Ben in appearance, but without the beard, walked into the reception at The Oaks. No one was in attendance, and for a moment, he stood there wondering what course of action to take. He was just about to wander through the building, unaccompanied, when a member of staff appeared through the double-doors at the end of the corridor. It was Tracey, another of the care assistants who regularly spent time with Ben.

"Mr Linton-House. We thought you was in hospital," she greeted him. "I like the new look, without the whiskers."

"Good morning. I am not Mr Linton-House. I am Saul Lindenheim, and I'm looking for Benjamin Linton-House. Did you just say you thought he was in hospital?"

"He had a stroke a few days ago. Mrs Linton-House phoned to say he might not be coming to the day centre for a while."

"That's not good to hear. How would I get to the hospital?"

"Are you in a car?"

"No, I took a cab from the station."

"The hospital is the other side of Maidstone. Would you like me to call for a minicab for you, Mr Lindenheim? I like that name. It has a nice ring to it. You're American, aren't you?"

"Thank you. That would be most helpful," replied Saul, ignoring the question about his nationality.

Tracey went behind the reception desk and surveyed a list of numbers pinned to the noticeboard.

"May I use the bathroom?" asked Saul, as she was raising the receiver."

"Through the double-doors, first door on the right."

"Thank you."

Saul marched down the corridor and Tracey phoned for a minicab.

"The minicab will be here in ten minutes," she reported, when Saul returned.

"Thank you. How long has Benjamin been coming here?"

"Are you family? I shouldn't really say."

"Something like that," responded Saul conscious that the different surnames might be hard to explain.

Tracey looked Saul in the eyes.

"It's been a few months now. He's the life and soul of the party. Everyone loves him. He's very funny."

Saul's heart swelled with familial pride. He remembered the last time he had seen Ben, trying to keep the children entertained on the train. There was so much to catch up on.

Obviously, Ben had married, because the care assistant had mentioned a Mrs Linton-House. Did Ben also have children? Was he, Saul, an uncle? The minicab pulled into the forecourt.

"There's your minicab. Say 'Hello' to Mr Linton-House from us. Wish him a speedy recovery. Tell him we're all missing him."

"I will. Thank you for all your help. Goodbye."

"Bye, Mr Lindenheim. I do like that name."

Saul gave a wry smile and went outside to get into the minicab.

How long's the journey?"

"Not long. We'll go cross-country to Barming. No need to go through the centre of Maidstone. Maybe twenty-five minutes."

Having no idea of the local geography, Saul sat back in his seat, trusting that the driver wouldn't take advantage of an American.

"On holiday?" inquired the driver, after half a mile.

"Something like that."

"You should come here in the spring, when the orchards are all full of blossom. It's a sight for sore eyes."

"I'm sure it is."

"You drive on the right, don't you? I'm guessing you're from New York."

"That's correct. On both counts."

"I've been to Vegas, but not New York."

"I've never been to Las Vegas."

"My mate got himself married there. No one thought it would last, but he's been with his wife for twenty years. Never found the right woman, me."

"Nor me," replied Saul, ruefully wondering why he had let the one woman he had ever loved slip through his fingers.

They passed over the River Medway.

"Not far, now."

Saul said nothing, starting to feel irrational, nervous apprehension. The journey continued in silence. They pulled up in front of the main entrance.

"Keep the change," directed Saul, handing the driver some notes.

"Thank you. Very generous of you."

Saul got out of the minicab and went into the hospital.

"Good morning. I'm looking for a Benjamin Linton-House."

"Good morning, sir. Do you have the date of birth?"

"Er, yes. 12 May 1922."

The receptionist scrolled down her computer screen.

"There we are. Edith Cavell. First floor, along the corridor, on the right," she directed him, pointing towards the lift.

"Thank you."

As he stood thankfully in the lift, his heart also seemed to ascend to his mouth. There was a nurse seated at the nurses' station. A buzzer disturbed her from her concentration.

"One minute, please," she acknowledged Saul, crossing the ward to attend to a patient.

Saul watched as she stooped down to retrieve something that had fallen under the bed. She returned to the nurse's station.

"Now, then. How can I help?"

"Where will I find Benjamin Linton-House?"

"He's at the end, left side of the window, but his daughter is with him at the moment, and we try to limit visiting to one at a time."

"No problem," responded Saul, glancing down to the end of the ward, curious to see what his niece looked like. "I'll come back in a bit. Please, point me in the direction of a café."

"Certainly."

The nurse took a piece of paper and a pen and drew a simple map for Saul.

"Try half an hour. She's already been here a while."

"Thank you."

A little frustrated, but feeling closer to finding Ben than ever before, Saul went to the café and bought a toasted teacake and a cup of coffee. It was lunchtime, and even though he didn't feel hungry, he wasn't sure when he would next have occasion to eat. When he had visited London just over a year ago, with Rebekah, his courtesy, great-niece, she had introduced him to what he could only describe as the English version of a raisin and cinnamon bagel.

"Please could I have an extra portion of butter?" he asked, with an avuncular charm.

"Alright, then," replied the elderly lady who was serving. "I can tell you're not from here. Have you come far?"

"New York, but not today. Just from London, this morning."

"I always wanted to visit The Big Apple. I'm too old, now."

"You're never too old," Saul encouraged her. "I mean, look at me."

"I'll bring it over to you. Take a seat."

"Thank you."

Saul had brought his briefcase with him. Inside it, he had letters and certificates of provenance for some of the property his family once held. Ben was entitled to his share in the inheritance. Saul had only succeeded in tracing the assets in the last twelve months, so the timing of re-connecting with Ben was perfect. Opening his briefcase, he removed a copy of the New York Times which he had picked up at the airport. He read the culture section, depositing buttery finger-marks all over the paper. Swallowing the last of his coffee, he folded the newspaper and left it on the table, in order to avoid transferring any grease to the documents he was carrying.

As he arrived back at the ward, a woman in her thirties, with long dark hair, and from what Saul could remember of Ben as a fifteen-year-old, obviously his daughter, was exiting the ward. Helen smiled at the stranger who stood back to let her walk through the doors. He glanced over at the nurses' station, nodded at the nurse he had spoken to previously, and continued walking down the ward.

Ben was leaning back against raised pillows, with his eyes closed. Saul stood silently for a moment, contemplating the brother he hadn't seen in just over sixty years, until he could no longer see through his tears. Taking a handkerchief from his pocket, he blew his nose. Ben opened his eyes.

"I'm sorry. I didn't mean to startle you."

Ben's face broke into a lopsided grin. Grabbing his pen, he scribbled 'STROKE' and 'CAN'T TALK' on his writing pad and held it aloft.

Saul stepped forward and placed his arms around Ben, who could only reciprocate with one arm.

"My brother," whispered Saul.

Ben patted his back several times with his left hand. They separated and stared at each other.

"Where do we start?" remarked Saul.

Ben took his pen and wrote, 'SORRY I LOST YOU IN ROTTERDAM. I SENT A LETTER.' He held out the writing pad for Saul to read.

"No. It's I who am sorry. I promised our mother I would look after you and I failed. Once I reached New York, there was very little I could do. A wonderful family, the Edelmanns, took me under their wing. I've been looking for a needle in a haystack ever since. Just over a year ago, I made a breakthrough. I spoke to someone who knew that you changed your name to Linton-House and were living in Kent. Why did you change your name?"

Ben scribbled on the writing pad again. 'LOTS OF OUR PEOPLE CHANGED THEIR NAMES' and held it up.

"And did you change your faith too?"

Ben raised one eyebrow, the one that he could control and wrote another phrase, 'I THINK I GAVE UP ON GOD. TOO MUCH PAIN AND SORROW. TODAY, I MAY JUST BELIEVE IN MIRACLES AGAIN'.

Saul sighed.

"And will you tell me about your pain and sorrow?"

Ben nodded and started to write again.

'I LOST YOU. OUR MOTHER AND FATHER WERE LOST. I FELL IN LOVE, MARRIED AT 16, WENT TO FIGHT IN FRANCE. I WATCHED MEN DIE. I WAS WOUNDED. NEVER MADE IT BACK TO ENGLAND. HELPED THE FRENCH RESISTANCE. ENDED UP IN MALTA. HEARD MY WIFE AND SON - DIDN'T KNOW

I HAD A SON - DIED IN THE BLITZ. WENT TO SOUTH AFRICA. LOVED AND LOST AGAIN. CAME BACK. MET A NURSE. MARRIED. OWEN WAS BORN 1961. HELEN 1963. OWEN LEFT HOME FOR 12 YEARS. CAME HOME BUT CRASHED HIS MOTORBIKE AND DIED A YEAR LATER. HELEN HAS A DAUGHTER AND SON BUT HER FIRST MARRIAGE WAS A BAD ONE. I SUFFER FROM CHRONIC PSORIASIS. AND TRAUMA. EVER SINCE THE WAR, EVERY TIME I HEAR GLASS BREAKING, I'M PARALYSED WITH FEAR. WHAT ABOUT YOU?'

It took a while for Saul to read what Ben had written, during which time his expression became increasingly strained.

"I am so sorry, my brother."

There was a lengthy pause.

"I fell in love but never married. I served in the air force, but as ground crew. Spent a few months in Huntingdonshire just before the end of the war. Needless to say, I tried to find you. I didn't know you had changed your name. After the war, I trained as a lawyer. No family. I heard our parents died in Auschwitz. I have remained close to the family who looked after me when I arrived in New York. Was that my niece I passed on her way out?"

Ben nodded.

"She looks like you."

Ben smiled. There was another lengthy pause.

"I'm curious. I understand from the need to contact you at the Oaks that you are hiding your past from your family. May I ask why?"

Ben wrote his answer. 'AT FIRST, I THINK I SIMPLY TRIED TO BURY THE PAIN. IN FRANCE I HAD TO LIVE A LIE. IN SOUTH AFRICA IT WAS EASIER TO FORGET THE PAST. WHEN I CAME BACK TO ENGLAND, I DECIDED IT WAS EASIER NOT TO BE JEWISH. GAIL, MY WIFE, KNOWS I HAVE A PAST BUT ACCEPTS IT IS TOO PAINFUL FOR ME TO TALK ABOUT. SOME THINGS ARE BEST KEPT HIDDEN.'

Saul read Ben's response and started to shake his head.

"But you have so much to be proud of. Firstly, you made sacrifices and fought for our freedom. Secondly, you have a family. It doesn't matter what our children do. They are our children. The greatest blessing that we can know."

Ben looked Saul in the eyes and wrote, 'ONCE YOU START LIVING A LIE, IT IS HARD TO ADMIT THE TRUTH. TOO MANY PEOPLE GET HURT. BOTH THE LIES AND THE TRUTH WILL DIE WITH ME. YOU WILL HONOUR THIS? PLEASE, SAUL.'

Saul nodded.

"Have they said if they think you will recover? From the stroke, I mean."

"TESTS. THERAPY. MEDICATION. THEY WILL DO WHAT THEY CAN. IT'S EARLY DAYS.'

"I will sit here with you for a while, and then, I must go back to London. I am returning to the UK in September. I promise to come back and visit. I will contact you via The Oaks. I'll write down my address and telephone number."

Ben wrote 'THANK YOU' followed by 'GAIL WILL BE HERE SOON' and added 'THANK YOU FOR NOT GIVING UP'.

"You're my brother. I promised our mother I would look after you and I failed. At least now, I've found you again. I'd better go if Gail is on her way."

Saul took the pen and writing pad and wrote down his address and phone number, tore it off, folded it and slipped it into Ben's pyjama-shirt pocket. As he was within arms' reach, the two brothers embraced, and Saul walked back to the nurse's station.

"Thank you for all you do here."

Halfway to the lift, he passed a lady he surmised was Gail, and afforded her a courteous but understanding smile, one that any visitor of relatives in hospital might give to another visitor. Gail returned the empathy, having no idea that she had just met her brother-in-law.

After three weeks in hospital, and daily speech therapy, Ben started to speak again. He was discharged to Gail's care. Railings were fitted in the bathroom and outside the front and back doors due to the doorsteps. Ben became adept at using the clawed metal walking stick he had been issued and the twice-weekly visits to The Oaks were increased to three, as much for Gail's respite as Ben's stimulation. Each month, he wrote to Saul, and each month a letter arrived for Ben at The Oaks. None of the staff ever questioned the letters.

Two weeks into July, Ben was descending the stairs, one step at a time, when he lost his footing. Unable to cushion his fall with his useless right arm, he tumbled down four steps and crashed into the front door. It was half-glazed with twenty small panes of glass, and as Ben's momentum carried him towards it, he had the presence of mind to lift his left hand in order to protect his head. His elbow collided with the door, and one of the panes smashed, landing on the brick-built doorstep outside. Searing pain shot up Ben's arm as he collapsed on the floor. Gail, who had been reading in the living room, came out to see what had caused the crash. Ben was slumped in the corner of the hallway staring blankly ahead. Gail wasn't sure if he had suffered another stroke or whether it was the reaction he always had when glass broke.

"Ben, can you hear me?"

Nothing. She called for an ambulance and found a blanket to wrap around Ben. After a few minutes he groaned in pain.

"Where does it hurt?"

"Arm."

"The ambulance is on its way. I'll let them in at the back. I'm not moving you away from the front door."

"Cup of tea, please. Three sugars."

Gail made a cup of tea, adding a spot of cold water, so it was drinkable. Unfortunately, Ben's right arm was paralysed, and his left arm was now incapacitated, so Gail held the cup up to Ben's mouth for him to slurp down some warm tea. He was about halfway down the cup when the blue flashing light could be seen outside. A paramedic appeared outside the door.

"I'm afraid you'll have to go round the back," explained Gail, through the hole in the glazing. "I can't move him out of the way."

"No problem."

A few moments later there were three knocks followed by the back door opening. The paramedics checked Ben's vital signs and examined his arm.

"Quite possibly a break. Let's get you to hospital, Mr Linton-House."

They manoeuvred him gently onto a stretcher and carried him out to the ambulance, which they had moved round to the car park at the back.

"I'll follow in the car," stated Gail, before one of them asked if she wanted to ride in the back of the ambulance.

After packing Ben's hospital bag, she went to the toilet, closed the cat flap, fed Misty, and went to lock the front door. At that moment, she realised that not only had she forgotten to clear up the broken glass, but any self-respecting burglar could easily reach through the hole and undo the yale-lock. There was nothing that could be done about replacing the pane, in the immediate future, but she could block the hole off. Outside in the shed, she found a saw, a hammer, some panel pins, and a piece of leftover plywood, and took them indoors. Twenty-five minutes later, she had cut a rectangle to fit flush with the frame, and secured it with panel pins, so that it would be difficult to knock inwards, but the panel-pins could be removed when a glazier came to replace the pane. Before locking the door, she swept up the fragments of glass along with the sawdust she had made, and bundled it all up in a newspaper parcel, which she placed in the dustbin with 'Broken glass' written in permanent black marker pen. Having tidied the tools away, she headed off to the hospital.

Ben had been x-rayed and was waiting to be plastered, when she arrived. He would be admitted because they also wanted to establish if the loss of footing had been caused by another stroke. More tests and observations. Gail stayed at the hospital until he was comfortable and clothed in his pyjamas, and then went home, where she rang Helen, who insisted on driving down the next evening, to stay for the weekend, with the grandchildren. It would be the last time she saw her father alive.

A week after he was admitted, and still undergoing tests, Ben contracted pneumonia. For several days he drifted in and out of consciousness. During his more lucid moments he reflected on his life and felt guilty for the lie he had lived. It was too late to admit to the truth, even if it deprived Saul of getting to know his niece, and it would probably cause more hurt to Gail than to had ever intended. Why had he hidden his past? Was he ashamed of being Jewish? Was he afraid that the South African authorities would catch up with him and charge him with the deaths of Hauptmann Brecht, Oberleutnant Fischer? Would he be charged with desertion? Surely, it had all been about survival and no one could blame him.

Ben was deteriorating fast. Gail visited daily, and as a trained nurse, recognised that he was on his last legs. Remarkably, she thought she had never seen him looking so at one with the world. A cannula had been inserted in the back of his left hand. Was he being drip-fed antibiotics or peace? The look on Ben's face suggested fulfilled hope, although Gail had no idea what it was that he had been hoping for, at least not since Owen came home, and was then taken from them again.

Ben passed away on 4th August 2000, having finally been re-united with his brother. When the nurse on duty rang Gail at just gone nine in the evening, even she commented on how peaceful he looked.

"Hello."

"Is that Mrs Linton-House?"

"Yes, it is."

"I'm really sorry to tell you this, but Mr Linton-House died a few minutes ago."

The news was hardly unexpected.

"Thank you. I'll come tomorrow morning."

"If you don't mind me asking, was your husband a religious man?"

"Not to my knowledge. Although, since he had his strokes, there are many things about my husband that I've only recently discovered. Why?"

"It's just that the last few days he's been so calm and peaceful."

"'Thank you. I thought so, too. Like many things about him, the truth will remain a mystery. Goodnight."

"Goodnight, Mrs Linton-House."

Gail poured herself a sherry. If she was being honest, the last few years had taken their toll on her own health. The strain of looking after Ben, not only his physical care but dealing with his personality, had caused bouts of tinnitus and dizziness, which the doctor diagnosed as Meniere's disease.

The staff at The Oaks were genuinely upset by Ben's passing. The event also became the cause of some anguish for Lindsay, who received the bundle of post from the postman, which contained Saul's August letter. Unfortunately, no one knew to notify him of Ben's death, because no one knew he was a close relative. There was a return address on the back of the envelope, and although tempted to open it, Lindsay feared her curiosity might lose her the job she both loved and needed, so she took a biro, wrote 'RETURN TO SENDER' in large letters on the front, and popped it into the letter box she passed on her way to and from work.

After the funeral, which was the same immediate-family-only affair Owen's had been, except for this time Helen was present, Gail scattered Ben's ashes on the North Downs above Hollingbourne, in the same place where they had scattered Owen's. When having left it a few weeks she decided it was time to sort out Ben's belongings, Helen came for the weekend to assist. A regular connoisseur of charity shops, which she scoured for props and garments that could be altered to become pantomime costumes, Gail was keen to donate what she could. However, most of Ben's clothing was beyond redemption, due to the ointment he had used regularly for his psoriasis.

He had been a man of few possessions. Things like his tools and typewriter Gail thought she would keep, but other items could be found new homes. Ben had owned a case of 78 rpm records, a handful of LPs and a small case of 45s. Helen took the case of 45s, and Gail held onto the 78s as she thought they might one day appreciate in value. The LPs went in the charity-shop pile. Although very little of his life before meeting Gail had ever been divulged, Ben's African language textbooks had always sat on the bottom bookshelf, along with the other large books. These too were added to the charity-shop pile along with the miniature trophy cabinet Ben had made to house his refereeing medals.

"Wait," interjected Helen. "Why don't we take the medals to The Oaks and give the staff one each to remember Daddy by?"

"If you think they'd appreciate it."

"I'd like to take them, if it's OK with you. I'd like to see where he spent some happy times."

"Be my guest. I think Lindsay was very unhappy about not being invited to the funeral."

The three trunks he kept in the attic at Moat Cottage had become one trunk, when they moved to Yalding. These days, even the trunk he had kept was almost empty, containing only manuscripts, stories he'd written and crosswords he'd compiled. Many years before, when Ben had been in the bath and Gail had been out shopping, Helen had crept out of her attic bedroom and peeped into the top trunk in the stack. Carefully displacing some papers that were written in an unfamiliar language of many double vowels, she had caught a glimpse of a wallet-sized photo of a woman holding a baby. Now, as Gail and Helen sorted through the contents, the photo was nowhere to be seen.

"May I have the stories Daddy wrote?" asked Helen.

"Of course," replied Gail, holding the manuscript for *When Glass Breaks*. "This must be the song he had published with Uncle Max. That reminds me, I still need to let Uncle

Max and Uncle Peter know. I don't know how I forgot them. Possibly because Daddy didn't have an address book to prompt me."

As far as Gail knew, the only people Ben knew outside of their mutual Christmas-card list were Uncle Max, Uncle Peter and the staff at The Oaks, so the various scraps of paper with anonymous numbers and addresses on meant nothing to her. When he had come home from hospital after the visit from Saul, Ben had hidden his brother's contact details in the trunk, where Gail never ventured, and now, in her ignorance, she was throwing it away. In possession of Ben's death certificate, Gail had hoped to find a birth certificate amongst Ben's papers, but she was disappointed. The trunk itself was assigned to the tip pile.

Later that afternoon, Gail took the charity-shop items into Maidstone, and Helen drove to the tip, followed by The Oaks. On arriving, she rang the bell in reception and waited. Lindsay came through the double doors.

"Hello. How can I help?"

"Good afternoon. My name is Helen. I'm Ben Linton-House's daughter. I'm sorry that none of you was invited to the funeral. No one was invited. It was just my mum and me. That's why I've brought these. I was wondering if the staff who knew my father might like one to remember him by," she explained, holding up the trophy cabinet. "He won them as a football referee."

"That is so kind. You know he was very popular here. Life and soul of the party, your dad. We was really sorry to hear he'd died. Our sympathies to you and your mum, by the way."

"Thank you."

"Did he have family in America?"

"Not as far as I know. Why do you ask?"

"Because every month since January, a letter's been coming here for him from America. I had to send the last one back 'Return to sender'."

"January? Why January?"

"How should I know? Although he did have a visitor in January, when he went into hospital after his stroke. I didn't see him, mind, but my colleague said he looked just like your dad, only without the beard. She thought he was Mr Linton-House, back from the hospital, clean-shaved."

"Oh," responded Helen, a little perplexed. "Anyway, please pass on our thanks for everything you did for my father."

"You're welcome. He's sorely missed."

Helen turned and left, her eyes filling with tears.

Back at Farmer Close, Helen started to peel some potatoes ready for the evening meal. She was just finishing up, when Gail arrived home.

"I just had a strange conversation with one of the carers at The Oaks."

"Really?"

"Apparently, in January, Daddy was visited by an elderly man from America who looked just like him. Then, every month, a letter arrived at The Oaks from America, addressed to Daddy."

"We didn't find any letters from America in the trunk, and I checked all his pockets. There's a lot of mystery around your father's life. Since he had his strokes, there have been a few times when he's said something that made no sense. He once asked me about his son, Roger. When

I corrected him, reminding him his son was called Owen, he was adamant he had a son called Roger. He never wanted to talk about his past and I didn't ask. As lightbulb moments go, it would explain why he was finally at peace with the world just before he died."

"But what if I have an uncle? I asked Daddy once or twice about the war, and he shut down the conversation, challenging me that I wanted to drag up the painful past."

She paused for a moment.

"Mummy, do you think Daddy was Jewish? Uncle Peter is, at least he and Aunty June celebrated Hannukah. I'm not sure about Uncle Max. Maybe we could ask him."

"If Daddy was Jewish, he avoided anything religious. I'm afraid, whatever the truth was, it died with him."

KRISTALLNACHT AGAIN

For twenty years, Helen wondered about her father's heritage. Since her Road-to-Damascus conversion, there were many occasions when she wondered why she felt so at home with the Jewishness of Jesus. She started to read novels such as Elie Wiesel's *The Night Trilogy* and some other novels set in the Holocaust, like *The Pianist* and *The Boy in Striped Pyjamas*, when it was on Mike's school reading list. Each book she read evoked a feeling she could never quite place, an inexplicable homesickness. She always felt both anger and sadness, at the experiences of the Jewish people, but there was also a deep sense of connection. When she watched *Schindler's List* she couldn't help wondering if she had paternal grandparents who had perished in the Holocaust. Who was she? Was she half Jewish?

In 2020, she finally took a DNA test. A third cousin on Gail's side of the family had already done a detailed family tree, so no surprises amongst her maternal forebears. When the test results became available, Helen hardly dared click on the link. She was suddenly very afraid that her father hadn't been Jewish. Eventually, she viewed the report. Fifty percent European Jewish. Tears started to flow. Now, she was angry with Ben for having kept the truth hidden. He may well have chosen to live a lie, but Helen desperately wanted to know the truth. It was unlikely that there were now any people left alive who knew him. Uncle Peter and Uncle Max had both passed away.

She searched out 'Linton-House' on the internet and found it didn't appear before her father. Was it a translation? Her next attempt was to email Winchester School, but they hadn't heard of him. Neither would the army release any records to her, especially the ones relating to Ben's war pension. It was all just one huge frustrating void.

One day, after she had written two novels, Helen was pondering the few fragments of evidence known to her about her father's past. It occurred to her that if Ben had experienced Kristallnacht and lost his parents in the Holocaust, if he had been one of the child refugees who came to England before the second world war, if he had come face to face with the horrors of war, no wonder he didn't want to talk about his past. What she had witnessed growing up were, possibly, symptoms of something akin to post-traumatic stress. Her anger subsided and was displaced by a strange mix of pity and pride. Reflecting on how she could honour him, she started to research the Holocaust and the events of Dunkirk, the diamond mines in South Africa and London in the fifties. Finally, she began to write about a sixteen-year-old boy and his older brother on Kristallnacht, and how by a bizarre turn of events they had become separated from one another during the Kindertransport.

Milton Keynes UK
Ingram Content Group UK Ltd.
UKHW010707201023
430994UK00004B/165